The Silver Oar

The
Silver Oar

HOWARD BRESLIN

New York
THOMAS Y. CROWELL COMPANY

Manufactured in the United States of America

For Pat
And Ann
And Carl

Contents

A silver oar, both in England and her colonies, was actually carried upright before a condemned pirate on his way to execution. The one that led such processions to the gallows at a point between high and low-water mark in Boston harbor of the Massachusetts Bay Colony was a thing of painted wood. This work of fiction is as thinly coated with truth. Certain characters, Puritan conspirators or royal officials, are truly historical. Certain events, like the Boston revolution of 1689, happened as described. Everything, however, is seen through the eyes of the narrator. There are times when he seems to be a great liar.

BOOK ONE

The Iron Shackles

Chapter 1

MY true, real name is Cormac O'Shaugnessy Doyle.

Since this is the log of my last voyage (and partly a land voyage at that) it is best at the start to tell the truth and shame the devil. The events which brought me here, after as crazy and crooked a track as a rabbit with drink taken, to freeze in their new stone gaol in this raw-fresh town called Boston of the Massachusetts Bay Colony on the continent of North America will be set down as they occurred.

That my trial for the crime of piracy still awaits me is as of little matter as my pleading innocence. The attitude of turnkey and guards, of preachers and advocates, of every long nosed idler who comes to stare through the bars makes that plain enough. The rope for my neck is already made, and they are putting fresh paint on the silver oar.

Even the hardiest, toughest old buccaneer blanches when that oar flashes silver in the sun ahead of him as the boat pulls down the bay. It beckons like the last trump, and there is time only left for prayers, or a round oath saved for the occasion. These Boston folk may not put on the pomp displayed at Execution Dock in England, but the result will be the same—carrion, sun dried, for gulls to peck.

Like all Puritan preachers those of this town are great ones for writing, almost as great as for sermons, and they have given me ink, and quills, and a great sheaf of foolscap in hope no doubt of an open confession which they are not going to get.

During the days of my life I have set my hand to many trades, but scribbling was not one of them. Still, I had schooling as a lad, manage a fair, plain script, barring blots, and a man goes nowhere unless he hoists anchor without fear of whatever reefs lie ahead.

So I set this down in December of the year of our Lord 1688, in the fourth year of the reign of His Majesty King James, second of his name on the English throne. There is time to pass, much to relate, and, in spite of the morsel of fire they give me, it is bitter cold.

With God's help I can finish before my fate. For, accused as a pirate, and admittedly a Papist, there's small chance of rescue or escape.

Sure, these Puritans will get double pleasure out of hanging *me!*

❖

The September storm that brought me to these shores came without warning. Seamen who sleep, without watch, in the North Atlantic deserve bad luck, but we were both worn to a whisper. Besides, these waters were strange to me, and my shipmate knew them no better. There were only the two of us to work the ketch, stand watch and watch, rustle up a mug and biscuit now and then, and put blue water between our stern and those who might come after us. We set our course for a far port where there'd be few questions, and stayed well off the coast of North America.

Our ketch was a sweet little craft named *Fancy,* not young but still frisky. We'd had busy days since we'd picked her out, and snaked her away from the others, and got her under weigh. There had been no sign of pursuit, nor any speck of sail in all the heaving sea around us. With the Grand Fishing Banks well behind us, scudding south before a brisk wind, with no sign of foul weather, we'd lashed the tiller and napped where we stood.

So the storm caught us unawares. Caught us asleep, drenched us with driving rain, drove us scurrying from bed like a blustery mate. Though no mate ever matched this storm for bluster. It roared out of an angry sky, roiling the sea quicker than a pot will boil.

The ketch fled before it, but there was no escape. I have seen hurricanes in the West Indies, and gales without number, but I could not put a name to what hit us. We couldn't get the sails in before they went to tatters. Before long the rigging was whipping around our ears like some giant cat-o'-nine-tails.

"Cormac," said the Swede then, his accent thick with worry. "Cormac, this be trouble."

"That it is," I said. "And when have we been strangers to it?" But neither words nor my laugh fooled the Swede. He stood there in the pelting rain, his whole huge frame swaying as the *Fancy* heeled from side to side like a teeter board. He looked down on me from his great height, and his broad face was as sullen as the sky.

"No good," he said. "No good."

Truth he told me. And as day turned to night it got no better. The storm drove us, and tossed us, and pummeled us, through a night made tumult by wind and rain. Nothing but darkness, pitch blinding darkness around us. A man could see the length of his arm, no farther. Except for the waves, grown as high and wild as the hills of Connemara. We saw the white foam when a wave broke across us, a black glass wall shattering to slivers.

The *Fancy* was brave. She fought for her life like a true lass, but she was not built for such a buffeting. Time and again she thrust her bowsprit through the vitals of a mountainous wave, and fought free. Then, the wind would shift and attack on another quarter.

Day, a mere thinning of blackness to gray, found us hard pressed. The dory was stove in, kindling. A wave had washed through the galley, quenching our bit of fire, spoiling the food. We did what we could, which was little, on empty bellies save for a tot of rum when the Swede fought his way to the cask.

Maybe we were light headed what with drink, and cold, and misery. The night seemed to come as a sudden clap of thunder. Bad it had been, but this was worse. The storm raged in new fury with the sound of a thousand banshees. Inside the Devil's hip pocket was a bright place to that night.

It was my turn at the tiller. There was naught to do but keep her head up, since all thought of a course had vanished in the first hour. The tiller was a wild thing, gone over to the enemy. My nails were split, my arms aching, my ribs sore with the battle. I wrestled that tiller; I straddled it, battered it, cursed and cajoled it. God knows who steered for it was not me.

That fight, in the bone-chill rain, with the seas leaping up at us like hounds after prey, took the marrow out of me. The fear of death was a taste in my mouth. My muscles turned to jelly, and my brain spent its time wincing. Once I think I wept, though I could not tell for sure with a face already so wet. I know I whimpered.

Then, I heard the Swede singing from the bow.

[5]

> So go, all you crawling lubbers, beg!
> For me it's gold chain or wooden leg!
> Yo, ho—heave, ho!

The snatch of song carried to me, for the Swede had a voice fit to match thunder. There was no seeing him, but my mind pictured him, a blond giant roaring defiance to the elements with that old pirate chantey. There was Viking blood in the man somewhere.

"Swede," I yelled. "Swede, are you all right?"

"Fine, Cormac, fine!" His speech, strangely, came thinner than his song, borne on the wind.

"How are we headed?"

"God, He knows!"

My shipmate's laugh boomed through the tumult at his own joke. The good Lord has made men smarter than the Swede, but none braver. We had been together in fair weather, and foul, and won through always. Few crossed us, paired, and none twice. His brawn matched my quickness. Though he was two years the older—twenty-five or so—he followed my lead. I led with a firm step, sure in the knowledge that the Swede was at my back.

Now, to hear him, unafraid, gave me heart. Anger replaced my fear. Good, warm, raging anger that made me stamp on the deck. We had come so far, risked so much, fought clear. No damned storm had the right to cheat us of our prize. I said as much too, cursing in its teeth. A futile, senseless act, truly, but better than grovelling.

"Hang on, Swede, hang on! We'll beat it yet!"

"Avast! Look out to starb—"

The rest of his cry was lost as a tremendous wave took us amidship. It folded across the deck, a great dark blanket. Nothing ever hit me harder; it doubled me over the tiller like a half-shut clasp knife.

She's gone, I thought, feeling the ketch heel.

The *Fancy* fooled me. She came back, bless her, shaking water like a doused mongrel. May the man who laid her keel receive a fair share of Paradise!

Sputtering, I got my feet back on deck when the Swede shouted again. This time I heard only one word—"casket." He always used that name though it really was a brass-bound sea chest.

My heart gave a frightened bound as I looked. But it was still there, lashed to the deck where we had put it. That chest was our cargo, worth the lives we had staked to get it.

"It's safe!" I screamed back. Then, I laughed. Safe indeed it was, if we were. Safe on a foundering ship in a vengeful ocean. It would, I thought, soon be even safer from any man's hold, twenty fathoms deep.

There were jewels in the chest, and gold, and coins from the nations of half the world. Share and share the contents could have kept the Swede and me in soft beds and fine coaches as long as we lived. No breathing soul had a more rightful claim than we did.

But that chest had brought us where we were, so now I cursed it as a millstone around our necks. We would not have the spending of a penny, yet it had cast us on the mercy of a merciless sea.

Preachers a-plenty have told me that one facing death should make ledger, count past sins and past blessings, credit and debit. A few claimed the whole past came unsummoned, turning through the mind like the pages of a book. These things may be, but it was not like that aboard the *Fancy*. Naught but the sorry present had room in my head. Always it was *now*—this moment's howling gust or towering wave—that made me raging brave, or a quaking coward.

For a while we shouted to each other, bandying courage. The Swede sang; I prayed and swore. There was no figuring how long we spent at such nonsense; we had no measure of time. When my throat grew hoarse I stopped yelling. Much later, I heard the Swede chanting some Swedish doggerel, but by then a hopeless lethargy had seized me, and I only wondered dimly at the meaning.

In that state, I was numb, dazed. Mind you, the stinging rain had me shivering. I wore only shirt and breeches, sodden and clinging, without warmth. Instinct kept me gripping the tiller, but I was jerked at its whim. Through chattering teeth I mouthed the prayers of my childhood.

> Our Father, who art in Heaven . . .
> Hail Mary, full of grace . . .
> St. Patrick preserve us . . .
> Matthew, Mark, Luke and John . . .

The sea and the storm betwixt them had beaten me. My sorrow for myself was deep, pitiful. Once I saw a sailor, high aloft, hang by one desperate hand until his strength gave. I had let go inside, in some such fashion. I was finished, through; drained even of despair.

"Cormac!"

"Coming," I said to no one in particular.

"Cormac!"

"I hear you," I said. "I hear you."

"*Christ!*" The shriek shocked me back to sense. "Breakers! Breakers ahead!"

[7]

The Swede's warning brought me erect and tense, but that was all the good it did. The black night had hidden the tell-tale line of white; the surf noise was lost in the storm's roaring. We were almost on the breakers when the Swede saw them. With the wind dead astern, gale strong, and our keel already in the swell's grip, no two men, nor twenty, could have kept us off that shore.

I tried. I summoned strength I did not know I had, throwing it on the tiller. That accursed bit of gear, bedeviled to the end, gave not an inch.

Suddenly the Swede loomed beside me, added his great weight to my own. The tiller gave! It gave with a snap that showed the rudder gone, and flung us headlong. Rolling in the scuppers I cracked my head.

At that moment we struck.

The *Fancy* went on the rocks like a horse bellying into a hedge. She ripped her bottom out in that first wild plunge. Her timbers screamed; the mainmast snapped with a crack, toppled. The sea picked her up, hurled her down with another shuddering crash. Surf in a vast cataract poured into her.

I saw it coming, threw my hands before my face. The wave swept me up and hurled me over the side.

Down, down into the smothering black depths of the ocean I plunged, into deep lightless cold. Few can match me swimming, but I was a chip in that surf. I lashed out, kicked, clawed for the surface, but no skill of mine brought me up. The sea, having swallowed, digested, and rechewed me as a cow her cud, spat me out.

The rain-filled night was a different black, with air. The breath I gulped steadied me.

"Swede! Where are you?"

My cry was nothing to the thunder of the surf. A new wave broke over me, rolled me under again. This time I did not go so deep, but swam with the surge.

When I rose again the surf seemed farther off, its pounding more distant. I shouted for the Swede, and listened. No sound but breakers, and the hiss of wind-driven rain. There was an undertow dragging at me, and, willy-nilly, I was forced to swim with it. To fight it was suicide.

Its pull took me far, a puny human in vast restless black water, with another vast darkness above. I swam, sobbing for breath—God, how long and how far I swam!—until my limbs were lead. That was a swim to brag of after, but I have uttered no word of it to this day. The mightiness of my task left me humble, too humble to curse or pray.

At last I heard the surf again, closer and clearer. This nearly made me despair, thinking I had been moving in circles, believing myself in

[8]

the current of some giant whirlpool that would carry me round and round till it sucked me down in its center.

Such marvels were common talk among seamen. Ships were said to have been lost in this manner. The thought was not pleasant. In panic, I forgot my fledgling humility, forgot all swimming sense. I spent my strength in a frenzied thrashing struggle to escape.

One foot smashed its toes against something. I scrabbled, kicking, touched bottom. Awe and unbelief overshadowed my joy. But there was no time for feelings. As soon as I stood upright a wave tossed me, heels over head. It rolled me, neat as any ball at bowls, bouncing along a rocky bottom to end face down in swirling foam. Even as the wave sizzled, receding, its follower slapped down on me.

There was sand beneath me, and I crawled. Edging on my belly, pulling with fingers, arms, elbows, knees, I crawled away from the grip of the sea. Inch by agonized inch I made a snail's pace across that beach until the rain that beat on me was free from spray.

My body seemed one great bruise; my aches outnumbered my bones. Worst of all I was sick, exhausted, shaking and retching with dry heaves, me who had no bit of morsel in me. The storm still raged about my ears; the rain still lashed me. I cared not if it were the end of the world.

Too worn to think, I had no mind for my friend, or the sea chest, or the ketch. I was not even grateful for life. I was out of the sea, and that was enough. Collapsing, I slept.

So I landed on the coast of North America, which was the last place anywhere that I wanted to be. But the shipwrecked have little choice, and lie at God's mercy.

Back home in Ireland they had a saying, old and true. Those born to be hanged, will never drown.

Chapter 2

SUNSHINE, beating down on my eyelids, woke me. For a long drowsy moment I lay quiet, enjoying the warmth baking into me, wondering only why my thighs felt clammy. In sleep I had turned on my back, but my main thought was a great reluctance to rise. Then I opened my eyes, blinked at a bright blue sky, closed them again, puzzled. Why was the sky motionless? Slowly the reason seeped into my brain. There was no ship moving beneath me; my fingers touched sand, not deck. I was ashore! At that everything came back with a rush. Memory of storm, wreck, and swim jolted the last dregs of sleep from me.

I came up with a bound to stand alone on a curving strip of beach with sand dunes piled behind me.

The day looked new, clean, fresh washed. A morning sun, butter yellow, beamed above, bleaching puffs of clouds, flecking the calm ocean with gold. Indeed, sea and sky seemed to sparkle at each other in pleasant blue rivalry. The long roll of surf that kissed the beach was as gentle and white as the clouds. It unfolded its lace along the sand with a friendly murmur. Spots of color caught my glance—the bronze strip that glistened at the water's edge; a sea shell that cupped a glory of speckled purple; a coil of seaweed, deep green against white sand. All nature preened itself, decked in its best.

It was as if God had made morning that minute. There had never been rain, nor gale, nor was any intended. The peaceful loveliness of it drove me to rage.

"You lying scuts!" I shouted, shaking my fist at sea and sky. "You treacherous, murdering, two faced harlots! Do you dare to smile at me now?"

The Swede was foremost in my mind. He was gone, almost surely; it was unlikely we had both been spared. Muscles had meant nothing to last night's seas, and the Swede, like so many seamen, was no swimmer. The blond head, a beacon in many a brawl, would be seen no more; the soft, accented voice would support me in no future quarrel. Tears of mourning blurred the landscape that I cursed.

A wave swept calmly in, gracefully strewed plumes along the curve of the shore, drew back. Whispering, it chided my anger. Everything else in sight went about its own shining business.

That stopped me acting like a fool. Men died; seamen died in ship-wrecks. The Swede had been a matchless seaman, had pitted his strength against the sea, and lost. He would not want me to stand keening, like an old woman with a shawl over her head.

"God keep you," I said to the Swede. "May your soul rest in peace."

With that acceptance came a sudden gladness that I was alive. A gull wheeled down from nowhere, whistled, and skimmed off above the cresting waves. The bird, a living thing, made me laugh with the sheer joy of life. I was grateful, and I thanked the God who had saved me.

First I took inventory of myself. My body was stiff and sore, marked with bruises everywhere, but there was nothing broken, no wound deeper than a scratch. My buff breeches were still wet, clinging and uncomfortable. Peeling them off, I spread the leather to dry, weighting it with rocks. Only a few rags remained of my shirt, and these too I pegged in the sun. There was no sign of habitation on this stretch of shore, and cloth, unraveled, might be needed for a fishing line.

Naked, except for the Spanish doubloon on its gold chain around my neck, I climbed a sand dune to get my bearings. The coin had a cross on one side, so I wore it as half-medal, half-souvenir, a talisman or trinket. There was devil a bit of priest's blessing on it if anyone thought the wearing smacked of Papistry, but it could buy a man out of starvation.

There was naught it could buy in that place, but it set me thinking of the sea chest. On the dune's summit my gaze turned first out to sea.

The shore line swept away to the south as if I stood on the sharp curve of a scythe. To the north there was open water. Dead ahead, off my strip of beach, was the bulk of a good-sized island, the dark of its shrubbery dotted with patches of sand. A spume of spray, flashing in the sunshine, lifted regularly at the island's northern end. Shading my eyes, I stared.

Those, I thought, must be the rocks that did for us. There was no sign of wreckage. That surf would have pounded the *Fancy* to pieces in a matter of minutes. I was turning away when the thing caught my notice.

It was no bigger than a dark splinter haloed with spray by every breaking wave. Was it a spar? Was it mayhap one of the *Fancy's* masts jutting out of the water?

The mizzen, I decided, recalling how the main had come down when we struck. Grinning, I strained my eyes, afire with plans. If the ketch lay no deeper than that the sea chest was not lost! The knots that lashed it to the deck would have held; the chest itself, cured wood and tarred, would keep out the sea for a long time. If that *was* the *Fancy's* mizzen-top, riches lay waiting. All I had to do was dive for them!

There was no certainty on such evidence; distance was too great for that. It need not be mast at all, but driftwood, a strange shadow. But there was a chance! When a man has nothing left a chance is a warming hope.

Head high, swaggering, I went exploring in search of water. Dune followed dune, making no easy walking, but the sun drew the soreness from my body. This portion of North America was a barren, tumbled sort of land, the sand broken only by clumps of coarse, rank grass, and some scattered scrub pine. These last had a forlorn, lonely look, as if misplaced.

In a rocky bit of hollow I stumbled on my water. Last night's rain, collected there, had not yet seeped away. To my parched lips and tongue the cool wet was heavenly. After drinking my fill I used the little pool as a mirror glass.

The face of a wild, wood creature gazed up at me. In the image my blue eyes were black, so was my dark brown hair, awry as last year's bird nest. Sure, I laughed, hardly knowing myself at all. That long O'Shaugnessy nose, with its slight tack to port, was the sole feature I recognized. The chin's cleft, the wide mouth, the dimple so praised by certain ladies, were all hidden by a three-day growth of beard.

Many a morning, after a bout with the bottle, I have scared myself shaving, but this savage would have scared Caliban.

After scrubbing my face, I combed my wet hair with my fingers. As I climbed the far slope of the hollow I laughed at my vanity. But all laughter went out of me when I reached the top.

Ahead lay the sea! Across the wide blue sheen of it was the dark line of a distant shore. The sun was at my back, and I gaped west. This was no inlet! Jaw slack I swung round to stare north. There again, like a blued blade, was the glimmer of open ocean.

I was not on the mainland of North America at all, at all! This was only the north end of some beggarly strip of God-forgotten island, not a mile wide! A sand pile fit only as a perch for sea gulls, where nothing could grow or graze.

The heart within me dropped like a shot goose. Marooned, I thought, turning cold. No man with a grain of sense would live on such an island. The mainland lay across a width of water that made even a swimmer of my power shudder, especially after the last swim I'd had. And I had seen neither strip nor stick for the makings of a boat.

Glumly, I dragged my feet back through the track I'd made in the sand. My breeches would be dry enough to don before exploring farther. For exploration was a necessity. Some other part of the island might lie closer to the main. A cove somewhere might have collected driftwood to fashion a raft.

This was just whistling when becalmed. The bright day was a mockery; its promise a lie. Children crossed so lie down and wail. Though a man grown, I was tempted.

In such a mood I topped the dune that fronted the beach. Then, I stood frozen, wide eyed!

There was a girl wading in the shallows! Her back was to me as she stooped over, searching, but the shape of her was human, female and young!

I couldn't believe my eyes. I opened my mouth to shout before she disappeared. Even as my lungs filled, I remembered my nakedness and dropped flat on my belly.

Praise the Saints that she had not turned! The very thought made me hot with shame. Besides, the likes of the fellow that had glowered from the pool would have frightened the poor soul witless.

Snuggling into a shallow in the sand, I peered down over the edge of the dune. I cast one longing glance toward my breeches, some thirty yards up the beach where I'd left them. It was a wonder she hadn't discovered them. Too busy after clams or scallops, I supposed.

The girl stood, calf deep, out beyond the gently breaking surf. She wore a gray dress of some homespun stuff, plain and sleeveless, but kilted up high in a froth of white petticoats for her wading. She had long, slim legs, very pale in the blue water. A bucket hung over one arm, and she used a short-handled bit of rake at her task.

When she straightened, to clunk a shell into the pail, the sunlight made a splendor of her hair. It hung in loose waves below her shoulders.

I caught my breath, staring. Red was too harsh a word, though right, for her coloring; gold was too pale. Only a painter maybe would know the right term. I have seen Spanish sherry glow like that with the sun shining through the glass. Sure, the beauty of it plucked at your heart like a harp string.

There was naught I could do but watch. Wading she moved with grace; she bent easily to plunge her arm in after the shellfish. She was having no trouble filling her bucket, but I doubt her enjoyment matched mine.

Warm and content I rested my chin on my hands, and gazed. I had seen no woman for too long, and none like this one ever. Once she turned, pushing the hair back from her face with a wrist, to frown shoreward. I saw the fine sweet figure of her and a face to match above.

Nothing clouded my happiness, not even my nakedness. That was, after all, just a temporary discomfort. When the girl left, I would nip out, don my breeches and follow. If, by any chance, she found my nether garment, I would speak her fair, hidden in my trench, gently so's not to frighten her. Butter and honey mixed would be grit compared to the tongue with which I'd address this girl.

Her very presence was surety for the future. There was nothing of the wild castaway about her, but an air of domestic serenity. She came from a home and hearth; knowing or unknowing she would lead me to them.

[13]

There would be food, and talk, and company, and herself to share all with.

She waded far in her search, away from my breeches and back. Once she stepped too deep, a kittenish wave splashed up at her, and she yanked her skirts higher. I saw the curved loveliness of a thigh and chuckled my appreciation into the sand.

When her bucket was full she came out of the water. Putting her implements aside she seated herself on a rock directly below my sand dune, not over a dozen yards away. She hitched up her petticoats, placed one heel upon the opposite knee, and unwound a length of seaweed twined around her ankle.

Maybe a Saint might have turned his head, which is why there are few saints among mankind. Holding my breath, I stared. There was no lust in my look, though my heart beat faster. In that long, joyful moment I would not have changed places with any crowned king that ever lived!

Then, she raised her head to look me full in the face! The move caught me by surprise, tongue-tied. With one swift blur of motion her arm darted out, seized a rock, flung it at my head!

I barely ducked in time. The breeze of it parted my hair. A raging shriek of a war cry jerked my glance up again. The girl was charging up the sand dune, her hair and skirts flying, a rock in each hand!

Mother naked, I fled. I bounded across the dune with her yells whipping my speed. There was blood and battle in her voice. She wanted my hide, and me in my pelt! One scared look over my shoulder showed her whooping in hot pursuit.

God save us, I thought, leaping for the next dune. In mid-air a blow smote me square between the shoulder blades. The rock hit with the force to drive me somersaulting in a cloud of sand off the dune onto the beach.

Stunned, for I landed sitting, I had enough presence of mind to scoop quick handfuls of sand as a covering over my lap. I was scarce decent before I heard the shrew storming above me.

"You gowk!" she cried. "You big, bulge-eyed oaf of a gowk!"

Another rock bounced off my shoulder. I cringed, throwing a fearful glance up at her. She was standing, stiff angry, atop the dune, hair tossing as her head turned in search of something more to throw.

"Please," I said. "Please, Mistress——"

"I'll please you!" she yelled, fire in her eyes and fingers curved into talons. "You—you peeping Tom! You indecent whelp, I'll teach you to ogle at me!"

[14]

"I meant no harm," I said. Sure, the blaze of her temper would have chilled Hell.

"No harm, and you naked as a babe!"

"There's a reason for that, milady, and——"

"Aye! Reason! Oh, where's a rock?"

"Listen a minute!"

"And me sitting there scratching—Argh, you lout!"

"Shut your jabbering!" I roared, stung by her unreasonableness. "You're not hurt, and you weren't scratching!"

"I might have been," she said. "And don't yell at me!" She stood, arms akimbo, glaring at me. Once she ceased shouting there was a touch of Scots burr in her speech.

"Will you listen, now?" I said, pleading. "I'm a shipwrecked seaman, and I knew not you were here or any living soul. I left my breeches to dry—they're leather. You can see them up the beach if you look."

"I don't believe a word," she said, looking.

"I couldn't come out," I said. "Now could I? Like this? It was against all decent modesty."

"But you could peep at me! You could ogle!"

"Well," I said with a grin. "In God's truth you were a fair sight, and I did not mean you to catch me."

"That I believe!"

"If you'll just turn your back now, I'll go get my breeches and——"

"Oh, no!" she said. "I've no willingness to trust you." With that she took a flying leap off the dune, legs flashing, to land between me and my clothes. In a shake she was on her feet with the rock that had bounced off me in her fist.

"You needn't fear me," I said.

"Nor do," said she. "For if you move I'll brain you."

"I am not moving," I said, convinced.

"Then talk," she said, watchful and wary. "And don't give me a daft tale of a shipwreck."

"But it's true. My ketch went aground on the island yonder in last night's storm. By God's grace, and some luck, I made it ashore here."

Her eyes widened. They were dark-brown eyes, rich and well set. As she glanced across at the island I regarded her face, close and quiet for the first time. Her nose was straight, with the tiniest pert tilt at its tip; her mouth, rose lipped, was neither large nor small. Some nice molding had been done on the bones under her fair skin—the forehead both sides her widow's peak was noble; the cheek-bones were high placed; the curve of the jaw was true. If her chin was a trifle too square, I found it attractive, like the track of freckles, golden dots, across the bridge of her nose.

"Another lie," she said. "Nobody could live in that tempest. It smashed half our fisher boats."

"I am here," I said. "How else did I get here?"

"True," she said. She sounded doubtful, no longer so angry. "What sort of ship was it?"

"A ketch. Not big."

"Your shipmates?"

"I had but one," I said, with a sigh. "The sea has him now."

The brown eyes softened. She tossed her head as if to drive the feeling away. She said: "From where and what cargo? Two men in a ketch."

There was no sense going overboard with truth telling. My answer came smooth and easy. "From the south with rum and molasses. Making for Boston." My gaze was straight in hers, for I was only half-sure Boston lay to the north.

"From Virginia?" she asked, easing my mind.

"No." I shook my head. "Jamaica." Then I decked the lie with lace. "We last touched the Carolinas. Place called Charlestown." That was the only mainland port I knew besides New York, and the latter was too close.

The girl nodded reluctantly. "It could be true, you're not so far off your course."

"Why should I lie?" I asked with loud indignation. "Would I admit my plight—bereft of goods and gear—if I wanted to spin a tale?"

"You might," said she. She squatted on her heels, but she hefted the rock on her palm. Sitting, she was not so formidable. "I cannot forget that you wandered like a daft, naked loon when a two-hour walk would have brought you to our village."

"And how was I to know that?"

"By using the sense that God gave you. But mayhap that's too much to ask from one who'd rather shame a poor girl spying on her hidden."

Poor girl, indeed. She was enjoying herself now. Her tone told me that, and the dance in her eyes. I said: "I was cast on a strange shore. I didn't know but that——"

"I might be a cannibal," she finished for me. "What's your name?"

"Cormac," I said. "Cormac O'Shaugnessy Doyle." There were others I could have mentioned, but there were prices on those.

"Irish," said she, and sniffed.

"So," I said, nettled. "And if my ears don't play me false there is Gael in you, too, cousin."

"Scots," she said with a shrug. "There is a world of difference. As

[16]

much as between O'Shaugnessy and Odysseus. Aye, and their actions."

"O-who?" I asked.

She laughed at me, a gay peal that flung her head back. Showing fine, even teeth she grinned, and said: "That's Homer. He once, Odysseus, that is, naked and shipwrecked, watched Nausicaä and her maidens on a beach."

"Did he now?" I said, my annoyance rising at the smirk on her. "And did they stone him for his pains?"

"No," she said. "They gave him *ceud mile failte*. But I forgot the Irish have no learning. That's a hundred thousand welcomes."

That much Gaelic I knew, though the Scot tongue of her made a shambles of it. Deliver me from women who've delved through books! The snip of a girl, no more than seventeen, sat there, with her eyebrows arched, and her smile superior. A good shake was what she needed.

"Would you mind," I said, cold polite, "removing yourself while I fetch my raiment?"

"Why?"

"Why? Why?" I was so mad I stuttered. "Because it is only decent!"

"But I have not finished with my examination." She was overmuch the great lady, frowning in effort to hide her amusement. "Nor you your explanation."

"And am I to sit here while you blather about Homer, and Nauseous, and O-something-or-other?" I was boiling, and loud. "Don't they teach maidens modest behavior in the Highlands?"

"Lowlands," she said. "And I've never seen them. I was born here. You've a great voice to be bellowing of modesty. I've not been taught superstition anyway." Her glance flicked at the doubloon hung around my neck. "Nor the Papist trick of spying on one's betters."

The cool contempt of her did it. "So be it," I said, "on your own head."

I stood up and walked past her. I went to my breeches, pulled them on. Neither glance nor thought did I give her till they were on. My anger overcame all sense of shame. When I turned I was clad, and ready.

She stood a few steps away. There was a pink flush on her cheeks, and she gazed out to sea, biting her lower lip. The rock hung heavy in her hand, as if forgotten.

"Now," I said, "if it's more talk you wish, I'm at your service."

Her glance flashed at me, and away. "You're a feckless, shameless man."

"Maybe," I said. "But we're quits. If I saw aught of you, you've seen more of me. And neither of us will be talking about it."

"You give your word?" she asked, facing me.

"Word and hand," I said, offering the latter.

She put out the hand with the rock, smiled, dropped it. She had a long, narrow hand, with a firm clasp. We shook, and let go, not friends but no longer enemies.

"My name," she said gravely, "is Judith Murdoch. But they call me Jill."

"Jill. And do you flirt then?"

She smiled at my knowing the name's meaning. Shaking her head, she said: "A flirt is an abomination and a hissing in the sight of the Almighty. No daughter of the Covenant would stoop to such unholy japes."

I near gave a shout of laughter, but realized in time she was serious. The lesson was recited with lips made for what she condemned. I judged the Scotch Covenanters were as dourly strict as reputed if Jill swallowed such talk.

"Are you really a Papist, Cormac Doyle?"

"In a fashion," I said, with caution. It was not a thing admitted to everyone, even with King James on the throne. "But there would be some that questioned it."

Her face cleared. "I thought so. Both your feet have toes. Those who follow the Whore of Babylon are marked with the cloven hoof."

The language made me blink, though among certain sects the term was common for the Church of Rome. Discretion, and hunger, kept me peaceful. I said, "Well, now, I never talk religion on an empty stomach."

"You poor man!" Jill said, all eyes. "Of course. You've had nothing this day." Clucking like a mother hen she herded me toward the bucket. "These will help till we get something hot in you."

From a pocket in her skirt she drew a knife, opened out a blade as long as my hand, and started shucking clams. It's a good thing, I thought watching, that she did not go for me with that!

After I wolfed a dozen or so, slaking my thirst with the juice, I called halt. They made poor fare, and salty, for a famished man. I wanted something that would stick to my ribs.

"Come then," said Jill, leading the way. She insisted on carrying the bucket, and off we went.

Without making a to-do about it, I marked the beach well, particularly the island where the *Fancy* lay. If the sea chest was there it was safe till my return. But I would need a craft for that.

"What sort of village is it?" I asked Jill.

"Southold? Like any other. We're fisher folk. Up this end of the island we're all part of Massachusetts Bay Colony. Down to the other the settlements are New York Dutchy. It's called Long Island, and it is."

"And that smaller isle out yonder?"

"That? Shelter Island. It's really in a bay, you know, though we can't see the other side from here."

"You've lived here always?"

"Aye." Jill was full of chatter. "My father when he was young fought with the Army of the Lord under the Covenant. He did not hold with selling the first Charles, nor welcoming the second. So he took wife and child and ship to America. He was a holy man, and a fisherman, sickened by the bloodshed of the civil wars. At least so I am told for he was called to the Lord when I was very young."

As she guided me, she danced around me, first this side then the other, with a light easy step. She was almost as tall as myself who lacks an inch for six feet. Her bare feet flashed in and out beneath the ankle-length dress.

"Your mother——?"

"She, too, some time later. When I was seven. My brother Alec rules the clan now. He is a good man, Alec, the best fisherman out of South-old, and a deacon of the kirk. Though of course it is not a true kirk, what with a Puritan preacher and all, but Alec bides well with his neigh-bors, and makes do. He even paid good shillings for me to read under the preacher who has a full shelf of books. That's where I learned of Homer."

The last was tossed with a laugh and a glance. I laughed with her, not being able to help it. She had that way with her.

"And of welcoming the shipwrecked hero?" I asked.

"La!" Jill cried. "We'll not talk of that. You'll get welcome pressed down in Southold. They'll talk for days how they sent me for clams and I fetched back a big fish from the sea."

Laughing thus, we came over the last hill. So the day fulfilled its promise after all.

Chapter 3

THIS village of Southold was on the same bay as my landing, but farther south, behind its own nook of a cove. The place had the look of fishing villages everywhere, houses huddled back from the harbor, nets drying, ropes and gear in heaps, boats pulled up on the shingle. A second glance showed most of the boats had suffered from the storm. One sloop lay on its side, high on the beach, stove in like a dropped egg. Others were in like state, some worse, all holed, battered, or crushed. Indeed the whole shoreline looked as if a giant hand had strewed it with broken vessels. I saw a round bottomed craft, much like the curragh of my homeland, impaled on an anchor fluke. Men were busy with repairs, but listlessly, subdued by the amount of damage.

"You see," Jill said. "The seas crippled half our fleet."

"None lost?" I asked the first question of all fisher folk.

"None. Praise be to the Lord God! They were all in before it struck." Jill hurried me on, tugged at my elbow. "Come along. There's Alec and the others."

But my pace slowed. This was a new port, and it was wise to take careful soundings. The houses were typical fisher cottages, frame and roofed, not thatched, facing the sea or the path that led to it. They were weather gray for the most part, almost the color of the smoke that twisted from their chimneys. Except for the church, which I recognized by its squat box of a steeple, there was more paint on the hulls than on the shacks. Each place had its little patch of green, and white stones or shells bordered path and plot.

A neat folk, I thought, and tidy. A cow lowed somewhere; my nose caught a whiff of pigsty through the salt-fish tang of the air. Prudent, too, I decided hungrily.

"Come *on!*" Jill said, with an impatient toss of her chin. Arm and voice went up in wave and call. "Alec! Alec! *Cooo-eeee, Alec!*"

There was no answering hail. The men had seen us all right for the murmur of talk died away as we came down the last of the hill. Hammers slowed, stopped; gulls, flapping and crying, were suddenly louder. Every face was turned toward us before we reached the first doorway, and sure wasn't there a woman in that, with young ones peeking around her! But not a smile, nor greeting, in the lot.

"Jill, which is Alec?" My tone was casual to mask my worry. The lack of welcome had me uneasy.

"The tallest." Jill, too, sensed something wrong. Her forehead was puckered with a puzzled frown, her lips pursed. "There by the sloop."

The tallest was easy to find. Alec Murdoch stood above the rest, a sparse man with a large head, and broad shoulders, like a mast with only the topgallant set. Hatless, he wore his grizzled sandy mane Roundhead fashion. In a faded chamois vest, homespun breeches, knitted hose, and scuffed buckle-less boots, Alec managed to look a chieftain.

Jill ran to her brother. "Alec, Alec. This is Cormac Doyle who was cast up by last night's storm."

A man behind Alec spat, and spoke. "Cast him back then. The sea must have its due."

"Aye," said another. "If not him, one of us."

I stopped where I was, ready for flight or fight. I had heard of the superstition that it was ill luck to save a man from the sea, but this was my first meeting with it. I did not know how far these strangers would go supporting it.

"Alec," said Jill. "What talk is this? The man was shipwrecked, and——"

Calmly I met Alec's gaze as he stopped Jill with raised hand. Beneath shaggy brows his eyes seemed black as char. He had his sister's nose, but much enlarged and sharpened to a harpoon's keen edge. His voice was deep, the burr rasping through it like the scrape of a holystone.

"The Lord giveth and the Lord taketh away. Blessed be the name of the Lord."

"Amen," I said, hoping it would serve.

"But, Alec!" Another Scots voice was quick with protest. "We would not the Lord to taketh from us what he giveth to this stranger."

"Peace!" Alec spoke loudly, but his gaze never wavered from my face. "Hold your tongue, Hamish MacInnis! Such talk is blasphemy in the face of the Lord God's will. Since it was my sister who succored the man, me and mine will accept the blame and burden of it."

Jill tossed her head, eyes blazing. "Such Orkney blather! I promised him shelter and food, and you shame my words with cowardly nonsense."

I said: "No hand is to blame for saving me. The sea didn't want me. The girl just showed me the way here."

"A bad day's work, Jill Murdoch!" a woman shrilled behind me, "if it costs a man of mine!"

There was a growl of agreement from the men. They sounded more frightened than ugly, but Alec Murdoch whirled on them at once. His fist pounded the side of the sloop; his voice clanged like a ship's bell.

"What manner of heathen talk is this? Do the chosen of the Lord harbor the fears of the Philistines? It's bad enough that Hamish brought such a belief from the Orkneys, but the rest of you shouldn't swallow it whole. The sea is no pagan idol that demands human sac——"

"Speak not against the sea!" said Hamish MacInnis. He was a short, scrawny man, long faced, with the quick, jerky movements of a bird. " 'Tis daft and dangerous!"

"More nonsense!" Jill said with a snort.

"Enough, Jill!" Alec Murdoch threw the rebuke over his shoulder. He scowled at MacInnis. "You might let a body finish, Hamish. I was saying only that the sea——"

"No, no, no, no!" This time the interruption rattled from the scrawny man in woodpecker beat. Shaking a finger he hopped from one foot to the other. "Desist, Alec Murdoch! Desist!"

"I'll say my say!"

"Not against the sea!"

Both men bawled at each other, weather reddened faces darkening in anger. Alec stooped over Hamish like a heron annoyed by a jay. They made me fearful; any bloodshed would be placed at my door. A glance at Jill startled me. She was grinning, no longer worried. Other grins showed on the faces around me; a few turned away to hide smiles. The group's whole attitude had changed. They watched the two embroiled Scots as if regarding a familiar, pleasing entertainment.

"Luck can make nothing happen," cried Jill's brother.

"Happen it cannot, happen it can!"

"Papist superstition!"

"Papist!" Hamish MacInnis snapped his fingers. His head jerked toward me. "Speaking of Papists, look at the ornament around the man's neck."

Every eye rolled my way like so many shifted gun muzzles. Jill's teeth showed as she bit her lip. Her brother, fiery with wrath but a moment before, stiffened as if his backbone had suddenly frozen. He raised a long finger in a point.

I said, smiling, "A Spanish coin. With which to pay my score." With a finger I flicked it from my chest, sending it spinning the length of the chain. Sunshine made the coin flare like a matchflame.

"Gold?" asked Hamish MacInnis, wetting his lips.

"It is that. A doubloon."

They were all staring at it. Alec Murdoch spoke in a musing tone. "We don't see much coinage here. What would that be, say, in shillings?"

Striking bucket with rake Jill Murdoch made everyone start. She said: "Alec, you'd not be charging the shipwrecked for a morsel of bread and——?"

"No, lass, no." Alec sighed, shook his head. "I was just curious, that's all."

"Aye," agreed MacInnis.

Others nodded, chirruped agreement. Alec said: "There can be no thought of payment from the naked and the hungry."

"Then it's high time," said Jill, "that we stopped the talk and fed the man."

Bless you, I thought, for the hunger was an ache inside me. Alec Murdock turned, led the way. Jill and I followed; the others trooped after us. Now that they had decided my arrival wasn't necessarily ill luck, it became an event. They crowded at our heels, curious and listening. Wives joined their husbands with whispered questions; children ran about whooping. Only Hamish MacInnis hung back, dragging behind the rest like a towed dinghy.

"The small man's nose is out of joint," I whispered to Jill. "Would he be making trouble for your brother?"

"Hamish?" Jill said, with surprise. "Why, he and Alec are cronies, partners." She laughed, the brown eyes twinkling. "You let their argufying fool you. They do that all the time, on every subject. Being the only Scots in the village, you see."

Not seeing at all, I nodded. The general chatter around me lacked Jill's touch of burr, but the Murdock cottage looked no different from its neighbors. Alec stooped under the lintel; Jill skipped over the threshold. I went in after them.

The front room was small and square, but friendly. There was a fire dancing, and the kettle on its crane. Sea shells flanked an hour glass on the mantel, the only decorations unless you counted a flitch of bacon hanging from a ceiling hook. A long, plank table stood before the fireplace, amidst a bench and three stools; an open cupboard took most of one wall. The cupboard shelves held dishes and mugs, a skein of wool, knitting, fish hooks, a cut loaf and some carrots, a heavy horse pistol. In a corner a tall gaff stood beside a musket.

[23]

The whole place was scrubbed speckless, every board and inch gleaming. With the fire and all, there was more home to it than a seaman sees in a year. Tears brimmed in my eyes, and I squinted to hold them. God save all here, I thought, but spoke no word.

"Tansey," called Alec, "will you come."

"Tansey," Jill said, "here's Cormac Doyle that I fetched back with me."

"Did you fetch back the clams?" asked Tansey, coming in from the rear of the house. She was a plump, busy person, no higher than Jill's shoulder, all smiles and dimples. There wasn't a gray hair in her neat, black head, and her eyes were very blue. Tansey Murdoch, I judged, was Alec's wife, as trim and as clean as her apron.

"I am sorry," I said, "to cause any trouble."

"Sit down there by the fire," she said, wasting no words. "And we'll get some food into you."

Then she went to work like the woman she was. Children, suddenly underfoot, dodged out of her way as she bustled. There were three boys and two girls, all with a likeness to Alec on them, but something of Tansey too. They were a sandy-haired crew with watered versions of Jill's bright crown.

The onlookers had crowded in after us, lined the walls, watching. Men mostly, with a scattering of women, they beamed at me as if I was a prize catch. Jill darted back and forth, in and out of the room, bringing salvage from where Alec was rummaging after clothes for me. Each garment was appraised, discussed, and approved by the villagers. Tansey, bless her, paid no attention, intent on her cooking.

By the time she had a steaming bowl of chowder in front of me, with bread and fresh butter, I was dressed. The shirt was homespun, speckled blue and white, sleeveless jerkin, and stockings were of the same knitted gray wool. Chowder and bread and clothes made a new man of me.

Boots were a problem, with my small, narrow feet. There was much comment over this. Man after man slipped off a shoe to let me try the size. Nothing was right; all were too big. Stuffing myself with food I didn't care.

"Pack rags in the toes of these," Jill suggested, showing a handsome pair with steel buckles. "They'll do till you find some others."

Over a spoonful I saw Alec Murdoch's face. His chin quivered in a signal that these were his best footgear. There was no sense in offending him, and anyway, I could have slept in one of his boots. I said: "Rather none than a bad fit. I'll not spoil good leather."

"Aye," said Alec, nodding.

[24]

Hamish MacInnis pushed his way through the crowd. "Try these," he said, thrusting out a scuffed and battered black pair. "They're Reverend's. He has a wee foot."

"Where is the reverend?" asked someone.

"Over to the main," came an answer. "Be back anon."

Alec Murdoch noticed my puzzled look, and managed a frosty smile. "He's a good man, the Reverend Bradish. For a preacher of his lights." Alec ignored the buzz that rose from his neighbors. "A pious and learned dominie."

"For a Sassenach," said Jill, giggling. The echo of her laughter went around the room like a breeze. Hamish MacInnis guffawed.

"Aye, Alec," he said. "You're a fair man at that."

"Try the shoon," said Alec, brow dark and furrowed.

They proved a fair enough fit for a beggar who could not choose. I stamped my heels on the floor, mopped my bowl with the last scrap of bread, and sat back. Noggins appeared from nowhere, leather mugs, pewter. Alec Murdoch poured rum, Tansey added hot water, Jill stirred in the butter. Hamish MacInnis helped serve until every man in the room had his palm cupped.

"Air do shlàinte," said Alec Murdoch.

That was near enough to the Irish for me to know that he wished me good health. Saluting with the mug, I raised it, drank deep.

The liquor slid down my gullet with a deceiving smoothness that would have ensnared Beelzebub. Its warmth spread beneath my belt; its fumes were a heady aroma. The company smacked chops over it.

"The King," toasted Hamish, eyeing me.

"Your King," I said politely. I had small trust in the MacInnis, and was wary of traps. These Puritan folk had little love for the Popish James. They tittered at my remark, but they drank. I drained my own mug. Before my lips were wiped it was filled again.

Hamish MacInnis said, "Your turn."

'Ware shoals, I thought. The scrawny man's tricks were so bold they tickled me. If he sought a careless word he was steering the wrong course. I can handle my cups as well as the next.

"All right," I said. "A seaman's toast. Fair winds, full hold, and safe port." And I took a hearty pull of the drink.

The fishermen cheered the sentiment; even Hamish hid his scowl behind his noggin. The applause and the rum addled my brain. My vision was clear as I smiled at Jill, but my wits were slightly fuddled. Food on top of hunger, ease after aching muscles, the potent brimmer, all betrayed me. Liquor loosened my tongue, thawed the talk out of me. These good people had fed and clothed me, and like the ancient minstrels I wished to pay with a tale.

Common enough coin it was for they expected it. They had been waiting for me to begin. Men crowded closer, nudged each other to silence. Alec Murdoch leaned his tallness on the mantel; Tansey, at the cupboard, paused to listen. The girl, Jill, sat down across the table, put her chin in her cupped palms, and gazed at me. Hamish MacInnis hovered at my elbow, replenishing my mug, but I paid him no heed.

For a fact my mind was off on a cruise of its own, and no good to me. Before I had reeled out a dozen sentences, I was beguiled by the sound of my own voice. Strangely, my speech came without thickening, easy and flowing, but I forgot my listeners. They heard one thing left better unsaid.

❖

My name, Cormac O'Shaugnessy Doyle, was given me in baptism. Some twenty-three years back I was born in Ireland, in the old kingdom of Munster, two long days' ride on a good horse, northwest of the city of Cork, which is a place named for a swamp, but a darling town. Didn't Cromwell take the bells out of its belfrys to make cannon for his army?

Before I could walk or speak my position in life was fixed. King Charles II, may his soul rest, had come into his own five years before I came into the world, but it made no difference in our part of Ireland. My mother, Kathleen Ruadh, the Red Kate of the legends, I only remember as a tiny, smiling woman, all eyes in a starved face. I know my father strictly by hearsay. Timothy Doyle, they told me, was a violent man, who refused to submit to the Act of Settlement, and had his head blown open one night while poaching. This was a half year after my birth and prevented me from knowing much about him.

The castle where I first saw day had been McCarthy land, after that Geraldine, with a claim from my mother's people the O'Shaugnessys, but held, since the wars, by Love Jebson, one-time captain of Parliament's cavalry, who had come over with Jones, ridden behind Broghill, and received it as payment from Oliver himself. It was a fair, sweet acreage of sloping hills, and green velvet meadows, with a twist of salmon-rich stream that fed the Blackwater. But my first recollection was the grass square of the bawn, the keep inside what was left of the fortifications. Like most small castles in the Ireland of my youth the walls were tumbled from cannonading, the towers broken off like bitten sausage, the living quarters shacks against charred masonry.

On that square I crawled; in a rubble of stones I wept when my mother died. Of politics I knew nothing, and of religion less, but on that black day I was a lone child in my own land, and that held by strangers.

The proprietor was kind. His full name was Love-Jesus-and-smite-the-Papists Arthur Jebson, but he let me go on living in the corner lean-to that I called home. His shout could make me lose balance as a toddler, and I learned to hate every blue vein in his red face, but to give the man his due he let me live there. There was an old servant named Bridget who looked after me, and some of the tenants helped.

On the whole it was not an unhappy life. There was little to eat sometimes, but when little is custom lot is not missed. There were always green hills, and the mist on the mountains, and the smell of turf. There were bright silver streams to dabble in, fish, and wade. There were sheep to tend, blue sky and birds, a dog, and horses.

Sure, especially horses. The stables on the place were in better shape than the houses. The dog, a red bitch of a setter, with a coat the color of russet autumn leaves, became my friend while still a pup. Her name was Niamh, later on she littered every fall, but from the first she lived among the stalls. She took me, leaning against her, to visit, while I was no taller than herself.

I was eight when Love Jebson noticed me. His voice exploded behind me one day.

"What son of Tophet is this? And, in the name of the Lord God Jehovah, what are you doing with that mare?"

"I am cooling her," I said. "She's been ridden hard, and she's skittish when anyone shouts."

Love Jebson towered over me, legs spraddled, thumbs in his broad leather belt. He was a big man, twenty stone at least, cask head on barrel body with legs like tree stumps. He couldn't speak below a roar.

"Are you telling me I shout?" he asked.

"Look at the mare," I said.

The one thing we two had in common was a regard for horseflesh. With all his faults, Love Jebson had been in the cavalry too long not to prize his mounts, and the mare, Sadeye, was a frisky creature. He looked from me to the horse and back, squinting through eyelids like sword cuts. When he spoke again the mare, rearing, lifted me off my feet, but he did that on purpose.

"Your name?"

"Cormac."

"Oh, the orphan."

"Yes, Captain."

"Well," he said, turning away, "rub her down when she's cool. I came out to do that."

This meeting fixed my station in the household. I was groom or hostler, with the run of the stables. The head stableman, Mickeen Oge Flynn, was glad of a helping hand. My work more than paid for my keep; my clothes were cast-off cutdowns. Till I was fourteen I never had shoe or sole on my foot.

No matter. Growing among horses is no bad life if you like them. But there were few chances to ride, and those only when Love Jebson was away. Still Mickeen Oge never told when I took the mare for a canter. Afoot I roamed the hills and woods at will with Niamh coursing ahead of me. The horses were the first part of my education.

Remember now, that Jebson's Court, as he called it, was like all Ireland, in small. There were old walls, scarred from old battles, containing the raw houses of the newcomers, and the hovels of the dispossessed. *They* lived on one side of the courtyard, out of the wind; *we* lived on the other side, worked for *them,* and remembered the glories of ancient days.

Even when kind Love Jebson was a conqueror; even when laughing we Irish were the beaten. These things I learned, as I learned most of the lore of my race, from Mickeen Oge and the native tenants. We spoke no Gaelic around Love Jebson—he forbade it—but we used it among ourselves. I have lost most of it since, but I had it once.

Mickeen Oge had fought at Waterford, and Knocknaclashy. He limped from that last great defeat. But there was nothing wrong with his tongue! He told me the legends and the stories, the grand days that were, the victories, the lost causes. Nights I would toss on the straw and dream of heroes from Chuchullin through Finn to Owen Roe O'Neill. A boy's dreams are brave dreams but let no one who has not lived, defeated, in land held by a victorious enemy smile at mine.

So the hate smoldered inside me, without purpose. For the English had the power, and the powder. They had even passed a law, I was told, that all Irish should move to Connaught under pain of death. They winked at that one for they needed our hands and backs in the fields, but the law existed.

Love Jebson had brought his wife over the water, and I hated her more than him. A pinch-nosed woman with a whining voice, big with child as regularly as the seasons, she resented my maleness. For Captain Jebson had better luck breeding horses, sheep and cattle than with his wife. He couldn't seem to beget anything but daughters. There were, living, four—Charity, Joy, Peace and Patience; six or seven had died, and Benignity was expected when I left.

[28]

That was long after the night Mickeen Oge woke me from my sleep. "Come away out of this," he said. "And not a sound."

"What game?" I whispered, ever ready for sport.

"Whist!" said Mickeen Oge. "It's time you learned something of religion."

"Religion?" At ten years of age the term meant psalms sung in the Jebson parlor of a Sunday. The night around me was black moonless November. Frost crackled underfoot and the wind nipped. "At this hour?"

"When else, lad?"

"Oh. Is it the little man at Ballykillala, then?" Love Jebson had not approved when the King restored the living of that chapel to an Episcopal minister. The captain was of a different persuasion.

"No," said Mickeen Oge, "this is another matter entirely. But stop the talk and follow."

We went through the darkness, Niamh padding beside me. I was awed with the quiet of it, the secrecy, the mystery. The dog never so much as growled when brush crackled near us.

"Is that you, Pat?" asked Mickeen Oge.

"It is," said a hidden voice. "Hurry now. Don't keep him waiting."

We pushed on another mile or more with me wondering who it was we mustn't keep waiting. Now there were more sounds of passage—the snap of a twig, the fall of a stone, the stamp of a foot. The night was alive with people moving. Here noise was muffled by the gurgle of a stream, there a cough sounded loud in a clearing. Not a light showing, nor a shadow, just the sounds.

"Ah," said Mickeen Oge as we came around the shoulder of a hill, "here we are."

There was a crowd standing in a bit of a hollow, all silent. Facing them a man leaned against a slab of flat ledge chiseled out of the side of the hill. Two tiny candles, flames dancing in the breeze, were the only light.

"God bless all here," said Mickeen Oge.

"And you too," said the man softly. "Is that you, Mickeen?"

"Yes, Father." Mickeen Oge pushed me forward until we reached the man. "Kneel down, Cormac, for Father Murphy's blessing."

"God's welcome, Cormac," said Father Murphy. Close, in the candlelight, his features showed plain. He had a thin face, smooth shaven, with a long jaw, and a high-bridged nose. His lips seemed sad, but his eyes were the blue of a robin's egg. His hand moved, a gesture that ended with the palm on my head. "What have you told him, Mickeen?"

"Nothing yet, Father. I wanted him to see first."

"Can you keep a secret, Cormac?"

"Yes, Father," I said, furious at Mickeen Oge for thinking me so ignorant. "They'll not get a word from me. You're that Father Murphy from Saint Gobnet's, and the good saint blinds your enemies, which is why you have escaped them so long."

The sad lips smiled. He said: "I baptized you Cormac, but I haven't seen you since. Learn all you can till I come again."

Mickeen pulled me back, and another stepped up. But I couldn't take my stare off the priest. He was no hero in stature or stance, just a slight, tired man, almost bald, in a stained riding coat, and patched boots. Yet I had heard more stories about this Francis Murphy than about fairies, leprechauns, or the black coach of death. Proscribed and condemned he rode the whole country between the Lee and the Blackwater, and beyond, as if he owned every bush. The government knew his name, but not who hid him, nor how he came and went. They never did find out.

He bent his head, listened to a message, spoke to the crowd. He kept his voice low, but it reached every ear.

"Dearly beloved, we must be away before daylight. We'll begin."

As he stepped aside to open a book, I saw the sheen of black silk on the altar stone in the middle of the ledge, arranged like a flat-topped little tent. Later, for I never blinked the whole time, there was the glint of the gold chalice, and the white disk of the Host. Mickeen Oge, beside me, whispered explanations, but I hardly heard him.

There were thirty or so people assembled on their knees in the frost-stiff earth. Their prayers were less loud than the murmuring of the wind through the leaves of the trees. As the night fell back I could see clearer; darkness fading to gray revealed groups and persons. Old men, gnarled and twisted as blackthorn, clasped boney, calloused hands. Shawled women, pearls of tears on their cheeks, lifted faces like taut flags. Lads I had known as hobbledehoys were suddenly grave with dignity. All the girls looked saintly.

Then it was over, and the crowd dissolved like the morning mist. The candles went out; the priest left. Fairies vanished from their rings with slower steps. On a hillside, under a paling, before-dawn sky, I stood alone with Mickeen Oge, and heard a single horse trot away into the distance.

"God and the Blessed Mother," said the stableman, "hold fast to his stirrups."

I said, "Amen."

Now, *that* part of my education might well have cost my life. All practices of the Church of Rome were forbidden. So, of course, driven into the hills it flourished like the heather. When a faith, any faith, becomes hunted it is guarded and cherished from the hounds. Which simple truth has not yet been learned by any government whatever.

Still, that was not the reason why I left—

❖

Here the tale was interrupted by a crash on the table, and an angry shout.

"Papist!" cried Hamish MacInnis. "Papist, after all, as I suspicioned!"

"I have not finished," I said, bewildered. "I was merely telling of my boyhood, before I put to sea."

"You've said enough!"

Glancing around, I saw he spoke only the truth. Alec Murdoch's face was black as sin. Jill was staring in wide-eyed horror. Every man in the room looked at me as if I'd suddenly grown horns. A cold wind blew down my back; my neck broke out in goose bumps.

"But that was long ago," I said, "and in another country. I told it just to illustrate——"

Hamish was dancing about in rage. A sweep of his arm sent my drink hurtling across the table. He spoke to Alec, but his words were for all.

"That was a Popish Mass he spoke of! He's an Idolator! A worshiper of the Whore of Babylon that sits on the seven hills of Rome. He's a Papist!"

They were all standing now, except myself. In the silence that followed I could hear the drip of my spilled drink.

"Aye," said a voice not heard before. "Aye. That and more. He's both Papist—and pirate."

Chapter 4

THIS new voice, deep, had a chill threat in it like the hiss of a sword as it comes from the scabbard. At least it made a sober man of me and that quickly. While the others, including Hamish MacInnis, turned toward the doorway where the speaker stood, I planted my feet, braced myself, and calculated the distance between my chair and the boat hook in the corner. The musket, unless loaded, was worthless, but with a barbed gaff in my hands I'd be less helpless.

"Pirate?" said Alec Murdoch, his mouth working like a landed fish.

"Pirate?" Jill whispered against the back of her hand.

"Aye," said the strange voice behind me, "I fear so, my friends. With a soul stained with crimes, and hands with blood."

At that I turned, slowly, holding out my palms. "With *clean* hands," I said. "And who is it that names a man thus, behind his back?"

"Shhh. It's the Reverend Bradish."

"Ephraim Bradish, servant of the lord," Bradish said, with a bow. He was a man of moderate height, but fat, with a paunch big as a pillow, purple jowls and two chins. He wore the black of his calling from tiny buckled shoes to broad-brimmed hat. Coat and breeches were broad-cloth. He had a dab of a mouth, a pug nose, but very shrewd, narrow, hazel eyes. The preacher's wig was as gray and frizzled as the lord chancellor's. It didn't fit; whenever he waggled his head the wig moved.

"You call me 'pirate,' Reverend Bradish?"

"I do."

"You lie."

A flush rose from the purple jowls to tint his cheeks. Bradish silenced the outraged buzz around us by a shake of his head that flipped the ends of his wig. Drawing a paper from inside his coat, he said: "The thief and the liar are vomit out of my mouth, sayeth the Lord. Let us see which of us merit the description."

"Who calls me 'pirate' lies!" This time I slapped my hand on the table top for emphasis. It also gave me a brace if I had to spring.

"Hush, man," Alec Murdoch said.

"Hold your tongue," said Hamish MacInnis.

My glance swung across both of them. I let my voice rise in anger. "I'll not. It's bad enough to be shipwrecked, cast ashore with nothing, but when an honest merchant sailor is accused of piracy without the slightest proof on——"

Reverend Ephraim Bradish cleared his throat. "Proof," he said, "we must seek to find. I have just sailed back from the mainland. There, in Saybrook, I was requested to convey a copy of this document to our constable here." He flourished the paper, snapping it open.

"It can't concern me," I said, easily. My brain tried desperately to figure the time since I'd left the Grand Banks. It couldn't concern me!

"We shall see." Bradish handed his hat to a bystander, spread his legs, held up the paper with both hands. As he cleared his throat again his wig seemed to quiver one way and his paunch another. He rolled out the reading like a man used to the pulpit.

"Proclamation from His Excellency, the Governor. To all constables, watches, militia officers, officials, and citizens of the united seven provinces constituting the Dominion of New England."

"Fash!" snorted Hamish MacInnis. "Does he still whistle that same tune?"

"Through information brought into Boston," read Bradish, ignoring the interruption, "by the schooner *Brothers' Venture,* Samuel Quimby, Master, we learn of pirates operating in our waters, his vessel having been seized by these villains while operating on the Grand Fishing Banks——"

Sweet and sainted mercy! I thought, not listening to the dates and other nonsense the clergyman was droning. I remembered the *Brothers' Venture* well. But how had she made Boston so speedily?

"—but being released upon the discovery by the others that two of their number had fled in the night aboard a ketch purloined for that purpose. These two being accused by those left of being the ringleaders and perpetrators of all their crimes and troubles."

Those lying bastards, I thought, listening hard now.

"The main bulk of the pirates sailing in pursuit of these two deserters, Captain Quimby and crew immediately put in to Boston at all speed, bearing with them a description of the pirates, especially the pair who may try to land on our shores."

"Man, dear," I said, "this is a grand document to be sure, if a bit long in the writing, but why read it here and now?"

Hazel slits glared at me over the top of the paper. Reverend Bradish went on reading: "First, foremost and chief of these is one Jack Irish, or Irish Jack——"

"Ahhhh." Jill's loud sigh brought all our heads around. She flushed, but relief was in her voice. "His name's Cormac. Cormac Doyle."

"Also known," continued Bradish, "as Cormac the Mick, and Mac Foyle, or Coyle."

"Common names, all of them," I said. Nobody bothered to look at me. Jill Murdoch's mouth was a straight line.

"About five feet, eleven inches in height," Reverend Bradish said, "and roughly one hundred and fifty pounds in weight. Brown hair, blue eyes, with a slightly crooked nose, and a star-shaped scar from an old pike wound high on his left thigh."

My fingers trembled with the effort of not reaching to touch the place

[33]

of the scar. I pushed my stool back, stood, and stretched. "Well," I said, "that's fine. Glad I am that the wicked devil was scarred. I've no mark on me."

Jill Murdoch's voice rang out. "But you have! A puckered sort of circle right where it said!"

Her brother's question broke a shocked silence. *"How do ye know that?"*

Reverend Ephraim Bradish coughed; Tansey Murdoch shook her head. Everyone stared at the girl. A blush rose slowly from her neck to the roots of her hair. She said, lamely, eyes wretched: "I—I happened to—to see it——"

Partly because I couldn't stand her face, partly because nobody was watching me, I made my move. A kick sent the stool toward Alec Murdoch; a wrench upset the table. As it crashed I leaped for the corner with musket and gaff. Hamish MacInnis grabbed for me, but I slammed the heel of my hand on his forehead. Someone shouted; another man swore. But I'd have reached the weapons only Jill Murdoch stepped in my way.

"No, no!" she cried. "You'll not get them." Her arms were raised to ward me off; there was no telling how she had moved so fast.

"Slut!" I said, between my teeth. My heel grated as I spun to meet the rest. There was nothing of courage, nor of sense, in fighting. On that island there was no place to run even if I fought free. Some hatred of captivity drove me. I had never been a prisoner, and, in a white blur of rage, every ounce of me rebelled against the thought.

They charged me in a pack. Alec Murdoch was among the leaders, and the Reverend Bradish cheered them on from the rear. The sensible course was to yield, but I met them with my fists. No stranger to brawls, my first punch dropped a young fisherman; my second doubled another over my wrist. This time the Swede wasn't whooping, and swinging beside me; so two blows were all I had. Then they swarmed over me, and I went down.

"Seize him!" yelled the clergyman.

"Grab him!" Alec Murdoch shouted.

Hamish MacInnis cursed me in Gaelic. His voice cut through the hubbub in shrill fury.

The fishermen, scrambling, managed to get in each other's way. Swings collided; grabbing hands clutched someone else; slashing kicks battered the nearest shins. With a twist I broke loose, rose.

Alec Murdoch loomed before me, arms curved to catch and wrestle. He was panting with anger. We were both planted, hip deep, in the struggling mass of men entwined on the floor. For an instant that seemed like a full minute we stared eye to eye, glaring.

"Lying Papist bastard," said Alec.

"Covenant hypocrite," I said.

I fended off his clutch, caught his fingers, pulled him close. The joy of battle rose in me; my fist swung back like a hammer poised to strike. By his eyes he saw it coming, but could do nothing. As God made us, I thought, I'll drive my knuckles through the long face of him.

Then, a keg of gunpowder seemed to explode on the back of my head. There was an instant of bright, shooting lights before engulfing blackness. I never knew how I fell, or another thing.

❖

People were talking in time to the throbbing pain in my skull. Buzz, buzz, buzz went the voices as insistent as hiving bees. Raising my hands to press my temples I found them bound with rope. Indeed, I was trussed like a bird for the oven, round ankles, wrists, and knees. Whoever had tied those sailor knots was no apprentice at the trade. Recalling the reverend, and the blasted description, I knew I was taken.

"Patrick, Kieran and Columcille!" I said to myself, "but this is as pretty a pickle as ever brined pork." The thought of my own foolishness was worse than my aches. None but a daft yokel would have let the cleric's reading panic him into action. My chances, as ever, lay with talk and dissimulation, not in attacking my accusers. As a warrior I was always prone to bite off more than easily chewed. It was sad to be wise after the event, and I groaned at my folly.

"He's stirring," said a voice. There was no mistaking Alec Murdoch's rolling of those r's.

"Aye," Hamish MacInnis said, "I saw him move just now."

"The way of the transgressor is hard," said the deep tones of the Reverend Bradish. "But their skulls are harder. He will live to grace a gallows tree."

That opened my eyes. I said: "Thank you for your well wishes. You've made a grave mistake."

They had placed me in some sort of boathouse; water lapped under me, and the moonlight made blue streaks through the loose boards of the walls. The three men were grouped around a lit lanthorn. Scrawny little MacInnis squatted on his heels. Alec Murdoch was sitting on a coil of hawser. The clergyman, most of his bulk hidden in shadow, had a chair. He leaned forward, hands on knees, to peer down at me from under his hat brim.

"Those who live by the sword," said Bradish. "Will——"

"Perish by the sword," I said, interrupting. "But that says nothing of dancing at a rope's end."

"The Devil, or a Papist," MacInnis said, "can quote Scripture."

Alec Murdoch gave a snort of impatience. "Don't parley with him, Hamish. I am glad his blood will not be on us, though he abused our hospitality, and shamed my sister."

"I shamed no woman," I said. "She lies if she says different!"

"Jill Murdoch will say nothing," said the Reverend Bradish. "Neither to complain nor explain. But her brother as her guardian, and myself—" his throat clearing disturbed the shadows—"as her future father-in-law would like—that is—my son Daniel—already called to a church——"

His fumbling speech, and their faces, told me what troubled them. I had the grace to hide my grin. Modesty had silenced the girl. Not even among the women who followed pirates was limb display common, and the Puritans were death on it.

I said: "Don't you know your own sister, Alec Murdoch? Sure, I had a twinge in an old wound walking here, and when she asked I told her of the scar. Not knowing, of course, that others would make so much ado about it."

"Praise the Lord," said Alec Murdoch.

Hamish MacInnis slapped fist into palm. "Didn't I say the lass was all right? Didn't she fell the wretch with a swing of the musket while the rest of us tumbled in our own way?"

"A brave girl," agreed the preacher.

"Too quick with her hands," I said, not thankful for the head that Jill had given me, "as you're all too quick to judge. For a similar name, a description that could fit two dozen, and a scar—mine happened when I fell on a boathook—you'd hang a man."

Alec Murdoch said: "And you started fighting to beat sense into our heads." He sneered, shaking his head.

"I went for a weapon," I said, "to hold you back till you'd listen to reason. The reverend here was convinced of my guilt."

"And still am," Bradish said. "But it is not up to us. You'll be turned over to the proper authorities, tried, and given justice."

"Here?"

"No. In Boston."

My bonds felt looser as he said it. I was not sure where Boston was, but doubted it was around the next turn. The more miles that stretched

[36]

between me and there, the more chances there were for escape. Guile, wile or gold would yet cheat the hangman. These three men, I judged, would scruple at a bargain, but others might not. There was the chain and coin round my neck to barter for freedom, or, if worst came to worst, a share of the sunken sea chest.

"Good," I said. "The sooner there, the sooner all this is mended. Since this is an island I suppose we sail."

"We sail," said Alec Murdoch. "But only across the sound. I am constable here, but my duty ends when I hand you to the next constable. He'll see you the next step on your journey."

"Well," I said, "I'm ready. I can't shake the unlucky sand of this place off my shoes—your shoes, Reverend, begging your pardon—fast enough."

"You may keep the shoes," said Bradish.

"Providence rules us, not luck," Alec said.

MacInnis said: "There's time, lad. There's time."

All three remarks were reluctant, subdued. A glance flapped from one to the other to the third like a fish in a net. Alec Murdoch stroked his chin; the preacher cleared his throat again; MacInnis drummed his fingers on the floor. Oho, I thought, there is something on their stomachs.

"My boy," said Reverend Bradish. "There is only one course for the sinner, be he black as pitch, and that is repentance, confession, and a change of heart."

"Confession?"

"Fash!" said Hamish MacInnis. "Not your Papist hide-behind-the-arras kind, but open declaration before God and man."

"Before a servant of the Lord," Bradish said.

"And an authority such as a constable," added Alec Murdoch.

MacInnis scowled, annoyed at being left out. I looked at each in turn, and spoke with as much innocence as I could muster. "How can a guilt-less man confess?"

A triple grunt of disgust came as one. MacInnis, squatting, jogged up and down on his heels in impatience. "Man, man," he said eagerly. "The paper the reverend has mentions your absconding with much treasure. If you should return your ill-gotten gains it will go easier with you."

"A sign of true repentance," said Bradish.

"And loyalty to the authorities," Alec Murdoch said.

Their faces, in the flickering wan light from the lanthorn, were avid, the whites of the eyes showing. My laughter hit them like cold water. I said: "You all lived through that storm. The ship I sailed lies at the bottom of the sea. Besides, I confess to nothing, admit nothing, and defy you to prove anything!"

"Aye." Alec Murdoch unfolded his long length from the coiled rope. "Well, it did no harm to ask."

The preacher rumbled to his feet. He sounded pained. "For the unregenerate there is no forgiveness. Take him away, Alec. The sooner we're rid of him the better."

Hamish MacInnis drew out a knife, opened the blade with his teeth. The gleam of the steel gave me a startled moment, but he only cut the ropes on my legs. His grumble was annoyed. "You're able-bodied enough to walk."

Reverend Bradish took the light; the others, one at each arm, jerked me to my feet. My legs tingled with the sharp prickles that set my teeth on edge; I stamped them into shape as we left the boathouse.

The night was clear, moon and starlit, with the water like silver silk, rippled by a breeze both brisk and cool. The shoreline was strange. I stared about, puzzled. There was no village, no lights nor outlines of houses, no cove, no line of battered vessels. This beach curved in a different way; there were only a few shacks, and a pinnace rocking beside the boathouse pier. Glancing at the moon I realized we were on the other, mainland, western coast.

The pinnace was a light craft, single masted, not much bigger than a jolly boat. Since the last ship under me had sunk, I drew back from trusting to a cockle shell.

"You're not putting that out on the ocean?" I asked.

"Ocean!" Hamish MacInnis pushed me forward. "A wee sail on the sound is all. Don't you think we know these waters? Get in." When I still hung back, he wrestled me to the edge of the pier.

The reverend held up the lanthorn. Alec Murdoch dropped into the pinnace, helped me down. He took out a horse pistol, cocked it, waved it toward the bow. "Except you try trickery," he said, "you needn't fear."

I crawled to my place as if sullen, but my fear was that MacInnis would need his knife. He'd put it back in his pocket, but his prodding had made it easy game for a man who'd studied under the light-fingered gentry of London. The knife was snug in my jerkin when MacInnis climbed aboard.

"God speed," called Bradish from above. "Make sure that Constable Pemberly understands the prisoner's importance. And inquire if there's a reward." He tossed a line over the gunwale.

"There'll be no reward," I said.

"We know," said Hamish MacInnis, gloomily, shoving off.

They rowed, one behind the other, until they were out a ways. Alec sat nearest, but both watched me over their shoulders. They were good strong oarsmen, bending in unison. Even small Hamish dug deep, and handled his sweeps with ease.

"If you'd loose my bonds," I said, "I can row with the best."

"Stay where you are," Alec Murdoch said. "The pistol's handy in my lap."

MacInnis laughed, a mocking titter. "Is it likely we'd trust you? Anyway, it's time we put the sail up." He shipped his oars, stepped to the mast.

The two had the single sail hoisted in four pulls. It bellied before the breeze, and the pinnace began making feathers at her bow. Hamish steered, hunched in the stern. Alec, long legs crossed tailor fashion, sat on a thwart amidships, watching me, pistol barrel resting on crooked elbow.

On the second tack, canvas hid me from them, and I got the knife out. On the fourth I cut my wrist bonds, careful not to let them fall away. After that I leaned against the gunwale, scanning the shore ahead like a homecoming passenger.

Inside I was humming happily, though I never spoke, sitting hunched over as if the world bowed down my shoulders. After a time they stopped talking to me; they chatted together, terse men, used to each other.

"Back by dawn, Alec."

"Aye."

"Unless they fribble."

"Won't. Can't waste the day."

"Aye."

I saw the schooner first, a low, black shape on the water to the north, running without lights, with darkened sails. Hamish MacInnis had quick eyes. He spoke a moment later.

"Sail to starboard, Alec."

"Huh?" Alec stood to gaze. "Aye."

"Beating in, wouldn't you say?"

Alec Murdoch settled back. "Mayhap. She'll not cross our beam. We who run in the paths of righteousness need fear nothing. Blessed is the the ship that sails in the service of the Lord God!"

When the preacher, Bradish, was around, I noted, Jill's brother wasn't so quick with the pulpit phrases. In his own boat he spoke more freely. Hamish MacInnis spat over the side, argued.

"Ain't likely our cargo's any more blessed than theirs."

"Hamish!"

"Well? A Popish pirate?"

"We are delivering a Philistine into the hands of Israel!"

The mainland was looming larger now, and I measured the distance. It was no more than a decent swim on a fine night. I would have to get shoes and clothes off under water, but I'd hang onto the knife. So I spoke for the first time in over a half hour.

"What was that, Alec Murdoch?"

The question startled them both. Alec jerked the pistol upright; Hamish made the pinnace veer.

"What?"

"What did he say?"

"Something about delivering a Philistine, wasn't it?" My voice was deliberately mild, and pleasant. In fact, I was enjoying myself.

"Aye," said Alec.

"Well," I said, "I'm afraid you're wrong."

As I spoke I planted my feet; as I finished I went over the side in a fast, flat dive. The pistol roared; I saw the flash from the corner of my eye as my hands split the sea. The water was chill for September but not cold.

Turning under water I swam back toward the pinnace. My shoes were gone, and the jerkin off before I surfaced. I came up close under the stern. The sail rattled down as my head emerged.

"Can you see him, Alec? Can you see him?"

Hamish MacInnis was shouting not five feet over my head. I gripped the gunwale, pulled, reaching. The scrawny man's back was turned, and my fingers hooked into his belt before he knew it. One heave had him over my head.

"*Alec!*"

He screamed the name as he arched through the air. A splash drowned out his cry. By that time I was in the pinnace, knife open in my fist, facing Alec Murdoch.

Alec stared at me, jaw dropped. The pistol still dangled from slack fingers.

"Alec!" MacInnis cried. "Help!" He was splashing, blubbering.

"Hamish can't swim," Alec said.

"You'd better get him then," I said.

"I can't swim either."

His doleful tone, the indecision in his manner, puzzled me. I cast a glance at the floundering MacInnis in time to see his hat float away as he sank. That bobbing blob of headgear made me suddenly anxious for the man's safety.

"Get your oars, then," I said, "and go after him!"

"Can't do that either," said Alec, dropping the pistol, and picking up a tin pannikin. "Must bail or it founders." He motioned toward the bow, and, looking past him, I saw water spurting as prettily as a fountain.

"What in hell?" I asked.

"Missed you," Alec Murdock said, shrugging. "But the cursed pistol ball shot a hole in its bottom." He dropped on his knees and began to bail. The pinnace's bow was already beginning to settle.

"Al—*hic!*" Hamish MacInnis's wail was choked and watery. It sounded the knell of my hopes for escape.

"God damn!" I said, bitterly. Closing the knife, I stowed it away, and went in after MacInnis. Accursed be all sailors who will not learn to swim! Here I was, safe and away, foiled by two Scot numbskulls. But I could not let the small man drown, and Alec was Jill Murdoch's brother.

MacInnis was no great weight, but fought like a poked weasel. My annoyance exploded into one fine, swift clout on his jaw. After that he sagged, and I dragged him back to the pinnace. He lay on the bottom, coughing and spewing up a tub full of water, as Alec tried stopping the leak with his socks.

"Glory be to God!" I said, bailing. "What was it you used in that pistol, a cannonball?" We were ankle wash in the wet, and the bow was dipping in a curtsy at each swell.

"Ahoy, the pinnace!" came a hail. "Are you in trouble?"

I looked up to see the dark hulk of the schooner beside us. She was still all dark; the faces along the rail were pale blurs.

"No!" My shout was thick with rage. I shook the pannikin at them. "It's a game we're after playing!" The failure of my scheme to escape was biting deep into my skin.

"We heard and saw your shot," the man on the schooner called. "Anything we can do?"

Alec Murdoch straightened. He gave me a sweet smile, before he cupped palm to mouth. "Aye, Tobias," he cried. "Alec Murdoch here. You can throw us a line, if you will. Hamish and me was taking a pirate to the main when he stove in the pinnace trying to escape."

The man's effrontery took the speech from me. They had a tow line taut, and muskets on me in a trice. So I came to the mainland of North America after all, towed in a leaking pinnace, captive of a fisherman constable, and his half-drowned crony.

I had only one thing to say to Alec Murdoch, more pained than angry.

"Why, you ungrateful psalm-singing spawn of a bitch," I said.

Chapter 5

SOFT gray spread across the sky from the east, dyeing the black velvet of night, covering the stars. Dawn was due, but not hurrying; a hush lay on the land. There was no whisper of wind. The pennon hung limp from the schooner's topmast like an empty stocking. On the shore not a leaf stirred; shadow still bound the foliage into solid clumps. As the pale moon died the "sound," as they called it, tarnished its silver, but it ran calm, lifting in easy swells. Nothing in nature moved loudly or quickly. Only the crew of the schooner, though they made little noise, worked at unloading as if driven by a lash.

They had berthed their ship alongside a sagging wharf that seemed to jut out of the dark square of a warehouse. The pinnace was beached, but its three passengers had transferred to the schooner's afterdeck. Hamish and I sat huddled in blankets, dripping. Alec Murdoch stood guard over me with a borrowed musket. Captain and crew were busy handling cargo, passing bales over the taffrail, rolling casks along the wharf.

They worked with a fast stealth that I thought I recognized, the precision of men who had long practice together. When Hamish MacInnis sneezed, a tearing explosion that shattered the stillness, every man froze for an instant, heads turned. Then, I was sure, and chuckled.

"God bless you," I said to MacInnis.

"Fash!" he said. "Keep it. It's you I've to thank for the wetting."

"And for your rescue," I said, but without force. There was no arguing with that unreasonable pair. Alec blamed me for the hole in the pinnace; Hamish blamed me for everything. In truth I was the biggest loser from my gamble. The scrawny man had his knife back, but, though Alec had fished my jerkin aboard with an oar, I was shoeless again.

Alec Murdoch leveled the musket when I stood up. Waving my hand at him, I said: "I'm merely getting my bearings. Where's the town?"

He pointed with a nod. "Along the beach a mile or so. Tobias puts in on his own place."

Well he might, I thought, pleased at the reply. My brain was busy with a new plan, a grand plan. Once the cargo was safely ashore I would broach it to the schooner's master.

"Tobias is captain?" I asked.

"Aye."

"Owner as well," said Hamish MacInnis, through chattering teeth. "This ship, *The Careful Mary,* is his own from bow to stern."

"Free and clear," Alec Murdoch agreed. "And there's the warehouse, the shipyard, and other interests. He's a credit to the town is Tobias." There was no envy in Alec's voice, just a decent respect.

Better and better, I decided. A man who stands to lose will listen before another. This Tobias seemed to be a skipper-merchant after my own heart. I hadn't had much chance to look him over, but I did so now.

He stood, stocky and barrel chested, directing his men. In spite of the tarred sea cloak wrapped around him he'd spring forward to lend a hand as often as he gave an order. In the dimness of the false dawn I couldn't see his face, but he wore his hat brim low, and a cutlass lifted the skirt of the cloak with a curve like a cock's tail. The way he moved, I guessed he was handy with his cutlass.

To the east, above that Long Island where I'd been cast ashore, the gray was changing to blue shot with pink and gold. The sun, still hidden, cast a glow before it that made a line white hot like a poker first from the forge. Day was getting ready to break.

"That's the last," said the schooner's captain, as a cask was rolled away. He walked aft toward us, then waited for his crew to return. Those on the wharf came back in a bunch, joined the others on deck.

"All stowed, Pa," said one, knuckling his forehead.

Startled, I stared. Then I realized that the whole crew, in spite of different heights, had the same stocky build as their captain, walked with the same wide, striding gait. Swiftly I counted heads. Ten men.

"William, Dick, Ned and Pym," said the captain. "Stay with me. The rest of you home to your mother. Tell her I'll be along presently." Four sons followed him as he climbed to the afterdeck.

"Alec. Hamish," he said. "You'll breakfast with me." His voice was gruff, made hoarse by many commands, but he kept it pleasant. "And who is this bully boy?"

"My name is Cormac O'——"

"His name," interrupted Hamish MacInnis, "is anything he cares to think of at the moment. But unless the description lies, he's a known and wanted pirate."

"Captain Tobias," I said, "that is not——"

"Speak when you're spoken to," said Tobias, spinning on his heel. "Bring him below where I can get a look at him."

We clattered down the ladder and crowded into the captain's cabin. It was a snug berth, bare but comfortable, with leather cushions, and a shining mahogany table, fastened down. One of the lads lit the candles in a candelabra that was never made in America, chased silver with a French escutcheon on the base. It reflected my grin.

Tobias read the document that Alec handed him, glanced from it to me. The candlelight displayed his face as well as mine. Close to he looked older, well past fifty, with a weathered, leathery face; webs of wrinkles sprayed from the corners of mouth and eyes. Hatless, his hair was mouse gray, worn long, tied in back with a black ribbon. Against the tan of his skin his eyes seemed sea green.

"This cap fits," he said, tapping the paper.

"A score of men," I said.

Hamish MacInnis sneered. "Even to the scar?"

"Even so."

Tobias twisted the paper into a spill, whistled against it. He said: "It's not like Andros to get such details wrong. I cannot stand the Cavalier cut of his jib, but he's accurate."

"Satrap of a tyrant," said Alec Murdoch.

"Aye," agreed Hamish, "but no lover of pirates."

The captain's smile was grim. "The governor loves nothing except at the king's command. He's had His Majesty's frigate, *Rose*, in Boston Harbor for a couple of years, sent to chase fellows like this and his friends."

"It would chase smugglers, too," I said.

I expected at least a change of expression, maybe a gulp from a son, or an oath. Captain Tobias didn't even blink. Alec Murdoch and Hamish MacInnis exchanged a glance; somebody laughed softly behind me.

"Yes," said the captain, bowing, "Sir Edmund Andros is death on smugglers. Seems to have some fool notion the Navigation Acts mean what they say. Which is proper for a governor, but hard on shipping."

That was bold talk, and neat. In case he thought I was just guessing, I pulled the blanket tighter around me, and said: "You all seem to be friends here. Or relatives. It's not my place to ask about a man's cargo. I'm all for friendship. Rum, now. Sure, it's a grand friendly drink. And tobacco."

"Both taxed," Tobias said.

"Yes," I said, "among other things. What else can you expect from a tight-fisted government that won't let so much as a nail travel to the colonies in any but English bottoms? That even frowns on a bit of friendly trade between neighbors. Now, I'll admit I've winked at those rules myself once and again." Smiling, I made my voice pleasant and easy. "The cargo I lost in the storm was molasses and some rum." The same lie that I told Jill Murdoch served me here. It was sensible not to be inventing different ones.

"Just what," asked the captain, "are you trying to say with that spate of words?"

"That *The Careful Mary* would not be running without lights, with tar-dark sails, and unloading before sunrise without good reason."

"The impudence of him," said Hamish MacInnis.

Alec Murdoch said: "It is not your business, ruffian, how a God-fearing merchant conducts his business!"

"No," I said, shrugging, "but it might be the business of the excise officer, or the collector of the port. Or even of the constable into whose hands I am to be delivered."

Murdoch and MacInnis gaped, but the captain remained composed. He made a steeple of his fingertips, rested his chin on it. "Pym," he said.

A youth, somewhat taller than his brothers, stepped from behind me into the light. His apple-round cheeks showed an unrazored golden down. Pym had the heavy shoulders of his clan, but not the years to fill his frame.

"Aye, sir?" he said, with a low-high break in his voice.

"Fetch the irons. Our prisoner seems to find means of cutting ropes." As Pym disappeared the captain politely explained. "We keep a few shackles aboard, Master Cormac. They pay their passage in case we transport a slave or two."

"That's your answer then?" Anger stirred through my question. The damned smuggler could put me in irons, but he couldn't gag me forever. An informer was a low creature to my mind, but Tobias had no right to guess that.

The captain raised his eyebrows, a signal for his sons to surround me. One closed on each side; another breathed on my neck. Outside, metal clanged as the irons jangled.

"That's my answer, Master Cormac." The captain rose, bowed deep. "You see, I'm afraid you're somewhat misinformed. Ned Pemberly, there on your left, is excise man for the Town of Saybrook. His brother William, abaft your starboard side, is collector of the port."

My mouth opened so wide my jaws ached. Murdoch and MacInnis guffawed; the scrawny man beat his thigh.

"And I," continued the captain, "am Tobias Pemberly, constable, at your service. Like my cargo, sir, you are already delivered. And like it, also, you will be passed on to the proper hands as speedily as possible."

Laughter burst around me. I shrank from it, feeling shame heat my face. My bargain was no bargain at all. Tobias Pemberly, smuggler, was also upholder of the law!

This knowledge so crushed me that I hardly felt it when they snapped the gyves on my limp wrists. The lad, Pym, hammered the pins home with neat care, but each blow marked my heart. They had me now, I thought, in iron cuffs with a chain stretched between. I had been so sure that my talk would win freedom, but it had dug the pit deeper under my feet. And a man without faith in his own talk is a lost man.

"Take him to the warehouse office," said the captain. "Dry him and feed him. We'll not abuse him for likening an honest trade to piracy."

The brothers hustled me out to Hamish MacInnis's crowing. That moment I cursed myself for not letting the scrawny man drown.

Pemberly's sons proved good-natured louts. They followed their father's orders without mocking my misfortune. Pym struck flint on steel before the wood laid in the fireplace of the warehouse office. William, the eldest, gray at the temples, sent the other two for food. This pair, as alike as twins, returned laden with dishes. To judge by the way that family broke its fast there was a fine profit in the honest trade of smuggling.

The house must have been near for the hot things came hot. While my clothes steamed I stared at the plenty provided—rashers of bacon, a dozen eggs, thick slabs of ham, a cold leg of mutton, white bread, half a pie, porridge, a pan of fried fish, a jug of steaming chocolate.

As the brothers fell to, I no longer wondered that Tobias Pemberly thought little of pirates. Sure, it was poor fare they had in comparison.

Without appetite, I choked down porridge and bread, drank chocolate. The last was sweet and thick, but even this treat couldn't lighten my gloom. When shackles were put on they pinched more than flesh. They linked wrist to wrist with a chain, but worse they joined the wearer to the brute beast, the slave, the madman. They set one apart from his fellows.

So, I munched, and gazed into the fire, feeling sorry for myself. Even the future looked very bad. Tobias Pemberly could carry me to Boston in *The Careful Mary* in a matter of a few days. There was no escaping from a ship's brig, on the high seas.

After a couple of hours the captain joined us. He had changed his dress for a suit of cinnamon color, with crisp lawn showing at collar and cuffs, but no lace. The tanned cheeks were freshly shaved and glowing. He gave orders as he entered.

"Pym. To the house. Get a pouch with some foodstuffs. Load and fetch the second-best fowling piece. William. Find that fancy footwear we never found buyer for. Third shelf on the south wall of the warehouse, five boards in from the corner."

Pym went out one door; William through another into the warehouse. The captain selected a long-stemmed clay from a sheaf in a jug on the fireplace mantel. Then, to my surprise, he handed me another.

"Thank you," I said, meaning it for I'd had no tobacco for a long time. He passed me a cannister stuffed with dark-brown leaf, fragrant with perique.

"I sent Alec and Hamish back in my sloop," said Pemberly, bending to spoon a glowing coal from the fire. When we had both pipes going he sat down opposite me, crossing his legs.

"Good riddance," I said, with a smile. The tobacco was strong flavored, and welcome, but I was wary of this new friendly attitude.

William returned, handed a pair of boots to his father. Tobias tossed them at my feet. "Here," he said. "You can't walk to Boston in your stockings."

"Walk?" I asked, fondling the gift. The boots were soft, cordovan leather, finely made, pliant and russet. Few gentlemen boasted better footgear; they came calf high with the fit and feel of a glove. My sudden fear was that Pemberly had heard of my chain and doubloon, courted them as payment. I'd not exchange my gold keys to freedom for a pair of boots.

"Walk," repeated Tobias. "I stable no horses."

"But the schooner?"

Teeth whiter than the pipe stem showed in a grin. "I care not to have *The Careful Mary* too familiar around Boston harbor. A sharp-eyed man, the frigate captain say, might remember her lines on some other occasion."

With his build, the pipe, his neat clothes, Pemberly looked more a stolid Dutch burgher discussing wool prices than a smuggling sea captain. This feeling must have showed on my face for he pointed the pipe stem at me.

"Master Cormac. You still misunderstand your position and my own. I have put you in irons, and will transport you under guard to the next constable, but hold no rancor. You are suspected and detained as a pirate. Nothing you say can harm me. My neighbors know my trade, give me their custom. The government can prove nothing."

He paused, and blew a great cloud of smoke as Pym entered, laden with pouch and gun. "Ah," said the captain, "here is your escort. As soon as your pipe is finished, you and Pym will take to the road."

Gazing at the lad, I found the tobacco more mellow. Old Tobias was a hard nut; the other brothers grew on the same tree. But Pym, for all his height, was only a boy.

Sure, I thought, if I can't flimflam a downy-cheeked stripling, I deserve to go in chains. I figured I'd be loose and away in three hours at the utmost.

So I puffed contentedly, well satisfied and in no hurry.

Chapter 6

IT was still early morning when Pym Pemberly and I started on our journey. The sky was clear blue, the sun warm, but the breeze coming in from the sea had a tingle in it as well as the smell of salt. Even with shackled wrists, a prisoner, I stepped with a brisk stride. What with the walking, and some thoughts about Tobias Pemberly I followed my guard in silence, content to be on the move once more. There was no plan in my mind. When my next chance of escape came I wished to be well away from that efficient family of smugglers.

Pym led us inland, away from the sea, avoiding the town by a path that twisted among tall trees where shafts of sunlight, slanting down, turned the leaves to shimmering greens not unlike reflected waves dancing on the ceiling of a ship's cabin. Soon we could neither see, smell, nor hear the surf. My only view of Saybrook was from a hilltop beyond it. It looked pleasant enough at that distance, frame houses facing across a road, each with a farm behind it. There was a tiny square of grazing common, and a church. But what struck me was the newness of it all.

At least that was what I decided after puzzling it out. In England, or Ireland, towns that size would have maybe a castle around, or a manor house, mayhap a tumbled ruin or two. The houses themselves, if no larger, would be either aged, or dilapidated. I didn't bother to make a comparison with the Indies ports I had visited for those places were foreign anyway, Spanish built for a tropic sun.

Young Pym was a careful keeper. Captain Tobias had given precise orders, and the tall lad was the kind who wouldn't sneeze without his father's permission. He clutched his fowling piece with a grip that whitened his knuckles, started if I whistled, watched me with the wide eyes of a scared rabbit. By the time we came out of the woods to the road, I'd had more than enough of it.

"Pym," I asked, "is the gun loaded?" It was an ugly long-barreled weapon with a muzzle as big as a fist.

"Yes," he said, startled.

"Well, then, I'd be obliged if you'd not point it at me all the time. I see it's cocked, and I've no great liking for a hole in my middle."

"Holes," Pym said. "It's charged with shot."

"All the more reason you wouldn't want it going off by mischance. Nor would I. I'll give you my word not to try to escape."

The round face reddened as he pursed his lips. With the fuzz on his cheeks he resembled a ripe peach. Pym wet his lips, spoke. "What good's a pirate's word?"

"Better alive than dead," I said, half tempted to take the gun away from him, and knot it around his neck. To be doubted, by a callow lout in a superior tone, was goading. Determining to be patient, I ignored the insult with a laugh. The next time I tried to escape I wanted to be ready, and certain. Besides, Pym warily kept his distance, gun level.

The road hardly deserved the name, a cart-wide track, wheel rutted and pockmarked with potholes. Stirring dust with my new boots, I started down it. Pym followed, eight paces behind, faithful as a shadow. It was too nice a day to stay angry, or even to sulk about the shackles on my wrists. Without turning my head, I asked a question.

"Is this the main road, Pym?"

He paused so long, I looked around. Pym was evidently reflecting before he answered, fearful of trickery. This will be a damned dull march, I thought, waiting.

"The post rides it."

"From Boston?"

"New York too."

"Often?"

"When he needs."

Having once owned a parrot that gave more information, I shut up. Pym, nice as pie among his family, seemed too worried by his responsibility to be friendly. The road led to Boston, was travelled, was a highway between the two colonies. Anything more I wished to know would have to wait.

We walked around a bend to come on a broad, gleaming river. The sight halted me, so suddenly that Pym squealed.

This river was worth a squeal, worth a shout. Nothing I'd seen on my voyages had prepared me for the breadth of it, the majestic sweep as it rolled to the sea between high green banks, dark blue with current in the middle, gray and lazy with tidewater near the shore. The Lee I remembered as ever-changing beauty; the Thames, busy and bridged, was a city river where I knew it. This stream, in its wide naturalness, caught me by surprise. From it I think came my first inkling that the wonders of this new land were big.

"Don't try anything!" Pym was shouting behind me. He sounded as if he'd stepped on a thorn. "Don't run! I'll shoot!"

Even his nervous trigger finger didn't bother me. I said: "Pym, I'm *not* running. The eyes in my head have my feet turned to stone. Whist, the water! And what would you be calling it?"

"Calling what?"

"The river, man. The river!"

"That?" said Pym, in the gentle voice used to a child, or a madman. "Why, that's just the Connecticut."

"Connecticut," I said, mimicking the drumbeat of the outlandish syllables. Somehow it was fitting that the name was strange and savage. The lad's very casualness was impressive. Life, I decided, would be grand in a land where such rivers were taken for granted. Given freedom without chains, and a chest full of riches, a man could sink roots in such a place.

"There's a ferry," Pym said, "below the bank."

There was a ferry, a flat-bottomed, oversized punt, with a toothless old man in charge of it. He ogled my shackles with popping eyes.

"A felon?" he asked.

"A pirate," Pym said, frog puffed with pride.

Rattling my chain, I bared my teeth, but the ferryman merely sucked his gums in disgust. "All very well," said he, "but I'll be months getting my fee from the vestrymen. The post is bad enough, but felons is misery. Nobody wants to pay for sinners to cross."

Charon probably said the same at the Styx. Crossing, we all pulled on oars. Refusal never entered my head; the river still fascinated me. I was only sorry the voyage was so short.

On the other side we followed the same road. As a seaman I was not accustomed to long walks, and Pym, lanky in the shanks, covered ground better and faster. He wasn't a prodding sort, for all his worrisome ways, and let me set my own pace. When we overtook a cart behind plodding oxen, laden with firewood, Pym was willing to beg a ride.

The carter, as solid and blank faced as his beasts, seemed glad of the company. He, too, looked askance at my fetters, but said nothing. We jolted along for about a mile before he spoke.

"Happen it's hanging cause?" he asked.

"Piracy." Pym nearly broke his neck nodding.

"Happen it's naught but a mistake," I said. Hanging was both sport and spectacle, but nothing I considered with relish in my situation. The carter's speech twanged a string in my memory; broad Devonshire that was once familiar. "But when did you leave Devon?"

"You know Devon?"

"I've ridden the breadth of it," I said, telling no less than truth, "when I was younger."

"Four years," the carter said with heavy gloom. "Four overlong years. 'Tis good to be here among the saints, with proper preaching, and holy life, away from the fleshpots and the Papists. But 'tis not Devon. Now and again I have a longing."

"You could go back."

"No." He said the word with finality. Then, twisting on his seat, he looked at Pym. "You've heard there's a King's Chapel now to Boston."

"I've heard," Pym said.

"That's your Sir Edmund Andros. That's he. That's King James's governor. What's the use of coming so far from Devon if suchlike comes after?" He leaned forward to goad each ox in turn. "But come I did."

So we talked a while of Devon, while Pym sat open mouthed listening, the fowling piece across his lap. Most of the talk was mine, with happy agreement from the carter. The oxen, treading like paired sentries, churned the miles under their hooves, slowly but steadily. In the midst of our talk, with the sun high overhead, I heard a horse galloping somewhere behind us.

"That'll be post," said the carter.

Pym glanced back, so quickly I had no move before he was watching me again. The drumming hoofbeats grew louder, but thick woods grew down almost to the edges of the road, and the track itself curved so that the rider overtook us at the same moment we saw him.

He was a slight youth on a sturdy pony, bay with black points, no higher than fourteen hands. The rider, pale cheeked under a too large hat, rode as if he'd grown in the saddle. He wasn't pushing the pony, but he wasn't ambling either; compared to the oxen the easy gallop seemed headlong. As he drew beside the cart he reined down smoothly, slowing without breaking stride. When a grin split his dust-streaked face I saw he was hardly more than a boy.

"Pym," he cried. "Jed." His glance raked me, held. "I'm late. But I saw Cap'n Tobias. They'll know ahead."

"About him?" asked Pym, pointing the gun at me.

"About him," the rider called, already moving away. He must have touched the pony's sides, for the gallop picked up speed again, and he was gone, dragging a train of dust behind him.

"Yon has a good name," the carter said, staring after the pony.

"And good hands," I said, "and a good seat."

Pym laughed. "That's Devon Neville. He rides post as well as any. But Jed, here, thinks he bears a fine *given* name."

"What better?" asked the carter, nodding with ponderous approval. "Orphan he may be, but there's good blood there with such a name. Yon's a decent lad."

"Hasty anyway," I said, not pleased that young Devon was hurrying ahead with word of my capture. Now every town on the road would be alarmed, and waiting. Crowds would gather to stare as they did in London when the condemned were taken out to Tyburn.

The carter finally turned off into a weed-choked side road. After Pym and I climbed down a hail made me turn.

"Happen it's hanging cause," said the carter, leaning from his perch to grip my shoulder. "I'll come see." His broad face beamed at me. "You knowing Devon and all."

We went on, making faster speed than the oxen had. Pym, evidently less fearful, stayed a stride behind my shoulder. It was a long, deserted stretch of road, and my legs began to ache. Pym seemed tireless, but at last we stopped to eat. He picked a place where a stream tumbled through a natural clearing. I bathed my face while he brought food from his pouch.

We ate bread and cheese, drank the cold water. The afternoon was hot and still. Overhead the sun, past its peak, had burned a haze around itself.

"Hot," I said, feeling better for the rest.

"Wait'll Indian summer," said Pym through a mouthful of bread.

"Indian summer?"

He stared, nodded. "Hot fall weather. The Indians call it their summer." He swallowed, gazed at the clumps of goldenrod that lined the road banks. When he spoke again he blurted his question. "You ever see a hanging?"

"Yes," I said, watching him, "in London."

[52]

"Was it—? Is it—?" The lad kept trying to get the words out. "I mean—Jed talking about it. I know they'll hang you, but I wasn't thinking what it meant."

"I was," I said.

"Does it take long?"

"Depends. Some die hard, kicking hard. Others go quick. But they all die." He was careful not to look at me, but his shoulders were rigid. Deliberately I told him a few more details. "I've seen the hung black faced with tongues hanging out. And I've heard the crack as the neck broke—like splitting wood."

Pym glanced at the rest of his bread, folded it back into a kerchief, put it in his pouch. He stood up, paler, but calm enough. He said: "We'd better move on. We've a piece yet."

"How old are you, Pym?" I asked, rising.

"Sixteen."

"I was about your age when I saw my first hanging. Just about." I walked back into the road, head bowed, letting thought fester, considering my next move. Pym was likeable, but young and alone. The passing of the post rider made escape more imperative. But there were arguments for waiting, too. I didn't know the countryside; I had an iron band on each wrist with a foot of linked chain between. If I hurt the lad, all the Pemberlys would be after me, with Captain Tobias leading the pack.

Pym said, "Pa says a righteous man never fears to meet his Maker."

"Pa should know," I said, shooting a glance at him. He wasn't watching me, but staring ahead into the distance, lips pursed. If the idea of hanging upset him a bit more I might get a grab for the gun. I said: "But about that hanging. They turned off three that one time."

"Three?"

"Yes. A pickpocket, a footpad, and a murderer."

"Three," Pym said again, shaking his head in awe.

"The pickpocket's turn was first," I said, thinking hard, trying to impress and revolt the lad. "He kicked and screamed, prayed and blasphemed, when they put the noose 'round his gullet."

"My," said Pym, "that must have been a sight! I don't suppose you'll have any company though when it's your time. Pa might take us to Boston for that. Us having had a hand in it, you might say."

His tone made me gape. He wasn't bothered, merely interested. Poor Pym, apprenticed to the family trade of smuggling, hadn't had many opportunities for entertainment. My hanging would make a nice holiday. I don't know why I was shocked; it was a common attitude.

"Aye," said Pym, still musing, "if we wasn't away on a voyage, Pa might take the lot of us."

Shock exploded into rage. I forgot plan and scruples, forgot everything but cold deadliness. He was keeping that careful pace behind me, gun in the crook of his near elbow. Swinging the chain in a loop, I whirled.

Pym dodged, ducking away from those lashing links. I wasn't after his hide, but the gun. I grabbed the muzzle with both hands, jerked, Pym hung on, and for a wild moment we circled in the dust like dancing bears. He was taller than I, as strong but off balance. I put a toe into his middle, stiff legged, and he doubled with a gasp. One twist and I was away, with the fowling piece.

I said, panting, "I'm sorry, lad."

He sat in the middle of the road, fighting for breath. His glare was a mixture of pain and hate. Head and shoulders heaved as he sucked in air.

"Take your time," I said. "I didn't mean to hurt you, but I had to have the gun."

"Pa," said Pym with a great sob. He began to weep.

"Now stop that," I said, embarrassed. He wasn't blubbering, and his tears were half anger, but they ran down his cheeks in glittering streaks.

"Pa," repeated Pym. He drew a cuff across his eyes, rose to one knee.

"Look," I said. "The worst you can get is a thrashing, but I might be hung. Just tell your pa I surprised you. He saw me get away from two men—Alec Murdoch and that Hamish—and you're naught but a lad."

Pym's teeth came together with a click. He stood up, rubbed his middle, looked at me. A sniffle ended his tears. His wet eyes gleamed in the sunshine, hard as steel and as cold. He spoke with slow purpose.

"Pa don't hold with excuses."

"This is once he'll have to."

"No," Pym shook his head, "I'd rather you killed me."

"Don't be a fool, Pym. I'll just tie you with your pouch strap. Likely you'll get loose before anyone comes along. All I want is——"

"No. Give back the gun."

"Pym, mind now. I'm desperate for my life!"

"Aye," said Pym grimly, "so be I." He crouched, arms out, fingers curved, moving toward me like a country wrestler. "I'll have that gun."

"Pym, I'll shoot!" The fowling piece was cocked, leveled.

"Shoot then, you cursed pirate."

He took another step. I moved backwards. He was ridiculous, crazy. Any sensible man wouldn't risk it. Pym was little more than a boy, with a boy's unreasonable courage. For all his height without the shackles I might have chanced a grapple. As it was my control of the situation slipped more with each passing second.

"You loaded it yourself, Pym. I can't miss this close. The charge will tear you in two."

"Shoot or give back the gun."

The brave, silly young ass. Here he was facing a dastardly, bloodthirsty pirate and he presented a choice like that. Any buccaneer worth a dram of rum would have blasted him down without another thought. I couldn't do it. Pym's unshaven face would have haunted me.

"Stand still," I said, with a pirate oath that should have startled him.

"Foul-mouthed scum," said Pym, and leaped.

I jabbed the gun butt in a feint, rapped the muzzle against his reaching arm, and danced away. That was pike work, or quarter stave, and my only hope. The next time he jumps me, I thought, I'll brain him.

Pym shook his bruised arm, crouched again. He was aware now that I wouldn't shoot. He circled, waiting for a chance to rush.

"All right," I said, stepping forward. The long barrel of the gun went back for a swing. "Come on."

He charged. At the last moment, as the barrel swished through the air, Pym stopped dead, weaved away. My blow missed him by a feather's breadth. With a shout he dived for my knees. Finn McCool himself, hero or no, never matched the leap that saved me. My heels cleared Pym's back by at least three feet.

He was no tortoise either. Before I could turn and pin him to the earth, Pym was up and away. He drew back a few feet, and we gazed at each other.

"Pym," I said, "I'll not be taken. Give it up."

"No," said he, "there's more than one way to trap a varmint." He walked to the edge of the road, hunted, stooped for a stone.

"You throw that," I said, "and I'll shoot. A man can stand just so much!"

Pym never answered a word. He reared back and let fly. The missile was wide, but it hit among the trees with a crash that turned my stomach. Jill Murdoch had pelted me good on the beach; my shoulder bore the mark to prove it. Against Pym Pemberly the girl could match neither force nor distance. He was ready with another stone before the first finished rattling among the branches.

Do they rear the babes on stoning in this God forgotten land, I wondered, ducking. The idea of fleeing before Pym was too much for me. Instead I raced at him, raising the gun as a bludgeon.

He ran, tearing down the road as fast as his long legs would carry him. Pym took the way we had been going, and me after him. To end the farce was the one thought I had. It gave strength to my thighs, breath to my lungs. All I wished was to plant a lusty clout on the lad's head. With him asleep I'd put miles between us. His skull was thick enough to take a clout without permanent harm, and I'd had enough nonsense.

Tall as Pym was, I gained. We hadn't covered fifty yards before I was on his heels. We swept around a bend, hammered along a straight stretch of road, turned another curve.

One last spurt, I figured, and he'll be within reach. Lowering my head, I sprinted. When I saw Pym's heels flashing through the dust I glanced up. He seemed close enough and I took a firmer grip on the gun.

"Halt!"

"By Gideon and Jupiter!"

"Will you look at them?"

"Stand, there!"

The voices rose in a babble, but the two commands were clear. Pym and I stopped as if we'd been reined. He was in front, and I peered around him.

There, ranked across the road, red coats bright in the sunlight, was a file of soldiers! Four men and a sergeant, I judged, all with muskets. Cromwell first put the red coats on them, and I had known the markings from my childhood!

For all my pleasure it might as well have been a full regiment. Five muskets to one fowling piece was too great odds. Besides, I could not use Pym as a shield against unknown soldiery.

The sergeant, a bull of a man with a face the color of his jacket, swaggered forward. He barked his words more than spoke them.

"What in the thundering hammers of hell do you think you're doing?"

Pym's spine quivered as he braced himself. "Running a race," he said lamely. His hand came around behind his back, fingers groping.

"A race?"

The bellow made Pym's fingers twitch. There was no sense in shaming the lad. Winded already I couldn't very well run for it, and I stood small chance against five armed troopers. So I put the gun in Pym's hand.

"Aye," I said, stepping beside him, "a bit of a foot race to pass the journey."

My appearance caused a commotion.

"That's him, sergeant."

"Look at the shackles."

"He's the one all right."

"And a hangdog cove at that!"

"Silence!" roared the sergeant. He swung to confront me, musket at the ready. "You one Doyle, the pirate?"

"I'll admit to the name," I said. "But not the title."

"You'll keep a civil tongue or get a swollen mouth!" The sergeant turned to Pym. "Is he?"

"Yes," said Pym. "I'm taking him to the constable at——"

"We know all that, sonny. All on account of you the ensign's made us march back these several miles."

Another redcoat swore. "A rutting ensign and a blasted whelp of a pirate!"

"In this bleeding heat!" said another.

"Silence!" The sergeant ripped out an oath. "We'll take him now, sonny. We'll march him in proper drill, we will, and not play games along the way."

"No," Pym said, flushing but firm, "Pa said deliver him to the constable."

The big shoulders shrugged. "Come along with us, then. Form—ranks! You in the middle, Doyle." In case I misunderstood he gripped the chain, dragged me into place.

As they formed around me, Pym in front with the sergeant, two beside, and two behind, my hopes went down somewhere in the pit of my stomach. This was capture, and no mistake. The common soldiers were bad enough, slovenly though they were, but the big sergeant was a competent veteran.

"What is this town we're going to anyway?" I asked.

"New London," said Pym.

"Forward—hup!"

We started with a jingle of weapons that drowned my groan. The name had put the final thorn in my crown. No place called London had ever been good fortune for Cormac O'Shaugnessy Doyle.

Chapter 7

We marched into New London in the soft glow of a September sunset with my spirits trailing like the soldiers' muskets.

The sun, sinking behind us, threw our shadows ahead, and bathed everything in a pink radiance that flattered eaves and clapboards. Farms and clearings were more numerous as we approached, and the place itself was bigger than the others I'd seen. It was happily situated on a height above a fine harbor about three miles in from the mouth of its own river.

As we crossed this high ground you could see, with one turn of the head, the line of blue ocean to the south, and the shipping in the river. To the south, too, the woods thinned as the land sloped down, giving place to the sand and scrub of seashore. Upstream the forest was beginning to collect twilight shadows so that view stretched dark, solid, cool looking. The houses lining the road, both sides, were neat and clean, though we walked on the same uneven dusty track. The settlers had picked their spot well; it was healthy as well as eye pleasing. I hated every stick of it!

Citizens began to appear as we followed the road down toward the river which they had called, with consistent unoriginality, the Thames. They looked a sober lot, clad in somber grays, browns and blacks, homespun mostly but some of finer cloth as befitted the merchants of a thriving port. These latter, and their women, were very like the Puritan gentry I had seen in England, and all seemed much sterner than Jill Murdoch's fisher folk, or the Pemberlys. Except for the scampering children no one smiled, or raised a voice, or moved faster than a sedate walk.

Every man scowled disapproval at me; all the women stared with pinch-lipped horror. One girl, more comely than the others, drew her skirt aside and flounced away as we passed. The soldier nearest her, on my left, chirped a coarse chuckle.

"What'd you do to her, Sime?" asked his partner.

"Winked," said Sime.

"Skittish, ain't she?"

"You'd think I'd pinched her bottom!"

"Wouldn't you like to!"

"Huh!" A soldier behind me snorted. "Not in this town. These wenches are colder'n Boston's."

"There's Katrina," Sime said, "she's a warm armful. Remember her when we marched down?" He had a thin, pointed face with perky eyebrows that made it fox-like. "I'll do better this trip."

Sime's partner tittered. "Not ruddy likely! That one can get all she wants any time!"

"Silence in the ranks!" cried the sergeant over his shoulder.

Sime spat, but spoke low. "Old Hanks acts like we was parading for the king."

They stepped a little smarter though, as we drew near a tree-shaded square with a white church on one side, and an inn opposite. There was quite a crowd gathered in the square, grouped mostly around the pillory in front of the inn. On the church steps the dominie stood alone, in black gown and white wig, regarding his flock. I have seen softer features chiseled on stone statues. Under the inn's sign—an oval of wood with a keg painted on it—bright color caught the eye. A tall officer almost glittered in that drab crowd. He wore the scarlet of the king's coat, with a gold-braid lanyard at one shoulder, sword hanging from baldric, everything polished to a high shine.

"There's the ensign," muttered Sime, "at the Tun and Trencher."

Standing beside the officer was a slender lady in a russet traveling costume. Her dark hair, jet black, looked from a distance as smooth as ebony, with the face under it paler by contrast.

As we passed a smithy there was an enclosed chaise blocking the doorway. The vehicle's fashion made me blink; it showed the skill of a London craftsman. The body, high and narrow, painted olive green with gilt trim, rested on blocks, minus its wheels. Seeing it, even horseless and forlorn, in that town was like finding a gaudy pin in a cask of nails. Somehow, instantly, I connected the chaise with the lady.

"Look, will you, Joe?" said Sime. "The smith ain't touched that broken axle."

Joe was the man on my right. He said, "What harm? Restin' is better than marchin'." Then, as the tall officer strode from the doorway, Joe hissed a warning.

The ensign clapped on his hat, cocked with a plume, as he pushed through the crowd. His arrogance was obvious in the way he moved, using his crooked swordarm as a plow whenever anyone was in his way. People muttered, darted black glances after him. He ignored them, elbowed to the front, stood waiting, tapping his scabbard against the side of a high, gleaming jackboot.

He had a high-bridged nose, long and narrow, a red-lipped small mouth, and a square jaw. His blond wig, full and curly to his shoulders, matched pale eyebrows from beneath which gray eyes peered. Except for a dusting of sunburn on his high cheekbones his complexion was so fair that he seemed to lack eyelashes.

"Sergeant Hanks," called the ensign in a voice tight with impatience, "look lively there!"

"Ah—halt!" ordered Hanks. "Ah—arms!"

Hands slapped, scabbards clinked, musket butts thudded on the ground. The drill was ragged; Sergeant Hanks was rigid at attention long before Sime reached the same position.

"Ease," said the officer.

"Ease," repeated the sergeant.

Sime slumped; Joe scratched an ear. The ensign took his gauntlets from his belt, slapped them against his thigh. "Bring out the prisoner," he said, still using that high-pitched tone as if his collar pinched.

The sergeant beckoned. Sime and Joe led me forward. The crowd, murmuring, pressed close, hemming us on all sides. The ensign's eyes never flicked toward them. He held his head up, and glared down his nose at me.

"Pirate, eh? Lousy wharf rat!"

I gazed up at him; he was taller by half a head. From my angle his nostrils quivered like those of a tight-bitted horse. As we stared at each other, gaze meeting gaze, color spread from his cheekbones down to his chin, and the gray eyes darkened. It was foolish of me I know, but I didn't like his tone. This one, I thought, is strutting rooster fashion before the lady. So I met his glare with a slow, insolent smile.

"Damn all!" As he ripped out the words he slashed the gloves across my face. "Show some manners to your betters, gallows' bait!"

The sting of the leather burned slower than my anger. Still smiling, I jangled the chain that joined my shackles, and said, "Aye, when I meet them."

Pym Pemberly saved me another, harder blow. He plucked at the uniform sleeve as the officer drew it back. The ensign's reaction, jerking away, nearly sent poor Pym staggering.

"Please, sir," said the lad, "Pa said deliver him to the constable."

"Keep your filthy hands away," said the ensign. "And what are you rattling about?"

"Pa," said Pym, "he's constable to Saybrook. He sent me along as guard."

A man wearing an innkeeper's apron and a brown nightcap bobbed out of the crowd. He was of moderate height, stoop shouldered, with a bulging paunch that belied his gaunt face. Under a nose as warty as a pickle the man seemed to be tasting vinegar.

"It's all right, Master Whitlaw," he said, bowing. "We all know Pym. He's Tobias Pemberly's youngest. How is your pa, Pym? Safe home, and hearty?"

"Aye," Pym said.

Ensign Whitlaw's glare shifted from Pym to the man. He said: "Twigg, go back to your spit and kitchen. This doesn't concern you."

Twigg bowed, yanking off the knitted cap to reveal a totally bald head. "Sorry to say, sir," he said, whining, "but it does. You see, sir, besides keeping the Tun and Trencher, Master Whitlaw, I'm—well, I'm constable, sir."

The voice of the minister rang out from the church steps. "Duly appointed in town meeting. Do your duty, Jotham Twigg."

Approval, audible as wind through trees, stirred across the crowd. The soldiers stiffened. Esnsign Whitlaw threw back his head to look thunderously at the preacher. I recognized a well-remembered feeling. The redcoats were not popular with the citizenry.

"And I," cried the ensign, "am an officer of his majesty, the king! This prisoner will be taken in my charge as I am sure would be the wishes of his excellency, the governor, Sir Edmund Andros, his majesty's representative." The high voice was haughty and loud. "We will march this felon under guard to Boston where we are escorting Lady Esterling." He pivoted, and bowed to the lady in the doorway, doffing his cocked hat like a play actor.

"There's no need to quarrel," said Jotham Twigg, wringing his cap in his hands. "I'll accept delivery, Pym. And I'll go along with Ensign Whitlaw and his command to carry the pirate to the next township."

It didn't sound like an argument with any good for me on either side. Twigg was a mean-looking devil, and the ensign, though no older than myself, was the kind that enjoyed using spurs, on man or beast. But the dominie, as I later found to be common in New England, had the final say.

"Compromise not with wickedness," he preached, in nasal but pierc-

[61]

ing accents. "Those that live by the sword, perish by the sword. Let the abomination of evil be pilloried in accordance with the laws!"

Ensign Whitlaw looked startled, then showed white teeth in a savage grin. He couldn't hide the pleasure in his voice. "I've no objection to that! A time in the stocks might take some of the surliness from the brute."

Beside me Sime whispered, "You're for it, me bucko, chains and all."

"Sergeant Hanks," said Whitlaw, "put the prisoner in the stocks!"

Hanks saluted, turned toward me with a scowl. The sergeant's broad, battered face was the only one that showed disapproval. Even Pym watched with eager interest; the crowd jostled forward for choice positions. Whitlaw waited for my objections, but I wouldn't give him the satisfaction.

"Sorry, lad," murmured Sergeant Hanks, "orders is orders."

The pillory was on a raised platform about as high as a table up one well-worn step. Jotham Twigg bustled ahead to open the stocks, swinging the top half back on a hinge to reveal the three smooth semi-circles for neck and arms. This pillory had obviously been much used, and I was glad it hadn't been built for taller culprits. My forearms, still shackled, rested in the proper slots, and I bent my head, trying not to flinch when the wood touched the skin of my neck.

Twigg slammed the gate down with such force that the post shook, and my ears rang. Two quick blows hammered the bolt fast, the soldiers stepped from the platform, and there I was.

The crowd greeted me with a sigh of pleasure. At first glance it seemed a solid mass, the faces featureless blobs. Twigg pushed into the front rank to leer at me. My back was to the inn; over the heads of the spectators the preacher frowned from the steps. Behind me, out of my vision, Whitlaw laughed, a hearty sportsman's guffaw. Individuals began to emerge from the gaping herd. A skinny youth hooted; a dumpy woman tittered; two overfed men nodded in unison.

To be trussed up for a mob's jeers branded me in a strange way. I had seen others in the stocks; God forgive me I had laughed at them. Now, something inside me wanted to crawl and hide. Pride kept my face blank, but I felt unmanned. Curses and tears came unsummoned. I swallowed both, but it was not easy.

Someone unseen threw the first stone. It smacked into the wood a foot from my head.

After that it was country fair on closing day. Mud came my way, offal, garbage, an occasional rock. A pilloried person was fair game, and the sport was part of the punishment. The older and more respectable citizens merely watched, and kept tally, but every boy shied something. Good shots were applauded; the match was spirited.

"A pint for the best marksman," called Whitlaw.

That, I decided, I will remember. Spattered, my neck rubbed raw from continual flinching, cold hatred filled me. I hated every member of the crowd, the preacher, Twigg, the soldiers, Pym. Most of all I hated Ensign Whitlaw. I wanted to kill. The feeling drove out the last vestige of shame; I glared back at the mob. At least I was a man again, and by that much a gainer.

Sime, the soldier, scored the best hit. He plastered me on the forehead with a piece of fruit, pulpy rotten. The mess ran down and dried sticky, but it was too far gone to name as peach or plum. Sime won the pint. I watched him drink it.

Thanks to poor marksmanship, and the fading light, no one else marked my face. The board was plentifully daubed, my left hand had a ripped knuckle, but that was all. They threw nothing large enough to do more than bruise, so I should be thankful.

Twilight, and the supper hour ended the game. The preacher seemed to signal the finish by entering the church and slamming the door. Husbands escorted their wives away; mothers shooed their children home. The crowd thinned, broke into groups, dispersed. Soon the square was deserted, its shadows deepening, and the only voices came from the inn.

Pym Pemberly walked around in front of me. "I'm off to home now," he said.

"Go to hell for all I care," I said with feeling.

"I threw naught. Pa wouldn't think it fitting."

"Small thanks for small favor."

"Well, goodbye."

Reluctantly, glancing back every few steps, Pym left. He took no good wishes from me. If the young idiot hadn't ignored the gun I might be out on the road instead of clamped in a pillory. I cursed him, and his pa, and the Murdochs, and everyone else I'd met so far in this misbegotten New England. My legs ached from the long walk of the day; I was stooped in a far from comfortable position. I would not have exchanged one Irish shamrock, or one Indies coral fan for the whole blasted country!

The shadows blended together, blotted out the last gray haze, and made night. I could see a sprinkle of stars above the church roof. Candles gleamed in the windows of the houses that fronted the square. The preacher's house had glass windowpanes. One of the others had yellow squares of paper, or hide.

[63]

From the inn came the noise of crockery and eating. My stomach rumbled with hunger. My leg muscles were twitching from weariness. No light reached me from the inn. I stood alone in deserted darkness.

For about an hour I enjoyed the solitude, trying to find the most comfortable posture. There was nothing I could do about my pinioned head or arms, but I stood, crane like, on one foot to rest the other. Nothing helped much, but the exercise kept me busy.

They hadn't sent me a bite of supper. I was too proud to beg, but bitter annoyed. If being used as target was part of my plight, starvation was not. The meanest prisoner was entitled to a crust and a sip. Filling my lungs with breath I began to sing.

> Let us drink and be merry, dance, joke, and rejoice,
> With claret and sherry, viola and voice!
> Tomorrow we sail,
> On rum punch and ale,
> To seek the cursed don and his wenches so choice!
> *Heigh-ho! Pass the bowl 'round!*

Nobody has ever called my voice musical, nor saluted its pitch or tone. Yet it had been tested by many a hearty chorus, afloat and ashore, as loud as the rest. In the stillness of that night I outdid myself. The very pillory groaned under the strain of my bellowing.

The town had never heard such singing, nor, I think, such a song. Shutters slammed open, doors banged. The preacher, gown flying, came running out with a candle. I could not see the inn but to judge by the noise the place emptied its custom into the square as if it had caught fire. Voices were raised, shocked, protesting, awed. I could hear the preacher's nasal shouting, and Whitlaw's cursing. Both called on the Almighty, but hardly the same way.

"In the name of God, cease that sinful song!"

"God damn your eyes, stop that noise!"

"Listen to him, will you!"

"Tophet, Sime, he sings worse than you!"

"It's a scandal!"

The first verse did so well, that I gave them another. I was getting a little of my own back. Not wanting to sound too much the pirate I shifted to a drinking song less specialized, but even more bawdy.

> Oh, the island females are black or dusty,
> But their hips are wide, and their bosoms busty,
> And the roving, randy sailorman
> Must find his port wherever he can!

Sing—yo!
Sing—ho!
Sing—yo, ho, ho!

By that time they were on the platform yelling at me. The preacher, candle held over his head, was practically dancing in fury.

"Cease!" he screamed. "Cease that Godless outrage!"

Ensign Whitlaw cuffed me. The back of his hand drove my head against the board that enclosed it. "Damn all!" he said. "We'll stuff a gag in your mouth, you bastard."

"You can do that," I said. "It's cheaper than feeding me, and even braver than striking a pilloried man."

Jotham Twigg squealed. "And who's to pay the score for your fodder?"

"I'll give a shilling," said Sergeant Hanks.

"That will do," Whitlaw said. "It's not your place, sergeant, to be coddling criminals."

The preacher was fairer. He brought his voice down from a yell to speak reasonable. "I didn't know you'd not been fed. Though you should fast for the words that sullied your tongue, and scandalized my people, I'd not have them saying in Boston we were too niggardly to keep you in health. See to it, Jotham Twigg."

"But——" Twigg spluttered.

"See to it."

"Thank you," I said. "For my part there'll be no more disturbance. You'll remember I've been seized on suspicion, and have not yet been tried."

"Out of your own mouth," said the preacher, "you're convicted. I would put no crime beyond you." With that he stalked away, stern as ever.

"I'd not give you a crumb," Whitlaw said. "But a thrashing you'd not forget."

"Oh, let the man eat, Borden." That voice, a woman's, low pitched and husky, called from the inn doorway. "He just sang for his supper." Her laugh was refined, without real mirth.

"As you wish, my lady." Whitlaw was suddenly gracious. He jumped down from the platform and disappeared.

"As you wish, milady." Sime's whisper mimicked his officer. "Make a leg and kiss my hand. Two to one he don't get more'n that before we gets to Boston."

"Stow that," said the sergeant.

They all went away. The moon came up over the square, brightened

[65]

it. It was about half full, and waning, not as bright as the previous night. After a time Sergeant Hanks came back, bearing a bowl of squirrel stew, an end of bread, a mug of ale. He had a wet cloth, too, and wiped my face. I could use my hands easily enough for eating. The sergeant kept me company as I ate.

"I don't hold with these here stocks," he said. "If you're a military prisoner, you should be treated military fashion. Ensign Borden Whitlaw, he thinks different."

I said, with full mouth, "What are you doing down here, anyway?"

"Escort duty. Sir William Esterling, he used to work for Sir Edmund Andros in New York. But he's joined the governor in Boston. So when his lady—her inside—was to come up from New York we was sent down as escort." Hanks snorted to mask a sigh. "These folk don't care much for soldiers."

"I noticed."

"We notice too. Our swearing sits a mite uneasy on these Puritan stomachs. Besides there's talk the regicides fled down this way, and a redcoat isn't welcome."

"Regicides? Here?"

"There's talk. They came to Boston for sure some years back. But nobody's seen them. Nobody that'll admit it."

I chewed thoughtfully. These people would hide a king killer, but they had no mercy for a pirate. It made me realize that any mention of the sea chest had better get into the right ears. Hanks seemed incorruptible; the likes of Sime couldn't be trusted. Most of the king's officers were not averse to lining their pockets, but Ensign Whitlaw looked the kind who would run you through for a sixpence. Strict Puritans, the preacher for example, were already convinced of my guilt, and any offer would be regarded as proof of piracy. The Jotham Twiggs seemed venal enough, but they would never believe me.

Truly, there was no solution. No honest man would conspire with me. The corrupt one who winked at my possession of the treasure would be blind to my interest. All I could do was bide time, and hope.

"Sergeant," I said, "how can I march much tomorrow, after a night in this thing?"

"We'll not be marching. Not till the chaise axle is fixed. It split on a rock just outside town." Sergeant Hanks scratched his chin, lowered his voice. "Look, lad. Keep your tongue still, and don't cross the ensign. He's touchy like, but his main concern is Lady Esterling."

He took bowl, mug and my thanks when he left. The sergeant, I decided, didn't like his officer and didn't like his orders. That was something to be stored away for future use.

The food made me feel better, but was no substitute for sleep. My eyelids seemed weighted with sinkers, but no matter how I leaned on the pillory I could snatch no more than a doze before I woke choking. All around me was the endless droning buzz-buzz of the insects; some found and feasted on me.

One by one the lights in the town's windows went out. The night grew colder; a breeze rose from the river, damp and stiffening to a pilloried man. Even the inn had settled to silence behind me before the last candle, the preacher's, was snuffed out. Then I was alone, with my thoughts, in the moonlit square, the buildings a dark wall around me. It was like being stuck in the bottom of a pit.

Loneliness seeped into me as physically as the chill. My head hung lax in its wooden socket, bowed by my troubles. Shackled and pilloried, a prisoner in a strange land, I felt that every man's hand was against me. That night I'd have keened to the moon like a baying dog but for fear of a gag. Fortunately my brains, drugged by too many worries, concentrated on my present plight, the smaller irritants created by the pillory. At least that was better than thinking.

Midnight, guessed at by the shifting moon, came and went. Minutes seemed like hours, but hours must have passed. I know not how long it was before my last visitor came.

A cloud hid the moon, and I could not see the edge of the platform. There was a light step; the boards underfoot creaked, sagged with added weight. An arm brushed my side as a figure ducked under the stocks to hold a mug to my lips.

"Shhh," said a soft voice, "speak down. Drink!"

"Who is it?"

"Katrina Krön from by the inn. I work for Twigg." Her accent recalled Dutch shipmates. "Shh and drink."

The drink was a rum toddy, steaming and strong. Though the mug burned my lips the liquor spread through me with a pleasant warmth. I could feel it make its way, tingling, from throat to heels.

"You did this by yourself, Katrina?"

"Ja. Why no? They let you stand in night air."

The moon came out again, and I could see her better. She was young, small, amply curved. She must have been very blonde for her hair, hanging in two braids that framed a round face, seemed polished silver in the moonlight. Bare ankles and feet showed under her skirt, but she was fully dressed with a shawl over her shoulders.

[67]

"You won't get in trouble, Katrina?"

"No. Drink." She laughed quietly, a bubbling sound full of good humor. While I sipped the rum, she whispered. "They all snore. Old Twigg he move from bed, his goodwife holler so. With Katrina in attic goodwife watch Twigg so." She found this amusing. Her shawl dropped away and her giggle bounced the ribbon-gathered bodice of her dress. Her breasts filled the bodice with two neat, separate globes.

"The soldiers?" I asked, gazing.

"Baby watch soldiers."

"Baby?"

"My son. Deidrich. Baby. Is five."

"You're married then?"

"*Ja!*" Head and bosom bobbed with the force of the word. "Widow woman. Not here. New York." She took the empty mug, put her hand in mine. "Have ring. See." As I looked at the wedding band her chuckle ruined her story. "Have baby. Have ring. Widow woman."

Her muffled glee made me sure she lied. Awkwardly, because of the stocks, I raised her hand to my lips. Katrina's fingers fluttered, but she stood perfectly still, not even breathing.

"Thank you, Katrina."

"Why you do so?"

"For thanks."

"But—like a lady?"

"A very kind lady."

Katrina stroked my cheek. Her palm, work roughened, scraped on my bristles of beard. "They throw at you," she said. "Is not right this—this pillory. Soldiers and Twigg say you wicked man. You not."

"Not as bad as they think." There was nothing much this serving girl could do for me, but she'd been kind. I was not refusing any kindness offered.

"Devon bring word, I think to see big, fierce pirate, beard to here, with swear words. I like Devon."

Her candor made me smile. I said, "Lucky boy."

"Others all liars. Devon just wrong. Mis-taken."

Raising on tip-toe, Katrina put her lips on mine, soft lips well practiced in kissing. My first surprise changed to pure pleasure. When she stepped back, she shook her head, chuckling.

"No. Not wicked. Katrina can tell."

The test, I thought, was more enjoyable than certain. There was no sense in my arguing about that. I said, "Thank you again, Katrina."

"Twigg and soldiers wicked. Bad talk. Pawing. Even ensign officer pinch me. When lady not looking. Devon not like that. You not."

She sounded sure, not vehement. Devon's conduct, and mine, was the surprise, the other customary. She expected such treatment, and, I gathered, was prepared to manage it. Her breasts were almost brushing my fingertips, but I kept my hands rigid.

"You have name?"

"Cormac."

"Cormac. Is nice. I help you, Cormac."

She kissed me again, thoroughly, gave me a friendly pat on the cheek, and was gone. Breathing hard, I was glad I'd behaved. She was a tempting morsel, but aid was what I needed. The taste of those kisses stayed with me as long as the rum.

The little Dutch girl was the one friend I'd made since my shipwreck. She was worth a dozen Jill Murdochs. She was here, and kind, and friendly. I wanted no more to do with that redheaded termagant.

So I told myself, again and again, until I almost believed it.

Chapter 8

By the time the soldiers released me, in the gray half-light before dawn, I could barely stand. In fact Sergeant Hanks kept me from pitching on my face. My legs were numb; my knees acted like greased hinges. For the last few hours of ordeal my arms had held my full weight. The square was still deserted. I had heard farmers stirring, the slam of a barn door, the rattle of a dropped pail, cows greeting milkers. No one had been visible before Sime and the sergeant arrived. They helped me down from the platform, led me back behind the inn to the necessary, walked the stiffness from my joints.

"For God's sake," Sime said, "be quiet."

The sergeant nodded. "Only the ensign's still abed, we'd not dare. He'd have me reduced."

"He'd have me flogged," said Sime, nervously. "You'd best be back up there before he stirs."

They made a queer pair of samaritans. Hanks, with a veteran's wisdom, didn't want a hamstrung prisoner slowing the march. He was kind, but would have given equal care to a supply mule. Sime helped me for sheer deviltry; he had the common soldier's delight at any chance to diddle an unliked officer. Whatever their reasons I was grateful to them both.

They sneaked me into the warmth of the inn's kitchen where Katrina was already bringing last night's embers back to a blaze. The huge gray-stone fireplace, with its crane and spit, dwarfed her as she knelt before it. Her posture tightened her brown homespun dress on the curve of a thigh, and a plump bottom. She turned, startled, as we entered.

"Nobody touched you," Sime said, with a leer.

"Nobody do so," Katrina said, giving me a wide blue-eyed stare. "Or I tell officer and preacher who let loose pirate."

"Hold your peace, wench," the sergeant said. "Let the man warm himself, and eat a bit. We'll have him back and no harm done."

She flounced away, tossing everything tossable, but she soon had a kettle steaming. Hanks roused the other two soldiers, posted one as sentry in the inn's hallway. Katrina gave me a wide berth until she slapped a bowl of gruel before me.

"*Dere,*" she said. "Eat and go from my kitchen." Standing as stiff as her voice, she winked. A dimple twitched beside her mouth.

"Hurry up," begged Sime, busy building the fire higher. "If he spent another night in his own bed I don't want to face him."

"Did so," said Katrina. "The lady is not loose."

Sime cackled, reaching for the girl as she passed. "Not like some, eh?"

Katrina merely weaved her hips away from his grab, and went on. For all her bounciness she was not ungraceful. The candlelit inn kitchen was a large pleasant room, eastern windows brightening with daylight. As I shoveled food in with a horn spoon, I watched the girl as if we'd never met.

By day her braids were the color of hemp rope fresh from the walk. Her dress was faded, her slippers scuffed, but she was spotless, cheeks scrubbed pink and shining. Her eyes were the blue of a tropic lagoon; her nose as cute as a rabbit's.

With quick, deft movements, skirt fluttering, she almost skipped about the room. She fried bacon, sliced bread, poured milk. Handling plates and mugs like a juggler Katrina carried everything to the long table where I sat. She put the things in front of Sergeant Hanks, but within my reach. The sergeant, eating with one eye on the doorway, fought a losing battle.

"Katrina!" cried a shrill woman's voice. "Girl!"

Katrina halted in mid-stride, spun around.

"The goodwife!"

"Mrs. Twigg!"

Sime crossed the kitchen with a bound as the sergeant tugged me to my feet. Grabbing bread and bacon, I ran. The three of us collided at the back door, but the others shoved me ahead. We scuttled around the inn, dashed for the platform. Sime raced ahead to open the stocks. They had me back in place, with Sergeant Hanks fastening the bolt, before I crammed the last morsel in my mouth.

None too soon for the dew was showing on the square's grass; the sky, still gray above, was yellow to the east; the first ray of sunrise was gilding the weathercock atop the church steeple. My bacon was barely swallowed when the minister clapped open the shutters under the peak of his two-story house. He looked just as stern in his nightcap. When I waved a hand in salute he popped out of sight like Punch from the stage.

Before it was full day the square became busy, and I realized it must be market day. Squealing pigs were herded in a corner; stalls were erected, wares displayed. Farmers carting produce slowed their horses to stare at me, but most of the town people now took me for granted. If I was a show to any, they were the same to me.

The market was much like that of any English town about the same size. I noticed that the dominie, again wigged and gowned, was in charge. He gave directions, settled disputes, opened the market by having a bell rung, and a drum ruffled.

All through the forenoon, while the sun rose higher and hotter, a pale yellow blur in a heat-hazy sky, merchants bargained with farmers, farmers bought from pedlars, hawkers cried. A group of apprentices, lads in leather aprons, jeered me, but there was no renewal of the throwing contest. The preacher and his deacons—all grave, well clad, and paunchy —kept order. Even the sailors, swaggering from the riverfront, were well behaved, though they examined me with professional interest.

Through all the babble of market-place chatter, the handbells, the haggling, I could hear the clang of the blacksmith's hammer. Ensign Whitlaw appeared late, gave me a glare as greeting, showed his authority by posting Sime as guard.

"Wonder how in Tophet he thinks you can get out," complained Sime. He felt misused; the other soldiers were wandering about the square, redcoats spotted the somber-clothed crowd like pimientos in a bean pot. There was ale, beer, and rum to be had, but none for Sime or me.

My interest was held by the foodstuffs new to me. Sime named the Indian corn, "tenpins with green husks and tasseled tops." The husks were peeled back to reveal shining pearls, as tight in rows as a lady's stomacher.

Game was in evident plenty. A man stalked by bearing venison for the inn. A fisherman traded fresh cod for a brace of ducks. Rabbits hung from one stall. This pleased me. If ever I escaped there was food outside the towns. My youthful poaching would prove an asset.

When the sun was directly overhead the heat seemed to descend on the square in visible, shimmering layers. The sky stayed the gray-white of smoke, but its glare hurt the eyes. All who could sought shelter indoors. Those forced to stay, watching their wares, hunted out every speck of shade. Activity dwindled for the noonday meal. It was that hot, and, of course, on the pillory I roasted.

Sweat poured down my face, ran in rivulets under my clothes. Sime was in scarcely better case. He turned ugly, cursing me and Whitlaw for his plight. By the time Joe relieved him, bringing beer and bread for me, I knew every oath in Sime's collection.

The beer, native brewed, was thin, weak stuff, but its wetness helped. I wolfed the bread, but hoarded the drink, spacing my sips at long intervals. The afternoon was half spent before I finished the last, flat mouthful.

By that time the square was busy again with buyers who had waited for late prices. Whitlaw went past, the lady on his arm, strutting as if they led a march at the king's ball. Lady Esterling paused beneath me to gaze up from under her wide-brimmed hat. She gave me a proper scanning, toe to crown and back, while I got my first clear look at her.

This woman, of all I'd ever seen, looked more like a painted portrait than flesh and blood. Mayhap it was the elegance of her attire, but more likely it was her startling thinness, not one whit hidden by the long riding coat, cut man style, nor the folds of the skirt draped modishly across her rear. Indeed her figure was more boyish than female, barely hinting at her sex in the curve from waist to armpit.

Her face, too, had the flat composure of a drawing. Skin as pale as beeswax, very sharp features, and dark eyes whose expression, mild curiosity, might have been sketched in by a pencil. Her hands were long and tapering, as white as the fluff of lace stock at her throat.

"Borden," she said, turning to show the smooth black hair gathered in a net snood at the nape of her neck, "he is not very stout for such a cutthroat." She might have been discussing a prize bull.

"They're all cowardly weaklings," Whitlaw said. "Brave enough with cannon to attack unarmed vessels."

"I see." The lady's voice was low, precise. There didn't seem to be a good shout in her. Once more her gaze met mine for cool appraisal. "How disappointing."

Whitlaw gave me a glance, eager to rebuke resentment. I kept my face blank. They went on to examine the other livestock and vegetables. That one, I thought, noticing the lady didn't walk like a boy, is a cold fish, too mean to sweat. She and Whitlaw made a fine, arrogant pair, but I doubted the ensign received any favors more mussing than a smile.

Thunder rumbled in a long ominous roll. I rubbed my skull against the stocks trying to look heavenward, but what sky I could see was unchanged. There was no whisper of wind; neither leaf nor hair stirred. Nothing existed but dead calm, and stifling heat.

Joe turned to stare upward over the inn's roof. He was frowning with worry. "Fixin' to storm," he said uneasily.

In the square before me all movement had stopped as if frozen by magic. Every face was turned toward me, but raised to watch the distant thunderheads.

Again the thunder fired a broadside. This time, after a pause heavy with tension, there came a tremendous crack of lightning. I did not see the streak, but the whole square was lit by its lurid flash.

"Lord Jesus!" said Joe.

A gust of wind, as sudden as the lightning, hit me in the back. It swept Joe's hat from his head, sent it twisting and turning across the square. The hat marked the path of the wind. Where it passed men clutched their own headgear, women's scarfs and dresses flapped. A boy shouted, a horse reared, people started scurrying.

Whitlaw and Lady Esterling came hurrying back. Her skirts were whipped flat against thin shanks. His wig streamed out like a pennant.

Men raced about the square, herding women, children and stock away. Others dismantled stalls, hitched teams; the preacher screamed orders. The bell that signalled the close of the market was drowned by another clap of thunder.

This lightning tore through the fabric of sky above my head. The jagged, forked lash of it ripped out a report that rocked the pillory. When its blinding instant of glare vanished, it left dimness behind, a queer livid dusk that was almost darkness.

The rain followed. One big drop splashed on the platform, another broke on my head. All the rest came in a stream like sea into a holed ship. The downpour matched the worst of the storm that wrecked the ketch. It was, I decided, a custom of the country.

Cursing, Joe abandoned his hat and fled. So did everyone else. The square was emptied in a matter of minutes. Before the last farmer drove his horse from sight I was soaked.

At first, after such heat, this was welcome enough, but it became too much of a good thing. The thunder and lightning were terrifying. The one nearly deafened me; the other seemed to send its white whip searching for me. Alone, penned in the stocks, I felt too exposed, the last man alive facing God's almighty wrath!

Sergeant Hanks and Sime rescued me again. They released me, dragged me through the tempest to the inn's stable. While the sergeant went after tools Sime, cursing me for a nuisance, kicked me headlong into an empty stall.

Hanks knew fetters from past experience. He overseered while Sime loosed my left shackle, driving out the pin with careless hammering that marked my wrist. There was a grid used as a manger in one corner of the stall, and they fastened the manacle around its middle iron bar.

"That'll hold you," Hanks said. "You can lie down or stand up, but you'll wander no farther than the length of the chain." He knelt beside me, examined the band on my right wrist, every link that stretched to the manger. Satisfied, he collected his tools, and left. Sime started to follow, turned back.

"This'll hold you, too," he said, with a snarl. "You stinking pest!" He took deliberate aim, and kicked me in the face.

His aiming warned me so I ducked. The heavy boot ripped open my cheek, but missed my mouth. Still it had force enough to slam my head against the floor. For a moment of pain the stable seemed to tilt in one direction, and my stomach in another. Before they righted Sime was gone.

After cursing him back through four generations, and vowing a future revenge, I tried to stop the flow of blood. The gash felt long and deep, but a sodden sleeve held against it dammed the bleeding enough to allow a crust to form.

Compared to the stocks the way they'd chained me was bliss. Lying down full length my gyved wrist was raised some two feet by the chain, but it wasn't too uncomfortable. The floor, after a night and day of standing, felt softer than any featherbed. I stretched out, listened to the storm, and rested.

The rain, rattling on the roof, gave no sign of slowing. Certainly the thunder and lightning kept on full tilt. Somewhere in the stable horses nickered nervously, and stamped. In spite of all the noise I think I dozed. The stall, shadowed when we entered, grew darker until it was completely black except for an occasional flash of reflected lightning.

When I felt stronger I rose, examining my bonds by touch. No human fingers could open either shackle. The manger was fastened by big spikes, driven deep. There wasn't a loose bar, nor a crooked nail head to pry. My only tool was strength, and I had not too much of that.

Taking the chain in both fists I threw all my weight on it. Nothing gave; the manger neither creaked nor budged. I took a fresh grip, climbed the wall, tugged till I panted. I tried jerking the chain, hammered it on the shackle. All I succeeded in doing was making some noise.

At last I stopped, beaten and exhausted. I stretched out on my back again. The stable was getting colder; my drenched clothes had me shivering. Sleep was something I needed, but this time it wouldn't come. I didn't think much, just lay in a melancholy stupor, head pillowed on my free arm, eyes shut.

"Cormac?"

Fine, I thought with disgust, now you're hearing voices! At that rate I'd reach Boston a gibbering madman. Then, light seemed to fall on my closed eyelids.

"*Ja!* Is you!"

The lanthorn blinded me for a second, but I knew that soft Dutchy voice.

"Katrina!"

"*Ja!*" Her laughter came to its easy boil. "I am late so because nobody sleeps. Storm is too loud." A shattering crash of thunder proved her true, made her pause. She was busily unpacking a basket. The dull yellow glow of the lanthorn showed her cheeks wet from the rain, but her hair was dry. She tossed a shawl aside, smiled at me, then gasped in distress. "Cormac! Your face!"

"What?" I touched the gash. "It's nothing."

"Nothing!" She jumped up, flouncing, darted away. "I bathe it." She returned in two shakes, plumped down on her knees beside me. She bathed the wound with a wet cloth, her fingers careful and tender. "Twigg and goodwife go to prayer meeting. Soldiers play cards. Lady talks to officer." Katrina's tongue clicked at the gash's size. "Who do so?"

"Sime."

"Pig!" She put a hand on my shoulder, recoiled. "Cormac! You are soak!"

"I'm starved too!"

"First take off things!" Katrina tugged at my shirt. "You catch death! Chills! Fever!"

"Katrina, wait!"

She sat back on her heels, puzzled. She looked pretty. Then her nose crinkled, the dimples appeared as she burst into delighted laughter. Her braids danced, but I was more aware of her bosom.

"You shy!"

"Well——" I felt a fool as my face reddened.

"No. Is nice." Katrina hugged herself, rocking with amusement. "Devon blushes so."

"Damn Devon," I said.

"We blow out light," she said, trying to sound stern over giggles. "You dry with blanket. Wrap around. *Ja!* I not look."

"Katrina——"

She dropped the blanket in my lap, picked up the lanthorn, opened the slide, and puffed. Darkness closed around us with startling swiftness.

Between giggles and thunder it seemed an age before I was rubbed dry, and swathed in the blanket. I couldn't get my shirt or jerkin over the shackle so I let them hang from that wrist.

"Cormac?"

"All right," I said. "You can light the candle."

"No." Katrina's chuckle was close. "No fire. No flint-and-steel. No light. Here."

She touched my free arm, put a flask in my hand. It smelled like brandy; it tasted like nectar. I took a long swig, and gave a grateful sigh.

"Good, no?"

"Good, yes!"

We ate in such fashion, passing things in the darkness, whispering. It was a good full meal, a fowl still warm from the spit, fresh bread, a ripe peach, the brandy. Katrina had really raided the inn's larder. She chewed noisily, but mostly to keep me company. Twice I heard the gurgle as she drank.

Katrina made a game of the whole business, finding the murmurs, the fumbling, of our blindman's-buff picnic great fun. Her giggles were so infectious that I shared the fun as I did the intimate darkness, the food, the drink. Sitting up I could use both hands, but the chained one was restricted. We thought this very funny. While the storm roared outside we were like two children eating forbidden sweets, snugly hidden from our parents.

Once, reaching, my palm stroked the swell of her thigh. Later she leaned close, breath warm on my ear, her breasts pressing my shoulder, to pop chicken in my mouth. Before we finished she was sitting on my lap, feeding me.

We licked our fingers, emptied the flask. Katrina sighed, settled herself like a nestling kitten. I was very conscious of the warm armful I held, the soft plumpness, the clean smell of her hair. My hug tightened, and she turned her head toward me. Her lips brushed my cheek, found mine in a long, lazy kiss.

"Katrina."

"Is nice."

We kissed again. This time her hands slid under the blanket, stroked my back. My own free hand caressed her throat, slid down.

"Ah, Cormac. Oh, wait."

Katrina slipped from my arms. For a moment I wondered if she was disappointed at finding me so like other men. From the darkness came muted movements, the rustle of cloth. Then the blanket was drawn aside and her smooth naked form came back to my embrace.

"Now, we are same," said Katrina.

"Katrina, my dear."

"*Ja*, Cormac. *Ja*."

"This chain——"

"We find way!"

Katrina's pale face seemed to float from the night as she bent to kiss me. She spoke only once as far as I heard.

"Is nice," said Katrina.

Chapter 9

WHEN the soldiers arrived they found me fully dressed, sleeping soundly. Oddly my dream was of Jill Murdoch, not Katrina, and there was nothing fleshy about it. Jill seemed to be wearing Lady Esterling's traveling costume, but her hair was that remembered fire, and she was giving me a proper scolding about something, shaking her finger under my nose. I was getting ready to bite that finger when the sergeant shook me awake.

"Axle's fit," Hanks said. "We march."

The other two redcoats were with him; they were less talkative than Sime and Joe. One hammered my shackle loose from the manger, back onto my wrist. The other handed me a bowl of hot porridge, and went to lead out the horses. As I ate my glance gleaned the stall for any sign of Katrina's visit. The wench had carefully collected every last chicken bone. Her farewell whisper still puzzled me. She had murmured something about asking the lady to help me.

Outside the stable the morning was young and lovely. It was a bright September day, crisp and tingling. The town was wrapped in sunlit quiet, so still that the birds carolling in the trees sounded hysterically gay. A group of blue jays held an angry parliament in a nearby tree. Gulls and ravens circled over the harbor. From a distance came the raucous cawing of crows. There were few man-made noises, and those hushed. The whinny of a horse seemed startling.

"Where is everybody?" I asked.

"Sabbath," Hanks said. "They're all getting ready for church."

The soldier holding my chain nodded. "That's why this early start. Some of these folk think it a sin to cross a river on Sunday."

That, I judged, was a pull at the long bow, but it wasn't my place to argue. They let me stand in the yard between inn and stable while they hitched one horse to the chaise, saddled the other. The horses interested me as horses have from boyhood. These were both sorrels, no bigger than the post-rider's pony. The ensign's mount may have shaded fourteen hands; the other was smaller. Both were well made, sturdy and lively, their coats glossy and smooth. The Suffolk Punch in England stood no higher, but they were yellow, long-backed, ugly steeds alongside these.

Lady Esterling's colt had a white star on his forehead, and one white stocking, left forefoot. The saddle horse had a blaze down his face and two stockings. They were teasing the soldiers, rolling their eyes, tossing their heads, frisking. That was play, not temper; each took the bit without fuss.

My interest in the blaze faced sorrel was more than casual. Borden Whitlaw's big frame would be no light weight, but this horse looked as if he'd run under it. Without seeing him race there was no telling how fast he'd go, and that was the important thing. Over any terrain where

[78]

a horse can go a rider was sure to catch a man on foot. Whitlaw's breed hunted foxes; he'd ride me down without a qualm. The little sorrel made my chances of escape very meager.

Jotham Twigg joined us as they tied both animals to a hitching post. The innkeeper wore a brown homespun suit, and had clapped wig and hat over his baldness. He'd paid no great price for the wig; it was coarser than the homespun. Twigg, as constable, walked with a swagger.

"Here," he said, handing me a leather pouch, "you're my prisoner, and you'll tote my sack."

The temptation to toss it in his face was great, but I controlled myself. Hanks and his squad were donning packs. Sime scowled like a man bedeviled by last night's liquor. The constable was the lesser of two evils. Anybody would rather haul for one than five. Besides, the sack wasn't heavy; it slung from my shoulder by a strap.

Katrina came bustling out for my porridge bowl. Her air of busy innocence almost made me laugh aloud. As she listened to Twigg's parting instructions, with demure attention, you'd have guessed her a maiden in her teens. But she gave me one tense whisper.

"Watch for lady's signal!"

As we marched through the silent town, past shuttered houses, along a road deserted except for a stray cur, I pondered Katrina's message. She could only mean Lady Esterling, and, for the life of me, I could not picture that chill, genteel woman raising a finger to signal, or help, anyone. She had shown me neither pity nor sympathy, but a disinterested perusal. For all the Dutch girl's well meant kindness, I was sure that the lady would do nothing.

An obliging sailor ferried us across the Thames. There were a dozen or more ships tied up to wharves or at anchor in the basin, but they displayed the same early-Sabbath-morning calm. On one schooner, indeed, a group of sailors were gathered while their captain read a prayer service. From the rail of another a striped tomcat paused in his primping to watch us pass. I envied the men, and the beast.

The tide was at young flood, but my thoughts were of slipping a cable, putting out to sea. To watch the sails fill, to feel the deck pitch again would have been a cleansing thing after pillory and fetters. I wondered if my sailing days were finished.

We climbed the eastern bank and went on. Here the road curved down toward the sea, and I could follow the blue splendor of it as it stretched, restless and free, to the horizon. Tidal inlets serried this coast like fork marks on the rim of a pie. At one place we were forced to ford; the water was only ankle deep, but cold.

[79]

There was little cover in the landscape to hide a fugitive. It was sand mostly, with some sparse growth, rank grass and an occasional weary tree. Nothing on that fine morning could have looked desolate, but that bit of land almost did.

We marched without order, but a fair pace. Sergeant Hanks and Twigg led, talking together. Sime and Joe were ahead of me, the other two redcoats behind. All had their muskets slung, and the four in front glanced back at me constantly. The rain had settled the road dust, turned the ground soft, but it was drying, and only the deeper ruts were muddy.

Dropping back I tried to start a conversation.

"Where are we bound?"

"Westerly," said the shorter soldier.

The forenoon sun was in my eyes; we were headed due east. I said: "We're not. You're turned around."

"It's the next village," he said.

"Still Connecticut?"

"Who knows?" the other redcoat shrugged. "Some of the towns down this way are Connecticut, and some are Massachusetts Bay. Others are Rhode Island Plantation. Six of one, half a dozen t'other."

"They're all a nuisance anyway."

"Rhode Island is worst."

They nodded in agreement, and the shorter one explained. "They was supposed to give up their charter three years back. They all was. Sir Edmund, he's asked them time and again. He even sent us down to get it. But they hid it away somewhere."

"They're pesky," agreed his partner. "They ain't Puritans, but they're just as pesky."

"They ain't *nothing!*" The shorter man shook his head. "In Rhode Island they got all sorts. Quakers even. That's how the colony started. Them as couldn't get along with Boston struck out for theirselves."

Rhode Island sounded attractive to me. I said: "Do they let everybody in? Even Papists?"

"Well," said the taller one, "I ain't sure they're *that* pesky. But there might be a couple around Providence. Hidden away with that there charter."

"They raise some pretty horses."

That reminded me of the ensign and the lady. With chaise and horses they hadn't needed to start so early, but I was surprised they hadn't caught us. The two redcoats grinned at my statement. The shorter one did the talking.

"Been the same all the way from New York. We get just about

tuckered when they come along smooth as butter. Mind you, the ensign ain't getting more than pleasant company, but it's a sight better'n walking."

We'd crossed another river, named the Mystic, before I heard the hoofbeats. Hanks heard them too, called back.

"Close up now. Look smart."

Sime blurted his favorite oath, but they obeyed the command. Arms, shoulders and legs began to swing in unison; they became a unit, marching like soldiers. They weren't too precise, but they moved together, heels thudding as they stepped. In their midst I picked up the same beat, and rhythm. Twigg couldn't adjust to it. He tried, skipping beside the sergeant, but only looked foolish.

Chaise and rider grew larger behind us as if rolling up the road like a carpet, with an ease and grace that made the beholder want to cheer. Both horses had a sure-footed natural way of pacing that gobbled miles. The lady drove for herself, and Whitlaw, for all I disliked the man, rode well. They made a handsome sight.

"By Pegasus!" I said. "Those are horses!"

"Hers," Sime said. "Both of them. Or her husband's rather."

"Make way!" Sergeant Hanks waved us off the road.

The chaise swept by, giving me a glimpse of an ample Negro woman sitting beside Lady Esterling. Her ladyship handled her reins as smartly as a coachman. Whitlaw, riding beside her off wheel, reined in after he passed, making his mount curvet in the middle of the road.

"Everything all right, Sergeant?" he called.

"Yes, sir," Hanks said, saluting.

"Keep on then. We'll wait for you." Whitlaw grinned, wheeled his horse, spurred after the disappearing chaise.

"Hope he breaks his neck," muttered Sime.

The wish was understandable. There was something in Whitlaw's manner, an arrogance that mocked walking, that made me long to see him come a cropper. Hanks stared after the glinting hooves, shrugged.

"They in a hurry?" asked Twigg.

"They'll rest up ahead," Hanks said. "They like to run the horses some of a morning."

We slogged on, no longer bothering to march, wearied by the very sight of easier travel. As the sun rose higher the redcoats grumbled. Twigg looked shocked at their language, but the sergeant ignored it. The road turned inland to wind among trees, and it was pleasanter striding through latticed shade.

About noon we caught up with the riders. Both horses were tethered, and grazing. The Negro woman was taking food from a hamper. Whitlaw and Lady Esterling were seated on the roadbank. The ensign rose to watch us approach. He stood, arms akimbo, legs spread, with anger in his attitude.

"A rogue's march in truth!" he cried. "Can't you prick that fellow along faster, Sergeant?"

"He's given no trouble," Hanks said.

But there's trouble in the wind, I thought. Something, perhaps the lady, had rubbed Whitlaw's fur the wrong way. You could see it in the gleam of his eye, in the way he leaped down the bank.

"Fetch him here," Whitlaw ordered.

Sime reached for me, but I pushed his hands away. Walking forward I tried to look respectful, but not cowed. Jotham Twigg hovered uneasily at my elbow; Sergeant Hanks stood aside, expressionless. The other soldiers grouped behind me. From the bank Lady Esterling gazed down at us, posed and detached.

"Doyle," said Whitlaw, "even though you're headed for the gallows, I'll not have you slowing my march."

"I didn't set the pace, sir," I said.

"Didn't you?" The ensign drawled the question. "Well, you'll set it in future. And in case you're still sluggish from the stocks, we'll stir your blood." He drew a riding crop from his jackboot, swished it once.

Knowing he was baiting me, I waited. If the highhanded bastard provoked me into going for him, a beating was certain, a shooting possible. For once in my life my head ruled my tongue. I cursed Whitlaw behind tight lips.

"Sergeant Hanks."

"Sir?"

"Take the squad a hundred yards up the road. Bivouac under that big tree. Leave your packs here. Anything you want this man is to fetch you. The faster he goes back and forth the more you'll have to eat. See to it that he keeps moving."

The crude jest appealed to most of the soldiers. Sime laughed aloud in anticipation of some sport. As they dropped their packs, Twigg stepped forward to retrieve his pouch.

"Any objections, Master Constable?" asked Whitlaw.

"No," said the innkeeper, "mirth and sport are not seemly on the Lord's day, but the punishment of the wicked is always righteous work. I'll just sit apart, and stay my hunger, until we move on again. Delivering the prisoner to the next constable is my sole concern."

Twigg sat down by the roadside, removed his hat, bent his head to say grace. Before he was finished the soldiers were in position. Hoots summoned me.

"You'd better go see what's wanted," Whitlaw said. He balanced on the balls of his feet, crop poised to strike. "Or do you want me to start you?"

"Borden," called Lady Esterling. "Phyllis has the food ready."

"One moment," Whitlaw said, not turning. "Well, pirate?"

I waited until his arm swung back, then ran. There was a small satisfaction in making him miss, but that was all the satisfaction I had. Hanks sent me back for his pack first, but the others chose precedence by lot, laid wagers on my speed, urged me with shouts, cuffs and kicks. For more than an hour under the noonday sun I trotted up and down the road. The gait I adopted appeared more tiring than it was, but even so by the fifth trip I was winded. Every run after that was more and more difficult.

Two things saved me from worse treatment. Hanks would not let the redcoats get too rough; when Sime sent me to search his pack for a parcel that didn't exist, the sergeant cursed him for a cheat. Ensign Whitlaw, sulky at my lack of spirit, lost interest and devoted himself to Lady Esterling.

Another might have preferred a whipping to being a tormented butt. Such pride seemed too high priced for me. Let them all think me mean and cowardly. Let them believe that, like most seamen, I could not run fast or far. There was nothing fake about my sweat or panting, but I pretended greater distress than I felt.

I do not think I fooled Sergeant Hanks. The big man watched my efforts with a quizzical twinkle. Perhaps he remembered my sprint in pursuit of Pym Pemberly two days past. He said nothing; he even slipped me a swig from his flask. Hanks was a tough old veteran, but he was fair.

Whitlaw gave me no chance to rest when we resumed the march. He swung into the saddle, shouted orders. I brought the last pack, Sime's, to the squad, leaned against the big tree while they made ready.

"Here," said Hanks, passing me a hunk of bread, and a gnawed half of mutton chop, "eat as we go. Don't let him see."

"Coddling him, ain't you?" asked Sime.

"If he keels over, you'll help *carry* him, Sime Watkins. You'll not like that to happen!"

Twigg hurried up to burden me with his pouch once more, and we all lined up in the road. Chaise and rider led the procession now, both horses walking. We marched at a slightly brisker pace, but moderate enough. Lady Esterling, I judged, was not one to overtax her husband's horses. The road twisted and curved back on itself in a wondrous fashion. If that one was a fair sample, the New England roads were made by chasing a blind cow through the night.

Sime, hunching along beside me, ranted at me. "You'll get no rest at Westerly either. It's only a score and some miles from New London. We'll be there in an hour. Twigg can ease his bones, but you'll press on with the rest of us."

"So be it," I said. "Maybe we'll find a constable who isn't afraid of the ensign."

The idea intrigued Sime, but only for a moment. He shook his head. "No fear. Whitlaw is weasel mean, but there ain't many that care to face him." He mentioned the officer's ancestry and habits as if to prove his point.

We climbed a hill, and paused on the crest of a tree lined bluff above another river. This stream was smaller than the Connecticut, or Thames, but larger than the Mystic. Thick woods, a virgin forest, bordered the road. There was a village on the opposite, east, bank, a cluster of frame houses with the usual church tower jutting up.

"Westerly," Sime said.

"What's the river?"

"The Pawcatuck. Don't they have the damnedest names?"

There were no boats on our side so the redcoats halloaed for a ferry-man, shouting together at the sergeant's word. A man appeared on a wharf, shading his eyes to gaze across the river at us. Hanks hailed him again. With a wave that meant he understood, the man went into a dock shack.

Lady Esterling stepped from the chaise, strolled along the bluff. She climbed the roadbank, stood there above us, gazing downstream. "Borden," she called in that calm, assured voice, "come admire the scene while we wait. It's a *signal* view."

As she beckoned, her head turned, and, for the first time that day, her glance met mine. She never so much as winked, but those cool eyes dared me.

The word she'd used, the glance, gave me a thrill of tension. If ever she intended to signal, she was doing so. My eyes roved, searching for exits. The woods looked close, and promising, but Sime stood by my shoulder, the others surrounded us. Surely, the lady wouldn't tempt me to certain failure!

Whitlaw dismounted with an indulgent laugh.

"Phyllis will hold the horse," said Lady Esterling. She watched him toss the reins to the Negro woman, turned away. She never glanced at me again.

The ensign was still in the road, a dozen paces from her, when she screamed!

It was a shrill, piercing scream, ear-splitting and sudden. The sound froze Whitlaw in his tracks, brought an oath from Sime. It even startled me, and I was poised, expecting something, ready for anything. The noise was an awesome thing to come from her ladyship's throat.

"Snake!" she cried, stamping at the tall grass. "Snake!"

She gathered her skirts waist high to reveal slim hosed legs, a flash of pale thighs. She was thrashing about, shouting as she kicked.

"Help me! Snakes! Help!"

"Zounds!" whispered Sime, open mouthed at the sight. The others dashed to rescue her, Hanks cocking his musket. Even as I gave the chain two quick turns to bring my fists together, I noted the yellow stripe of her ribbon garters. Whitlaw was halfway up the bank when she flung herself on him. They went down under a flurry of petticoats, and flailing legs.

Sime gulped, took a step forward to see better.

Phyllis let go with a scream practically on the sorrel's blazed nose. The horse reared, tore the reins free, plunged back up the road at a gallop.

Raising both arms high, I brought the whole weight of bunched chain and shackles down on the back of Sime's skull. Mayhap the memory of his kicks made me strike with greater force. He crumpled, soundlessly. Before his nose was in the dirt, I was across the road, over the bank, and away.

The women were still shrieking, the soldiers yelling, the sergeant beating the grass, as I broke through the underbrush, entered the forest. My direction was north, of course, away from that hemming ocean. Fetters held in front of me, Twigg's sack slapping with each stride, I put my head down, racing as I've never raced in my life.

The trees were spaced enough to permit weaving between them; the ground was firm and even. Wild hope spurred me on, graced me with sure-footed speed.

This was my best chance, and I used it to the full. The tumult died away behind me until there was no sound but the quick drum of my feet, the flap of brushed bushes, the steady bellows pumping of my lungs. Any estimate of how far or fast I ran would seem like a brag. I kept on until a stitch in my side slowed me. Even then I walked, listening for the first sign of pursuit. There was nothing.

When any thought beside headlong flight returned to me the first was to bless Lady Esterling. Whether from pique or jest, kindness or mischief, she had done me the greatest of favors.

The device she'd used made me laugh through my panting. Only for Katrina's warning I'd have thought both fright and snake real. As it was, her performance deserved every admiration. I owed the lady an apology for misjudging her. Under that bland façade she had hidden talents, perhaps even hidden warmth.

Sure, and it was not the first time that a snake and a woman had joined to befuddle a man!

Through the tall trees to my right came the glint of the river. That gave me a bearing; I pushed on to the north, sometimes at a trot, sometimes walking. It was cool in the forest, passing through dappled patterns of shade and sunshine, but that was not what added bounce to my step, fresh strength to my muscles.

Shackled or no I was free! The very air tasted sweeter; the birds, the murmuring leaves, made music once more. Each step took me farther from the gallows tree, brought the recovery of my sunken sea chest from a dream to a possibility. It would be a bad day, and a violent one, before they took me again.

Chapter 10

FLIGHT without plan is sometimes necessary, but seldom successful. Fortunately it was still early afternoon when mine began. There were hours of daylight to be used, not only by running feet, but by thinking head. Before nightfall found me safely away, or securely hidden, a practical scheme for the future would have to be contrived. There was bound to be pursuit. Whitlaw, for one, would be scarlet with fury at my escape. Jotham Twigg, too, was duty bound as constable to preach a pious search for the ungodly fugitive. To evade recapture would take all my wits, a strong spice of luck, and any help the good Lord could spare.

When I reached a hilltop, with a fine, clear view behind me, I sat down to eat and think, having need of both. Twigg's pouch provided the fodder. The innkeeper either had eyes bigger than his belly, or had carefully provisioned for his return journey. There was bread and sausage, two red apples, a remnant of cheese, a leather bottle half full of beer. Even on half rations, which I sensibly imposed, there was enough for a meal.

Nor was this all the sack yielded. From its bottom came an extra pair of knitted stockings, a battered prayer book, and a heavy deerskin purse. The book was welcome as reading matter, but when I opened the purse I nearly shouted with joy! It held flint and steel and tinder. Twigg had removed the snaphance from an old gun to make a very welcome, if cumbersome, fire starter.

That was the kind of boon that gave me an urge to whistle a lively tune. Finding the snaphance was like getting the card you needed, the one that brings the feeling that maybe you'll rake in the winnings after all!

Happy that I'd have fire for cooking, and warmth, I ate, with a wary eye on the valley below. No banker ever figured his ledger with more care than I did my situation.

First I counted my disadvantages. The fetters marked me for an escaped felon, at sight I was something to set the dogs on. All the towns along the main road knew of me, name and description; whether I could beat the news of my escape inland was a question. Also I was a stranger, ignorant of this big new land. I might get lost, wander the forest in circles, or blunder into captivity at the next turn.

On my side was the fact that it was Sunday. The villagers would be loath to leave their peace and rest. My fear was of the native yeomen, not the redcoats. To judge from their talk the soldiers knew no more of the land than myself. But the farmers and hunters knew their own bailiwick as they knew their doorsteps.

In my favor, too, was something they didn't know. This was not my first time of being hunted over hill and dale. Their broadside called me pirate; they would think me a sailor as helpless in the woods as any landed fish. But I had been quarry both in Ireland and England, where a man learned a few tricks, or never lived to use them.

Finishing one half of a tart, juicy apple, I decided on a scheme. Based on out thinking the hunters there was little new or original about it.

My plan was a recipe of four ingredients. A fox runs down the wind; a felon flees the gallows; a rabbit doubles back; a shackled man cannot swim a river. All were true enough maxims, but some, in my case, could be turned contrariwise.

After repacking Twigg's pouch, I turned east, toward the river, and, as far as I knew, toward Boston. Though I had seen no motion from my hilltop, I was sure the redcoats were beating the woods after me. My notion was to cross the river, double back down the other side, find out how the wind blew.

The Pawcatuck wasn't far, nor where I reached it too wide, but I wasted minutes searching the bank for a fallen log. Panic began to unsteady me, but I fought it down. Finding a man in a forest was harder than finding a log! There had to be one!

Then, I heard voices, and dived for cover.

Praise God, I was snug behind a tree when the boats swung into sight. Through a screen of rushes I watched them come. There were two boats, eight men in each, the oarsmen pulling upstream. Jotham Twigg was in the bow of one; Sergeant Hanks, like the last rose on a bush, was evident in the other. The rowers, townsmen, were finding it hot work, and heavy going.

"He can't have come this far," one said.

Hanks shrugged. "He can run."

"The evil flee where no man pursueth," said Twigg. "But surely this is utter foolishness. The man will seek the depths of the forest, the mountains to the west, a safe stronghold like King David's at Adullam."

"What stronghold?" jeered Twigg's bow oar.

"I used the scriptural expression as an example only," Twigg explained. "But the criminal will of a certainty flee to lonely desolation."

"*I'd* make tracks," said another oarsman.

"Listen," said Hanks patiently. "My men, with the flanker on the riverbank, in open order, are beating the woods in pursuit. Ensign Whitlaw, with the mounted folk who volunteered, are riding hard in a wide circle to cut him off to the west. Some of your people are closing in between the soldiers and the horsemen. The whole idea is to pen him against the river. He can run in those shackles, but he can't swim."

"That's what I say," Twigg argued. "Since he can't swim he'll not come near the water."

The oars flashed, dripping, dug in. Slowly, too slowly for my taste, they pulled up river till a bend hid them. Their voices faded to a rumble, blended with the stream's noises, were drowned. When I could hear no splash or mutter, I emerged, sweating and scared.

Their military arrangement of forces to catch me was a good one. I wagered it was Sergeant Hanks who proposed the cordon, suggested fox hunter Whitlaw's sweep to the west. Now finding a log I could drag and float was imperative. Any minute I might hear the redcoats.

As I searched, I stripped, wadding shirt and jerkin over my fetters, stuffing all else in the sack. At last, in despair, I grabbed a fallen branch. Wedging the pouch in a crotch, I carried the branch into the stream.

[88]

I waded as far as I could. When the bottom dropped from under me, I placed my wrists on the branch, prayed it would buoy them up.

That branch gave me good service. Kicking, I managed to make headway, even steer, though I was forced to kick deep, with care, lest splashes betray me. The current helped, sweeping me far downstream, but aiding my efforts. Cold as the water was, it was nothing to my fear of discovery. But I heard no shout, no shot. When I was safely across I looked back, scanning the opposite bank. There was no soldier in sight.

Jerkin and shirt were soaked, of course, but the rest of my clothes were dry enough. Damp, but joyful, I hurried away from the river, seeking a vantage point that overlooked the town.

From a perch in a tall tree, high on a hill east of the village, I could see the road, and, at an angle between two houses, most of the common. Lady Esterling's chaise was there, looking at that range no bigger than a child's toy. There wasn't much activity so I jammed myself between branch and trunk, and dozed.

It was late afternoon when my pursuers returned. The first group that entered the common, I guessed, were the boatmen. Only one redcoat showed, bright as a flaring ember, among the drab citizens. Next, Whitlaw rode in from the riverside. He checked the sorrel back on its haunches, an angry man's reining. Four other horsemen followed him, wearily dismounted. Those on foot, soldiers and villagers, came last, straggling, until the square was crowded with people.

They stood in bunches, talking and, from their gestures, arguing. The sight made me grin. I imagined the ensign's high-pitched curses, Twigg's outrage, the sergeant's grim silence. The ill feeling between soldiers and natives should be boiling over. Each would blame the other for my escape. Whitlaw, in his arrogance, had claimed me, but I was still Constable Twigg's charge. These Puritan colonials openly resented the king's governor, and his troops. The joint cast of the net that missed me would fan that resentment.

To my surprise, for the sun was low in the west, already turning the sky pink, Lady Esterling's chaise led the soldiers from the village. Whitlaw trailed the little column, walking his tired horse. Evidently her ladyship refused to delay her journey longer.

All five redcoats were marching, but one, hatless and packless, wore a white bandage for a turban. My blow, then, had not cracked Sime's thick skull.

Once they were gone, I roused myself, slid down the tree. The village was alarmed, watchful. To enter it, even long after dark, was inviting disaster. My greatest need was tools—chisel, hammer or file—to rid my wrists of the hampering gyves, but common sense told me to seek them elsewhere. Some isolated farm, with barn not too close to the house, was my best bargain.

That called for an inland settlement away from the coast. Accordingly, I went north, keeping the river on my left, following its course.

Even before the daylight faded I found that the Pawcatuck curved as crazily as the road. When it barred my path, turned me due east, I followed still. I had my fill of fettered swimming and wet clothes. Besides, as the light faded the wind rose, lashing the treetops with a cold breath that promised frost. As soon as the shadows crept up to fill the spaces between columned trees, I was shivering and bewildered.

My intent was to walk by night and hide by day, but that New England forest fooled me. No woods I had ever known over the water matched its impenetrable blackness. Five yards from the river I was lost, surrounded by a solid black wall. Moonlight, if there was a moon, found no chink in that bulwark. The only stars that showed were over the river. Now, I can steer by the stars as well as any, but that twisting, topsy-turvey stream had me so mixed up that these looked like so many glittering ice chips.

When I decided that the Pawcatuck, against all reason, had done a complete about-face and was heading back to the sea, I gave up. There was wood for a fire, and rocks to mask it; with the help of Twigg's snaphance and tinder I soon had a blaze going. The bright flames warmed me; the warmth cheered me. Even my shackles thawed to some degree. Toasting a sausage on a pointed stick, I dozed off twice.

Weariness and cold turned me reckless. All my running and walking, the excitement of escape and chase, had me witless with fatigue. The night grew colder with every heart beat. Heedlessly, I piled the fire high, pulled one of the innkeeper's stockings over my ears, used the other as a muff. With my feet in the leather pouch I curled as close to the flames as I dared.

Only half of me was warm, but before all the wood was burning, I was asleep.

❖

Morning found my clothes rimed with frost. The fire had burned to ashes that matched the color of the sky above. My stocking cap stuck to the ground that even before sunrise glittered with hoary crusts crackling underfoot. A rim of white lace-like ice trimmed the river's edge; the Pawcatuck itself had the cold gleam of polished, black marble. This change of weather frightened me; if autumn came so early in these latitudes my unsheltered future looked bleak indeed.

Shivering, blowing vapor through chattering teeth with every breath, I gathered twigs, rekindled the fire. That helped, though caution kept the blaze tiny. Those orange flames were a beacon for any early riser. After a meager breakfast of half a sausage and a bit of bread my hoarded food supply resembled a mouse's pantry. Kicking the fire apart, stamping out the sparks, warmed me more, and I started off as briskly as if I knew where I was going.

All morning I tramped beside the Pawcatuck, travelling roughly north-north-east. The forest was filled with the muted noises of nature. Birds sang, birds I couldn't name; a squirrel scolded as I passed; unseen creatures rustled leaves. Once a partridge rose almost from beneath my feet, whirring up with a rattle that made me jump.

These encounters reminded me that I must find means of catching game, or starve. As I marched I gathered stones, hunting for a sharp edge to use as a knife. There were few enough under the trees, and none suitable. With tree trunks as targets I practiced throwing. The results were discouraging. My aim had lost its boyhood skill; the chain hindered a free throw.

I came upon a track, a footpath. It looked unused, overgrown with calf-high grass, but it had been cut through to the river. Carefully, walking softly and alert, I traced it inland. After a couple of hundred yards it ended at the edge of a small clearing.

This was man made, but long neglected. The stumps of trees, rotten dark, stood barely higher than the weeds. In the clearing's center, like a gouge in the green land, was a charred black hole.

A house had burned there, fallen in on itself, burned to the ground, and left a scar. Somehow the sight, in the sunlit clearing, made me shudder. This new land had its ruins, after all, lonely ones, and pitiful.

Thirty feet away, in the tattered remains of a bean patch, I tripped over a hoe.

The tumble barked my knee, but that was of no matter. Reaching, I picked up the rust-red blade, long since rotted away from its shaft; rotted, not broken. In a raw country where tools were more precious than gems this hoe would not have been lightly discarded, left forgotten where it dropped. Something, fire or worse, had caused the user to leave it, prevented his return.

Breathing a prayer for the former owner I took my prize back to the river, and marched on, sharpening the hoe edge against a flat rock. This was tedious work for the rust was crusted thick, and the rock hardly a proper whetstone. My fingers ached before the hoe had a bright rim, jagged but fairly keen.

Inserted sideways in a split stick and fastened with thongs trimmed from the pouch's strap, it formed a crude hatchet. The blade could not dent the iron of my bonds, but it would skin an animal. My handiwork pleased me. As I walked I swung the cudgel at imaginary opponents, pretending it a stronger weapon than it was.

A stream that tumbled into the river delayed me for over an hour. Two steps and a jump forded it, but fish moved in one pool. Cutting a switch, I bent it into a hoop, attached the open end of a stocking to make an improvised net.

Motionless, on my belly beside the pool, both arms elbow deep in the cold water, I fished. Little fish darted near, nibbled my fingers, but I wanted the pool's monarch. This was a trout as long as my forearm, a big brown fellow, sluggish with years.

He would not be hurried. He didn't care that pursuit might be hot on my trail, that he was wasting precious minutes. Never was there such an inconsiderate trout! He didn't even show the normal curiosity of his kind. The dolt examined every cranny of the pool before he came near me.

"Coward," I said, "it's your own pool. Nobody's ever bothered you, have they?"

Finally, after a year or so, the trout swam my way, slowly, barely moving his tail. Then—blast him!—he floated, just out of reach, eyeing me.

"I'm good to eat," I said. "Choice. Something new. *Come on!* Do you want to die of old age?"

He edged a trifle closer, wriggled his nose at the rim of the net. I held my breath, not moving. I could see his gills working, the whole fat brown length of him. My mouth was watering.

"Please," I said. "Please."

The tunnel of the net fascinated him. He poked his snout in, one inch, two.

With a swoop and a shout I had him! He fought; he slipped from the net in midair. My heart stopped, but my heave had tossed him landward. For a few seconds we both flapped wildly on the bank. He was still struggling when I fell on him.

No trout, not even my first, gave me more thrill than this beauty. I packed him, cleaned, in wet leaves in my sack, and marched on, singing.

My song was wordless, tuneless, and low, since I wished no audience.

The lack of pursuit was beginning to worry me. By pure chance I had fled through unsettled woods. This good fortune might curdle. The longer I wandered, wearing fetters, the more people might have my description.

While daylight lasted, I hurried on, meeting no one. That night, in a cave on a bluff overlooking the river, after feasting on trout baked in clay covered by embers, my sleep was deep and dreamless.

During the night it grew warmer. Breakfast emptied the sack without filling my insides. The morning sunshine soon burned the last wisps of mist away, and with it the chill. A brisk pace raised a pleasant sweat.

In the early afternoon I heard the strokes of an axe. It sounded nearby, to my right. Creeping cautiously toward the chopping, I heard the axeman singing an old hymn as he worked. Each stroke crashed as he ended a line.

> Praise God from whom all blessings flow!
> *Whack!*
> Praise Him all creatures here below!
> *Whack!*
> Praise Him above, Ye heavenly host!
> *Whack!*
> Praise Father, Son, and Holy Ghost!
> *Whack!*

The singer was a big man, hatless and shirt sleeved, with cropped, grizzled hair and a broad, leathery face. He paused to mop his brow, and take a long pull from a jug. The gurgle sounded cool; the smack of his lips made me envious. There was no temptation to rush him. He was twice my size with a sheathed knife in his belt and a musket propped handy, besides the axe.

"Paw," cried a boy as he pushed through a bush. "Maw wants you, Paw."

"What for?" asked the giant.

"She didn't say."

Startled by the boy's appearance, I shifted position to find we were near the edge of another clearing. In the open was a tiny house with a peculiar roof that sloped lower in back than front. Smoke billowed from a crooked chimney. Three small children romped before the door; an older girl helped a tired woman lay wash on the grass to dry. There were two animals, a staked cow and a sleeping mongrel.

Dog and youngsters made the place dangerous. Waiting to see if the farmer, so near his peaceful home, would leave axe or musket behind,

I tried to watch everything in sight. The boy took the axe; the man carried the musket. As they went toward the house, I crept away.

Guessing at a nearby settlement I passed the clearing in a wide arc that brought me to a track on its far side. Following this for about a mile brought me to a tiny village, a cluster of eight houses, shining new, grouped around a wide curve of the road.

If this little hamlet had heard of me, my fame was all too widely spread. No place could have better fitted my purpose; every house had its outbuildings. There were tools in those sheds, perhaps even food stored for the coming winter. Isolated and snug the settlers obviously expected few visitors; they would be less watchful. No one had seen me come. No one, I hoped, would see me go.

Slipping from tree to tree, careful as a stalker, I climbed the hill behind the settlement. From its crest every field, every dwelling, the slightest movement was in plain sight. For an hour or so I studied the ground, choosing the likeliest, safest outbuilding, selecting the quickest path to it. That was the one where someone hammered.

Hunger was growling inside me. The pouch held nothing but a few crumbs. Still a chance to get a tool that would rid me of my fetters was worth a fast, so I wasn't too dismal. As soon as the settlement was quiet again, I decided to sleep.

The night was cold, starry clear, but there was no frost. My sleep was fitful; chill kept rousing me. I didn't dare risk a fire where I was, nor did I wish to go blundering about in the moonless dark. Betwixt dozing and stamping to keep warm the hours dragged past.

Black sky fading to the east gave the signal for my raid. Knowing farmers for early risers I waited no longer. When the first star winked out, I started down the hill.

For some reason an old adage popped into my head at that very minute.

> The evening red, the morning gray,
> Sets the traveler on his way.

Naturally I hoped it was true. Once I came out of the forest I could see fairly well. There was mist on the fields; the grass was wet. A stone wall was slippery as I climbed it.

My memory of the route was well-nigh perfect. The shed I sought loomed out of the graying mist like the piles of a fog-bound wharf. Crouching, I listened. The hamlet was dark and silent.

Dogs were my chief worry, but if I had picked owners correctly the nearest was two houses distant. Nothing stirred as I crept across the barnyard. The first breeze of morning made more noise.

I reached the shed, felt its rough planks. Now, all that was left was to sneak around to the door.

Practically in my ear a man yawned.

A gunpowder explosion could not have surprised me more! The voice that spoke through the yawn was inside the shed, a plank's width from me. Every word increased my horror.

"The varmint's miles away by now."

"Maybe not," said another man's voice.

"Abel saw him this afternoon."

"True, but dawn's the favored time for mischief."

My face must have been a picture; my mouth was wide open. They couldn't be talking about me! Nobody saw *me!* Not Abel, Cain, nor any other son of Adam! It wasn't possible! But the talk droned on.

"Skulking rat!"

"Planning thievery, I suppose."

"Or deviltry."

"Thanks to Abel we're forewarned."

"I hope he does try his tricks."

"Uhuh. We owe him for a night's sleep."

My only choice was a quick, silent retreat. These men had taken their position after dark. Another shed might conceal more guards. Robbing a sleeping hamlet was one thing; avoiding watchful armed men was another. I felt as if I'd put my head in a trap!

In my haste to get away my feet betrayed me. Three strides from the shed, I stumbled. My chain was muffled inside the sack but a rock clattered.

The back door of the house crashed open. A shouted challenge shattered the stillness.

"Who's there?"

There was a stamp of movement inside the shed as the two guards rushed the exit. Hesitation was fatal. I ran!

"There he goes!"

From the house doorway a gun roared, a blunderbuss by the ripping sound of its blast! Pellets rattled around me like tossed gravel. They missed, but lashed me to greater speed.

"I see him!"

"*Shoot!*"

Two muskets slammed off to my right. I saw both flashes from the corner of my eye. One ball whistled past, struck the stone wall, whined as it bounced. I cleared that same wall with a hurdling leap.

"Reuben! Sam! Around behind your shed!"

"He's heading up the hill!"

As I neared the woods I glanced back. Several forms, mist-wrapped shadows, were strung out behind me. A gun fired, yellow flash and dull report. They seemed to be keeping together, pursuing with caution.

That was fine for I intended to run for another hour. The brief days of freedom, tramping the woods, had made me much fitter for such a race. Panting, thankful that there was light enough to see fairly well, I plunged in among the trees. They would never catch me now.

Almost immediately someone leaped on my back! I staggered, tripped, went down. Other forms flung themselves on me! I was the bottom of a heap of writhing bodies! A hand was clamped over my mouth; another clutched my throat.

The assault was so sudden that I was shocked into stunned lethargy. My struggles were feeble, futile. Dimly aware that the bodies atop me were naked and greasy, I was gagged, pinioned, yanked to my feet before I realized why.

My captors, already hurrying me along with savage stealth, were painted Indians!

For the first time I considered death on the gallows better than some others.

Chapter II

FROM the very beginning the savages gave no sign that they planned to deliver me to the settlers. That was evident from their attitude, the way they hustled me away, the fierce scowls and fingered knives. They were not concerned with my fellow white men. As they shuffled, at a curious, fast, muffled pace through the forest, I realized that I belonged to these lithe tan-skinned warriors. For although the countryside, as far as I knew, was at peace, I was the prisoner of a war party!

The thought chilled me. My previous experience with Indians had been with a few bedraggled remnants of Caribs on the West Indies Islands—scarecrow serfs drained by two centuries of slavery. These were of a different breed, tall men, clay colored, with swift, graceful movement, and the faces of hunting hawks. They wore loincloths, leggings, moccasins; naught else besides ornaments and weapons. They slid, dusty wraiths, between the trees, but they carried themselves like supple blades.

For some reason they were annoyed with me. This showed in their shoves, prods, grunted commands. Their glances, from eyes as dark as their coarse black hair, smoldered with resentment. This did not make me feel any better, but I jogged along in their midst, careful not to give fresh offense.

All day we travelled, trotting like a foraging wolf pack, without slowing or sprinting. My escort numbered seven, two striplings, the rest in the prime of manhood. The leader seemed oldest, a squat, beady-eyed scoundrel with a paunch above short legs. When he set the pace the others gasped and I nearly collapsed.

At last we paused while the leader raised his voice in a series of squawks. It was amazing to hear birdcalls, bugle clear, come from the throat of that paint-streaked, leathery visage. An echo seemed to answer, trill after trill; the savages uttered grunts of applause. The leader grinned, waved us forward.

We came out on the edge of a pond, or lake, a sapphire puddle dwarfed by surrounding green hills. Skirting the water we filed into an Indian encampment.

There were a dozen huts, scraggly clumps of sticks as unkempt as hayracks, and half that many campfires. The whole place had a dilapidated look, cluttered with refuse, littered with offal. One glance told me that the band that captured me was the flower of this tribe; the stay at homes were a collection of ragamuffins.

Squaws in tattered, shapeless garments barely turned from their cooking to watch our approach with bovine placidity. A few listless children, both sexes, gathered. The very curs didn't bother to cease scratching fleas in order to snarl a greeting.

Grouped around the central fire were three old men. Except for their faces they might have been mounds of turf. The man in the middle, gnarled and weathered as an ancient sea-grape stump, puffed at a feather-bedecked pipe.

We lined up, and the squat leader addressed him. After a number of grunts, I was pushed forward. Dark eyes, well set in nests of wrinkles, regarded me. This chief old man had a face that might have been carved from a polished peach pit.

He gestured with his pipe. The gag was removed from my mouth. A knife flashed; the thongs that pinned my elbows to my sides fell away. Instinctively, I took my shackled wrists from Twigg's sack, and stretched.

The chain, link clashing against link, jangled. As if it were a tocsin a tremor passed among my captors, stirred the two flanking old men.

The central old man blinked, spoke through the slow puffs from his pipe.

"You wear chains?" His English was harsh, rasping as if rusty from disuse, but perfectly clear.

"As you see," I said.

"Why?"

"I had no choice."

"Who had?"

"Those who made me prisoner."

"Prisoner." He chewed the word. "This we know. Chains we know. But why have you spoiled the raid of our young men?"

"Raid?" The reason for their annoyance became clear, and I grinned. Abel, whoever he was, had seen a scouting Indian instead of a fugitive pirate. No wonder the settlers had opened fire so readily.

"We sent our young men for corn, and they return with a chained white man. This is not good."

"I think your young men spoiled my own raid," I said. "I wished tools to remove these chains, but the men of the village had been warned, and were watchful. They shot at me."

The squat warrior said something, and the old man nodded. "Why do they drive you away in chains?" he asked, still puffing. "A trick to fool the Narragansetts?"

"No," I said, "they did not know me. I believe they took me for one of your braves, and fired their muskets for that reason."

"Ninigret, Sachem of the Narragansetts," the old chief's bow identified himself, "finds this hard to believe. He knows his people are fallen from greatness to beggary. But who is so blind that he cannot tell a white beggar from a red?"

Not too pleased with the comparison, I explained my plight. Most of what I told was true, and they listened with grave interest, Ninigret translating for the others. The squat leader, Mononchet, seemed to understand a little English. At least he grunted applause when I described my escape from the soldiers.

The tribe was a mere remnant, as bedraggled as it looked. These Narragansetts numbered some twenty odd, ten warriors counting the three ancients, the rest women and progeny. Most of the squaws were fat, middle-aged drudges; there was one wizened old crone. Mononchet's band had all the looks, all the vigor. The poor youngsters were as emaciated as a scurvy-ridden crew.

"Sit down, brother," said Ninigret, when I had finished. "Let there be peace between us for we have suffered from the same foes."

The raider captain clapped me on the shoulder, seated me beside Ninigret, went away. The old Sachem passed me his pipe. It reeked of foul tobacco, and the stem was filthy, but his gesture was the same as Tobias Pemberly's. I puffed gingerly, not wanting to cough.

Mononchet came back with a hammer and a chisel, squatted before me. Excitement stirred me at sight of the tools.

"It's a shackle with a pin——" I began.

"We know," said Ninigret, "to our sorrow. We have met your chains and shackles."

"Not Ninigret," Mononchet said, hammering with swift, expert strokes. "They never chained Ninigret."

"Not my limbs," said the Sachem. "Just my heart."

One shackle fell away, the other. I rubbed my wrists, threw my arms wide. The freedom of it felt wonderful.

"Now, let us eat," Ninigret said, "like brothers, not like chained slaves!" He gave an order in his own language, and the squaws brought the meal. We all dipped in turn from one heavy cauldron. The stuff was bubbling hot, thick with grease, a very devil's broth. Sure, the taste was strong, and the chewing tough; in my famished emptiness I licked my fingers hungrily.

"Good," I said, scooping out a large chunk. "Deer?"

Mononchet said a word; Ninigret translated.

"Dog."

The morsel on my palm was suddenly heavy. My filled stomach twitched. I had made a hearty meal of mongrel.

Still, my hands were free for eating, my wrists unencumbered. These savages had proved friendly, hospitable. Who was I to scorn their fare when it had restored my strength? They gave from their own small store, and had treated me better than my own kind.

I crammed the portion into my mouth without bothering to wonder whether it was cut from haunch, tail or paw.

The taste was no different than before.

❖

For three days, while the foliage turned colors, I stayed with Ninigret's Narragansetts. The weather continued warm and fair; the trees of the forest changed their leaves to hues that I had never beheld. There were golds, browns, russet, flaming crimson. Nothing in Ireland, England, or the tropics had prepared me for this brilliance. Autumn in this new land flared out with a loud glory that took the heart right out of a man. If it signalled the death of the falling leaves, sure it was a gorgeous way to die!

The third morning it was evident that the savages were breaking camp. Squaws were making bundles of possessions; the huts were stripped clean. Ninigret and Mononchet appeared with a bulging deerskin sack. As the warrior unknotted the thongs that tied it, the Sachem spoke.

"These were gifts of the Boston men. They may help you. The wise animal changes his fur when the trees are bare. This fools the hunter."

Mononchet drew out a handsome coat, dark blue, the edges trimmed with crimson braid. With it he produced a wide-brimmed, black-felt hat. From the creases neither article had ever been worn, but they were brushed and clean.

"Can you wear?" asked Ninigret.

The coat was a trifle tight, but, since it was worn open with the gray jerkin as a vest-doublet, it made a very proper outfit. With the hat pulled down over my eyes I looked like a respectable member of Parliament.

"Weapons," said Mononchet.

He gave me his own sheath knife, a wide, buckled, leather belt, and a long pistol. The brass-bound gun, another gift from Boston, was empty; the canny Puritans had failed to send loads. Still, it was a gentleman's arm.

I could hardly thank them. Now, I was dressed differently from the description, armed, unfettered. If the coat's cut was old that was unimportant in a colony where homespun was the rule. Thanks to the Narragansetts, I could make bold plans.

The tribe went one way, Mononchet and I another. We headed northeast, covered an amazing number of miles. Mononchet knew the country the way a sailor knows spars and rigging. I wished to strike the main road north of a village, enter it as if coming from Boston or Providence Plantation. My role was to be a government official searching for myself. The citizenry would expect some official interest in the recapture of the notorious Cormac O'Shaugnessy Doyle.

Toward sunset, Mononchet left me, ankle deep in curled brown leaves, in the middle of the road. His farewell was as brief as his handclasp.

"Mononchet hate chains. Much hunting, brother. Many scalps!"

With a swirling crackle of dead leaves the brave was gone.

Chapter 12

ONCE more alone, I marched south, half relieved by the savage's departure, half lonely to be again friendless. Striding down the road, through the lovely quiet of the day's end, my thoughts were on my coming gamble. Because of Ninigret the odds of hazard favored me, not the settlers. If a man played at all, he had to play firmly.

Crossing a bridge over a tidewater stream, I came on a village, not as large as New London, but far bigger than the raw settlement that had so nearly trapped me. Some of these houses were freshly painted, a few had glass windows. To my surprise there were two churches instead of the usual one. Twice as much trouble was my immediate reflection.

Flickering lights from fires brightened the windows, made me aware it was dusk, but there was no one about. Supper hour, I supposed, well pleased at the lack of attention. One building bulked wider than its neighbors, had a sign board suspended over the road. Closer, this displayed a rearing, weather-mottled horse, black against unpainted wood. An inscription read, "The Old Snip."

By rights a sign like that marked a tavern. The door was on ground level, and opened into an expected common room. There was the familiar smell of stale ale, smoke, cooking odors. It was a long, low-raftered chamber with benches, trestle tables, a fire dancing in a big stone fireplace.

A trio of rustics in a corner turned to stare at my entrance. The only other occupant, alone against a wall, was a small man who stopped eating to greet me.

"Come in, friend. Come in, and close the portal. Thou brings a draft with thee."

Dress and hat, matching gray, as well as his speech stamped him as a Quaker. I had nothing against the Friends myself, but his presence surprised me; New England was noted for hating the sect. This one was fussy. He ate a pasty with quick nibbles, like a squirrel, his knife darting between pie and mouth.

"Where's mine host?" I demanded, rude as a lord.

One of the rustics called out: "Matthew! You're wanted."

The innkeeper, a swarthy man, moderately tall, heavy shouldered, appeared from the back. His eyebrows flicked up when he saw me, but I gave him no chance at questions.

" 'Do," I said, with a curt nod. "I want a bed for the night, a horse for the morrow, the best meal you can get ready, and a bumper of mulled wine right away."

He scratched his head. The three farmers glanced at each other, back at me. Even the little Quaker stopped plying his knife to stare.

"That's a large order," said the innkeeper.

"How's that?"

The way I snapped my words made him blink, redden. He'd heard such haughty tones before, but he didn't like them. "Well," he said, "the wine now. There's ale and rum——"

"Rum!" I slammed Twigg's sack onto a bench, pulled out another seat for myself. "The wine of the country. All right! I've come far and I'm thirsty. Let it be rum—hot, with a pat of butter, and a few sticks of cinnamon. *If* you have cinnamon!"

My sneer nettled the poor man. That was what I'd intended, but you needn't rake a horse when you spur. Shrugging, I spoke with patient resignation.

"Oh, bring what you have. The governor's business has directed me to worse places."

The room was so still the fire seemed noisy.

"The governor?" asked the boniface.

"Sir Edmund Andros."

" 'The insolence of office,' " quoted the Quaker. He said it softly, but I heard. Bless him, he gave me a wanted opening!

"Shakespear," I said. "At least the words are his, the ill manners are not." Rising, I bowed across the room. "Henry Walters, sir. At your service, sir."

The little man flushed. He had the pained look of the peaceful confronted by a bully. "Thee has me fairly," he said. "The remark was unworthy."

"Master Oliphant meant no harm," said the tavern owner. "You spoke of a horse, sir. Shall I stable yours?"

"Would God you could! The cursed beast threw a shoe a score of miles back, and then went lame. I left him at the nearest farmer's, and walked. Which accounts for my temper." At that, I smiled and saw my expression mirrored on the host's honest face. "That drink, please, my good man."

"At once, Master Walters." He went to fetch it.

"And another for Master Oliphant with my compliments," I called.

"Thank thee," said Oliphant, "but I do not use spirits."

"Then, mayhap, you, or one of these other gentlemen could instruct me as to where to find the constable. My business is urgent. Sir Edmund wished me to make haste."

"Be it about the charter?"

The question, from the tallest of the three, recalled the redcoats' gossip, solved the puzzle of the Quaker's acceptance. This, then, was a Rhode Island town.

"No, no," I said. "I've come because of that pirate who escaped a week or so back. You've heard of that, I suppose?"

"Oh, aye. We heard."

"Yes."

"Soldiers told us."

"He did not come this far," Oliphant said, "nor has there been word he was retaken."

"Which is why I was sent to direct the search." Oliphant's glance warned me to be careful. He had assumed me an arrogant official, but not a catchpoll. "I know the felon, you see, or think I do. He sounds much like a rascal that shipped out of New York when I was harbor clerk there." That established my station; Andros had imported trusted officials from his former post.

The innkeeper returned with my drink. I raised it to the company, took a deep swig. The Old Snip instantly rose in my estimation. The rum had a grand taste.

"Master Walters," said the boniface, who had evidently listened as he mixed, "I have sent my boy to fetch our constable. Would you care for a roast fowl, or a mutton joint?"

"Both, my worthy host. I'm famished. If you cook as well as you pour, I am a fortunate man."

He grinned with pleasure, more broadly when Oliphant added another commendation.

"Master Pritchard keeps a fine house."

"So I am learning," I said, tilting the noggin once more. "I have had no toddy as good since Boston. Not even in Providence."

Pritchard beamed; his fellow villagers nodded approval. Praise from the traveler confirmed their own opinion. So far, I thought, so good. They knew me for a moody, testy fellow, but a good companion if not provoked. I was assured a meal, and bed, in a good inn. My doubloon would more than cover that, if necessary, though I had no intention of spending it. The best coins in my purse were a glib tongue, and a crafty hand. What I needed most was a horse, but that would take time.

"About this pirate," Pritchard said, "Cormac Doyle, the ensign named him. He was last seen beyond the Pawcatuck River."

"That's a far piece south and west," one farmer said.

"How far would you think, Matthew?" another asked.

"Can't rightly say," Pritchard said. "Ask young Devon when he comes through next week."

That placed Devon Neville for me. The post rider was the one I feared for he journeyed the road at intervals and he knew my face. But by next week I'd be far away to New York colony.

A chaise rattled to a halt outside. Pritchard's beam came close to rapture at the sound of more custom. He hurried to the door. The three local men rose, followed. Even Oliphant skipped to the doorway for a look. An arrival, I gathered, was an event.

"Is this the inn, man?" called a voice.

"It is," said Pritchard, stepping outside. The others crowded after him.

"Praise the Lord God," said the voice, "for bringing this land craft to a snug harbor before darkness overtook us."

Sweet saints of Scotland, I thought, as the burr in the man's tone rubbed my spine like a currycomb. That sounds like Alec Murdoch!

In one bound I was at the front window. It *was* Alec Murdoch! There was no mistaking that frame, taller than ever in best black broadcloth, as he unfolded himself down from a covered chaise. This was not the elegant rig of Lady Esterling, but a well-worn vehicle drawn by a tired horse.

There was still daylight, though the shadows were darkening, and the evening star was bright in a fading sky. Men had come out of the houses opposite; there were a dozen grouped around Alec. The Quaker's polite greeting to one portly man sounded to me like the sputter of a fuse.

"Good evening, Constable."

"Evening, Master Oliphant."

A quick glance showed my safest retreat to be an advance. From the inn kitchen came the noises of Pritchard's help. I wanted no notice of my leave-taking. The curious massed before the inn's door had their backs to me, blocked Alec's view.

Grabbing my sack, I slipped through the door sideways, staying behind the others. Then, I edged along, slowly, toward the horse's head, attracting no attention. Alec, fortunately, was busy with Pritchard.

"You'll be wanting rooms?"

"Aye. Not too fancy."

"And stabling for your horse?"

"Aye. He's no mine, though. Borrowed."

"Well, step inside, sir."

Pritchard steered Alec toward the inn; the crowd shifted to follow. The movement drew them away from me, which was fortunate, but it left me in the open. Head down, I strolled in front of the horse.

Someone gasped; I looked to see.

There, standing in the chaise, ready to descend, was Jill Murdoch! By her wide eyes she was just as stunned as I! But woman like, worse luck, she was not too stunned for speech. Her cry froze the living; it would have roused the dead.

"Why, Cormac Doyle! What are you doing here?"

Alec Murdoch whirled as if spun. Over the heads of the others his glance found me at once. His shout was sharp with wrath.

"The Papist pirate!"

There was no time to dally. They were a dozen to my one. Whipping the Sachem's pistol from under my coat, I leveled it.

"Stand back!" I yelled. "I'll shoot the man tries to touch me!"

The crowd scattered. Oliphant popped back into the inn as if sucked inside. Pritchard and the constable collided at the door. Warnings added to the panic.

"Look out!"

"He's got a gun!"

"It's the pirate!"

"Matthew, give way!"

Only Alec Murdoch stood, thundering like a prophet of doom, my doom! Bellowing, he shook his fist at them all.

"Hold, ye cowards! Do you quail before one man as the Israelites before Goliath of Gath? Smite him with the strength of the Lord!"

He was ready to lead the charge, and a charge would have finished me, for the gun was empty. But three leaps took me along the far side of the horse. With another I was in the chaise, grabbing for the reins. I lashed the horse, screamed at him.

The animal bolted, starting with a jerk that toppled Jill back into the chaise. She shrieked, and that scared the horse still more. We tore down the road full speed, the chaise rocking worse than a skiff in a hurricane.

"Stop!" cried Jill.

"Not I," I said, "not this day."

"He's running away!"

"Thanks be to God!"

"We'll be killed!" She struggled up as if to jump.

I yanked her back. "You'll be killed for sure if you try that. Hang on, you silly fool."

Jill was white and scared, clutching the hood strut with both hands, but she still had spirit. "Fool yourself!" she said, the words jolted out of her by our bumps. "Feckless, reckless lout! Argh, you'll be the death of me yet, Cormac Doyle!"

She had said much the same the day we met. First and last Jill Murdoch had brought me nothing but bad fortune. The girl had a curse on me.

So there we were, pelting along behind a runaway horse, liable to break our necks the next minute. Yet, as we raced into the gathering darkness, to tell the truth, I felt strangely happy.

BOOK TWO

The Gold Chain

Chapter 13

THE finest steed in all Kildare, riderless, could not have matched our runaway that day. He was an old cob, autumn brown, but he galloped like a two-year-old stallion, as if the chaise weighed nothing. Though my fingers gripped the reins, I did no driving. By sheer good fortune, and God's grace, the beast stayed in the middle of the road.

We bumped along at a speed that made the trees on both sides seem as thick as a box hedge. Dust rose in clouds behind us to blend with the fading daylight. On the curves the shadows were already darkening so that we darted through patches of shade and twilight in turn. That first wild spurt covered a dozen miles in less time than a man can smoke a pipe.

For avoiding immediate pursuit that was fine. For living to old age it was not so good. If the chaise didn't pound itself to pieces under us, as was very likely, we were liable to overturn at the next jolt. Unless the horse slowed before nightfall a tumble was a certainty, and broken bones a dangerous risk.

Realizing that, I tried pumping the reins, drawing them taut with longer, steadier pulls each time. The cob still had the bit in his teeth, but was running more evenly, head down. Weary when he bolted, a soothing tone might calm him.

"Slow, boy," I said. "Easy, boy."

"His—his name's Di—Dickon," Jill stammered.

"Good Dickon. Whoa, Dickon. Slow, Dickon." My voice sounded like an amorous pigeon.

Jill giggled. When I glared she giggled again. It was a nervous titter, close to hysterics. Memories of hysterical women, hooting in grating peals, frightened me. Such a performance behind poor Dickon would send him into fresh frenzy. This was no moment for patience. Deliberately, in a fierce whisper, I called her a name that would have shocked a concubine.

The girl's cheeks blazed; fire kindled in her brown eyes. Lips tight she let go her hold to swing at me. She missed; a heave by the chaise bounced her back in her corner even as her hand fanned me. Hysterics, I thought, might have been preferable.

"Hang on!" I shouted.

"Filthy pig!" said Jill, shrill with anger. Heedless of danger she half rose to swing again.

This time the bouncing vehicle tossed her against me. Her wrist hit my chin but the blow was nothing to my fright. Her weight nearly drove me overboard. Only a hasty grab saved me. Clinging to the roof with one hand I lost whip and reins as I warded Jill off with the other. She was beside herself with temper, as raging as at our first meeting and, betwixt her clawing and the chaise's leapings, twice as terrifying. God alone knows why she wasn't spilled onto the road; she rattled around inside the chaise worse than a die in a drunkard's dice box. Her sole purpose was to get her hands on me, fists and nails, to teach me a lesson. It was like being swung in a sack with an angry vixen.

Twice she cuffed me before, diving, I drove her back on the seat. Even then, kicking and thrashing, she fought, her face only inches from my own.

"You'll get us killed!" I bellowed.

"Just you," she said, between her teeth, spitting the words at me.

"You too!"

"Worth it!"

Shaking sense into her was impossible, what with the shaking we were both getting anyway. Her face, that close, was coral pink but taut to the smoothness of marble. Her eyes seemed very large, brown as a sunlit mud flat. On sudden impulse I kissed her.

Jill's lips flattened beneath mine. Her gasp of surprise fluttered them. Then, as Dickon swerved, the chaise snapped like a whip tassel! I felt the sickening pitch, heard the clatter of hoofs and wheels on planks. A bridge! With the thought I whirled to snatch for the reins.

I never reached them. There was a jar like a cannon's recoil, and then the chaise flew up in the air in an insane attempt to leapfrog over the horse!

Neat as stone from slingshot I was flipped through space, into a whirling world that turned upside down to meet me. The very surprise of the thing saved me. Somewhere, detached behind me, there was a splintering crash of rending wood. But there was no time for wonder, or fear, no time to brace muscles. The earth rose so fast that I barely shut my eyes before I hit.

The slap of collision drove breath and brains from my body. I lay there, spread-eagled, gasping in the agony of airless lungs, thoughtless and, mayhap, senseless. Through the giddy pain came screams that held me on the brink of consciousness when my whole being wished to drop into the abyss.

"Oh, stop," I said, annoyed. With speech I drew in breath, and hurt, and awareness. My face, with nose for plow, had dug a furrow in the roadbank; my trunk was sprawled across the broken bush that had cushioned my fall. Nearby it was a horse doing the screaming, shuddering, high whinnies like blasts on a whistle.

No one who likes horses could abide that sound. I struggled to my feet, scrambled back down to the road.

Dickon was thrashing in a tangle of reins and snapped shafts. The chaise, overturned, was a crumpled wreck rocked by his lashing hoofs. My collapse had been momentary for one visible wheel was still spinning.

Whipping the Indian knife from its sheath, I managed to free Dickon, and calm him. The horse's recent frights proved too much for his years; he stood, head drooping and trembling, in weary resignation as if awaiting the next catastrophe.

Then, for the first time in my befuddlement, I remembered the girl! "Jill!" I cried. "Are you all right? Jill?"

There was no answer. The only sounds were Dickon's wheezing through flared nostrils, and the thin murmur of the slowing wheel. In the gathering darkness it was just possible to read the tale of our accident. The far end of the narrow, plank bridge was already shrouded in shadow; the stream it crossed was mist far below. Dickon, bless him, in spite of a right-angle turn had managed to get us across to where a boulder on the edge of an equally sharp curve had caused the crash.

With mounting panic I searched the road, both banks. There was no sign that Jill had been thrown clear; she must be pinned under the wreckage. Fortunately the chaise, light built to start, was no great burden in its battered state. One heave shifted it over on its side.

The girl lay crumpled on the roadbed, limp as a rag doll.

"Oh, God!" I said, with cold dread. There was but one thought in my mind in that terrible second before I knelt beside her. The fear of it brought a sob to lump in the base of my throat, sent a quiver from the pit of my stomach to set my fingers atremble. God forgive me, I prayed, I have killed her!

Gently, fearfully, I turned her, raised her against my chest. The sight of her breathing made me weak with relief! It was a momentary reaction; there was still cause enough for sorrow and anguish. Jill was unconscious with an angry bruise darkening on her forehead. Her garments were dusty, disheveled and torn; the back of a hand was scraped raw, bleeding. She was alive, yes, but at what cost in broken bones?

"Jill," I said, brushing the hair back from her face. "Oh, Jill. I'm sorry. Sorry."

Lifting Jill, surprised at her weight, I carried her to the road bank, stretched her comfortably with my coat wadded for a pillow. Dickon nickered at us plaintively. His bleat sounded as helpless as I felt.

Sweat was cold on my forehead as I examined Jill, relying on touch in the failing light. Nothing seemed to be twisted; no swelling or sickening gap met my probing fingers. I was no doctor, but in my crude fashion I tested every bone I knew from ankles to neck, opening her cloak to press each rib, raising the girl to feel the length of her spine. Thank God, her stays were flimsy affairs, not armor like some. She didn't really need them.

As far as I could tell the girl's frame was sound. She even seemed to be breathing better when I finished. Her breast rose and fell a trifle faster; a tinge of color replaced her pallor.

Fearfully mindful of pursuit, I plunged down the incline beside the bridge to wet a rag in the stream. Clawing my way back up I cursed every sliding pebble. When I bathed her face Jill stirred, sighed, but that was all. Evidently the clout on her head had been a stout one!

By then it was night. Darkness surrounded us; the air grew colder. Overhead stars appeared like distant tapers, but it was too early for moonrise. Behind me, I was sure, Alec Murdoch and others were already on my trail. Alone, with woods to use for cover, I would have scoffed at an army of such searchers. But I was not alone.

There was Jill Murdoch, stricken and unconscious. I didn't blame myself for her condition, but I felt responsible. The girl, again, had brought misfortune with her. It would, I thought, serve her right if I left her there.

Sure that thought didn't even fool myself! To desert her thus, for chance finding and succor, and never know if she lived or died, was beyond me. After all, the ill luck worked both ways. She'd not asked to come along. Besides I could not walk away from even a hurt dog in a ditch and know a moment's peace afterwards.

My other choices were two: surrender, or hide her with me until she recovered. The first plan was unattractive. My freedom was too nearly won to give it up easily. As God is my witness, if Jill's life were in danger I think I'd have done it, but as things stood I chose to play for time.

Action took the place of worry. Unless I wished to be caught bald-faced in the middle of the road there was work to be done. A small traveling case had been jolted loose from under the chaise's seat. That, my sack and the harness were all I salvaged. With Dickon's help—the poor beast, still trembling, was wearily docile—it was no great task to drag the vehicle from the road to the edge of the cliff above the stream. A shove sent it over. The crash, and splash, startled the evening quiet, but at least the wreck would be hidden till daylight. It was too large a marker of my plight.

Shouting, thinned by distance, sounded faintly behind me as I strapped pouch and case on Dickon's back. They joined with the darkness to make my fingers clumsily slow. Cursing to keep down the haste that tangles fishlines, I finished at last.

Then, again, I lifted Jill in my arms. With careful steps, leading Dickon on a rein, I mounted the roadbank, plunged through underbrush into the woods.

That was no easy journey. Once out of the starlight the forest was as black as the bottom of a tar barrel. Before my eyes adjusted trees barred my way, branches plucked at me, the uneven ground tripped me. At ten paces I was sweating, at a score panting, at two score my arms ached.

Fortunately, at about a hundred and fifty yards, I stumbled into a little glen, noisy with leaves, but well screened and starlit. I set Jill down, gasping with relief.

Almost at once I heard the drumming gallop of horses! I leaped for Dickon's nose lest he whinny a greeting. He took my grip for a caress, nuzzled me with tired gratitude. Poor Dickon wanted rest, not company.

From the slope I could see them come, a bulked mass with two lanthorns bobbing wildly like binnacle lights in a squall. They clattered across the bridge, seven riders. Pritchard, the innkeeper, had one lanthorn tied to his saddle. The little Quaker had the other. Judging by his tallness, and the way he rode, the last rider, two lengths back, was Alec Murdoch.

Still it was Alec's sharp eyes that noticed something kicked up by the horses ahead.

"Hold!" he cried, damn near unseating himself as he reined in. Alec swayed dangerously as the horse skidded to a stop.

The others slowed, halted. Their impetus carried them well down the road, and they milled there, seemingly bewildered.

"Backwater!" called Alec. "Fetch a light. I saw something!"

Oliphant's prim Quaker voice sounded querulous when he raised it. "Thee saw what?"

"How do I know without a light?" Alec was impatient. "Something moved in the road. It may be the mark of the beast, the spoor of the Bull of Basham!" Trumpets and hautboys echoed in the lank fisherman's angry tones. "Fetch a light! This may be a sign of the Lord!"

They all came back into a circle, the heated horses restless and shifting across the road. A big man, probably the constable, spoke with cold command.

"Dismount and search."

Nobody moved. Heads turned as the riders glanced at each other; turned again as they scanned the darkness. The pursuers were far from confident. Oliphant, nervous as his mount, tittered. The innkeeper, Pritchard, unfastened the thongs that fixed the lanthorn to his saddle.

"Murdoch saw it," he said. "Let him search."

Alec's crow of laughter was rueful. "Mine host," he said, "once down from this benighted creature and the Four Riders of the Apocalypse could not mount me again. I am a fisherman, not a dragoon. Already our endeavor has numbered all my bones, loosened every tooth."

An amused murmur stirred the group. I almost joined their chuckles. Alec certainly bestrode a horse like a witch on a rail. Then I stiffened as the Quaker swung from his saddle, lanthorn swinging from his hand.

"I'll look."

"Over that way." Alec pointed. "The steeds kicked it to the side."

Breath held, I watched the teardrop of light as it moved behind their bulk. Oliphant searched slowly, holding the lamp low. I saw the legs of the horses, the heavy linked shadows of mounts and men outlined against the yellow glow. Questions throbbed in my head. What had I missed, left to be found? Would it give the trail to the hounds?

"This is a fool's errand," said a voice.

Alec Murdoch growled. He said: "Mayhap. But I saw something."

"Ah!" The little Quaker darted, swooped, snatched an object from the dust. He slapped it against his thigh, held it out. "'Tis a maid's headdress."

That brought them forward like hens to feed, jostling their horses. For all his clumsy seat Alec, with a leaning stretch, plucked the prize from Oliphant's hand. He held the cap to the light, folded it with gentle care.

"Aye," he said, "that's my sister's. That's Jill's. She was wearing it."

His tone was steady, very low, without ranting or vehemence, yet a tone to bring prickles to the backbone, lump to throat. He was not being the prophet now, the head of a clan, the Covenanter. He was just a brother who feared for a beloved sister. The men around him felt it; I felt it. For a moment I was near to hailing him.

"So they came this way," Pritchard said.

"That much we knew," said the constable.

"She lost the thing," Oliphant said. Even from my post his sympathy for Alec was obvious. "That's all."

"Was that all?" asked Alec. "Was it? Or did something more happen here?"

He wasn't demanding, but he brought them from their saddles. They dismounted, used both lanthorns, examined the ground. Watching, I thanked the good God that their restless horses had ruined most signs in the road. Besides, these were villagers, farmers and tradesmen, not hunters. Alec himself, skilled in the crafts of fishery, was useless. While he could probably name a school of fish, scintillating the sea, a mile away, the road's tale was hidden from him.

"Nothing," Pritchard said.

I breathed freer. I had not noticed Jill's lost cap. I might as easily have missed some more telltale scrap—a trace, a buckle, the spoke of a wheel.

"Are you sure?"

Oliphant, his face a wizened triangle next the yellow lanthorn beam, nodded. "The ground is much disturbed, but there is naught else."

"They're ahead!" cried another, swinging onto his horse. "We'll never catch up at this rate."

"Let's ride!"

Alec glanced down at the folded cloth, tucked it inside his coat. He said: "Aye, let us ride. If he harms so much as a single eyelash——" He didn't finish; turning his horse with uneven tacks he kicked its sides. The resulting bound forward snapped Alec like a sprung mast. Mount and rider plummeted down the road, both bouncing in his own fashion.

His mates pelted after him. Oliphant hung back a moment to raise his lanthorn high, and gaze about. At last he shrugged, spurred away in pursuit.

I let my breath go in a relieved sigh. Dickon pulled his nose from my hands to whinny an echo. He'd been well behaved, and I told him so as I unloaded him, tied him to a tree.

The girl was still unconscious, or, perhaps, since she had shifted position slightly, asleep. She seemed no worse than before.

Which was more than I could say for myself. The night threatened more frost. Not daring to risk a fire I stamped and beat my arms for warmth, but the cold nibbled, gnawed, and finally bit bone deep.

Jill moaned, a whimper of distress. The sound startled and worried me. Even in her state the chill had penetrated.

I berated myself for a thoughtless ape. A well Jill would not have been bothered beyond discomfort, but there was no telling what the cold night air might do to her condition. I was tempted to ride for help, surrender, or at least to chance lighting a blaze.

Instead I tried a jury-rigged scheme. Lying down beside her I spread my coat over us both. Back to back our bodies would warm by contact. If this didn't work I would kindle a fire though it cost my capture. Jill Murdoch had suffered enough because of me.

She grew warmer. After a while she turned, snuggled closer against me. I lay rigidly still, feeling the healing heat where we touched, conscious of the shape curled so innocently alongside me. The breathing that stirred my hair was even, untroubled.

"That's sleep," I murmured to the cold darkness. "Thank God that it is. *Slainte geal, cuilin.*"

Sure the Irish came back into my memory unsummoned, but the wish was true. The meaning of the words fitted. *Bright health, maid with beautiful hair!*

So I settled myself, pleased that she slept, limp with tenderness at the nearness of her. As guard for us both I would not close my own eyes that night.

The next thing I knew a tug jerked me awake. There was the dawn in my face, and Jill Murdoch's voice ringing in my ears!

"And now, you gowk, if you make a move I'll blow your head off!"

Chapter 14

THERE have been more pleasant awakenings. Bewildered, still drugged with sleep, I twisted toward the girl's voice. She was standing, waist deep in mist, not three feet away. Whirls of vapor, yellow stained by the first light, coiled about her so that she looked like some phantom witch rising from magic smoke. But the face was Jill Murdoch's, and the glare on it, and the angry stance of her. There was nothing wraith-like either in the long pistol leveled at my teeth.

"Whist," I said, thick-tongued. "Easy with that now, Jill lass." My heart gave a leap of fright, but the sleep was still on me.

"Easy!" Jill snorted, turned it into a short laugh. "And when did you go easy on man or beast?"

"You'd not shoot an unarmed man?"

"Would I not?"

"Now, Jill——"

"Don't be soiling my name in your foul mouth!"

By that time the cold damp air had brought a wee bit of sense back to me. The gun was my own. Her taking it was the tug that roused me as she snatched it from under my coat. She had no time to do more than cock the hammer. With a great yawn, I sat up, rubbed my eyes.

"Move careful, Master Doyle."

"You'd really shoot?"

"I would. And know how." Jill bit her lip, shifted the pistol's aim. "Not in the head, though. In the leg."

"You're too kind."

"I'd not be cheating the gallows!"

Enjoying myself, since I knew the weapon for an empty ornament, I said: "You're a cruel one. You'd let them hang a cripple. Sure, there's no heart in you at all."

"You will march back to where we left my brother." Jill sounded coldly positive. "And I will deliver you to the constable there."

Shaking seed-like droplets from my coat, I donned it. "That's a long walk for a chill, foggy morning," I said, with a shudder. My whine was pretense, but the shiver wasn't.

Jill shrugged. "Blame yourself. You wrecked the chaise."

"*I* wrecked it! And who was it behaved like a madwoman?"

"I've been called worse," Jill said, and flushed. Her cheeks were rosy from the raw damp, but the mounting blood was evident.

"Aye," I admitted, aware that my insults still rankled. There was no recalling them, but I didn't like her thinking them intended. Truth seemed the best apology. "But only to prevent a case of screaming hysterics. If I hurt your sensibilities——"

"Sensibilities!"

I ignored her outburst. "—if I did, I am sorry." Suddenly last night's fright again gripped me, tightened my speech with anger. "You little fool! You might have been badly hurt!"

"A lot you'd care!"

"Aye."

My reply hung for a moment between us. Jill lowered the pistol a trifle to stare.

"What?"

"The meaning's plain," I said. "I did care. I do. And—God help me—a lot." The words came blurting out against my will.

"Gammon!" said Jill.

"No," I said, rising to plead a hopeless cause. "No. This is God's truth. From that very first day on the beach——"

"Do you dare to mention that!"

"Jill——" I took a step toward her.

"Oh, no." The gun snapped up. Jill's voice was as steady as her arm. "You'll not get around me that way! Argh! You've a crafty, fancy manner of speaking, Cormac Doyle, but the truth is not in you!"

"You've a bad habit of interrupting," I said, nettled.

"Have I now? How rude of me. I must mend my manners when addressing such a fine gentleman." Jill was tossing her head with mock gentility. "Care for me, indeed!"

"Oh, well," I said, with a shrug and a laugh. "It was worth a trial." I was proud of that laugh's ring. It both saved my pride, and masked my gloom. Sure, the girl was right. She had no cause to believe a black pirate. My wink and leer were that of a rogue. "I was hoping you recalled our kiss."

"That you stole!" Jill blazed, stamping her foot.

"Well, now," I said, "if you keep me here jabbering away the morning,

[118]

I'll die of the ague." With that I gestured to our surroundings. "We'll be fortunate to make port in this. It's as thick as treacle."

Jill glanced around, chewed her lip. She was lovely even then, with the dampness dulling the bright hair, her face glistening. Where her black cloak fell away the gray homespun of her dress blended with the thickening fog. It was rolling in from the coast, long combers as heavy as oil smoke. You could only guess at the sun's position where the haze seemed lightest.

"Fog," she said. "Alec hates fog."

"Most sailors do," I said, cheerily, "except us pirates. We find it friendly. It helps us slip up on fogbound vessels without being discovered."

"That will do," Jill said, every inch the queen. "Fetch the horse, and we'll be moving."

"Without breaking our fast? Surely there's a bite or two in your traveling chest?"

"No, that's my—" Jill paused, frowned at me. "You didn't open the case?"

"Do you take me for a common thief?"

"Yes! But it's just clothes and linens anyway. Alec and I finished our provisions from home yester noon. We planned to revictual at that inn."

"So did I." My insides were grumbling with emptiness, but there was no cure. My forethought in taking no food from the Indian camp had fixed that. I had wanted the contents of the sack to support my story if searched. There was nothing in it but Twigg's prayer book and tinder pouch.

"Well," said my lady Murdoch, "the sooner we're away out of this the sooner you'll be fed."

Using the reins for lashings I loaded Dickon. With Jill's case strapped behind for cantle my sack, emptied, made a serviceable saddle. Jill stood close, pistol ready, watching me work. The fog wrapped all three of us in its gray wool.

Then I freed Dickon, led him forward, and said, "We could easily ride double."

"With you? No fear!"

"Then let me give you a hand up."

"Full of tricks, aren't you?" Jill waggled the pistol at me. "You'll stand well back, or I'll put a hole in your middle."

"Do you drink blood, too?" I asked, stepping back. It suited as well as amused me to have her think herself in charge, safe behind a loaded pistol, captor instead of captive. Her commands would be obeyed like a man-o'-war captain's, as long as they didn't cross my plans. This made for smoother sailing, on my own course, until she was close enough to some safe harbor to be cast adrift.

"That's far enough," Jill said, afraid of losing me in the fog. "Stand there."

As she walked to the horse, Jill limped. The sight gave me a twinge. Was she badly hurt? There was one way to find out without seeming solicitous; it was a callous jeer.

"Shoe pinch?"

"Never you mind," she said, snapping. She patted Dickon's neck, hesitated, glanced to where I stood holding the bridle. "Turn around."

"You forget," I said, "I've seen your legs. Why should I be wanting another look?" Then turning my back before she exploded, I spoke to the fog. "And for God's sake ride astride. It's safer on this wet ground, and neither Dickon nor I are the least interested."

"You looked long enough the other time!" Jill spluttered.

She grunted, Dickon grunted, the halter twitched in my grasp. I risked a quick glance over my shoulder. The horse wasn't very tall, but she was having trouble straddling him. One leg dangled, exposed from knee to heel. Her head was behind the horse's mane so she wasn't looking at me, but from the way she held that pistol Dickon, had it been loaded, was the one in danger of death. The patient beast stood quiet while she hitched herself aboard.

"All right," Jill said at last.

Her voice sounded funny, and I saw why. She'd arranged her skirt the best she could, but still showed stocking to the calf. The wary glance she gave me was annoying. Women, I decided, think they're all a man thinks about.

"Come on, Dickon," I said, and started.

The horse followed at a plodding walk, picking his way down the slippery slope. He trusted me to guide, and I was careful not to hurry him, or go yanking at the bridle, but to choose the best path. Once or twice I glanced back to see Jill twitch up the pistol with one hand, and her skirt down with the other, but it was Dickon's paces I was watching. He was no champion, still he carried the girl as if she was a feather, without objection, and he worked sensibly. Dickon would bear me to safety well enough, once we were rid of Jill. He was built for distance, not speed, and he'd give the one if you didn't demand the other.

When we reached the road I told him so.

"Good boy, Dickon. The going's easier now." I led him out and turned him.

"Wait," said Jill. "You're going the wrong way."

"How do you know?"

"We crossed the bridge before we smashed." Jill pointed to where the end plank of the bridge, slick wet, edged through the fog like a slab of floating driftwood.

Only that single plank showed. If we'd come into the road a few paces farther away she'd never have seen it. I shrugged, urged Dickon forward.

"We go this way."

"No! My brother's back there."

Certain she had the pistol aimed again, I didn't bother to turn fully, but spoke over my shoulder. "He's not. He and some others rode by in the night. I saw them. He's ahead of us now."

"Oh, that's right," Jill said. Then, when I did turn to stare, she smiled down at me. "I thought I heard riders, but I wasn't sure it wasn't a dream. I—I had a lot of dreams."

"With the bump you had it's no wonder."

She touched the bruise on her forehead. "Is it too unsightly?"

"It's no fleabite, but I've seen worse. Does it hurt?"

"A little. But it—it feels as big as a duck egg."

"That's the swelling. In two, three days you'll never know it's been there. It won't scar."

"I didn't fear that." Jill laughed. "You forget I grew up in a fishing village. When I was small I was always tripping and skinning my—self."

The slight hesitation made me grin. "Mine were knuckles," I said, "and my nose."

"Fighting?"

"No. Though I did my share of that, too. But there was never a tumble I took, nor a bump in the dark but I'd come out of it with a nosebleed. Sure, it poured easier than claret at a wedding. I mind a horse hit it once in friendship with a toss of his head, and a cow, again, with the slap of her tail. I just had one of those noses that couldn't keep out of harm's way."

Jill laughed as I'd not heard her since our first walk back from that beach meeting. It was a grand, friendly sound that made my heart beat faster.

"So that's why the tilt," she said. "But it's not bad at all. Just a wee quirk to the left."

"A shade of a point on the compass. Aye. But the O'Shaugnessy nose is no beauty to begin with."

"I've seen worse," Jill said, "but what about your knuckles?" She glanced down at her own hands, folded around the pistol. "Mine were always chapped raw red each winter. They'd get rough as a grater and crack open at a touch."

"Girl, dear," I said, "you are talking to the original, the nonpareil, the Brian Boru of all tribes of skinned knuckles. Winter was only the worst season. There was never a tool I'd handle, nor a fish hook, but that same would turn on me. Why the first time I saw pig's knuckles served as a dish I couldn't eat for sympathy."

It was banter, of course, and the long bow, coin to buy more of Jill's laughter, cheap at the price since it brought bright warmth to that dreary day. The girl had a gay quality that made me lighthearted, forgetful of past trials, or future schemes. She gave herself wholly to mirth, throwing back her head, letting it peal past her white teeth. Few men could have watched her, listening, unmoved, and I laughed with her. That was a mistake.

She checked herself suddenly, frowning with suspicion. The long pistol swerved toward me.

"Don't think I'm forgetting what you are!"

"I'm a damn fool," I said, bitterly. I yanked my hat brim, soaked limp, lower over my eyes, and turned to lead Dickon. For a minute or two I'd managed to forget, to think us no more than any man and maid.

The journey promised long misery. Dickon's hoofs plopped into the soft road; my feet splashed through mud and puddles. On both sides of the road the trees held the fog like great gray festoons, garlands of dirty clouds. Ahead the murky wall retreated as we advanced; behind it followed on the horse's heels. We slogged on in our own small circle of visibility. There were no sounds but the ones we made, and the steady, soft weeping of the dripping forest around us.

A snick of metal gave me sharp warning. My ears went back like Dickon's, alert for trouble. I knew the noise. Jill had opened the pistol's lock to check the priming in the pan. It was a sensible move in such weather, but there wasn't a speck of powder to be hurt by dampness.

She uttered neither cry nor gasp of surprise. We plodded on in silence. The lock snapped shut with a loud click!

For a dozen paces, while I wondered, there was no sound behind me. Then, I heard a murmur of suppressed laughter that spun me around.

Jill Murdoch, palm over mouth, was shaking with glee. When she saw my slack-jawed amazement, she laughed aloud.

"You oaf," she said. "You pig! You knew it wasn't loaded all the time!"

"I knew it last night when I held it on a dozen."

"You let me go on——" Jill stopped to shake her head. "You even pretended— Ah, Cormac, Cormac, the Lord rebuked Ananias, so Satan made you. Aye, in his own image!"

"Well, now," I said, pleased but puzzled at her manner of taking it, "I may have a nodding acquaintance with the second gentleman, but I never heard of the first."

"Ananias, the liar. In the Bible."

"Oh, are they in there too?"

"Both of them!" She tried to look stern, but her lips curved at the corners. "The Devil is called the Prince of Liars, but I'm afraid the crown is yours. Why you do it as—as natural as breathing."

"It just *looks* easy," I said, "but it takes a dint of practice."

"Well, you needn't be proud of it!"

"That I am not. It's been a bane and curse since I learned talk. Handy at times, I'll admit, but more trouble than it's worth. Now, you take this morning. There you were all brave and sassy, with the armament in your fist, holding the beast at bay. Would I be the one to be spoiling your fun?"

Jill blushed, giggled. "Who's making sport now?"

"Not I. You took me prisoner. Your prisoner I am."

That sobered her. She looked from me to the weapon, and back. "I'm not sure just who is the prisoner, Cormac."

"Let be," I said, "must we be one or t'other? Can't we go on as we are—friendly like—for a while? After all——" I waved at the fog around us. "—I got you into this, I would like to take you out."

"All right," Jill said.

Not daring to force my luck I swung about again. But in spite of mud and ruts I stepped out with a lighter step. There was truce between us. I wasn't certain how it had happened, but I never objected to a fair truce in my life. Even the fog had a different look—eerie, but friendly. We were closed away from the world, wrapped in a fairy ring where the king's daughter rode her palfrey, and her squire held its bridle.

Sure if Dickon made a sorry palfrey, and the squire answered to worse names, at least the girl was real. I was building fancies more solid than the fog when Jill spoke again.

"Cormac."

"Aye?"

"You had no need to fear the pistol."

"No." I didn't face her, trudged on.

"You could have taken it from me any minute."

"Well—aye."

"Then—what you said—wasn't a trick."

"I said a great many things."

"I mean about—caring for me."

"Oh." Fear of her laughter came into me, tightening the muscles between my shoulder blades. I could think of no easy quip or jest that would save me. I said, gruffly, "No, it wasn't a trick."

After that, for a long time, we went on in silence. Jill didn't laugh, made no comment. Still, it was a good silence, without tension, almost friendly.

The road, such as it was, ran north and south so that I knew the sea was to my right, east. Curves and surface made me wish again that the Romans had discovered America early enough to do a little road building. Dickon and I were mud-splashed to fetlock and calf. We met no one, saw no sign of habitation. My one fear was that we would blunder into some fog-hidden village before I was forewarned and ready.

Late in the morning we came to a crossroad where a prow of forest made a Y out of the track. Without hesitation I led Dickon into the road that curved to the right. It was narrower, less trodden, and it led toward the ocean. The choice stirred Jill to speech.

"I think that's a wrong turning, Cormac."

"There's little to choose."

"But—my brother——"

"Even if he took the other way, he'll not be too distant." I turned as I spoke, walking sideways beside the horse. "Look, Jill. I will see you safe, and in good hands, but I mean to escape."

The girl gazed down at me, frowning. She said, at last: "That'll be no easy task. You stole chaise and horse—and me. There'll be hue and cry after you."

"There was before. This fog will help."

Jill bowed in a slow nod. "I should not wish you well. Wickedness and crime must be punished in the eyes of the Lord. You have been guilty of both." Her voice was low, troubled. "But——"

"But?"

"I—I'd not want you hanged. Especially if you're repentant." She leaned forward on Dickon's neck, very intent. "Are you repentant, Cormac?"

"Aye. But then I'm in flight for my life. That makes any man repentant." I thought of the sunken sea chest, the gallows, my chances. Her eyes were on me, and I tacked as close to the truth as I dared. "I'll not lie to you, Jill. Naught I've done, in my mind, deserved the gibbet. But there are those that feel differently."

[124]

"Piracy," Jill said.

"The term has many meanings. What was Drake? Or Hawkins? What, indeed, was Henry Morgan while he earned his knighthood? Oh, they're quick to fetch the hangman for a common sailor, but they make admirals out of captains with connections."

"That doesn't change the Lord's Commandment."

"True, and I'll answer to the Lord."

"I'll not argue with you," she said, shaking her head. " 'Tis useless. I fear for your soul. But I'll not lift voice or finger to hinder your flight. I'll tell them true, that you've not harmed me."

"Thank you," I said. It was little enough, but it was something. Journeying together had at least changed her opinion a trifle. My gladness at that made me wary of further talk. If fog and forest had laid a spell between them, I'd no desire to break it.

A mile or so later I found myself whistling a forgotten tune that I'd heard somewhere. I wasn't aware of doing it until Jill's chuckle brought my head around.

"Cormac, do you know the song of that?"

"Why—no."

"Listen then."

Smiling, she began to sing. Her voice was husky, but true. She picked up the melody where I'd left it, waved me to go on.

> O father, O father, a little of your gold,
>> And likewise of your fee!
> To keep my body from yonder grave,
>> And my neck from the gallows tree.
>
> None of my gold now you shall have,
>> Nor likewise of my fee;
> For I am come to see you hangd,
>> And hangèd you shall be.

"Faith!" I said, "now there's a pretty ditty for a man in my position! I'll not be pursing my lips with that again!"

Jill, the minx, was laughing at me. "There's more," she said.

"I've heard enough."

Even as we gazed at each other, grinning, her eyes went wide, and she screamed!

Dickon reared, and I threw my weight on the bridle to bring his head down. Then, a voice, deep and guttural, shouted at my elbow and I reared myself.

"Hold, sah! Yield, sah!"

[125]

There in the road beside me, as startling as any demon summoned from the depths, was a giant Negro! No wonder Jill had shrieked as he bounded from the fog. The man was hatless, in dark livery, only eyes and teeth showed white. His size dwarfed the bell-mouthed blunderbuss he shoved in my face.

My action was pure instinct, spurred by fright. I flung myself under the gun in a dive. My shoulder hit the giant's knees, drove his legs from under him.

The blunderbuss boomed above me as I slid face down through the mud.

"Ride for it, Jill!" I yelled. Whirling, I whipped around in a crouch. The black man had fallen heavily, but he was already on hands and knees when I jumped.

Both feet landed in the middle of his wide back. He flattened with a grunt. All I wanted was a start; stumbling, I turned to run.

"Stop, man! Ah shoot!"

Surprise froze me more than the command. There, across the road, holding Dickon's bridle, was the same giant Negro! Blinking, I stared, glanced back at the man I'd felled. He was still down, puffing and shaking his head.

The black by the horse aimed a musket with one hand, as easily as a pistol. Inch for inch he was as like the other as a mirrored image. His voice had the same throaty depth.

"You all right, Pollux?" he called.

Twins, by God, I thought, and sneaked a step. The musket didn't waver; the big head thrust forward.

"You, man. Stand still!"

He forgot to watch Jill. So far she'd sat in stunned fright, white-faced, not moving. Now, suddenly, her heels clapped Dickon's sides. As the horse bounded forward Jill's arm swept up and down. The pistol crashed on the man's head with a sound like a dropped coconut.

He crumpled, but he held on to the bridle so that poor Dickon spun around his lowered muzzle, hoofs slithering, nearly unseating Jill. She dropped the gun, clutched with both hands.

"Run, Cormac! Run!"

I ran, but toward them, reaching for the knife under my coat. I wanted that loaded musket. Each of the big black men looked strong enough to break me in half without trouble. Besides I couldn't leave Jill to those two! For all I knew they were renegade savages, berserk slaves!

I was a stride away, knife still sheathed, when a horseman loomed out of the mist! A new voice rang out.

"Stand and—surrender!"

The sudden apparition, the slight hesitation in the command, brought back memories. Open-mouthed, I stared at the rider, tall above his mount, a dark bulk shrouded by fog. A brace of pistols, rigid and gleaming, menaced me. They helped make the voice familiar.

I laughed, aloud. Jill gave a gasp, stared as if I had gone mad. Still laughing, I showed my empty hands, helped the Negro to his feet.

"Are you daft?" asked the rider.

That was all I needed for certainty.

"Ah, Jockey," I cried, "Jockey, man! Well met! Are you riding this highway now instead of Hounslow Heath?"

Chapter 15

NOTHING stirred, for a long moment, but the creeping tendrils of the fog. The big Negro beside me broke our immobility by shaking his head; his eyes cleared, focused. His partner, Pollux, loomed behind me to clamp a hand on my shoulder, as wide and tight as a joiner's vise. I made no move to throw off the grip. My gaze stayed on the horseman. The two pistols, fully cocked, didn't waver. A chill started at the nape of my neck, trickled down along my spine. Dread choked off the laughter in my throat, and I swallowed. Then the horse tossed his head, halter jingling, and walked forward.

"Who are you?" asked the rider.

"A friend to Jockey Grandison," I said, with more assurance than I felt, "or was."

"That name's unknown here. What's yours?"

"Now, did you never hear of the Irish Captain?"

That brought a muttered oath, and a neat swerve of the horse so that it danced closer. The rider leaned down to peer at me, showing a broad, fleshy face, full lipped, puffed at the jowls. Under his hat brim dark eyes, narrowed now to slits, inspected me. There was disbelieving wonder in his voice.

"Paddy! The Real Paddy!"

"Himself," I said, trying to bow against the pressure of Pollux's grasp.

"The wench called you Cormac."

"It's his name," said Jill.

"Aye," I admitted, "so it is. Here. Sometimes one has different names in different lands. 'Tis the custom of the country, it seems."

Inspection works both ways, and I had made my own. It was Jockey, all right, older and fatter, and decked in a great peruke wig, but recognizable. The big nose was the same, with its wasp-stung swollen tip; so was the barrel chest, the wide shoulders, the long-muscled horseman's legs. Some seven years had passed since our last meeting.

"Cormac," he said. "Cormac Doyle is the name of the pirate we were seeking."

"Oh?" My whisper was barely audible, meant for his ears alone. "And when did Captain Quickly ride with the watch, Jockey?"

"Mind your tongue!"

"That was always my habit. I've not changed."

"Hmm." He rubbed his chin with a gun barrel, glanced at Jill. "Castor. Pollux."

"Master?" The twins spoke as one.

"Take him to the house. I'll ride behind with the wench." He leaned so close that his breath warmed the fog on my face. Jockey, I smelled, was still in favor of a morning dram. His speech reeked of spiced rum. "You've a good memory, Paddy. Remember my skill with arms, and don't run."

His admission, his use of the old, half-forgotten nickname, made me smile. I said: "I've been running these many days. It will make a nice change to sit and visit with an old friend."

Jockey grunted, made his horse curvet beside Dickon. He had a good mount, a bay mare, taller by a hand than any I'd yet seen in New England.

"You're the girl he abducted?"

"Well—I'm Jill Murdoch. But, I wasn't abducted. I—I happened to be in the chaise, that's all. Cormac didn't harm me, Master Grandison."

"My name is Anderson."

"Oh, I thought——"

"Thomas Anderson, gent. I'm a horse breeder. A message came last night that all were to turn out in search of this pirate who had stolen a horse, a chaise, and a girl. Naturally, I offered my services and my slaves."

"You'll turn him over to the constable?" asked Jill.

Not he, I swore, but waited for his reply.

"When it clears. This is a bad day for travel. We were blundering through the fog, ready to turn homeward when we heard you. First we must get you dry and warm."

That sounded like a grand plan to brighten my future. Jockey, I judged, was in no hurry to deliver me to the authorities. There'd be time for a bit of talk.

After we marched several miles the smell of the fog changed. Through the moisture-laden air drifted the salty tang of the sea. The forest, both sides of the road, seemed to dissolve; the thick mist dropped lower, became a smoke pall clinging to flat land. From my right came the welcome sound of surf; at intervals, to the left, a black line of fence striped the gray curtain. Somewhere behind that barrier horses nickered, and galloped, but none appeared.

"It's not far now," Jockey told Jill.

"I'm glad. I—I'm not used to riding."

The road curved through gate posts, rock cairns glistening with wet. We trudged along a driveway until a house edged toward us out of fog like a vessel creeping into port. It looked to be a long, two-storied building, with its upper floor set forward, frame clapboards painted dark red. Light showed as streaks from between solid, closed shutters.

Pollux took the horses; the rest of us entered. A wide central hall, empty save for a narrow staircase, split the house in two. Here Jockey handed Jill over to a withered crone of a housekeeper, and motioned me into a room at one side.

This was a handsome room, a man's room, spacious with a raftered ceiling, and a massive stone fireplace. There was a blaze roaring, with wide armchairs drawn close. The puncheon floor, scrubbed bright as any deck, had no carpets, but the walls, planks polished to mellow ivory, were far from bare. Studs held a row of saddles, one above the other, fine-tooled leather; bridles dangled from a trio of deer antlers. There was a gun rack, padlocked, in one corner, fishing tackle in a cupboard opposite. Shelves of books bordered the fireplace.

A long table held a tray of bottles, and noggins. Above the rough-trimmed, half-log mantelpiece was a picture of a stallion, colorfully but badly drawn. Under a sleek head, neck and torso, were reed-thin legs, impossibly fragile. Inked on the frame, to avoid mistake, was the horse's name—Old Snip. He was evidently the Arab pride of the countryside.

Castor shoved a chair forward, stood behind it. Jockey carefully latched the door, tossed hat and coat aside, strode to the fire. He put his pistols on the mantel, bent to the blaze. As he warmed his hands, he regarded me over his shoulder. The broad face suddenly broke into a grin.

"The Real Paddy! God's fingernails! I thought they'd hung you long ago!"

"They keep trying, Jockey."

"Jockey's forgotten," he said, frowning. "Let him stay that way. Castor. Rum."

While the slave mixed drinks, I examined Jockey. He was certainly heavier by several stone, and the puffy, purple rings around his eyes were new. He still held himself well for a man in his fifties, but the old muscled solidness was gone. Good living and easy years had softened the rogue into a country squire. Clothes and wig completed the change. He was dressed well, in rich blue, but not lavishly. His high jackboots were unpolished, much used. He removed his wig to scratch a grizzled, close-cropped poll.

"The days that were," I said, raising my noggin of rum.

"Ah, no," Jockey tossed the wig on the mantel, twinkled at me over his own mug, "I've the better toast."

"And that is?"

"The days that are, me boyo. I ride my own acres now, and sleep safe under my own roof. All that's left from the old times is a knowledge of horseflesh, and at that I'm breeding a new strain known as Narragansett pacers."

"Pickings must have been good."

He shrugged, drank. "Castor," he said, "get some food ready. We'll have it here by the fire." He waited until the slave left, then pulled up a chair, sat. "They're good boys, and my slaves, but there is no sense in relating my whole history in front of them."

"Better they than strangers."

He didn't like that remark. He blinked, and his face went bland, impassive, though he kept his smile. He spoke very softly.

"Is that a threat, Paddy?"

"No." The liquor was burning my empty stomach. "Not from me. You're scot free, and away out of it, and I'm not one to spoil a friend's game. You know that. But I could use a bit of that same luck myself."

"God's teeth, you could!" His speech matched his savage grin. "You were a fool to turn pirate, lad. That's ever a rum go that ends either on the gibbet or in the gutter!"

"Are *you* preaching that text?" I was amused. There seemed little to choose between halting a coach on the highroad, and boarding a ship on the high seas.

"You can't compare piracy to a gentlemanly venture on the open highway!" Jockey flushed, emptied his drink with a toss. "And anyway I'm out of the one, and you're in the other as deep as your armpits."

"Aye. But I could put the Spanish Main behind me as easily as Hounslow Heath." I drained my noggin, rose. The rum was on the table behind us, but my move was a test too.

For all his extra pounds he hadn't lost his speed. Jockey was between me and the pistols on the mantel with one easy movement, neat as a dance step. There was no bound or jump about it, he merely flowed from chair to stance and stood there, balanced on the balls of his feet, smiling at me.

That showed where I stood. A cup comrade only, at Jockey's pleasure, and a captive. While I fetched the bottle, and poured, I did some thinking.

"All I ask is a chance, Jockey."

"What sort of chance?"

"Captain Quickly's chance," I said, using the name he'd acquired from his exploits. "A good horse and a fair start."

Frowning he considered, then shook his head. "No horse of mine. They're marked and known. And you'd not get ten miles on the plug the girl was riding."

"I think I could."

"I think not," Jockey said, as if that settled it. He was still standing, back to the fire, and with an over-careless glance he confirmed the position of the pistols. "How could I explain your escape?"

"A squad of redcoat soldiers couldn't hold me. How did *they* explain it?"

"That Murdoch wench would wonder. You and your tongue! Jockey this and Jockey that." His head turned as he gazed around the room. "I have been some years building this, me boyo. Horse breeding takes time. I'll not risk losing it just when it's starting to pay."

"Where's the risk?" I asked, worried by his tone. I had heard him speak like that when planning a foray, giving reasons why he'd decided to strike at such a place and time. "Few over the water knew Jockey Grandison was Captain Quickly. None here."

"One," he said. "Maybe two."

He meant Jill and me, of course. The way he put it left no doubt of that. I laughed, to dispel the queasiness coming over me. Jockey laughed with me. I didn't like that either.

"You see how it is, lad?"

"No," I said, "I don't. You let me run for it, and I'm out of harm's way. I'm no informer, Jockey. And Jill—the girl knows naught. I cried a name in the fog. A mistake."

"A mistake it was."

He was standing there, legs spread, like an oversize archery butt letting me shoot arguments at him. There was nothing to do but keep trying to hit the clout. Jockey never killed needlessly, I remembered, but with one memory came another. When his safety was threatened he was ruthless.

"She's forgotten it already."

"Mayhap."

"Leave her out. Send her on to her brother with one of your lackeys to tell of my capture. Then we two can deal together."

Jockey glanced at the windows. The wind had risen to rattle the shutters, but I hadn't noticed. Now, I could hear the pelting of rain. That signalled the end of the fog.

"I've trusted only one woman," Jockey said, "in all my life. To my sorrow. You are still very young, Paddy."

"This place is on the sea, isn't it? I heard surf."

The abrupt change of subject puzzled him. He frowned, said: "We face the bay. Narragansett Bay. Why?"

"Do you have a ship?" I asked.

"A lugger. Forty foot." He was interested, willing to give information to see where I was leading. "More like a captain's gig than anything else, but handy for crossing the bay. Again—why?"

For Jill's sake, as well as my own, I played my highest card. Drawing a breath, I said: "Because I can put you in the way of more riches than you took out of England. Hundreds of pounds. Enough to buy this place twice over."

Jockey's nostrils flared, and he sat down again. "And how can you do that?"

"There's a sea chest crammed with wealth—gold and jewels—but I need a ship to get to it. A ship and some help. It's in a sunken ketch, not too deep for diving. My shipmate drowned when we were wrecked in the breakers. You can have his share."

"Pirate loot, of course."

"There's no claims on it," I said, shrugging. "It's finders keepers now. Lend me the lugger with Castor and Pollux and we'll fetch it back in a week. Send the girl to her brother and—"

To my amazement he interrupted with a guffaw. It was real, hearty mirth that tossed his big head back and came out as a roar. The laughter

[132]

shook his girth; he beat a fist on his thigh. I stared, open-mouthed, flabbergasted.

"Paddy," he said at last, wiping his eyes. "The Real Paddy! Ah, lad, you've not changed a bit."

"What does that mean?"

"It means I know you of old. You always had a rare tongue for cock and bull." He put a finger alongside his fat nose, and grinned at me.

"I was only a lad back then," I said, sullenly.

"True. Your lies are bigger now. A sea chest full of jewels and gold." Jockey shook his head, laughing. "God's knuckles! You sound like Henry Morgan. You, who couldn't hold the bridles on a night's venture without shaking so hard they jangled like London's bells!"

The shame was on me, burning my cheeks, hot in my throat. There was something in what he said. Because the highroad frightened him a green hobbledehoy of a lad had boasted bigger than his boots. Still, all that was long ago, and in another land. I was not lying now.

"I'm speaking truth, Jockey. Sail with me, and I'll prove every word. The wreck is there, the chest is there."

"And wouldn't that look handsome when the girl peaches? Oh, yes, indeed." His voice went up in a mimic falsetto. "Master Anderson captured the pirate all right. But he's not at home now. He decided to go apirating himself."

Resentment sharpened my voice and wits. "Jill will do naught to hurt me. You heard her shout for me to run, didn't you? And she struck down your slave."

Jockey leered, screwed up one side of his face with an elaborate wink. "Oho! So she did. After one night together in the woods! You didn't waste any time, me bucko."

"There was nothing like that, but——"

"Come now! 'Twas a chill night. I'll wager you shared a coverlet." He chuckled at my startled expression. His elbow moved in a nudge though we were too far apart for contact. "You sly dog! I remember you were always a gay hand with the trollops. Conquests by the score!"

That, too, had been a boy's bragging, as false as the rest. But somehow I did not like him thinking such about Jill. I said: "The girl's no trull, Jockey. She's had strict upbringing."

"Better and better," said Jockey, mouth loose above his noggin's rim. "That's the way to still a maid's lips. Especially here in New England. They don't go blabbing your secrets if you can tell how you loosened their stays. The preachers are hell-fire and brimstone about *that!* Yes, lad. That changes the mare's color all right."

I didn't quite know what he was driving at, but I didn't like the gist of it. The change in his attitude stilled any protest. In spite of his becks, leers, and nods—for all the world like a lecher in a London comedy—he was more friendly, less worried. He began to pace; his speech crispened.

"We'll leave it at that for the nonce. But no more 'Jockey' and 'Paddy'. In front of her you're the prisoner, Cormac the pirate. I'm your captor, Master Thomas Anderson. You'll be guarded, and you'll eat apart. None of us can leave here until the tempest abates anyway."

"You mean you'll let me go?" I asked.

"We'll wait and see," he said, "but, mind, no tricks!" He took the brace of pistols from the mantel, balanced one in each big palm. "Understand?"

"Aye," I said.

He watched me for a moment, nodded. Then as he clapped on his wig he shouted with ear-cracking suddenness.

"Castor! Where's that food?"

The slaves entered bearing dishes, and Jill followed them. She had changed her dress to the sleeveless, speckled homespun she'd worn clamming, but under the top part now she had a shirt of the same material, sleeved to the wrist, buttoned high at the neck. Without lace, ribbon, or ornament it made a demure, yet handsome outfit.

It was the first time Jockey had seen her without the cloak hood covering her hair, and the glory of it struck him so he gasped. Sure, the sight was worth a gasp. But I did not like the smirk of approval that Jockey flashed toward me, nor the way he slobbered over her hand.

"Mistress Murdoch," he said, making a leg like a rakehell out of Whitehall, "you must be famished."

"Aye," Jill said, popeyed at the plenty being piled on the table, "I'm hungry."

My mouth was watering, too, and my stomach was urging the slaves to hurry. We'd not eaten for a full day.

Jill, bless her, looked a little startled at the seating arrangements. There was I, a good ten feet away, far below the salt at the foot of the long table. Jockey placed her at his right, took the head himself, scowled down at me, and explained.

"My apologies that this rogue must grace our dinner like Banquo's ghost, but I want him under my eye. Don't let his presence spoil your appetite."

My glare was villainous, and venomous. Under my breath I recited a before-meals grace that each morsel would choke him. For Jockey Grandison to put the name of rogue on anybody was sheer effrontery.

[134]

And if Jill, overawed by his grand manner, hadn't turned me an apologetic smile, I'd have hurled my plate in his teeth. That and the fact I was famished.

It was a rare meal. Castor stood behind me with a pistol; Pollux waited on the others. Mayhap it was t'other way round. In their purple livery with matching stockings I couldn't tell the two apart. But not even a stolid giant looming over my shoulder could spoil my appetite. I ate with both hands.

So did Jill. Jockey, always a good trencherman, wasn't far behind us. As course succeeded course, I realized where he'd added those extra pounds. There was mutton soup, a bit of salt codfish, the mutton itself with mashed turnips, collops of venison. To give Jockey his due, he saw that I had my share. The only difference was that my drink was ale; the top of the table had claret.

The wine was new to Jill. She kept her smile stiffly polite, but she glanced sideways at me as she sniffed the aroma. There'd been no wine in her brother's Covenant household. Was it then a sinful luxury? When she did sip, she didn't like it much. In spite of Jockey's urging she drank only half a glass.

Jockey drank enough for both. He grew more expansive with each draught, louder, happier. There was too much of the celebrating gamester in Jockey to suit me. He managed to change the room into a tavern, and a Newgate stew at that. You expected him to clatter his coins on the table top and send out for strumpets.

Not that he was ribald. He was too canny for that, especially when Jill missed his first bawdy witticism completely. He was very much the host, talkative, attentive, overpoweringly solicitous of his young guest. He kept piling her plate; he squeezed her hand three times before she put it in her lap. Then he patted her shoulder. Once, when he bent for a dropped spoon, Jill flinched, shot me a startled stare. But he was up in an instant, blandly apologizing for his clumsiness.

That brought a half rise out of me, but a stir behind me made me sink back. A pinched leg wasn't worth a broken head. Besides, remembering Jill's temper, I wasn't too worried. She was out of her depth; this was all novel—the wine, the man, the chatter, the fatherly pats. But God help him if he tried something she did understand!

When the meal ended the afternoon was well spent. Even then Jockey lolled in his chair, cracking nuts, munching raisins as he finished his second bottle of claret.

I will never understand what he did then. Maybe it was the wine, or the young girl so close, or the atmosphere of tavern conviviality, or my presence recalling the old days.

Whatever the reason he launched into a story about himself that I'd never heard before. It was a risky thing to do, and, considering his determination to hide his past, surprising. Of course he mentioned only the name he used as a High Toby, and he told it as if it happened to somebody else.

Which with one added parenthesis, is the way I'll tell it here.

Chapter 16

THE highwayman who was known as Captain Quickly to all who frequented the roads during the reign of the second Charles in England (and as Jockey Grandison to some fewer) always considered himself of noble birth. Since this was, naturally, on the wrong side of the blanket, he had none of the advantages of that breeding, but grew up, parentless, as a groom in a stable on a gentleman's estate. This fact was in itself suspicious since the gentleman—a round, short, red-faced squire, who could not possibly have sired the fine-boned boy—always insisted his groom had been found in a hedgerow nine months after a certain fair that the king himself had attended. Though his master was kind enough, and even promoted the stripling to ride his horses in all the neighborhood races, this life didn't fit the high-strung lad.

Young Quickly ran away as soon as he could. He took his master's best horse with him, and he knew exactly where he was going.

The horse helped him join the squadron of Claud Duval, though the boy lied about his age. Duval was just beginning his fame as a highwayman, but already he had attracted the finest collection of gentlemen of the road ever gathered under one leader. The king's own cavalry ate their dust on several occasions.

But what attracted the neophyte was Duval's history, common gossip in the inns, known to every coachman, sworn to by all postillions. Duval was French, and a gentleman. He had crossed the channel at the Restoration in the train of the Duke of Richmond. Loss of favor, gambling, or drink forced him onto his final career. There were some who hinted that a woman was the cause of it all, but Quickly himself scoffed at this.

"Nothing forced him," Quickly is said to have said. "He chose the high road of *adventure!* And he made it pay."

At any rate Duval was, with the possible exception of Quickly himself later, the greatest of highwaymen, the highest of High Tobys, the ruler of the roads. He welcomed his new recruit, and taught him much— manners, reading and writing, as well as the tricks of the trade.

In fact the leader gave Quickly his name, for the boy earned his spurs on his first foray. They had selected the coach of a wealthy merchant journeying from London to Bath. Duval's spies had sent word the man's coffers were bulging. The squadron struck at dusk, at the top of a rise where the team was catching breath. Duval was always careful about the proper time and place.

There was a quick patter of hoofs in the fading light. One swift movement and the coach was surrounded. Duval's challenge rang out.

"Stand and deliver!"

Excitement gripped the boy. In the second of pause while the command froze the victims, he had to break his own tension, and his shout echoed Duval's.

"And quickly! *Quickly!*"

Then, he whipped his pistol up and neatly shot the coachman's hat from his head.

Nobody moved. Duval broke the stillness with a crow of laughter. "*Mon dieu!*" he cried. "We have caught us a gamecock, a young firebrand. Things will march fast while Captain Quickly rides with us!"

Captain Quickly rode with Duval through all the great years, the times of success and riches. He learned his lessons well; his name and order became as familiar and dreaded as the professional catch phrase it followed.

"Stand and deliver! Quickly, quickly!"

Few hesitated, and, after he shot a lethargic post rider out of his saddle, none disobeyed.

In the years with Duval, the years of his youth, Captain Quickly never lacked gold, jewelry, fine raiment, and willing wenches. Among the latter was Nell Gwyn. Of course she was only selling oranges in the theater at that time, and was very young, but Quickly wasn't old either. Nell had a discerning eye even then.

Nothing lasted very long. As soon as the gold and jewelry were gone, so were the wenches. But Captain Quickly didn't care. He just rode out after more.

The squadron had its failures. Members were taken, shot down, surprised or recognized. Quickly himself had his narrow escapes, his flights across country throwing his horse at hedge, fence, ditch, with the pursuit ever closer behind him. Once, wounded by a chance shot, he hid out in the hills for three wretched days.

He was well out on the Bristol road, on business of his own, when Duval was taken. From the packed anonymity of a London mob he watched his leader climb the scaffold on Tyburn Hill. There was no attempt at rescue. It would have been a foolish gesture.

"It was the last lesson he taught me," Quickly is said to have said. "Don't get caught."

After that he rode alone, and it was a question of the pupil outdoing the master. Quickly started saving gold, a third from every venture. He was getting older, shrewder, more careful. When he needed followers for some venture too big for one man he could pick and choose from among the gentry of the road. All were eager to ride with Captain Quickly. But these changing gangs never matched the quality of Duval's great squadron. They could ride well enough, but they lacked spirit.

Those lonely, prosperous years came to an abrupt end in a London bootmaker's shop. The girl was nothing more than a slavey with a broom, part of the furniture, until she swept close to his feet.

Quickly had a sixth sense, and he moved fast. His fingers closed on the girl's wrist while her hand was still in his pocket.

"Oh, no, doxie. You could hang for that."

The girl said nothing. That was what impressed him first. She didn't whine, beg or curse. Nor did she struggle. She merely stopped her one-handed sweeping and stood still. The bootmaker began to sputter imprecations and disavowals, but Quickly silenced him with a look. He spoke only to his captive.

"A nice jape. The broom makes a covering noise, and usually requires both hands. I suppose most never look around."

"While they look I use both."

"You thought of this yourself?"

"Yes."

Her speech surprised Quickly. It was low, unperturbed, but he placed the accent as that of Kent, as yet uncorrupted by London. That accounted for her freshness, her cleanliness, but not her ingenuity. She was very young, very slender, boyish, in fact, until one stared down the front of her dress. But what struck Quickly most, stressed by her immobility, was the placid quality of her face. The black hair under her mob cap made her skin seem very white, and this, added to the perfection of her features, gave her the cool, glazed, unmarred loveliness of a china figurine.

From the first Quickly wanted to jar her into some visual reaction, a wince, a frown, a smile. He gave her a little shake.

"You'll swing for your cleverness."

"Not through Captain Quickly."

"You know me." He wasn't flattered. He knew that every light-fingered cove in a crowd touched his hat to Captain Quickly. Some of them gave him information. "Yet you'd try your tricks on *me?*"

"That—is why."

Quickly thought he understood her answer. He himself had felt the heady attraction of the difficult, the dangerous. Or had she chosen him for a cheaper reason—because he could not betray her if she failed? The urge to make her show feeling grew stronger.

"Losers pay, wench. Come."

Loosing her, he walked away without looking back. The slap of the broom handle, dropped on the floor, told him that she followed.

Though he made her cry out with passion, laugh, murmur endearments, she remained an enigma, essentially unstirred. She was not a maid, but she was no harlot. Even in the most intimate moments, naked and tumbled, an instant of repose restored her face to its calm, untroubled dignity.

Her history was simple. Country bred, her different beauty, a Norman by-blow in a family of fair Saxons, had set her apart from the first, made her the target of every amorous rustic. As soon as she could she had walked away from the farm to London. Except for two casual experiences, a farmer and the bootmaker, she considered herself chaste.

Quickly was not surprised, on awakening next morning, to find both the girl and his purse gone. The surprise came when she returned, laden with garments. She had purchased an entire outfit of male clothing. She cut her hair short, and, from boots to plumed hat, transformed herself into a lithe youth.

"You will have to buy the horse," she told Quickly. "And teach me. I have ridden only plow horses."

Intrigued, he taught her to shoot as well as to ride. She was both mistress and partner, a sure aide on a venture, a loving mate in bed. Anything he asked her, she did. Only her reckless daring bothered him. That and the fact that she retained always some untouched inner core.

For over a year they rode the countryside with never a failure. His name and fame now were linked with another. Those unfortunate travelers who heard his crisp demand, heard a low voice seconding it.

"Stand and deliver! Quickly, quickly!"

"And gently, masters. Gently."

Quickly and Gently. The naturalness of such coupling, contrasted with armed banditry, made it at once a joke and a slogan. London footpads guffawed at the sally; court ladies tittered over gossip that someone had been waylaid. Captain Quickly and Captain Gently became so notorious that they were credited with four different, distant robberies on a night they spent in bed.

Such notoriety, of course, led to their downfall. Quickly knew that the best thief is the least suspected. But by that time he was in love, enslaved, as fatuously proud of her exploits as a hero's father. In spite of complete possession, constant intimacy, he had failed to break through the girl's inmost reserve. Though he still rode in front, she led.

The trap snapped on them without warning. They had picked their victim carefully. He was a minor colonial official home on leave, rich and knighted, but not *too* powerful. There was no reason to think he would travel with an armed escort. There was no sign of trouble when they halted the coach.

As the knight stepped into the road Quickly felt the first qualm. The man was too calm, neither frightened nor upset. He seemed to relish the idea of being robbed.

Quickly dismounted, prepared to rifle the baggage. Usually he worked with precise speed, but this time he hesitated, pistol raised, warily watching his victim. The knight wore a sword; he was otherwise unarmed. But Quickly sensed danger.

Then he heard the thundering hoofs as the escort charged. The girl shouted; he leaped for his saddle. Even as he swung his horse around, Quickly knew that this one was bad. They had laid their snare cleverly, keeping back and quiet until ready. Now the road was choked with onrushing cavalry.

"Run for it!"

The girl fired one pistol to show their teeth, and he snapped a quick shot at the foremost horseman. That was to slow the pursuit but it brought a rattling return of fire, stabbing flashes, that startled Quickly. He realized that they had a score of troopers after them.

They fled across country, leaving the road at once. Quickly was a half length behind the girl. Her face was merely a pale blur in the moonlight as she glanced back. She took the first fence cleanly, as smoothly as himself.

So, unfortunately, did their pursuers. He saw them cross in a dark wave like a keen hunt. They were shouting. Hallooing, Quickly thought grimly.

Both horses were good, but his was the better. He drew alongside his partner. They rode stirrup to stirrup, lashing and spurring, for their lives.

The terrain was too open, the moonlight too bright, for subterfuge. They could only race, outrun the chase. They drew away a little but not enough.

Pistols cracked behind them. Quickly felt the whining wind of one ball. The girl twisted to fire back. He shook his head at her. No horseman could shoot decently at such speed. They might have need of that powder later.

A ditch yawned ahead of them, sliding toward them across the ground. It didn't look troublesome but he concentrated on his riding. The horse was willing, still unwinded. He crossed the ditch with one powerful thrust. Behind, guns banged in applause.

Silly fools, thought Quickly just before he realized he was riding alone.

The girl was gone from beside him!

He looked back, still not believing it. She had handled dozens of jumps worse than that. He knew her horsemanship, he'd taught it to her.

Then he saw the riderless horse galloping away alongside the ditch, saw the small crumpled bundle on the ground. The pursuit was clustering around her already.

Shot from the saddle, he thought. He didn't go back, didn't slow. There was no point. Dead or alive they had her. He would never see her again.

Captain Quickly was a hard man, iron hard. He escaped easily enough after losing his partner. It wasn't until he dismounted before a safe, friendly inn that he discovered he was weeping.

He stayed drunk for three weeks. He was sodden drunk when he heard the tales that confirmed his misery. Killed, not captured, saving the expense of a trial. One of the knight's retainers was bragging of his marksmanship. No grave to visit either. Any pit did for a dead highwayman.

Quickly had little taste for his trade after that. He was rich enough. He decided to let Quickly die with Gently. But it takes time to wind up a business after twenty years or so. He rode twice more, in a gang, as a favor and because of great temptation. His loot from those final raids made him secure for life.

After a year he had almost forgotten what the girl looked like, when he saw her face again. He stood in a London street, staring, paralyzed.

She was in a coach, dressed like a duchess, but he knew that face better than his own. He knew the coach, too. It was the coach they had tried to rob.

Grief had made Quickly drink. Jealous rage made him deadly sober now. The knight had preferred a plaything to a prisoner. For that Quickly planned to kill him.

He was careful. He found out where they lived, and he went in the dead of night. He stood under her window and whistled the signal they had used as High Tobys. He thought it would flush her, and he was right. He was inside, waiting, when she came down the stairs, very pale, barefoot, in a hastily donned white robe.

Quickly only half expected her to show fright in face or speech. Her hair was uncombed, but she brushed the dark strands from an untroubled forehead. When she spoke it was softly, with calm recognition.

"You."

"Did you think I'd not come?"

"I hoped you'd not."

Her quiet admission enraged him. She was as unruffled as if they were meeting at a levee. Anger thickened his voice, though he kept it low in the silent, sleeping house.

"God's teeth! When you fall off a horse, you land soft!"

"No. I was shot. See."

She loosened the robe, opened it. Quickly felt the surge of desire, strong as raw drink, for her pale, tantalizing body. The scar, still red, was like a puckered burn just above her hip. He had to fight to keep from trembling.

"A graze. Did he kiss it and make it well?"

"He was kind."

She retied the robe carelessly, watching him. Quickly wanted to tear it from her, strike her, stamp, shout, curse. As always her guarded, unshaken attitude maddened him. Jealousy gave him the cue; he took out a pistol, cocked it.

"Your wound cost him his life."

"And yours. A shot will rouse the house."

She sounded infuriatingly reasonable, patient. He was too clever a highwayman to risk death needlessly. Calculating his chances, he nodded, told her the alternatives.

"If you come with me now, he lives. If you scream or call anyone, he dies. Maybe not this night, but soon. If I swing, my dear, you'll swing beside me."

She stood thinking, seemingly unmoved. Finally, she sighed, gave a slight shrug.

"All right. I must dress."

She pattered away up the stairs. Quickly braced himself, checked his exits, ready for betrayal. He would wait, return again. She knew that, too.

Within two minutes she returned. She stayed a few steps above him on the staircase, still clad only in the robe, one arm hidden behind her. Quickly, wary and suspicious, raised his pistol.

"Change your mind?"

"No. I decided long ago. I knew you might find me. I knew what you'd do. I made my plans. This."

She took a fully cocked gun from in back of her. She held her robe clutched together with her other hand.

"It's not for you. It's for me. I will not go back to second best when I've had everything. You thought me dead—so——"

Quickly didn't believe her. He had his mouth open to speak when she turned the pistol against herself, pulled the trigger. The flash lit the white robe; the report shook the house.

She gave a cry, doubled over, dropped the gun. He saw the red stain blossom on the robe, spread. She crumpled, rolled sickeningly down the steps.

He stood, stunned and staring, while doors slammed, and voices shouted. Such a finish had failed to enter his mind. From the first he had never understood her. There were men on the stairs when he fled.

That same dawn he left London. He knew he would be blamed, that the hunt would be relentless. He rode his best horse, full tilt, to the nearest port, and left the country.

Nobody has heard of Captain Quickly from that day.

Chapter 17

By the time Jockey Grandison finished his wine and his story Jill was yawning. She had my sympathy.

The warmth of the room, the fire, food and liquor after our chill night and raw journey was too relaxing to withstand. Drowsiness weighed as heavily on my eyelids as coins on those of a dead man. My clothes were dry again, my stomach filled, both helped smother my energies.

One of the slaves replenished the fire; the other brought Jockey a fresh bottle. To give the man a nod, he held his drink well. He was flushed, glistening with sweat, but his speech was clear, his eyes sharp. When Jill made her excuses, pleading fatigue in spite of the early hour, he rose at once, jovially solicitous. Jockey's bow was a grand one. "Good night, my dear Jill. You'll forgive the usage, I'm sure. I claim the right as rescuer, and host." His chuckle was friendly and paternal.

The old goat, I thought. But Jill, pausing on the threshold, smiled over her shoulder.

"Good night, Master Anderson."

"Oh, come now. First names for first names."

"Well," said Jill, blinking but gracious. "Good night, then—Jockey." She closed the door behind her.

Her use of the name jerked me wide awake. Jockey turned with a brow like thunder. I expected the lightning to follow, but he didn't even swear. He took bottle and bumper to the fire, tossed his wig to Pollux, stretched his legs for the slave to pull off his boots. When that rite was finished he unbuttoned his waistcoat, loosened his laces, and belched. The slave brought him pipe and tobacco, held a coal while he puffed.

I stayed at the table. Castor sat at the other end, pistol in front of him, a black stone idol on guard. Jockey had me worried. A man who sits smoking, without offering so much as a pipeful, is not in a friendly mood.

"Jockey," he said at last, and drank deep.

"A slip of the tongue."

"How many does it take to hang a man? Look you, me boyo, this Governor Andros is an iron-fisted tyrant, death on anyone who breaks the king's law. Even the Puritan gentry find him hard. I want no slips of the tongue in his hearing."

"I don't even want to meet him."

He smiled, a bleak thin-lipped grimace, refilled his bumper. "For yourself, Paddy-Cormac, I am not afraid. I'll hand you to the constable, right as right. I must. But I'll make sure you're rescued if you don't talk."

"Devil a word, Jockey. On my honor."

"On your life, and don't forget it." He scowled at the blaze, thinking, puff and sip, puff and sip. "Rescued the day following, before you're near Boston. I know some rascals will do it for a few shillings."

"You won't regret it, Jockey." I sounded sincerely grateful, but actually I didn't believe a word he'd said. It was too pat, too glib. He'd rescue me all right, since he didn't want me preaching his past around Boston, but the escape he'd contrive would be a fatal one.

"You'll leave it to me, then?"

"Aye. In what better hands? But—what about the girl?"

"Why, nothing. I'll just have to chance it. We'll find this brother, and hand her over. The lass is too pretty to be harmed."

That, too, was a changed tune and a false one. His mildness hid some plan, but I was too sleepy to fathom it. He dropped the subject then, offered me more rum as if determined to make a night of it.

For a while I drank with him, noggin for bumper, then I put my head on my arms on the table, pretending to sleep. Pretense changed to reality. I drowsed, woke to peer through my fingers, found Jockey a blurred figure framed against the fire. He was still drinking. I dozed off again, woke again. But the third time, like the drowning man, I went down for keeps.

Something roused me, probably a log falling in the fireplace. Near me the sound of snoring warned me to stay still. It was grand, loud snoring, rasp and whistle, like rubbing a file across the steaming spout of a tea kettle. Then, when I had my bearings and remembered where I was, I raised my head.

Jockey was gone. The fire was a mass of embers, but still showed licking flames. The candles were low and guttering. Halfway down the long table one twin, face down on crossed wrists, was doing the lusty sleeping. His brother, on guard, watched me from the end of the table. He put his hand on the pistol as I straightened.

My knife was still sheathed inside my coat. Jockey hadn't bothered to have me searched. After all he had two armed slaves to guard me, both giants. Against Castor and Pollux that knife was about as dangerous as a gold toothpick. But guile might put a fine, nasty point on it.

Yawning, I rubbed my eyes, rose in a giant stretch. My guard picked up his weapon. I grinned at him, scratching my head.

"Mind if I stretch my legs?" I asked. Without waiting for an answer I walked around the corner of the table.

With a click he moved the hammer from half cock to full. Castor, or Pollux, wasn't taking any chances.

I made my movements slow, easy, wandering between fireplace and table. I kicked a little life into the fire, moved away from it. Always, I edged closer to the sleeping twin. The table was still cluttered with bottles.

"How about a drink?" I asked, waving toward the litter. "I need one."

The guard shrugged, said nothing. The gun muzzle followed me like a compass needle, but he wasn't really taking aim.

Stepping to the table I held a bottle high, shook it. The other hand darted beneath my coat, closed on my knife. In a flash I had it out, and its point on the back of the sleeper's neck.

"Don't shoot," I said, low but tense. "Or you have a dead brother!"

The Negro's mouth opened; he looked from knife blade to my face and back. He raised the pistol, hesitated, was lost.

"I mean it," I said, pricking a little harder with the blade. The sleeper stirred, choked in mid-snore, muttered. "Better tell him not to move."

"Castor," he said hoarsely. "Castor. Don't move."

"Huh?" said Castor. He woke, started to push back, stiffened. I could see his back muscles suddenly bulge the livery jacket.

"Tell him, Pollux."

"Don't move, boy. That's a knife."

"Aye, Castor. *My* knife." The sweat was cold on my forehead, but I made my voice steady. "Pollux, slide that gun down here. Slide it along the table."

"Master kill me."

By pressing with the knife I made an ally. Castor was breathing heavily. He spoke with a pleading whisper.

"Pollux. Do it!"

He wet his lips, placed the gun on the table top, shoved. It slid, lock side up, close enough to be grabbed. The heft of it felt like a kiss on my palm, but I kept the knife on Castor's neck.

"Now, fetch those bridles from the antlers."

Pollux was cowed. He might have rushed the pistol if I'd been careless, but he was afraid of the knife plunging down through his brother's soft neck. I had counted on the bond between twins, these two must have been sold and bought together.

Carefully I moved to Castor's side, shifted the knife point before I let him raise up so that Pollux could lash his arms behind him tight to the chair. It was easy enough to give Pollux the same treatment. When they were both trussed, I went over every knot to make sure they were seamanlike.

Then, I had that drink. I needed it.

The twins watched me sullenly, glowering under their brows. They couldn't very well cry out under my pistol, but their silence made me nervous. I kept listening for something. There was no sound but the fire. It finally occurred to me what was missing. The rain had stopped. It wasn't even dripping as far as I could hear.

With my heart pounding in march time, I gagged the brothers with their own kerchiefs before I went to the window. The shutters hooked from the inside. When I opened them a gush of cold air set my nostrils tingling, whipped my excitement. It was a clear, fresh morning. Clouds were still scudding overhead, but they only menaced the waning stars. To the east a faint, pale glow was climbing from the horizon. I could see the white rollers where the surf kissed the shore, and I could hear its rumble.

God is good, I thought, for the day promised well. In flight, or on voyage, there was never choice of weather, but blue sky puts heart in a man.

Somewhere out there was a lugger, if Jockey hadn't lied. Hurriedly, soundlessly whistling the tune Jill had sung, I made my preparations. Armed with a brace of loaded pistols—the second had been in Castor's belt—I rummaged for powder and ball. A drawer beneath the gun rack yielded the pistol box, complete even to wads and extra flints. It went into one coat pocket. The stone rum bottle, three quarters full, went into the other.

The slaves rolled their eyes as they followed my movements around the room. Those white eyeballs, shifting together, never took their glare from me.

Food was my next need, and getting it was risky. There was no knowing if Jockey had other servants besides the old crone and the twins. The kitchen larder couldn't be far, but the moment I left my prisoners they were likely to raise a commotion. I had no wish for Jockey to surprise me pillaging his pantry. I decided to pass through the kitchen on my way out, in a quick grab and run.

One pang spoiled my merriment. To leave Jill, without so much as a decent farewell, hurt more than I'd expected. The girl seemed to have put a spell on me, a spell I refused to name. She'd been a heart scald, a dragging anchor, an enemy at almost every turn. But the man who said I'd not miss the sight and laugh of her was a damned liar.

Sure, there was no room for any love nonsense in my life. At least until my sea chest was safe in bank. All I could do was cherish a few memories.

Jill was safe enough with me gone. Jockey wouldn't dare harm her, or hold her, with a live witness free. She'd rejoin her brother, and go about her affairs. I'd sense enough to wish her the luck she'd never get with me.

This feeling added strength to the threats I made to Castor and Pollux. With my strongest oaths, I swore horrible punishments for the first sounds they made. Their malevolent regard never flickered. As a last caution I blew out the candles.

Then, I eased open the door, wincing at each creak. The hallway was as dark as a bilge hold, quieter, more empty. Holding my breath, I tiptoed into it.

On my fifth step Jill screamed!

It was a chill, startling sound from somewhere above, but I knew it was Jill. My shoes were off, and I was halfway up the narrow stairs before that scream stopped ringing in my ears. Instinct made me quick and quiet, but there was no quiet in my heart. That was as loaded with murder as the weapon in my fist.

Finding the bedroom was easy by the noise of the scuffle. Jockey's drunken laughter was mixed with curses; Jill was railing at him in panting fury. The door, thank God, was only latched. I didn't crash through heedlessly, but swung it wide.

He had her bent half back across the bed, holding her arms pinned in a hug, as he pawed. Jill's shift was in ribbons, breasts bared, but she was fighting with every muscle. Her single petticoat flared as she kicked at him, her body writhed as she twisted. Jockey, in brocaded nightrobe and tasseled cap like a blasted sultan, couldn't hold her. Even as I leaped across the room Jill jerked a hand free, raked her nails across his cheek.

With an oath Jockey raised a fist to strike.

The blow never fell. I jammed the pistol into his spine with all my force. It brought a grunt of pain.

"Jockey," I said, and meant it, "let go, or die."

He let go, shocked sober, and straightened. Jill squirmed back on the bed. Kneeling, her eyes blazing, she cuffed him, right, left, with her fists, wide-armed swings that rocked his head.

[148]

"Filthy beast," she said, with a sob.

Jockey quivered, but I ground the muzzle on his back. He spoke through his teeth, deadly cold.

"I will kill you for this, Paddy."

"Not this day," I said, and swung the pistol in an arc that crashed it down on his skull. It struck so hard the tassel on his silly nightcap bounced. Jockey pitched forward onto the bed; his knees hit the floor.

Jill flounced from the bed as if he had the plague. She was weeping a little, trembling, but the tears were angry ones. Her breasts heaved, and she tried to cover them with the remnants of her shift.

"He—" she said, "he——"

"Are you hurt?"

"Hurt? Well—" She glared at me, then managed a smile. With it, through the tears, came a blush. "Just bruised. Praise the Lord God I didn't fully undress." She noticed a fallen stocking, a trailing garter, bent to retrieve them, remembered, and snapped upright, folding her arms across her bosom.

"It's all right," I said, turning my back. "Get dressed. We can't waste time."

"No." A lilt came into her voice. "*Cormac!* You're loose!"

"Aye. Again. But I can't leave you here now."

"Oh, no. Please." Clothes rustled as she hurried into them. "I'd be safer with Satan himself. I—I was asleep when he came. The first thing I knew he had the blankets pulled back, and—and——"

"Blankets," I said, "we'll need them." Her faltering was embarrassment, and I wanted to spare her that. I almost wished Jockey conscious so I could hit him again.

"He kept saying he'd stop my mouth with kisses. And—and something about sharing secrets."

"He was drunk."

"He was—unspeakable!"

"Darling, please, hurry!"

I heard her gasp, cursed myself for using the word. Especially in this room. But her voice had lost its anger when she spoke again.

"All right. You can turn now."

She was fully dressed, standing one-legged as she donned her last shoe. She stamped on the floor, reached for her cape. She wore the same dress as at dinner.

"Where's your chest?"

"In the corner. All packed."

"Get the blankets."

Jockey was lying across them. Jill stretched out a foot, gave a disdainful push. He slid off onto the floor. She swept the blankets, good strong wool, from the bed.

My pouch was with her chest. She slipped it on while I wrapped the rest into a heavy bundle, slung it over my shoulder. She followed me out of the room. Her hand touched my shoulder as we descended the stairs.

"Cormac. Thank you."

"Come on," I said, glowing. "Come on."

When I stopped to get my shoes there was racket coming from the living room. Castor and Pollux must have been taking turns bouncing their chairs. As we hurried past something overturned with a crash. Jill gripped my arm.

"They're safe," I said, "but there may be others. Here." I handed her the second pistol. "If anybody tries to stop us use it."

"I hope this one's loaded," she said, grinning.

That was the first time I remembered about our tussle over the other pistol. I almost laughed with pleasure. We'd come a long way since yesterday morning. We were in this together now, at least for a while. It was a grand feeling.

The old crone was hovering in the kitchen but she shrieked and scurried away. Jill filled the pouch with what food we could find handy. The remains of the mutton leg, a round of bread, half a cheese, some carrots. She emptied the bowl of raisins and nuts on top of this. Not enough for an ocean voyage, but we couldn't dally.

We went out the back door, into the cold gray of morning, and around the house. When we turned away from the stable, Jill glanced at me.

"Not Dickon?"

"No. Too slow. Jockey has lots of fast horses. There's a lugger we have to find. On the shore."

She nodded, staying at my shoulder, matching strides. We moved fast, through the brightening stillness, but she wasn't limping this morning, restored by a night's rest. She seemed as anxious to get away as I was. This one, I thought with sudden pride, would make a good shipmate. There was something comradely about the way her skirt swished beside me as we hastened through the wet grass. After we crossed the road, a mud channel now, the land sloped down to the bay.

The distance wasn't great, and sure the heart within me danced a jig at sight of the water. Across that wide stretch of sea, night black still but chopped with white caps, the far shore was merely a low, flat line against the paling east. The surf was running high, too, and rough, a charge of white steeds rearing and plunging on the beach. But the salt smell of it was perfume.

"There's your lugger," said Jill, pointing.

Bare mast tossing as the vessel pitched, the lugger lay about twenty yards out. Jockey's shoreline was a shallow cove, no deeper than the moon on a thumbnail. A dinghy was drawn up on the shingle.

"Let's hope the oars are in it," I said, leading Jill to the boat.

They weren't. I tossed the bundle in disgustedly, threw my hat after it. An oath came readily, but for Jill's sake I swallowed it. She saw my face as she ducked out of the pouch strap.

"What's the matter?"

"No oars, Jill. That'll be a cold swim." I swung around to glare back at Jockey's house. "Can you swim?"

"Aye, if there's need." Her untroubled tone brought my head around. "There's driftwood, Cormac. See, there. And there. 'Tis but a wee paddle, man."

With a laugh she raced for the farthest slab. Grinning, I fetched another. They made clumsy sweeps, heavy and awkward, prickly with gray splinters, but her spirit lifted my own. Without fuss or comment she sat on the farther gunwale to strip off shoes and stockings.

"Fisher folk," I said, bending to do the same. Only a pleased toss of her head showed she'd heard.

We got the dinghy through the surf, though we were soaked to our middles. The water was warmer than the air, but betwixt the two my teeth chattered as we struggled our way to the lugger, Jill paddling on one side, myself on the other.

The lugger's sail, unfurled, had been draped as a covering, but she still needed bailing after the rain. Jill, her feet blue with cold, her lips purple, worked like a bosun. We were both aware, I think, that Jockey's house overlooked us, that the beach was within musket shot. Any moment we might hear shouts as Jockey led his slaves in pursuit.

My worries were plentiful. Tide, channels, and winds were all new to me in this strange bay. Daylight was coming rapidly; already the sun's rim was a gleaming brass arch above the eastern shore. Besides, the lugger, a low, broad-beamed, little craft, with a tiny cabin amidships like a square snuffbox on a palm, was not my idea of a sea-going vessel.

I said nothing of this, naturally, but worked to get under way. My planned course was south, for the bay's mouth and the open ocean, but the wind decreed otherwise. When at last we upped anchor, and raised the yard, I steered north, up the bay, with a crisp breeze on our port quarter. Distance was what we needed first of all.

[151]

So again there was a deck under me, and canvas, even if only a lug-sail, overhead. The lugger was no racer, especially with the dinghy in tow, but she couldn't help move with that spanking breeze driving her. White water boiled back beside me, and the tiller answered like an old friend.

Sure, I was heading in the wrong direction, but that didn't matter so much. Not with Jill Murdoch aboard, rubbing her feet with a blanket, and grinning in triumph at the shoreline dropping behind us.

No, it didn't, for the moment, matter at all, at all.

Chapter 18

THAT bay, called Narragansett after my Indian friends, was a handsome piece of geography, the brag of Rhode Island, but it proved a bane and a thorn to me.

Our first few hours of sailing gave no warning of this. Daybreak turned into a glorious morning, gold sun and fleecy clouds in a bright-blue sky. The sun, all looks and no labor like a plowman in holiday dress, held little warmth. Even blanket-wrapped and reshod we shivered in the wind. White caps raised frosty hands in salute as we cut through the deep-blue bay water. Spray, when it hit, was a breathtaking spatter of sleet.

These discomforts were nothing. We were content to be moving, out of danger, going somewhere. The near green shore slid past, its solitude broken occasionally by a house; the far shore drew closer. We felt no need to speak, but our silence seemed to strengthen the bond between us. Jill was below, exploring the tiny cabin, when I saw the rooftops and chimneys of a town off our port bow. As I spilled the sail and came about she joined me.

"That'll be Warwick," she said.

My gaze took in the masts, thick as a spike fence, bobbing in the harbor. In New England I'd found towns poison dangerous, warned about me, suspicious. And I didn't want any speedy ship chasing the lugger.

"You know the place then?"

Jill shook her head. "Just must be. Providence is a sight bigger to hear tell. I've only been in the bay twice, Cormac, and never this far. Alec took me to Newport with fish."

"Newport?"

"That's at the very entrance."

Our tack wasn't getting us anywhere, and I tried another. The lugger didn't want to lie close, and I wasn't used to the lugsail. We damn near hung up in the wind's teeth. Jill took the sheet from my hand, nudged me from the tiller.

"Let me. I've sailed luggers."

The way Jill trimmed her, tacked, showed her skill. But we made scant headway. Right then the bay lost my admiration. With the wind where it was we'd be hours beating down to the entrance.

"Course?" asked Jill.

That made me skipper, and her helmsman, but I was too troubled to smile. I said: "Well, I had a plan. To sail out of the bay, and westerly. To make a landfall near your own village, land you, go on to New York."

"It's a good plan, but——" She bit her lip, watching me.

"Yes?"

"Well, I'm supposed to be going the other way. To Boston."

"So was I." Jill sounded so uneasy, I laughed. "If some people had their way. But why were *you* making for Boston?"

"To—to be married."

She looked down, busy with her steering as she spoke. The warmthless sun was suddenly without beauty; the cold felt twice as bitter. All right, I told myself, *all right!* You've brought the girl nothing but trouble. She's deserving the best, not you. My face felt taut, frozen stiff around the cheekbones. When those brown eyes glanced up I had to say something.

"Married, well! That's fine. Married."

"Cormac, it's been planned for some time."

"Is it——?" Memory recalled a forgotten conversation. "Your village preacher said something about his son——?"

"Aye, Daniel Bradish," Jill said. She was finding speech difficult too. "He left Harvard last year. Had a temporary church all summer. Now he's been called."

Not the things I was calling him inside. The smile I put on was one of the hardest things I've ever done. I said, "It would be the Reverend Ephraim's offspring."

"His eldest."

[153]

From the first I'd run aground because of that fat clergyman. If he hadn't brought the broadside to Southold, I'd not be a fugitive now. In my mind I even blamed him for the storm that wrecked the ketch. He'd probably prayed for a tempest to strike all evildoers.

"He's a fortunate man. Alec must be pleased."

Jill caught my tone. She threw her chin up, stared at me squarely. She said, as if reciting a lesson, the Scots burr as thick as her brother's, "It's a very suitable match."

"No doubt." In spite of all my resolution jealousy was taking hold of me. My voice was sharper, angrier, every second. "I am sorry I interrupted your bridal journey."

"You should be."

Her disdain was too much. It snapped my last control.

"It's soon mended," I said. Rudely shouldering her aside, I took the tiller, shoved it over. The lugger veered so sharply Jill nearly lost the sail, but she brought it around in time. She watched it fill, noticed we were on a long tack for shore before she spoke.

"What are you doing?"

"Putting you ashore."

"Here?"

"As close to Warwick as I dare. Within walking distance anyway. I'd go all the way, but they might grab me. A hanging's too big a price even for a wedding."

I knew she was looking at me, but kept my gaze on sail and steering. The town swung back in front of me again, off the starboard bow this time because of our tacking. Although farther away each house and topmast seemed clearer than before, as if scanned through a spyglass.

"Cormac."

"Go to the constable. Or a preacher. Tell your story. They'll soon fetch Alec."

"And you? What'll you do?"

"Sail as planned. To ship out of New York." I glanced at her then. She was standing against the rail, gracefully balanced in spite of the bulk of cloak and blanket. Sunlight brightened the gold-red glory of her hair, loose now, and streaming in the wind. Her eyes were clouded.

"I'd take it kindly," I said, "if you'd not repeat that."

Jill put her hand to her mouth, brought it down as a fist. Her wind-whipped hair seemed to throw off sparks. Her voice rose with sudden fury.

"You—you gowk! Do you think I *would*? After—Have you then such a low, poor opinion——"

[154]

A sudden report, a sharp pop in the clear air, interrupted her. My first thought was the rigging, and my eyes searched the stays for the break. Jill touched my arm.

"You can't land me here," she said, sounding strangely pleased, almost smug. "Look what's waiting to greet us."

On a bluff behind the beach ahead were three horsemen, no bigger than fingers at that distance, but unmistakable. One was lowering a smoking musket. He brandished his fist at us. The purple livery topped by the black-button heads of the others made recognition easy. Jockey, I thought, must be wild with rage to try a shot at such range.

Without a word Jill and I exchanged places and put about. Watching the shore we saw Jockey whirl his horse and gallop for the town. One twin followed. The other walked his horse along the bluff abreast of us.

"To keep an eye on us," I told Jill, "while the master finds a ship to catch us in."

Jill was tight lipped; her knuckles were white as she gripped the tiller. "*He'll* not take you," she said. "Not that one! Not if we have to sail this tub across the ocean!"

"What about your bridegroom?"

"He can wait." She laughed suddenly, wrinkling her nose. Her glee made her impish. "You're just as important as Harvard College, Cormac Doyle. I'm in no such great rush to wed as all that."

"Now, and I'm glad to hear it," I said, not daring to shout my great joy.

We cut the dinghy loose for greater speed. It helped a little, but not much. In the face of the unfavorable winds it was not easy sailing to get out of the bay. Jill was good, but the tacking seemed endless, to and fro. A long western leg would bring us back under the watchful scrutiny of the distant horseman, Castor or Pollux. So we worked over toward the eastern shore, beyond his vision, and stayed there. Trapped in that pesky bay we were as exposed as a fly swimming in a saucer of water.

Noon came and went with no sign of pursuit. We were too anxious, too busy to bother with food. We kept a watch aft, waiting for that tell-tale flash of canvas. They would be beating against the wind, too, but a bigger, better ship would eat away our head start knot by knot.

Jill, pink with windburn and excitement, was enjoying herself. She was without doubt the loveliest shipmate a sailor ever had. Time and again, as the hours dragged past, I wondered at her skill. Even in a fishing village women hugged the hearth, prayed for a safe return. I told her so.

"I know," she said. "I have been rebuked for it. But I was ever tagging after Alec. There were just us two, and him so much older. He'd scold one day, pray for me the next, but on the third——" She giggled at the memory. "On the third he'd teach me a new sailing trick. Cormac! Isn't the wind changing?"

The wind was our life, and we knew it. It seemed to be veering around to the north, but so slowly that a breath might discourage it. The breeze slackened, spurted, almost died completely. No sooner did our sail fill again than I saw the white gleam far behind us.

"Sail," I said. "Sail in chase."

"How big? How fast?"

"Can't see yet. Bound to be faster than we are."

"No. No!" Jill stamped her foot. Covenant-bred girls didn't swear, but she looked fit to bite nails. "We've the wind with us now, Cormac."

"So have they."

The lugger was low in the water, and I don't think they had discovered us when I could make out their jib and mainsail. By the way her mast grew larger I knew she was closing fast.

"Sloop, I think, Jill."

"Fast?"

"Aye."

"Then we hide."

With that she started giving orders that had me handling that lugsail like a magician's scarf. Even the lugger seemed to outdo itself obeying her.

We had passed a couple of small islands offering little cover while working our way south. Now Jill, on a long, scudding tack that took every advantage of the changed wind, steered the lugger straight through the strait that separated the two good-sized islands on the eastern side of the bay. Our course took us well into the passage between the more southern of these islands, Conaticut, and Rhode itself. As we tacked again the island cut off any sign of the pursuing sails.

"Girl," I said, "you're a pilot."

"Alec took me through there once," Jill replied, laughing but pleased. "At least we're hidden for a while."

She would, I thought, have made a good pirate. Hers was essentially a pirate trick, worked widely in the West Indies. Using smaller vessels the pirates played hide-and-seek among the islands, darting into land-locked channels where frigates and such-like heavier craft could not go. The sloop, manned by bay-wise sailors, might follow us here, but only if they'd seen us. As time and our wake slid behind us with no sail appearing, my cheerfulness increased.

[156]

"Tide's turned, too," I said. "Cresting for us."

"Aye," Jill said, with a glance at the shore eddies. She frowned thoughtfully. Her face looked a trifle weary.

"They've passed the strait by now, Jill."

"Aye. But there's one thing. This whole bay narrows down to a gap at the entrance. It's about three miles wide. This passage leads to it. The other side of Conaticut Island the mainland comes about as close. If that's a real fast sloop——"

She didn't finish. She didn't have to. If they beat us to the bay's entrance, and they should, they just had to patrol the gap. The lugger wasn't fast enough to slip by, and outrace a sloop. We were bottled up, neat as a minnow in a jug.

"We can beat off till night," I said, gauging the position of the November sun. "A few hours. We'll stand a better chance with darkness."

Jill shook her head. "We dassn't, Cormac. Given time to, they'll rouse more ships from Newport town. That's right beside the entrance. Newport men are merchant men. They'll gladly set sail to catch a pirate."

"We're not caught yet, Jill. We'll run ashore this side of Newport. You walk into the place, and I'll take to the woods again."

"You mean *give in?*" Jill clutched the tiller as if to guard it. "Admit we've lost? Without even *trying?*"

"I'll not go running you into danger. If we try to break out there'll be shooting."

"Not if we beat them to the gap."

"In this?"

"Don't you be insulting my lugger!" she said. "She's done everything we've asked of her, poor lass. And I'm taking her out to sea." Like a child Jill stuck out her tongue at me.

"But, Jill——"

"Enough. No more! That's twice the same day you've tried to get rid of me. Another word and I'll cast you overboard." She chuckled at my amazed gaping. "We'll make it through, Cormac."

"Sure," I said, "sure." We had less chance than a turtle on his back, but there was no arguing with the girl. Sure, it was my neck she was risking, but when she talked that way I'd have sailed the lugger up the scaffold steps.

So we beat down the passage through the fading day, and came at last to Newport. The lugger hugged the opposite shore, but it looked a busy place, well named, for the houses and wharfs had a fresh newness not yet shabbied by usage. There were ships of all shapes and sizes tied up, but one was moving.

The tide had reached full crest, and a big merchantman, several hundred tons, was warping her way into the channel. Square rigged and bulky, she was loaded deep. I figured her for the last vessel of the season. Winter would catch her in mid-Atlantic. She was sluggish with cargo; the men in her boats were straining. Her yards were dotted with men ready to unfurl at the first touch of the off-shore breeze. Her name, emblazoned in gold letters across the high broad stern, was legible in the paling sunlight. *The Gentle Anne*: Newport.

Jill didn't bother with the merchantman. Her gaze was fixed between it and the island. Her gasp of dismay brought my head around.

Beyond the bay entrance the last sunshine caught on a turning white shield. Together we watched the sloop come about, slide out of sight. Jockey's ship was on patrol, waiting.

"They beat us," Jill said.

"Aye."

"Cormac, we can't let that—that buzzard take us!" She was near tears with disappointment, but fighting them.

Jockey hadn't roused the Newporters. Glances from wharf or boat were casual. One of the merchantman's riggers even waved at us. At that wave excitement stirred within me.

"Jill. Give over."

"What?"

"We've found a friend. We're sailing tucked under *The Gentle Anne's* wing!"

Jill glanced from me to the merchant ship, to where the sloop had reappeared crossing the entrance. Her eyes narrowed in puzzlement, widened with realization, began to dance. She clasped her hands together, chortled.

"Oh, Cormac! Between the land and the big ship. They'll never know we're there!"

"If we are fortunate."

Luck or the Lord favored us. We timed the sloop's appearances, tacked across to the merchantman's port side while Jockey's crew was hidden. This put us almost under the wharves of Newport, but enough wind reached us. It was even colder in the shadow of the big vessel.

Canvas dropped, fluttering, from the top yards of *The Gentle Anne*, as she swung around, catching the tide. Her boats were recalled; her prow bit into the waves as she moved down the passage toward the gap. Beside her, faithful as any pilot fish, rode the lugger.

The merchantman went slowly, under half canvas. We caught all the wind we could get. Seamen looked down from the high rail above us, grinned, waved. Jill waved back with happy abandon. We were close to the shore, which seemed to be sliding by as we stood still. There was no sign of the sloop. No helmsman would dare cross the merchantman's bow for fear of going aground.

Soon, though it seemed hours, we reached open water. The land on our left folded back on itself like a slowly bent arm. We felt the long swell of the ocean under the lugger's keel. We were out of the bay!

Shouted commands sounded above us, on our giant escort. More canvas was spilled out, bellied as it filled. The white plume at the prow of *The Gentle Anne* spread out like an opening fan of feathers. Her speed increased. First the wide shadow that sheltered us moved ahead, leaving the lugger in the weak rays of sunset. Then, the big ship itself left us behind. As we dropped back, bobbing alongside the merchantman's wake, we both looked aft.

Far behind, at the entrance to the bay, the sloop was just starting on its eastern tack. Away to the west the sun, already half set, rested like a bronze egg in a nest of hay-colored clouds.

"Cormac! Cormac!" Jill, dancing, gripped my shoulders, hugged me. "We beat him! We're away! Will you mock my lugger now?"

"Never," I said, returning the hug, but watching our pursuer. Jockey was not a man one could diddle easily.

Her hull was visible, which meant our sail must be. We had no concealment now, but I didn't dare drop the yard. Every minute we ran before the wind increased our lead. But, if one sharp-eyed sailor gazed our way, the race was far from finished.

Aye, there it was. The sloop's shape changed as they bore away after us. We were seen. View halloo, and after them!

"They've sighted us, Jill. They're coming."

"They can't catch us now!" Jill was vehement, but she was too good a judge of shipping to fool herself for long. She gazed back across the water, turned to me in dismay. Her mouth drooped as she asked a plaintive question. "Can they?"

My only answer was a shrug. The lugger didn't belong that far out in the ocean, and it was no racer. Jockey had managed to find a fairly serviceable vessel. Our pursuer wasn't the fastest ship afloat, but, in spite of the old fable, it doesn't take a hare to catch a tortoise. On the wide, bare, open sea, with no place to hide, no shallows to take advantage of, our flight was bound to end in capture.

I cursed myself for letting the girl persuade me to quit the bay. Now there was no chance of grounding the boat and running. The sloop had us cut off from the shore. To stand helpless on deck while an enemy in a faster vessel comes ever closer was not a new experience, but I felt worse this time than any other.

Grimly, I checked the priming of my pistol. Jill's brown eyes widened as she watched.

"Where's the other one?" I asked.

"I left it in the cabin."

"Fetch it, please."

"But—" the gathering dusk couldn't hide her worried frown—"there'll be a dozen on that ship. What good——?"

"There's only one I'll aim at. Still, I want both guns in case I miss the first time."

Her mouth opened, closed without comment. She started toward the cabin, turned halfway to stare aft, past me. Turning my head I grunted to see how much the sloop had gained. If the light had been better, I could have named paint and trim. As it was her sails looked faded gray. Only a half mile separated us now.

"Cormac!" Jill cried, "tack to port!"

Her voice was so quick, insistent, that I obeyed without thinking. The tiller went over, the lugsail was shifted, before my brain worked. Then I thought this was a mistake. A glance back confirmed the opinion. The sloop was changing course smoothly, even seeming to gain by the maneuver.

"That's senseless," I said, glaring at her.

Jill leaped across the deck, ripped the clew of the sheet from my fingers. She was fairly spluttering with excitement.

"Jill, what——"

"The wind! The wind's dying!"

It was true; I could see it. The wind, as it often does at sunset, faltered and stopped.

That was what saved us. For when the breeze came again it blew toward shore, forcing both vessels to beat to windward. This gave the lugger the advantage, increased by the short November twilight.

Under cover of darkness we changed course twice, in rapid succession, trying to outwit our pursuers. We ended with the lugger driving in a totally new direction, south-south-east, out to sea. If the sloop's captain thought only idiots would take a forty-foot lugger so far from the coast, he thought as we wished, but he was very nearly right.

At last we dropped the yard, drifted under the bare pole. That was our final desperate effort to escape. They would search, of course, but with the sail furled they might pass close without sighting us in the night. We huddled together in the stern, under all the coverings we could find aboard, too cold and weary for speech. Jill nodded through several dozes, but I couldn't sleep.

When the moon rose, late and pallid, there was nothing around us but the black, endless heaving of the sea. At every point of the compass it stretched to the horizon with terrible, dark and lonely menace.

"How beautiful," Jill said, sleepily.

So it was. For us, anyway, under the circumstances.

Chapter 19

AFTER what must have been midnight, we hoisted the lugsail, started to cruise back toward the coast.

The weather was freezing, throat drying, ear tingling cold, but the sea, fortunately, was calm. Waves crested gently under the lugger's keel, lifting us forward; we shipped no water. The wind set our course, which, at a guess, was roughly southwest. That same wind was unfolding a lead-colored curtain to the north; it screened the few stars, turned night's black velvet to smudged shoddy. But the weak moon, ragged as a nibbled wafer, still rode serene, untouched, making a wake of its own across the ink-dark water. To the man in the moon our lugger must have looked puny indeed in the vast, empty ocean.

We supped on rum and bread, famished past hunger but aware we must eat something. Jill coughed on her drink but the liquor was warming; there was no galley on the lugger, nor sandbox for a fire. I insisted on standing first watch, sent her to bed down in the cabin, out of the wind. She went, stumbling weary, only after my promise to wake her in an hour. She wanted to take turn and turn.

Alone, with the tiller between my knees and the sheet belayed, there was naught to do except watch the sail. Drawing the blanket tight about me, I warmed myself with thoughts of Jill. The Atlantic, with all its majesty and power, never struck me as a cheerful friendly place to dream on, especially through a bitter November night. As a seaman I respected it, with fear and admiration, but it had done me dirty before, and, from the looks of that northern sky, would again at its whim. Yet, as the lugger slid along with a gentle, lulling motion, I felt a sort of lonely peace.

The sea did that, those times when it wasn't shaking your teeth loose, in the quiet hours of darkness. A Portugee shipmate once told me about the prayer of the fishermen along his native coast.

"O Lord, Thy sea is so great, and my ship is so small."

Aboard the lugger that prayer came back to me. Even for a non-praying man like myself it had a humility and trust that pleased me. While it asked the Creator of the ocean to keep you in mind, it didn't beg for any special favors. For Jill's sake more than my own, I murmured the Portugee's prayer aloud.

For Jill's sake. Sailing into the path of the moon, with boundless space above, and swelling waves below, there was no sense in lying to myself. I loved that girl. It was as true as it was hopeless.

She was promised, betrothed. Jill would not have given her word lightly, and she would be very loath to break it. Besides, 'twas little I had to offer any girl, much less Jill Murdoch. A fugitive, in a stolen lugger, owning only the clothes he wore. There was a charge of piracy against me, and the silver oar waiting to guide me to the gallows. Now, there were bright prospects to thrill a young maid!

True, there was the sea chest if ever hue and cry ceased long enough for me to return for it. In my melancholy, I even doubted the position of the wrecked ketch. It might be years before I recovered the chest, and Jill was betrothed to a lout named Daniel Bradish.

Sure, what if I did fill her apron with gold coins? Jill, with her strict upbringing, might toss them in my face as the wages of sin. She was a daughter of the Covenant, after all.

Then, I grinned at the moon, reliving the day just passed. At the lugger's helm, glorying in the race, Jill had left Covenant and scruples ashore somewhere. We'd been shipmates, partners in foiling Jockey, and she'd shown no unwillingness to aid a pirate's escape.

With such thoughts, as foolish as any callow swain, I happily ignored the future. Let Daniel Bradish, rot him, worry about Jill's whereabouts. She was with me!

Keeping the sail filled, with a wary eye toward where the leaden sky kept spreading, I did what many a lone helmsman does to pass the night. A song gathered inside me, and after another brief swig at the rum jug, to ease the tune, I sang it, soft and low.

> The king sits in Drumferling town,
>   Drinking the blood-red wine:
> "O where will I get good sailor,
>   To sail this ship of mine?"
>
> Up and spake an older knight,
>   Sat at the king's right knee:
> "Sir Patrick Spence is the best sailor,
>   That sails upon the sea."

There were many verses to the old ballad, and those I misremembered I hummed through. There was no one to make the true comment that when voices were handed out I was behind the door. The gurgle of the wash alongside sounded musical; the sail flapped a bit of applause.

Dawn came at last. Now, dawn at sea, with the sun bursting like a rocket from the far edge of the ocean, can be a wondrous glory, but this was a sad imitation. No golden disk, but a fading torch, tear shaped, rose out of the eastern horizon. With it came only enough light to lessen the shadows, to change the sea from black to cold, glittering steel.

Jill's hair, as she appeared over the top of the cabin, mocked the drab day. Her face, in spite of a chiding frown, was polished, buffed by sleep.

"Cormac, you didn't wake me!"

"No need." Strangely, I mumbled through frost-stiff lips. My voice came out as a croak.

"No need!" Jill sounded angry; she darted across the deck as if ready to shake me. "You're half frozen. There's no blood in your face at all. Are you daft, man, or did you never hear of frostbite?"

"You were in want of rest."

"Aye, but not that much! Give me the tiller."

Now I have stood colder watches, in worse weather, but as I swung my leg over the tiller, I nearly fell. My joints were surprisingly awkward; my feet were numb stones. Jill caught my arm, trimmed the helm with her other hand. She spoke with that mixture of scolding and anxiousness I have heard mothers use.

"You've no more sense than a child! Argh, men! Do you always have to be proving how stout you are? Defying the elements for some feckless notion? My standing watch would be a sight easier than nursing you if you sicken! If you were mine——"

"Yes?" I asked when she paused.

"Never mind! Get away below before you fall overboard."

I obeyed, grinning foolishly at nothing. The cabin was no bigger than a doghouse, dirty and stinking. There was a bunk against one wall, piled with rumpled covers, skins, a piece of sailcloth, another blanket. There was no mattress, but the coverings were still warm from Jill's body. I burrowed under them without bothering to remove my hat.

The last thing I remembered was a vague wonder at my complete trust in Jill. As helmsman she could steer any course she wished. Only a day or so ago—was it two, really?—she'd sworn to deliver me to my enemies. Now, given the chance, I was sure she wouldn't take it.

Sleep came as abruptly as a fall through a chasm. I didn't even dream.

❖

A hail woke me, brought me upright trying to place it, and myself. The roll of the lugger, the slap of the waves alongside, recalled the present. We seemed to be pitching more, moving faster, but not alarmingly so. I was on my feet, groping for the companionway when the hail came again.

"*Cor-mac!* Wake up! Sail, ho!"

Jill lapsed into muttering, evidently planning to lash the tiller, and fetch me, so I called back as I staggered blinking onto the deck.

"Sail? Where?"

Any sail was hostile. Captain and crew might never have heard of me, but we didn't dare approach close enough to find out. Coasters out of New England ports would carry word of my taking and escape; for all we knew Jockey's ship was still prowling in search.

The first thing I noticed was the weather; snow coming was my instant guess. The steel-gray sea rose and fell under a motionless, low-slung canopy, heavy with storm. Our mast wasn't very high, but its top seemed almost to scrape the sky. There was a brisker wind, and that warmer. We ran before it, on a somewhat more westerly course than before, but the lugger wouldn't outrun a snowstorm.

"To starboard," Jill said, pointing. "No, farther aft." She had her cloak hood raised, a blanket tied around her. These gave her the shape of a strange, sea-faring monk. The wind held her skirt taut against her calves, fluttered it in front of her ankles to display a gay froth of petticoats, an eye-catching touch of frivolity.

There was nothing to starboard but the dark bulk of an island about a league away. At that distance it resembled a half-clenched gauntlet resting on the water. I stared at it, head turning as I scanned its length.

"That's an island, Jill, not——"

"I know that. Block's. The sail was more to the north. I steered behind the island purposely."

"You did well. There's no sail now."

"But once we're past the island—" Jill said. She had her head turned, gazing back over her shoulder, and the phrase was almost inaudible. I finished it mentally. Without the island to screen us we were exposed.

"Was it the sloop, Jill?"

"I couldn't tell. But it seemed to be making south, as we are."

The weather was the greater danger. A heavy snowfall would be blinding, might even swamp the lugger. As the island dropped away behind us, I regarded it thoughtfully. There was solid ground, the first sign of the nearing coast, and land offered refuge. Reluctantly, I dismissed the idea. If the other vessel were ahunting, and had seen us, she would come sniffing around that island like a terrier at a rat hole.

"Steady as she goes," I said. "I'll get breakfast."

As we ate we both watched for the sail to reappear. The meal was no banquet. We chewed chips of meat, hacked from a frozen mutton leg, and hard bread. Carefully judging rations, I allowed us a palmful of raisins and a swallow of rum apiece, but saved the cheese.

About an hour or more later, in the early afternoon, we saw the sail again. It was no more than a fluttering scrap of paper across the heaving waves, but now it was directly to starboard, full abeam and sailing a parallel course. Both Jill and I raised our arms to point, exchanged a glance, found no need for speech.

"The same ship?" I asked, at last.

"I don't know. I think so."

So did I, from pure instinct. And the wind was wilder now with each gust; it hummed across the few taut lines of our rigging, a warning of what was to come. Flecks of moisture began to dot my cheeks, cold drops that hadn't waited to be snowflakes.

"Jill," I said, "I don't care for this. The storm is getting ready to break, and that lad yonder is between us and the shore."

A white wave broke across our bow, as Jill pushed the tiller. The lugger shook as if surprised; dirty water washed along the scuppers. We swung on to a due west tack.

"You're not putting out to sea?"

"No,"—the hood's point twitched as she shook her head—"there's an island dead ahead."

"You're sure?"

"Aye. You see, Long Island splits at this end like a two-pronged fork. This island—Gardiner's—lies just inside the southern prong."

Of course, she knew these waters much better than I did, but I peered ahead without seeing anything. The distant sail looked a trifle larger, and I wondered if they had tacked, too. We were going to have to find a port somewhere, but not, I hoped, under the eyes of a following craft. I said as much to Jill.

"There's a cove I'm thinking of," she said, "at the top end of Gardiner's. We can slip in there, and no one the wiser."

Since she was pilot, I left it to her. The lowering day, losing light by the minute, made vision difficult. At last there was a blur visible ahead of us, a stain like spilled ink on the ocean's steel. Jill gave a cry of joy as she saw it.

"That's it. That's Gardiner's! Now I know where we are!"

Sure I was glad that one of us knew! From the looks of the sky, and the feel of the wind, there wasn't much time left before the snow came. Only the blessed Saints had held it off this long. Making a landfall on a lee shore in a snow-whipped gale was not my notion of a frolic.

The northernmost point of Gardiner's Island thrusts itself into the water like a harpoon blade. Jill's cove was a nick in the straight edge, a harbor of no great size or shelter, but snug enough for the lugger. We swung into it, dropped the yard, and let the surf do the rest. Our will-o'-the-wisp follower had disappeared again. If that captain had a grain of sense he'd be running for shelter himself.

We grounded the lugger on a strip of sandy beach that fairly kissed the keel. A feather bed wouldn't have made a softer berth. There was no shock; the little craft listed slightly to port, but didn't shed a splinter. Surf hissed around us, but it wasn't rough in the piece of cove we'd picked.

From the bow I jumped ashore without wetting a shoe. My first concern was the lugger. The anchor rope tied her to a nearby tree trunk; a pounding sea might drive her higher, but we'd be able to float her when we wished.

Then we made camp, working fast and breathlessly, aware that the snow was imminent. We found a good place behind a curve of sand dune, sheltered on one side by a little copse, scrub pine and bare, gnarled trees, that served as windbreak. There I pitched the lugsail in a sort of half tent, open side facing the sand bank, using the yard as pole, pegging the canvas down with ropes and improvised stakes. While I hammered with a rock, Jill stripped the ship.

The beach was littered with driftwood which we gathered into a handy pile. As I clicked the snaphance into a carefully arranged nest of brush and tinder, sprinkled with gunpowder for faster action, the first snow fell, tiny flakes like wisps of ash. My fire puffed, burst into flame.

Jill was atop the dune, struggling as she dragged a timber through the sand. Before I could reach her the snow thickened to a curtain of whirling feathers. The force of the storm nearly knocked us both down, but we clung to the timber, added it to our fuel stock.

Firewood was our prime need, for the temperature was dropping as quickly as the snow. We fed the blaze like a pair of worried goldsmiths, weighing the selection of each piece of wood. We kept the fire large enough to warm our canvas hut, but not wasteful.

The bright flames did their work well, brought us both warmth and cheer. Snugly tucked against the sand dune, guarded by the tent, the crackling fire hissed defiance at the few flakes that reached it. Occasionally the wind howled through the scrub pine, but for the most part the snow fell in smothering silence.

For a time we sat without talking, huddled in the tent's entrance, letting the heat, that blessed thawing heat, sink into us. I became almost drowsy with the content of victory. We had beaten the storm; we were safe ashore, dry and warm. When, at last, Jill pulled her hood back, shook her hair loose, my hands made a half move to touch those tresses.

"Well," I said, changing the gesture by extending my palms to the campfire, "this is a sight better than fighting this blizzard in the lugger, now isn't it?"

"Mmmm." Jill combed her hair back with the fingers of one hand. "The Lord God was merciful. He heard our prayers, and held back the tempest until we reached safety."

"Your prayers anyway."

"You didn't pray?" She looked at me, grave-eyed and serious. "Not at all? Not once?"

"Maybe once." My admission brought a smile. "But do you think He gives much heed to the praying of a pirate?"

"He heeds everyone."

"All right," I said, thinking her very kissable. "Let's not argue, then. You have my gratitude, Jill. For whatever brought us here—your prayers or your seamanship."

Her fire-lit flush deepened; she twisted her fingers together. "Thank you. You're welcome indeed. It was little enough."

"Was it now? Aiding a criminal to escape is a hanging offense, girl. But, don't worry, I'll not peach on you."

"You're not escaped yet."

"Well, I'm closer to it than I've been for some weeks. Thanks to you and the lugger. When the storm abates we'll beat down to your home—it can't be more than a day's sail from here?"

"Less," she said. "It's not far." She gazed into the fire, sighed. "But you'll not be safe then. Not even after you reach New York. Governor Andros has probably sent expresses about you."

"I'll worry about that when I get there," I said, rising to throw wood on the fire.

"I—I'll worry too."

That murmured remark caught me standing like the stick in my hands. Jill evidently felt my stare, turned to meet it. She was smiling, but with a sad gentleness.

Then she dusted her hands briskly, twisted to crawl back into the shadows of the hut. When she spoke again, it was with brusque raillery. "If you'll stop standing there, gawking, and raise the fire, I'll cook us a bite of supper."

"Cook?"

"Aye." She returned to the firelight, clumping on her knees, brandished a battered tin pannikin. "I found this in the lugger's cabin. Likely they used it for bailing, but it will serve for a cook pot."

A new brass kettle would have been no more welcome. Jill melted a fistful of snow in it for water while I carved chunks from the mutton leg. Some meat we saved for the morrow, the rest, with the bone, was added to the stew. Jill cut the carrots into it, laced it with a splash of rum. After a bit of juggling I managed to balance the pannikin close to the blaze, so that it bubbled merrily at a slow boil. Steam rose from the mixture with an aroma that made the nostrils twitch, and my stomach rumble.

While we waited, I placed the stone rum bottle close enough to warm, after dropping a couple of raisins down the neck. After all, we had not enjoyed a hot meal, or a warm drink, since leaving Jockey's!

But we enjoyed this one. I counted it among the happiest suppers I have known. We ate ravenously, scooping the stew from the pannikin with slices of bread for spoons. The dish tasted even better than it had smelled. I was half finished before I noticed that Jill was letting me have the lion's share.

"You're bigger," she said. "You need more."

"We are messmates as well as shipmates, Jill. Share and share."

She argued, but I would eat no more, made her scrape the pannikin. With her hair tumbled over her forehead, and her mouth rimmed with grease, she looked years younger. For a final course I toasted slabs of cheese; we gobbled this on bread, scorching our lips against the charred, melted gruel, and licked our fingers.

By the time we reached the warm rum we were stuffed, sated and lazily gay. There was about a quarter of the bottle left, and we sipped it sparingly, savoring the taste, the expanding inner glow, the heady sense of well-being. Jill, from a fishing village, was no stranger to rum, though she was unused to the raw liquor without spices or doctoring. But she tilted and tippled in her turn, without coyness, and seemed to enjoy the drink.

We spoke softly, watching the flames weave different patterns, listening to the hushed murmur of the snow, the whistle of the wind. Our nest, cosy and protected, gave a feeling of aloneness; an island on an island, far from the rest of the world.

Without thought, I put my arm around Jill. With a breath like a purr she let her bright head rest on my shoulder.

"Cormac."

"Aye?"

"Is the rum all gone?"

"There's a swallow or two still."

"We should save a little. For tomorrow."

"Let tomorrow do its own worrying. Drink."

She sipped, letting me hold the bottle. As I took my own dram, she hiccupped, and giggled.

"I feel—just wonderful, Cormac."

"Share and share, Jill. I wouldn't call the king cousin myself."

"It isn't all the drink."

"I know."

Silence lay easy between us for a while. There seemed no need for speech. Jill dozed in the curve of my arm. I felt myself a man of might, full of a grand, tremendous strength, ready and able to defend her against dragons, ogres, and devils. Sure, right she was, it was not all the drink, but our closeness, the moment, the things shared, meal and work and dangers.

Around us was the cold night, the quiet rustle of the falling snow. A drift formed at the base of the sand dune, inside the edge of the firelight's circle, kept back by heat. That white windrow glistened, sparkled, captured and changed flickering shadows until it dazzled me.

Jill stirred, sat up, yawned. She put a hand to her mouth too late, gazed at me with eyes that were dark pools of sleepiness. My fond laughter was answered by a drowsy smile.

"Get to bed, lass. You're stove in."

"The fire——?"

"I'll tend it, make sure it lasts the night."

"Well. All right."

[169]

She crawled into the tent. I heard the noise as she gathered her coverings into some sort of couch. She muttered what could have been a good night, and seconds later was breathing in the steady rhythm of deep sleep.

I did more than build the fire. After all, I was captain, guardian, protector; Jill was my charge, and care. In that spirit I made a tour of our rookery, circling the tent, feeling in the darkness to be sure lashings were tight, pegs secure. Away from the campfire it was icy and bitter. The snow was a deluge of great flakes, overpowering, thick as fog. It was already almost knee high; I had to beat my own path. I found everything snug. The peaked slant of the sailcloth had chuted the downfall into an encircling drift, but this merely gave us an extra, windproof, wall.

When I stumbled back to the fire I was soaked, and breathless. I took a long time drying my clothes, and longer still piling on fuel for slow burning. The cold air had sobered and exhilarated me. I wasn't sleepy; only fear of disturbing Jill kept me from shouting, or roaring a song. Then after our heaviest timbers were arranged to my liking, I crept into the tent.

I was on my knees, groping forward carefully lest I wake her, when Jill spoke from the darkness.

"Cormac."

"Did I disturb you?"

"No. Tell me something. What does *cuilin* mean?"

"*Cuilin?*"

"Aye. I know it for Gaelic, but I don't have that word."

"It means—maid with the beautiful hair."

"Oh."

I have small enough store of Irish words, and suddenly I recalled my last use of that one. I'd murmured it that night in the wood while she lay unconscious, knocked out by the overturned chaise. Startled, I peered toward the sound of her voice. The fire made a red triangle at the hut's entrance, but all else within was darkness.

"So, now, you heard that? You were shamming, not hurt at all."

"My head hurt," she said, with a hint of mirth, "but I heard."

"You let me share your cloak, sleep by your side, and never so much as spoke a syllable. Not aye, yes, or nay!" My indignation was feigned, but my puzzlement wasn't. She was very close, within arm's length. I heard the coverings when she moved, the demure answer.

"Well, I was cold."

"Oh."

"And—and Cormac I'm a wee bit cold now."

"You are?"

"Aye. 'Tis a raw, wild night."

That it was, but I was sweating. My suggestion seemed forced through my tight throat. "We—we could pile all the coverings atop both of us."

"That might help."

With the speech her hand touched me, shoved a blanket in my fingers. Hurriedly, I piled everything on the low mound of her form, barely visible in the blackness. Then I slipped in beside her, carefully avoiding contact.

She turned toward me, snuggled close against my side. Her head rested on my chest; her hair was fragrant and ticklish under my nose. Before we were settled comfortably my arm was around her.

Huddled under the heaped coverings no cold reached us. Through my clothes I could feel the whole warm shape of her, but I made no move. The memory of Jockey Grandison's fiasco was too recent bright. Jill trusted me. I'd give her no cause to regret it.

That wasn't easy to do. Tenderness fought with desire, lost, joined forces like a pliant turncoat. Gritting my teeth I tried to control my impulses.

For long, long minutes we lay quietly. I stared into the darkness, listened to her soft breathing, the whisper of the snow on the canvas above us. Finally, I began to tremble.

"Cormac, what are you doing?"

"Just shaking."

"Shaking! Why?"

"It's nothing."

"You're not cold."

"No."

"No. Shaking, is it?"

Jill stirred, raised her head. Her eyes, her lips were very close. She put an arm around my neck, drew my head down. We kissed, slowly at first, then with fierceness.

"Ah," Jill murmured against my mouth when we drew breath, " 'twas worth the waiting."

"Jill——"

"Hush."

Our second kiss, while we held each other tightly, lasted twice as long. What followed, followed. Jill was innocent but unafraid. There was nothing furtive about our lovemaking. She helped undo the fastenings of her bodice, quivered when I touched the pale softness of her breasts. She matched passion with passion, welcoming each caress with a clean, joyful abandon.

"I love you," I said, at the final glorious moment. "Love you, love you!"

Afterwards Jill wept a little, gently, muffled against the hollow of my throat.

"Jill," I asked, worried, "did I hurt you? Are you sorry?"

"No. Neither." She drew back, wiped her eyes. "It's just that—I feel so weak inside. Nobody told me what love was."

"I will spend a lifetime at it."

"Will you now?" She stroked my cheek, slid the hand behind my neck, drew herself toward me. I kissed the wet tears from her face.

So, on that night, in that cramped cubicle, with a blizzard falling around us, the trumpets blared for us, the pipes skirled and the harps rang with golden melodies.

Tell me no different, for didn't I hear them?

Chapter 20

THE New England weather again showed itself more lunatic than anyone chained in Bedlam. Morning brought clear sky, bright sunshine, and pleasant warmth. Snow covered the ground, white, glistening, reflecting the sunlight with harsh glare, but already the thaw was at work. Melting flakes dripped from the entrance edge of our tent; a tiny rivulet trickled down the sand dune; the drift nearest our fire was softening to slush. The air, too, had a gentleness that gave November the lie. There was still need for the campfire, but it was no longer necessary for survival.

Daylight was full bright before I stirred, reached sleepily for Jill, sat up startled to find her gone. She was busily building the fire. When I crawled out to join her she edged away, giving me one swift glance that held the shy wariness of a penned doe.

"A grand morning," I said.

"Aye."

She was fussing with the pannikin, head bent. There was a constraint about her, the stiff way she held herself, her low tone. Feeling it, I was troubled. If she regretted what had been between us, it could curdle our whole future. Not knowing what to say, I gazed at the snow and the sun. Tenderness dried my throat, but there was fear, too. I was sore afraid that she was sorry.

"Can—can I help you?" I asked at last.

"I'm just boiling some water."

Still there was neither look nor smile from her. I couldn't stand that. Even a tongue lashing was preferable to not knowing. I went to her, took her by the shoulders gently, turned her to face me.

"Jill, darling, what is it?"

The brown eyes were brimming, but she tried to smile. " 'Tis no blame to you, Cormac. I want you to know that."

"There's no blame at all."

"No? Not for a silly wanton—a—a Jezebel? 'Twas a sin, and I knew it, and—I didn't care! They'd do right to put the red letter of shame on me, for I——"

"My dear, what kind of talk is that for a man to be hearing from his bride?"

"Bride?" Jill's mouth dropped open.

"Aye. I love you, lass. I told you."

"But—we had neither banns nor book nor——"

"Nor anything else on this island. But did you think I'd be leaving you now? That is—well, it's little I have to offer, besides rough sailing weather and——"

"Cormac, Cormac." She was half between laughing and crying. "I love you, too, but——"

"But, what?"

"Oh, we were daft last night!"

"If we were 'tis a grand disease."

"How can you laugh——"

"I am not laughing. I am waiting for an answer."

"An answer? Are—are you asking me to—to marry you?"

"Hell, no!" I said. "For my part we're wedded now. But maybe I'm taking too much for granted. Perhaps it didn't mean to you, what it did to me."

"It meant—it meant so much!"

"All right, then." I held her face between my hands and gazed on it to gather courage. "Jill, I want you for my wife. Sure, we've no chance here for the proper ceremony, but we'll attend to that when we can. Still——"

Ripping my neckband loose, I undid the gold chain. The doubloon glowed in the sunshine, but it was dull compared to the look of Jill. Sure, her heart was in her eyes. No woman had gazed at me like that ever. My knees shook; the fine, brave words I'd planned wouldn't come easily. I forced them out in a stranger's voice, thin and squeaking.

"Then with this—this chain—I—thee wed."

Somehow, with clumsy wooden fingers, I clasped it around her neck. Jill closed her hand over the doubloon.

"And with all your worldly goods you me endow?"

"Faith, and you're holding it!"

"Oh, Cormac!"

Her laughter trembled, but it was happy. She stepped into my arms, and we kissed. For long minutes we held each other tight, not speaking. The sky was very blue above us; her hair mocked the pale snow.

The pannikin boiled over, sputtering into the flames. Jill pushed free, leaped for it, burned her hand. I wanted to help her, but she dodged away laughing.

"No, no. It's nothing. A fine wife you'll be thinking me, that can't even boil water."

"You'll learn, Mistress Doyle."

She was gathering more snow to melt, but she stopped to touch the doubloon. "Aye. I'll learn. I'll have to. My man wants his victuals on time."

Now, why did that simple speech make me want to shout, or jig, or sing? Instead, I sat quiet, watching her bustle at cooking. There was beauty in her every movement. I wasn't surprised at my daring to marry her. The vows I'd taken with Jill that morn were as truly sincere as any ever pledged before a bishop. Sure, in the bright hours of our mating anything seemed possible.

We broke fast with the remnants of our food, finishing every crumb of bread, meat and cheese. Such a meal didn't even compare with our previous supper, but we never noticed. As we ate, we talked. Some of it was lovers' prattle, amusing only to ourselves, but some was serious. It was as good as a feast to hear Jill gravely discussing our problems.

"If we take the lugger down the sound, Cormac, we should make New York town safely."

"It seems best. I've heard of it as a thriving port with busy trade up Hudson's river. A sea-faring man might find employment there. Especially one who has a lugger for hire."

"That wasn't your first plan."

"No. I intended to ship out on any vessel needing a hand. But I've married since, and have obligations."

Jill's smile ebbed before her frown. "Mayhap, that was wiser. Since they've lumped all the colonies, including New York, under Sir Edmund Andros, you may not be safe anywhere in his dominion."

"Why, then, we'll sail farther south. Virginia or Carolina. But we'll try New York at first venture."

"You may be watched for—as a pirate."

"So we must steer carefully."

"I've no wish to be widowed, Cormac."

"Nor I to hang, my own. But among the Dutch I can earn a wage, buy supplies. We can find a preacher to wed us in proper fashion, and you can send posts to your people. You're leaving them, you know."

"I was anyway." She glanced toward her box stowed away under the tent. " 'Tis fortunate I have all my belongings with me as——" Her face changed to sudden dismay. "Oh, my!"

"What's the matter?"

"There's Daniel. I'd forgotten Daniel!"

"Oh, yes. Young Bradish."

"Cormac, what can I tell him? He's waiting, expects me to wed him!"

"Write and explain you've had a better offer." Old Bradish's son would get no tears from me.

"But I was promised. It was all arranged."

"Storms change many courses, Jill. Thanks be to God our paths crossed before you reached this Daniel. Of course he's a reverend, respectable and rich——"

"And you're a wild Papist pirate, and I love you!"

"Sure, I wish you joy explaining *that* to your folk."

"Aye." Jill, biting her lip, slowly nodded. "There's Alec, too."

"I was thinking of Alec. There's naught will make this sugary for your brother. He'd enjoy cutting me up for bait with a dull knife. You're jettisoning a heap of cargo, Jill, to sail with me. Home and friends, fiance, brother, reputation. At best they'll say I took advantage of you."

"Argh! Don't be talking nonsense."

"Alec is bound to think it."

"He'll be far wrong, then," she said, coloring. "I'm thinking I set my cap for you from the start. Aye, though I wouldn't admit it, and fought you at every turn. But last night—I knew! 'Twas the thought we might part on the morrow forever did it."

"We'll not be parting."

[175]

"I did not know that then. My fear was that I would never—never have you. That made me—bold." Her cheeks were fairly crimson, but her eyes were bright. "So, let's have no talk of taking advantage." Jill chuckled, gave a gamin grin. "To tell true, Cormac, you were netted sure as cod or herring."

"Easier," I said, "with no struggle at all. But that will not ease the shock to your family. We must send word, Jill. We cannot just let them worry about you."

"Aye. But we must pick our messenger with care. I will not have Alec storming after us because we sent post from New York. We might get the preacher to write that he married us."

"We will. Once it's done."

"Cormac, about that. You'll not be wanting a priest? I know little of Papistry, but——"

"And where would I be finding a priest in this Puritan stronghold, or even among the Dutch? There's the Frenchies to the north, and a scattering of Spaniards on the Indies isles, but both are far away, and I've no smattering of either language. No, Jill, we'll take the first dominie who asks no questions. In a new settled land we've small choice."

Rising, I scooped more snow into the pannikin to melt and boil. Jill, hugging her knees, watched as I tested the edge of my knife. It was on my mind to shave for my whiskers were as stiff as a boar's bristles, and I must have looked a ruffian. When I mentioned it, she nodded.

" 'Twas a mite prickly at that. But, can you manage? Alec had a very special razor."

"Alec is fortunate."

While I scraped, she didn't speak, but regarded my manipulations with open interest. When I was finished she gave a sigh of relief.

"You might have cut yourself."

"It has happened. It's not mortal."

"Cormac."

"Aye?"

"Are we leaving now?"

"Well." I gazed at the sun, calculated. " 'Tis past noon, and we must load and launch——"

Jill rose, waited until I turned. She said, softly: "Could we not stay one more night? Here, where we're safe and hidden?"

"We've no food, lass."

"We could hunt. There must be some game."

"You wish to stay then?"

"I would like it, if we could."

[176]

"Why, so would I. And we will."

We were suddenly very happy, and active, as boisterous as two truants. We checked the lugger's mooring, gathered more firewood. Then, we hunted, splashing hand in hand through the melting slush. A dozen strides had us soaked to the knees; we loved it. Jill pelted me with a snowball, was chased, caught and paid toll. Betwixt the romping and the kissing we were both rosy and breathless.

By rights our noise should have scared away any animal within earshot. But one plump rabbit hopped out of a thicket to watch. He sat a yard away, long ears and pink nose twitching, a ball of brown fluff against the snow. It seemed a shame to kill such a tame, curious creature, but we needed food. Holding my breath, I was easing back the hammer of my pistol when Jill, the accurate, felled him with a thrown rock.

We took our prize back to camp, skinned and dressed it. Jill prepared some pieces to broil on sticks, made the rest into a stew. We washed with snow, and built the fire high.

Our damp clothes were steaming when Jill, holding her petticoats fanned to the blaze, looked across at me. The flames tinted her skin, glorified her hair, made the dark eyes glow.

Then, as one, we turned and crawled into our canvas hut.

Thus passed the day, and the evening, and the night. We ate when we were hungry, kept the fire bright. This was our honeymoon, though I do not think either of us glanced to see if the moon rose. There was love and laughter, some talk, a new intimacy. Truly we were wedded and welded, husband and wife, with a surer knowledge and a greater happiness.

We fell asleep in each other's arms. Dawn was gray outside, the neglected fire a pile of embers when Jill tweaked my ear to bring me from sleep.

"Cormac."

"I'm awake."

"Lie still. It's nice like this."

"Are you comfortable?"

"Aye. But your arm must be stiff."

"No. You're a perfect fit."

"I've been thinking, dear one. You never did finish telling your story. You know, that time in our kitchen, your childhood in Ireland."

"I remember."

"Well, would you tell me now? I—I would like to know all about my husband."

"If you wish. But there's no moment in it that matches this one."

So, after a while, lying there in the darkness, while the embers faded and the day brightened, I related a few further adventures. Now, I never spoke above a whisper, but remember that I was singing to my love. Most of what I told then, and set down now, was true, but some was changed to please the cherished ears that were listening.

Chapter 21

My name, as will be read on my wedding papers, is truly Cormac O'Shaugnessy Doyle. So I had been baptized, according to the religion of my people, by that same hunted Irish hill priest, Father Murphy, whom I have mentioned. Though in truth I can't say I ever set eyes on the good man before that secret outdoor Mass when I was ten.

Whatever be thought of Papistry, and the term is intended as an insult, that faith, in that land, was as Irish as the lakes. Like our weapons it was forbidden by the Sassenach come-latelies who had conquered us, so like them too it was hidden and kept shining sharp while we waited for the day to bring both into the open.

To us Irish that fine future day is as certain as death. No man can name the month, the year, or even the century, but there is no doubt about its coming. The invader will be driven out, the clans will be clans again, there'll be acres and carriages for all. Oh, the goose will hang high, and a few score English as well!

A dream, mayhap, but one shared by the defeated. And, at the age of ten, I believed every wish and whim of it.

Captain Love Jebson, of Jebson's Court, would have laughed to hear the plotting between his groom and his stable boy. Sure, Mickeen Oge Flynn, for all his age and past soldiering, was as childish in his musings as myself. We weren't daft enough to let the captain catch us whispering, and every secret Mass attended, every bit of church lore learned, was another stone added to the cairn of victory.

Four years passed before I was deemed ready to start receiving the sacraments. During that time my education had progressed in a different field entirely. This, too, like riding his mare, and mocking him, was practiced behind old Jebson's back. And, moreover, it was something hidden from Mickeen Oge and my fellow Irish.

A month or so after that first Mass I was out on the mare, riding down near Ballykillala. My setter, Niamh, was coursing ahead of me, enjoying the grand afternoon by flushing birds as she roamed. Knowing I did no hunting by daylight the bitch was being as foolish as a puppy.

She crested a hill, disappeared. As I cantered up the slope, birds rose, fluttering shapes against the skyline. The blast of a fowling piece rasped through the quiet.

"Niamh!" I yelled, and heeled the horse forward.

We crossed the ridge to find two figures, stiff as neglected statuary, on the other side. Overhead the birds winged away, congratulating each other. Niamh, on her haunches, was gazing sheepishly at a short wisp of a man. He, dwarfed by his gun, regarded the dog with sorry patience.

"You shot," I said, reining in.

"Yes," said the small man, "but too soon because of yon blundering beast." His speech was the thin, clipped, pebbles-in-mouth diction of college-bred English. Brisk, three-second mumbling, for it took one to hear it, one to consider, and one to interpret.

"Sorry she is, Parson Lamb," I said, for I knew him by sight, though we'd traded no sentence. His history was common gossip. After King Charles came back from his travels certain Church of England chapels were restored in Ireland, as scattered as caraway seeds in a loaf. This wee man, Lamb, had the living at Ballykillala.

"You know me, lad."

"Through hearsay, sir."

"You're not of the manor?"

"No. I'm Jebson's boy of all work."

He smiled a bit grimly as I named the captain. 'Twas no news to either of us that Love Jebson's dislike of the Anglican establishment was only a thumb weight less than his hate for Papists.

"You'd best get along then," Parson Lamb said.

"The captain's away. Or I'd not be astride his mare." Saying which, I grinned impudently. Protestant or no, any man that had Love Jebson's enmity was my friend.

His surname, Lamb, suited him for he had a ewe-like pointed face, all eyes and forehead, with a woolly fleece atop his poll, his own, no wig. Hatless, in clerical black that showed the rust of wear, he stood no higher than my stirrup.

"You'll rue it if he hears of it." The parson's mouth twitched as he

[179]

spoke. His hazel eyes misted with kindness and amusement; I liked him from that moment.

Niamh came up, tail wagging, to pay her apologies. Parson Lamb scratched behind her ears, carelessly, knowingly, as one will who has had dogs of his own. While this went on we humans talked, he, as I know now, with a disarming interest that sprang from loneliness.

"You would not be a member of my congregation, young Cormac?"

"I would not."

"Roman, then." He waited, smiled at my innocent blankness, went on in his clipped manner. "No matter. That is closer than some sects. Cousins. Disagreeing as to which branch of the family is the elder, and who is head, but at least on speaking terms."

"Not always," I said.

"True. And a sad admission. But we can be friends, can't we?"

"I don't know, Parson." His gentleness made me bold. Ten is not a discreet age, nor polite. "I've naught against yourself as yourself, but your very presence makes you one of *them* that has stolen our land away."

Parson Lamb winced. He said: "My dear boy. Actually I was born within the pale, though my studies took me to Oxford." He saw that in my ignorance he could have claimed Nineveh and Tyre. "No matter. Will you honor my board for a bite?"

In those days I was always hungry, would have supped with the Devil without the long spoon. We went down to the cottage behind his chapel, where I hid the mare in an empty stable. When I saw the clutter of books and papers that filled his room the food became secondary.

He noticed my interest. "Would you like to borrow one, Cormac?"

"Aye," I said, "but—I couldn't read it."

"Well, now!" Parson Lamb rubbed his hands together. "That can be remedied. I'll teach you!"

"Go on with you, Parson. I've neither time to spare, nor pence to pay. And I'll not be joining your flock either. You'd get naught but trouble with a thick-skulled lout like myself."

"I'd get the pleasure," he said, "of making and helping a friend."

We had our first lesson then and there. And for four years, barring Sundays, I scarce missed a day at the parsonage, including harvest time. Nights when Mickeen Oge thought me out poaching I'd be there, squinting in the candlelight. Whenever Captain Jebson was missing from the court, so was I.

A living saint, Sylvester Lamb, for all he's in the wrong church, and a natural-born teacher. He'd drop his own tasks to help me, rise from bed if I arrived at midnight. As I did often enough for I came there on Shank's mare far more than on the captain's. Parson Lamb, God keep him if he lives, and rest him otherwise, taught me to read, and write, and cipher.

That was my schooling. The arithmetic was hardest for I've a poor head for figures still, in spite of a master who was on writing terms with Isaac Newton. Aye, many of the famous penned notes to my bog-country parson, Dryden and George Fox among others.

Ah, 'twas the books came quickest and easiest. They are the things I've missed most at sea and on my travels. I've scarce had time these past few years to read ship's articles, but in those days every nibble made me ravenous. Sure, for a while I was scowling my way among letters I couldn't yet shape with a quill. In strange snatched minutes, too, for the parson let me borrow as I wished.

Now, unlike certain female scholars with idle hours, I had no time to waste on Latin and Greek. The parson read to me out of *Caesar's Commentaries,* and some *Livy,* and *Cicero's Orations,* translating as he went. But learning one language was trouble enough.

Grand writing was in those books. There were hymnals and sermons aplenty, but these were just to cut teeth on. Of the latter I liked only Donne, and him more for the swing than the sense. But there was *Canterbury Tales,* and *Don Quixote,* and *Plutarch's Lives,* all rendered into decent English. As was the parson's copy of *Annals of the Kingdom of Ireland* by the four masters—the three O'Clerys and Fearfeasa O'Mulcrony.

I read his friend Dryden, of course, and Lovelace, and a thunderous fellow named Milton who found this earth too tame so recorded the warring of angels. Last and best, read and reread till the very pages wore thin, was William Shakespear.

❖

Jill stirred in my arms. "I have heard of him, of course," she said. "But Alec frowns on players' frumpery. Even the Reverend Bradish had no copy."

"You have missed much. There's the whole of living in that man's work."

"But—the theater is the Devil's workshop!"

"Well, I'm not saying you'd not blush at some comedies I've seen in London. But Will Shakespear! Why, when the parson mentioned him, he tipped his hat!"

"Had you no Bible at all?"

"Of course. In the fine, grand language that the first James paid for. Parson Lamb explained it wasn't the Papist version, but it made lovely reading."

"It's a very holy book," said Jill severely, as she settled back. "You should put no book before it."

"It has my entire respect."

"Well. And maybe you can buy me a Shakespear some day. But, go on, Cormac."

So, after a moment's reflection on the ways of women, I went on with my tale.

❖

All four years of my schooling remained a secret between Parson Lamb and myself. Which is remarkable in a country where the best-concealed poteen still collects topers overnight. If ever a boy gloried in deception, in fooling adults, I was that boy! Sure, I showed one face to the Jebson family, another to the tenants, and had a third that only the parson saw.

In the end old Shakespear proved my undoing. Cocksure, I took to carrying the volume about, reading aloud to Niamh whenever we could sneak away. Charity Jebson followed me one day.

She was the captain's eldest, even more vinegary than her mother, and my mortal enemy. She surprised me in a glade beside a stream.

"What's that you have there?" says Charity, her shrill voice could turn cream.

"A book," says I, "and no business of yours."

"A book! Where would *you* get a book? You can't read!"

The temptation to refute her was strong, but I had the good sense to keep quiet. Indeed, I was rising to make a swift retreat when she snatched for the book. Without thought I slapped her hand away.

"You—you dared lay a hand on me!"

"Twice as heavy if you try that again!"

"Wait'll I tell Papa," she says, and runs off shrieking.

I had no doubt that she'd tattle, but I resolved to deny everything. Even Love Jebson wouldn't thrash a day's labor out of a servant on the unsupported word of a known liar such as Charity. But the girl must have spied on my hiding place for the book, because when the captain rode up to the peat field next morning he had it in his hand.

While he dismounted I went on with my turf cutting, though my

[182]

heart was choking me. I had almost reached my full height, but there was little flesh on me, and that work muscle. Jebson's shadow made four of mine.

"You!" he said, in his usual roar. "Where did you get this book?" The veins on his angry red face were like mold on a raspberry.

"It's mine," I said.

"Yours!" The captain opened the volume to read. "Sylvester Lamb, his book! You've been stealing from the pipsqueak parson at Bally-killala. He's a High-Church nincompoop but better than an Irish thief!"

Mickeen Oge had stopped work to stare, *slaun* on shoulder. Niamh, close by, had her tail down before Jebson's wrath. Anger came into me, but I could not inform on Parson Lamb after all his kindness. My retort was foolishly rash.

"Lowest of all steals from the Irish!"

The captain blinked. His great arm could still move with speed. A clout of his fist sent me sprawling.

Sore hurt by the blow, I heard Niamh go for him as I hit the ground. The dog's growl was lost in Jebson's bellowed oath. Both brought me upright in time to see the captain meet her rush with a mighty kick that sent Niamh, twisting and whimpering, through the air.

With that the world turned to a swimming blur of rage, glaring white with red edges like a bar fresh from the forge. My *slaun,* the spade-length turf cutter, was still in my clutch. I came to my feet swinging.

The tool made a grand sound as it swished through its arc, a bugle call to battle! It caught Love Jebson right below the ear. If the wing blade had been turned in, I'd have taken his head off!

As it was he fell like an undermined tower. David, in your Bible, stood over Goliath with less satisfaction.

"Holy Mother of God!" said Mickeen Oge. "What have you done, Cormac?"

Staring down at Jebson's still bulk, I trembled at the enormity of my deed. "Is he dead then?" I asked.

At that the captain twitched.

"He is not," said Mickeen Oge. Then he neatly booted the man in the head.

"Mickeen——"

"Sure, when will I get another such chance? You'd best be gone and away before he's roused anyhow. Take the mare. Hide out till I can reach Father Murphy."

"Niamh?" I asked, for the bitch was bad crippled.

"I'll care for Niamh. Mount and ride."

[183]

"I'll take this back to Parson Lamb," I said, picking the Shakespear volume from the dirt. "He lent me it, and taught me to read it, too. He'll know where I'm hiding."

"Can you trust the wee Englishman, lad?"

"Aye."

Mickeen Oge asked no more questions. He motioned me to hasten, and went to tend Niamh.

The mare carried me almost to Ballykillala at a gallop. Then I turned her loose, not wishing to involve the pastor in horse thievery. Though, when I reached the parsonage, he listened to my recital as if it were an everyday occurrence.

"I'm sorry about the crumpled pages," I said, "but he dropped it when the dog charged."

"No matter," said Parson Lamb. "It's under the eaves for you, young Cormac. There's a cubbyhole that could hide two your size."

"No, I'll bring no trouble on you, sir."

"Then do as I ask. Captain Jebson will hunt high and low. You're safest here till we can sneak you away." His smile was as patient as ever. "I'll miss our lessons, Cormac. Give me a last few days."

So I hid in his attic cubbyhole for a week before Mickeen Oge found a chance to bring news. The captain swore to have my pelt, and had horsemen scouring the countryside. Niamh was hardly limping; the mare had been found.

"A certain person," said Mickeen Oge, "has heard and is coming. But he has to be careful with riders all about." He did not look at the parson, and that small man asked no questions.

Two nights later Father Murphy slipped into the house. To my delight both clergymen shook hands without hesitation.

"Good evening, Father," said Parson Lamb.

"God bless all here," the priest said. "You're risking a lot to do this. Cormac, Cormac, did the teachings of both of us go for naught that you had to strike that blow?"

"He was provoked, Father."

Father Murphy's lean, tired face split with a grin. "He must have been. I'm told Jebson's jaw is swollen to thrice its size."

They stood there, the dusty, threadbare priest, and the smaller, neat parson, sharing a moment like old friends. Both sobered as they turned toward me.

"We'll have to get him out of Ireland," Father Murphy said.

"With the alarm out, Father?"

"There are ways, Parson Lamb."

"Yes. You would know better about that."

"But—where would I go?" I asked.

"Kinsale first. Then to England by ship." The priest smiled at the parson. "You didn't hear that, my friend?"

"Nary a word, Father."

So they planned and decided between them. Parson Lamb gave me a purse, and my first shoes, second hand to be sure, but a decent fit. Shod, and rich, I felt equal to any new venture. My eagerness to get started even hastened my farewells to Parson Lamb.

The priest took me on the first long stretch of my journey, his horse carrying double. Father Murphy knew every twist and turn of the countryside. Once we hid in a copse to let a file of horsemen pass down the road, but we met no one else. By dawn we were well away.

He left me, in a high hill cottage, with a blessing and a warning.

"God keep you, Cormac. Stay out of trouble."

Then I was passed down to Kinsale, hand to hand so to speak, without incident. Sure, it was little I saw of my native land, since we travelled always by night, and slept hidden by day. My hosts and guides were grave men not given to talk; they hurried me along. I was expected and transported, not the first to go by this route, nor the last.

Nobody would accept a coin as payment, not even the fisherman who took me from Kinsale. He could have robbed me easily for I was sick blind from the tossing, tumbling in the scuppers and vowing the voyage would be my last. We were in the Thames itself before my stomach settled.

London's size scared me. I wasn't there over an hour before my pocket was picked. With the parson's purse gone I was forced to seek work. What I found was neither honorable, nor profitable. Oh, there was high living at Whitehall where old Rowley lost count of his mistresses, but in Newgate it was steal or starve.

We can pass over the next few years quickly. I learned the tricks of some trades not well regarded. The best was with horses, acting as hostler to a squadron of highwaymen, riding with messages about wealthy travelers. Finally, because I could read and write, I managed to get employment as a printer's assistant. Honest work!

I didn't have it a week before a ship's mate found himself short of a crew, and came looking for hands. I was having a quiet supper in a tavern when——"

❖

"Ahoy, the lugger!"

[185]

The hail came faint and clear. A shiver shot down my spine. Jill's hand closed on my arm; she caught her breath.

"By the beads of Saint Pachome," I said, "what's that?"

"Didn't you hear——?"

"Aye."

We scrambled for clothes and pistols. Jill's voice was a trembling whisper.

"Cormac, be careful. If they've seen the lugger——"

"That they have. You stay back. I'll do the scout."

"Hurry. They haven't hailed again."

"I know." Pausing only to check my priming, I blundered out into the morning.

The fire, thank God, had died to ashes. It was throwing no smoke that would mark our position. The sun was up, but there was mist still clinging to the ground. Whoever had hailed our ship must be off shore, coming in from the sea. Would they prove friend or foe?

Scrambling to the top of the sand dune, I lay flat, scanned the beach, the restless water.

In the middle of the cove was a longboat. The oars bit white spume as they drove it toward shore. I counted four rowers, and a steersman. As they drew closer he looked the hardest of a hard lot.

They pulled alongside the lugger's stern, and one boarded her. The others stared toward shore, the burly steersman shading his eyes with a hand. He had a musket slung across his back.

Jill, breathing hard, plumped herself beside me.

"Cormac, who are they?"

"I don't know. Sailors by the look of them. But armed to the teeth." The boarder was leaning over the lugger's gunwale, talking. I could see the naked cutlass in his hand. Other weapons glinted in the longboat.

They didn't hail again. That, and the way they acted, plus the weapons, gave me a fair idea of their occupation. They kept their voices low, and moved with stealth.

Another boarder joined the first. They passed a line to the longboat. A cutlass flashed as it cut our mooring rope. The pair aboard the lugger jumped from bow to beach. They shoved on the prow while the oarsmen in the longboat rowed in unison. It was done fast, and efficiently. Even the steersman left his rudder for an added pull at the oars.

"Cormac, what are they doing?"

"That I do know, Jill. They're stealing the lugger!"

Chapter 22

As we lay prone on the dune and watched the lugger slowly being towed away, my feeling was helpless rage. The circumstances made action impossible.

We were too far from the thieves to shoot from cover; at that range the pistols were barkers without bite. They were five to our two, and one of us was a girl. If we showed ourselves the result was inevitable. Against their muskets and numbers we'd be either slain or taken. I could not risk that happening to Jill. Afloat and ashore I had seen enough seafaring men like these to know them for pirates, or little better. Their manner proved it. One of the two who landed, a swarthy Spanish type with earrings, had unslung his musket to guard their deed, but they had made no search for the lugger's people like honest seamen would. Nor, after that first hail, had they raised their voices. They stole our ship as quietly as possible.

"Cormac," Jill said, beating her fist on the sand, "we must do something!"

"What?"

"Stop them somehow."

The cove was as calm as the water in a basin. Spray from the longboat's oars made glittering droplets in the morning sunlight. Both craft moved as smoothly as drifting toys; the lugger was no burden, it bobbed along like a cork on a fishing line.

"There's nothing to do, Jill," I tried to sound calm, though curses were bubbling inside me, and put my hand on hers, "except be thankful they didn't discover us."

In silence we watched the longboat swing around the cove's headland. A moment later the lugger, too, was hidden. The cove, smiling blue, looked very bare and empty. Jill's fingers squeezed mine.

"At least we know which direction they took, Jill."

"Does that matter?"

"They never came out here in that longboat. They've a vessel anchored somewhere."

"Maybe not," Jill said, frowning. "They could be friends of Master Gardiner's. 'Tis rumored he has some queer ones—smugglers, pirates——" Her eyes widened.

"Aye," I said, nodding, "they could be. But we must find their anchorage and steal the lugger back."

She smiled, swung my hand. "Well, let's get started. There's still rabbit enough for breakfast. You light the fire and——"

"We'll eat it cold with such neighbors close. They may come looking for us, too." I didn't think they would, unless rum heated their curiosity, or they needed hands. They'd gained a lugger without trouble; pirates never worked when there was no need, and fighting was work.

After we finished the cold meal we broke camp. We trudged through the slush with the sun at our backs, veering south. This was a chill November day, but windless. Snow clung in patches where the sun didn't reach, for the rest it had turned to a sort of pasty gruel. Once we entered the woods that had been our windbreak it was colder.

We marched in silence, single file, Jill following in my tracks. Partly this was due to the strange quiet, broken only by the crunch of our steps, the drip of melting snow, an occasional soft plop as a chunk of ice dropped, thawed loose from a tree. For the rest we went cautiously because we didn't wish to blunder into strangers.

After we had gone about a mile, due south, I was startled to find the blue of the sea glinting through the trees ahead. I stopped, and Jill came up beside me. We put our bundles down, looked at each other.

"We must be on a neck of land," I said. "The shaft of the harpoon blade that jutted into the ocean."

Jill bit her lip, thinking. "I've sailed around the island with Alec, but never landed. Gardiner's house is at the other end but if I recall aright there's more than one cove. Some are large."

"Leave the bundles while we explore."

Even before we reached the edge of the trees my nostrils sniffed at an old familiar smell. I caught Jill's arm, drew my pistol.

"What is it?" she asked, whispering.

"Take a breath. Sulphur and hot tallow. I think we've found the longboat's vessel."

She gave a puzzled toss of her head, but checked her own pistol. We pushed forward carefully toward the bright, beckoning blue of the sunlit water. A snatch of song drifted to us, tunelessly bellowed by several voices. That, too, was familiar.

> So go, all you crawling lubbers, beg!
> For me it's gold chain or wooden leg!
> Yo, ho!—heave, ho!

"Aye," I said, grimly, "as I thought, Jill. That's a stave from a pirate chantey. 'Tis not likely honest seamen are singing it."

"Nor that they'd steal a lugger!"

We parted bushes to gaze out over a splendid little bay, a snug harbor, many times larger than our cove. It lay, almost landlocked, in a perfect triangle, with its apex to the north. We had emerged near that angle, and farther down the same leg, was a sight that brought a gasp from Jill.

It was a scene of much disorder and activity. The center of it all was a sloop, about fifty tons, that was being careened!

The ship lay on its side, properly affixed by blocks and tackles to trees ashore. Men in boats were working on her bottom, scraping, calking, daubing on sulphur and tallow.

There was the longboat, and a dinghy. And there, in use under the stern, was our lugger!

"Cormac."

"I see it. They've found it handy."

They had taken the topmasts out of the sloop, and everything else movable. That was the only way to careen, of course, but this crew was sloppy. The beach was a welter of stores and goods, chests and sea bags, puncheons, casks, kegs, canvas, rigging, tools and weapons. Everything was piled helter-skelter; only three mounds were protected from the elements with tarpaulins. From the shapes these were the cannon and gunpowder. Overhead, attracted by refuse, gulls wheeled and called.

Atop a roaring bonfire a vat of tallow was smoking and bubbling, stirred by a wizened old sailor in a yellow yarn cap. Other fires held cook pots, and other men attended them. They had made a few crude shelters for sleeping, but these were deserted. For all I had seen neater crews everybody seemed to be busied at some task.

"Jill," I said, beginning my own tally, "count them."

As I counted, I recognized the longboat's burly helmsman, the earringed Spaniard, their fellow oarsmen. The helmsman, wide and squat, called orders from shore to boat. I placed him as quartermaster. Twice he conferred with a lanky, hook-nosed man in a bottle-green suit who could have been the captain.

"I make it twenty-two," Jill said.

"So do I. Twenty-two rascals."

"Why are they cleaning the ship here?"

"I don't know. This is an unseasonable time and place. They're too far north, but they've found a snug berth." I touched her cheek, kissed it. "Stay here. Keep your pistol dry."

"Cormac, where are you going?"

"Don't worry. I'll be careful. I want a closer look." Actually, I had a plan, but wasn't sure it was practical. Snaking on my belly, I crawled along the ridge above the beach, finding what cover I could. The men in the boats I dismissed; they were busy and I'd notice if a boat moved. Those ashore won my full attention. I tried to be sure where each was every time I moved.

The trickiest stretch was the last one, when I'd left the shelter of the bushes. Any sailor going to relieve himself might stumble over me. But it had to be risked; the fools had stationed no sentries.

Inch by inch I wormed my way down the slope, darted the last yard, ducked behind a pile of sea bags. There was no outcry.

Somebody began a bawdy ditty, an unprintable, repetitive recital of Jack Tar's exploits in waterfront brothels. Soon the whole crew was roaring verse and chorus, about as musically as the gulls. The words must have singed Jill's ears, but the noise was welcome to mine. In such a din, with all hands piping their ribald best, a horse could have galloped unnoticed through their camp.

My search was fast, but thorough. I slipped from stack to pile, keeping them always betwixt me and the sailors. Rifling bags and chests was a matter of delicate choice. I took sparingly, here a little, there a little, careful to select nothing that the owner might prize. I could not get near the food supply. From what I could smell through the odor of tallow, they were boiling salt pork for dinner.

In one hut I found the log and the flag. The sloop's name was the *Quarand,* which I knew for an Indies fish. There were few entries in the log, no prizes listed. Which supported the evidence of my search. This ship's company had found piracy poorer fare than honest work! There wasn't a heavy purse fore or aft.

The flag was a gaudy rag, blood red with a crude, full-length skeleton painted on in whitewash. Old Bones held a cutlass in one hand, a torch in the other, and danced above a lettered slogan—*Deth To All Dastards*.

Sea-faring men have a proverb: *the fancier the flag, the sorrier the belly timber*. I didn't doubt there was rough duff and short rations aboard the *Quarand*.

Having learned all I could, I made a package of my loot, and crawled away. Bucket men were getting fresh tallow at the vat, and no one noticed me.

Jill was waiting where I'd left her. She'd had sense enough to hide her hair under her cloak hood, and was curled up, tight and tense, legs tucked under her, eyes as big as peach stones. She watched me coming, called a whisper that shook with reproach and relief.

"You took so long!"

"It just seemed long," I said, which was true. Few there were who could manage faster pilfering. But then, I'd been busy and Jill hadn't. Smiling, I tossed the things I'd gathered into her lap. "These made it worth the trouble."

"What's all this?" She pulled the bundle apart. "Clothes?"

"Aye. For you."

"For me? Breeches? A shirt, and——?"

"Jill, girl, for safety's sake you must become a young man for a change." Looking at her, even as I made the statement, it seemed a daft and impossible scheme.

❖

The *Quarand's* careen, I judged, was already half completed; the crew was working on the second side. That meant if we were going to act at all we would have to act fast. Once the work was finished the sloop's company would waste no time putting to sea. No pirate crew, however careless, liked to prolong a careen; a ship on its side was helpless. They might take the lugger with them, scuttle her, use her planks for firewood. In that case Jill and I were marooned on the island, forced to hunt out the unknown Gardiner, or wait to hail a passing ship. In either case, with winter's vanguard already making forays along the coast, our stay would be long, my capture most probable.

My scheme was based on the fact that Jill should not appear, but if it went awry, or if she were discovered, it was safer to have her clad as a youth than a girl. Anyway, breeches would give her much more freedom of movement than skirt and petticoats. Our flight, if flee we must, would be desperate; our lives might depend on our fleetness of foot.

"Cormac, you mean to go down and beard them alone?"

"I have sailed under a pirate flag. I know the countersigns among the brethren of the coast. There will be no danger." That was not strictly true, but fortune could make it so.

"Why not just steal the lugger while they sleep?"

"They'll not all sleep at the same time. The minute I saw this bay I knew stealing was well-nigh impossible. We could not take the lugger without making noise. Before we could get the sail aboard and up, they'd be upon us. Even with oars the dinghy or the longboat would catch us."

She gave in at last, reluctant but convinced. We repaired to the place where we'd left our belongings, and spent hours on our preparations. I turned my back while Jill changed clothes.

"All right," she said at last, teeth chattering with chill, but as pleased as a child dressed up in adult garments, "you can look now."

She stood, posed and preening, with knuckles on hips and legs spread in what she thought a boy's stance. Her smile was anxious; her eyes danced. She greeted my stare with a cocky jerk of her head.

I was torn between laughter and tears, despair and affection. She looked ridiculously adorable, completely outlandish, and completely feminine. Venus rising naked from the sea, as I have heard she does in some painting, was probably more like a male!

"Well?" asked Jill.

Sitting down on a tree root, I put my head in my hands and groaned.

"What's the matter?" There was an edge in the question. When I glanced up I could see anger beacons spotting her cheeks.

"Now, wait," I said, fearing a tantrum, "wait. Don't go exploding like a grenade! You're still a lovely girl, that's all. You wouldn't fool a blind man."

"Why, you—if I'm a butt for——" She flared into rage, her voice rising as she sought words. Her fingers flashed to the neck of the shirt. I leaped to grab them before she ripped.

"Hold on," I said, as she struggled, "nobody's laughing at you. It just calls for a bit of fixing." Scowling like a crossed infant, she averted her face, but I waited until she glared at me. "You've a woman's figure, praise the Lord, and in places it takes more craft to hide it."

Then, holding her at arm's length, I slowly scanned her from toes to hair. She was blushing furiously by the time my gaze reached her face.

"You—you know me too well," Jill said, pouting.

"A husband's privilege."

"Well—what's wrong?"

Finding flaws was easy; the clothes, picked haphazardly, were a gypsy collection. Besides shirt and breeches—coarse cloth, clean, shore-going best but of no recognizable weave—I'd snatched a big kerchief and a wide leather belt with a brass buckle. The shirt, belted tight, was too snug across Jill's bosom.

We loosened it by slitting a seam. Jill fetched a sewing kit from her chest, and we contrived a makeshift jacket from her cloak, ripping off skirt and hood. Even without sleeves it made a warm, bulky tunic, shapeless on any figure. The tailoring was crude, but seamen often wore odd garments in freezing weather.

Jill kept her own knit stockings and unadorned, sturdy shoes. They could easily pass for a man's footgear. She sewed an unnecessary blue patch on the right knee of the black breeches to fool the owner should he see them. They were too big for Jill, but that was all to the good.

The hardest part was cutting her hair. Jill didn't care, but I felt like a murderer.

"What are you waiting for?" asked Jill, twisting to see why I hesitated.

"I'd sooner cut off my thumb!"

She laughed at my anguish. "Fool! It'll grow again."

So I hacked it as short as a man's, and hid the shorn locks in her chest like hoarded gold. We used the kerchief, a faded tan, to cover that striking glory. With my hat pulled low on her forehead she could have been bald.

I added certain refinements culled from the beggars of London. From a remnant of her cloak, I fashioned a black eye patch for her left eye. Jill dirtied her face and let the mud dry on it. Her only objection was to holding a pistol ball in her cheek.

She mumbled at me, spat it out. "How can I talk with that thing in my mouth?"

"You can't. You're my weak-witted cousin Murdock, and you garble your talk. It changes both face and speech, Jill."

"I do wish we had a mirror."

"I wish nobody else sees you. But if they do don't forget to pop that bullet in your mouth."

To me she still looked like a girl, my wife, herself. But we'd done the best we could. Her walk, at least, was no giveaway, she even managed a swagger. An uncritical viewer might think her an ill-kempt, ragamuffin youth, though I still hoped to avoid that test.

We went back to the careen in time to see the *Quarand* righted. Ropes squealed through their blocks, men shouted and heaved; the sloop heeled over, rocked, finally floated free. The crew dropped her anchor, but made no move to load her. She was a good-looking vessel even stripped. The pirates had cut her cabins out, and raised the bulwarks for better concealment, a customary procedure, but they hadn't spoiled her lines.

The whole crew came ashore, and began dipping out their meal. They beached the lugger, with longboat and dinghy, right in the middle of their sprawling camp. Even Jill realized we couldn't reach it without discovery.

"I might as well go now," I said.

"Oh, Cormac." She hugged me tight, kissed me. Sure, it was the first time I'd ever kissed anybody wearing an eye patch, but pleasant.

"You wait here with pistol ready. If I have to run I'll head this way. Take a shot at any pursuers."

"Suppose they seize you——"

"Suppose they don't. Now, mind. You're not to show yourself until I come for you. Promise?"

"But if you're bound——"

"I'll not be. Promise!"

"All right," Jill said, unwillingly, "I promise."

I left her more jauntily than my true feelings warranted. I was fairly sure the pirates would accept me as a fellow, once I had a chance to talk. The squall would come when I bargained for the return of the lugger. That would have to be met as it happened.

There was no point in concealment so I strode down from the ridge as if I owned the beach. Most of the *Quarand's* crew was too busy wolfing food to notice my approach. I reached old Yellow Cap, the tallow-vat tender, without attracting attention.

He had taken the big kettle from the fire, and was trying to tug it away from the blaze to cool. The task was too much for his ancient muscles. He called to the others with quavering annoyance.

"Say there! Somebody come give me a hand."

"That I will, Gaffer," I said. I took a grip and pulled the vat a foot.

"Thank ye," said the old pirate. Then his mouth gaped open to show his toothless gums. He spluttered. "Why—why—why! Who in blazes be you? Where'd you come from?"

"From the sea," I said.

His wizened face worked as he squinted at me. He backed away and started shouting.

"Cap'n! Turk! Isaac! Boarders, here! All hands to repel boarders!" He fumbled at the hilt of his cutlass.

"Stow that," I said, "there's only one of me." I gave him a friendly smile, and held out my hand. "Sure, I'm in the brotherhood myself. Take me to your captain."

The crew, thoroughly alarmed, was stirring like a hornet's nest. Men were leaping to their feet, bared steel flashed. The burly quartermaster bellowed and reached for a musket. I went toward them boldly, swinging my arms to show that my hands were empty.

"Avast," I called. "No need for gentlemen on the account to pipe a friend aboard with musketry."

In a moment they were all clustered around me, muttering and hostile but checked by my coolness. The quartermaster shoved his way through the circle. He was even uglier at close range, built like a capstan with his arms for bars. His nose was so broken it spread across most of his wide face.

"Friend!" he said, glowering up at me, a bull ready to charge. "Who says you're a friend?"

"Chips saw him first," a voice cried.

"No blame in that," said old Yellow Cap. "Walked up to me he did. Bold as brass."

"Correct," I said. "Walked right up and asked to see your captain. Same as I would in Papaya Tina's just off the square in Coxen's Hole."

Some of the younger pirates looked blank, but grins appeared on leathery, older faces. The bull of a quartermaster blinked in surprise. Chips cackled with tittered laughter.

"B'God and Davvy Jones!" he said. "If he knows Tina's he's one of us right enough, Turk!"

"Or he's heard tales of Cuba," said Turk. But he turned his big head, searching. The group parted to reveal the lanky man in the bottle-green suit.

Beside his beak of a nose he had tiny, button eyes, and a pursed dab of a mouth. There was an air of clerk or bookkeeper about him. When he spoke his voice was deep, slow and hesitant.

"I'm captain here, duly elected according to—ah—rules. Name of Logan Root."

"Doyle," I said, knuckling my forehead. That was all the name I gave. It produced no excitement. They had evidently touched no port where I was wanted.

"You've sailed—ah—on the account?"

"Aye."

"With whom?"

"Hollister, for one. And Bon-bon LaFleche. And one voyage with Johnny Barney." They were all captains I'd met in the Indies, though I'd sailed with none, and the Frenchman was dead. It was a good list, and I gave it glibly. "Three years under black flags, and huzzah for Jolly Roger."

Turk, scowling, said, "I sailed with LaFleche."

"Not in my time," I said, smiling. Then, I mimicked the tone and expletive that had given LaFleche his nickname. "Bon-bon. Bon-bon. A canny fighter, but given to carrying too much canvas in a storm."

"Aye," said Chips, "b'God and Davvy Jones, he did! Cost him ship

[195]

and life, that trick." The old man put up his cutlass, and gave me a friendly nudge. "I sailed with Morgan meself." He looked old enough for the brag to be true.

"Like this cock did with others," said Turk, jeering.

"Did too!" Chips squealed.

"Now—ah—belay!" The captain motioned for quiet, turned back to me. "What—ah—are you doing here, Doyle?"

"Well," I said, "if you mean in these waters I was about to ask the same question. It's daft to outstay the season. There's a king's frigate in Boston harbor, and your careen is under its nose."

"Jest what I said," said Chips. "Me very words!"

A couple of heads nodded. Captain Root sniffed. Big Turk swore a stream of round oaths.

"No—ah—choice," said Logan Root. "We took this sloop off Sea Island two months back. Since then we've had no chance to careen. Our last chase took us this far north. We lost it because our bottom was like a dragging anchor."

"It was," agreed Chips, "a stinking, crawling coral bed!"

"He ain't answered," Turk said, nodding at me. "What's he doing here and now?"

"Oh, I've just come for my lugger."

Heads turned toward where the boats were beached. Captain Root stroked his hooked nose. Turk gave me a wicked, triumphant grin.

"I figured so," he said. "Finders' keepers."

"You were welcome," I said, shrugging. "Shares among brothers. But you won't need it now, and I do."

Logan Root shook his head. "We can use another hand, Doyle. You can sign on—ah—for the usual full share. But we'll not leave you behind."

"No," said Turk.

"I won't peach," I said, "but I've a nice bit of smuggling arranged out of Newport. That's the reason for the lugger. If I go with you——"

"You go," Turk said. He crouched, stepped closer, musket level. "And not as a hand either. In irons, you go. You're worth twenty pounds, and it's been a slack voyage."

The others murmured, stared at him. Logan Root pinched the tip of his nose. Old Chips scratched his head. They all seemed as puzzled as I was.

"Twenty pounds," repeated Turk. "You see, we spoke the *Unicorn* a while back. Dandy Jeffcoat's ship. Real riled, Dandy was. Seems two scuts had robbed their shipmates. Which low trick is death."

"Who's Dandy Jeffcoat?" I asked, while my stomach turned ice cold. Of all ships at sea, honest and pirate, this crew had to speak the *Unicorn!* The Swede and I had left her without fond farewells. I'd get short shrift from Captain Dandy.

"I'm thinking you know," Turk said, watching me. "I'm thinking it's under him you sailed. I'm thinking your true name is Irish Jack. That you and a big hulk of a Swede broke your articles and robbed your shipmates blind."

"You're thinking wrong then."

"We'll see. The *Unicorn* was making for Jamaica. Dandy will fork over twenty pounds for your carcass, right as right. He was that eager to get his meat hooks into you."

So there it was. My luck had twisted under my hand. Instead of a safeguard my pirate lore had proved a deadly coil. And Jill was watching from the ridge. Turk was quartermaster, in all but sailing and fighting the ship, the captain's equal. I'd stepped into an adders' nest for fair!

Chapter 23

"LIAR!"

As I said the word, I threw a punch. Foolhardy courage was my only chance. Turk wouldn't listen to my reasons; the others might if he were silenced.

It was a good blow, swiftly delivered with all my strength. My fist cracked solidly on his jaw; the jar shivered up my arm.

I might as well have hit the cliffs of Dover. Turk didn't even sway. He growled, dropped the musket, reached for me. Even as I dodged I changed tactics. A fist fight with Turk would be disastrous; from the sting of my fist I'd already sprung a knuckle, a melee would leave me with few bones whole.

"Fo'c's'le rules," I cried. "I'm a thief or he's a liar! Word against word! No man *here's* been robbed. I claim settlement according to the custom of the brotherhood."

"You—ah-ain't signed with this crew," Logan Root said.

"Quartermaster makes the rules," Turk said. He was angry, darkly scowling.

"Oh, no," I said. "Not if the crew thinks different. That's been true since Morgan's day. Isn't that right, Chips?"

"Aye," said Chips, flattered. "Ship's quarrel, shore duel. Morgan knew the rules, he did."

"Blast Morgan!" said Turk, "and you, too!"

"Morgan at least was no coward," I said. "I claim the crew decides— jury wise. Quartermasters have been deposed before because they lacked the belly for battle!"

Turk called me an obscene name. I almost laughed in relief. He knew I'd touched a raw spot. No pirate quartermaster could handle a crew that thought him a weakling. Besides, a duel always was entertainment. And these men had been working hard, careening, for days. They were ripe for any amusement.

"Now-ah-wait," said the captain. "If Turk's right you're a hostage. Dead you're not worth a penny. You won't keep till we sight Jamaica."

Turk nodded. "Which is why I ain't gutted him already."

"Mayhap you're just craven." I turned to the men, grinning. "Twenty lousy pounds. Between a company of twenty-two. Two shares for Captain Root, two for this Barbary ape, one share per man. Why, for less than a pound you'll see a bonny fight!"

Chips cackled. "B'God and Davvy Jones! It makes me young to hear you. When Morgan——"

"Chips," said the earringed Spaniard, "shut up. *Si*. But it is true I have bet more at the cockpit."

"Better than that," I said, my glance flicking across the line of faces. "Better than that. If I'm not the man this walking cesspool claims, you'll never see twenty pounds at all. But you don't even risk *that*."

Most of the crew were listening intently. One licked his lips; two others traded winks; there was here a nudge, there a nod. Like all pirates these were simple men, given to crude sports, not averse to blood spilled in horseplay. It was easy to judge that Turk had his enemies. I held their interest; my voice and mind raced in desperate tandem.

"Sure, how can you lose if I sail with you? Aye, for a common one share, signed on the articles. To Jamaica, Barbadoes, Roadtown, wherever! You can all help me empty a bowl of bumboo with this captain of the *Unicorn*. And hear him laugh that this fool mistook me for his missing shipmate!"

The crowd gave voice, broke into murmurs that were almost a spontaneous cheer. Their oaths sealed their approval. Chips cavorted in a spavined jig step; the Spaniard flipped his pistol in his hand, stuck it in his belt. Captain Root looked at them, removed himself from the dispute with a shrug.

Turk, cursing me, surrendered. He said: "You'll not sail anywhere. Not while my name's Turk Farris! Your head will go in the hold, pickled in brine like pork."

"Now-ah-that might serve," said the captain, brightening. He regarded me like a fussy butcher. "Though I imagine-ah-that Jeffcoat wants him alive."

The quiet tone, the calm speculation, gave me the first inkling why Logan Root was captain. He was no blustering bravo like Jeffcoat, who would relish having me flayed, but a practical, hard-headed pirate. Root thought in terms of pounds, shillings, pence; he would cut a throat only for profit.

"I've my own pistol," I said, "but I'll have to ask loan of a cutlass."

A dozen were instantly offered. Chips brandished the brass hilt of his under my chin.

"Take mine," he whispered. "Morgan hisself gave it to me!"

Ignoring the lie, for the blade was new, I took a few practice swings to test the balance. It was a fine cutlass, bright and keen edged. I did not intend to use it. Against Turk's massive strength, for his muscles bulged his shirt, my chances of survival, if it came to swordplay, were poor indeed.

The crew's remarks, as they scattered to give us room, bore this out. The men were excited, boisterous, shouting wagers to one another.

"My share in the next prize on Turk!"

"What odds on the stranger?"

"Even at the pistols. One gets you three if they go at it with a cutlass."

"Si!" said the Spaniard, "I wager my dagger—the ivory-hilted one—that the Turk chop him down in five minute. Chopped like the red pepper for *chili!*"

"Taken," I called. "My pistol is yours if I lose." That was sheer bravado, done for effect. Inwardly, I was quaking, horrified by the coming combat. I wondered if Jill, watching, understood what was planned.

The wager was cheered. With a bow the Spaniard tossed me a salute. Captain Root eyed me with the detached amusement of a bystander watching a reckless gambler. He was canny enough to realize that my life was the important stake.

Since Turk was a combatant, old Chips appointed himself temporary quartermaster in charge of the affair. He stuck his cutlass in the sand, marched twenty paces, and marked Turk's position with another cutlass.

The procedure was familiar, followed the usual pirate custom. Both opponents stood, backs turned, whirled and fired at command. Unless the shots killed, they snatched up the swords and fell to. Such duels were always to the death.

Daylight was almost gone, but the campfires made the beach bright enough. I didn't care for the flickering, shadow-tossed illumination provided by the flames. It made marksmanship chancy, and I could not afford to miss.

"Take your places," shrilled Chips.

Only a few steps separated me from the upright cutlass, but it was the loneliest walk of my life. Jill was too much on my mind. Her fate, like the pistol, hung heavily from my sweating fingers. What would she do if I fell? I tried to shake the thought away. Worry over a loved one never yet added to a duellist's calm.

Quiet now gripped the *Quarand's* company. The pirates waited, breathlessly still, for the fray. In the stillness the crackling of the firewood seemed loud; the crunch of my feet on the damp sand was slower than the pounding of my heart. For a moment I was tempted to run for it.

Then, I reached the cutlass. Steadily, I gazed down the strip of beach at Turk. He stood, broad as a tree stump, glaring back. The firelight turned his eyes to yellow disks.

"Back to back," said Chips.

I wiped my hand on my shirt, took a fresh grip on the pistol, cocked it carefully, and turned. A sigh like a freshening breeze stirred from the crowd.

Chips, enjoying himself, decided to make a speech.

"You both knows how this goes, according to rules and regulations. I'm the one giving the order, and the word I'll say is 'fire.' Jest that, nothing else. You turns and shoots straight off, neither holding back. And—and may God have mercy on your souls!"

Been before a judge in his day, I thought, has old Chips, and never got over it. My stare was toward the ridge where the shadows were thickening. The wood was a dark clump, and somewhere in its blackness Jill waited. Stay there, I urged silently, praying. Stay there whatever happens!

"Ready?"

"Aye," Turk said, and spat.

Digging my heel in the sand to pivot, I raised the pistol. Sure, it took doing, but my voice was steady.

"Aye."

One second passed, two, three. Chips was wringing every vestige of power from his office. I drew a breath, held it. God, I thought, be with my aim. Keep Jill safe if——

"*Fire!*"

Spinning, I snapped my wrist to center the pistol on Turk's chest. We fired together. I saw the flash of his gun as my own bucked in my palm. My pistol, Jockey's, kicked high. I cursed it as Turk's ball whined past.

Turk jerked as if shoved. His feet shifted, he bellowed, flung down his gun, grabbed up the cutlass. The wide, curved blade caught fire-light as it swung through an arc. Then, with a roar Turk charged.

As he came, surprisingly light on his feet for his build, my heart dropped. For I hadn't missed. I could see the stain on his left shoulder, the spreading dark flow. But it hadn't stopped him; it had been no more deadly than a bee sting.

The pirates shouted as Turk bounded across the distance that sepa-rated us. Stunned by failure, I barely heard their noise. Sand spurting with each leap the burly man came fast. His face, crimson with fury, grew larger. Now, I would have to fight for my life.

He was almost on me when I moved. I still held the pistol, and I hurled it like a hatchet. The butt, whirling through the air, caught him on the cheek. It broke his stride, slowed his rush.

Moving with all my speed, I swept the cutlass up, thrust forward in a jumping lunge! I drove the point toward his middle.

Turk parried with a force that almost upset me. As I staggered he slashed wildly at my head. Only his rage saved me. The blades crashed and clashed, scattering sparks. Each mighty cut nearly ripped the hilt from my grasp.

God, he was strong! There was a roaring in my ears very like surf, but my whole body concentrated in avoiding the sweep of Turk's cutlass. He hacked, backhand, front, sideways, driving me before him as a thresher might flail wheat. All I could do was defend, and the fear of death was strong upon me.

I did not count the blows. I only know that the clangor seemed end-less, that my sword arm shivered under the constant shocks.

There was no time for fancy fencing; we were too close for a decent thrust. Turk kept on top of me, driving forward, trying to split my skull.

At the first pause, I smote back. It was a cut aimed to kill, swung with reckless desperation. I had to do something!

The blades met almost hilt to hilt. Turk, breathing heavily, his shoulder a wet pulp from spilled blood, cursed. I felt his breath and spittle on my face. His cutlass flashed up, down.

He beat my own blade back on my head. The force of the blow sent me sprawling. I measured my length on the sand.

And now I die, I thought.

Turk swung again. The sword bit into the sand inches from my brow. As he reared back I scooped a handful of muddy sand, and flung it in his face.

He howled, clawing at his eyes. I think now that the wound had weakened him. Then, I didn't *think*. I thrust upward from the ground with the whole force of my body, pulling my legs under me, driving with them!

The cutlass went in until the hilt slammed his breastbone. As I let go, stepping back, Turk looked at me. The broad face was puzzled; the expression melted as his mouth sagged open. He coughed once, and, falling, died.

I stood, trembling, gasping great breaths through a mouth dried by fear. I was the victor, alive, and I didn't quite know how I'd managed it.

"B'God and Davvy Jones! You done for him!"

Chips was standing over Turk. The old man genuinely triumphant, reminded me of a bantam crowing over a fallen sow! Others were shouting; the cheers had a ring of surprise. Some, still urging on the fallen Turk, choked off in mid-cry. Few had thought me capable of winning. My most ardent backer must have groaned when I went down.

The Spaniard shuffled forward, stooped to retrieve my pistol, offered it with a handsome dagger. "*San' Iago*," he said, "you have much luck, *Señor*. I, Dago, tell you this."

Panting, I took the weapons, answered. "We'll see, Dago. Later. At dice."

Captain Root touched Turk's body with a toe, glanced at me. He pulled at the tip of his nose. Evidently his quartermaster's demise brought problems, not sorrow. "You-ah-fight a tricky fight," he said.

I shrugged. Pirates respected victory by any means. They preferred always to attack weaker ships. Root knew that as well as I did. I said: "When I must. I fight to win, Captain."

He nodded. "Scruples are-ah-ballast in our trade. You've won your right to serve with us. Except for one thing."

"No," said Chips, "he won it clear!"

"*Si!*" Dago gave the captain a surprised stare.

"According to rules," said another.

The crew crowded round in a tight circle to hear. Nobody paid the slightest attention to Turk; several stepped over him. They all seemed disturbed by the captain's attitude.

"State your objection, Captain," I said, gathering my wits to meet it. This Logan Root was dangerously shrewd.

"I will not-ah-sign on any man who will rob his shipmates." Root's head turned as he surveyed his company. "Killing Turk only proves-ah-that he can fight."

My grin appreciated his cuteness. He didn't mind losing Turk, but he still wanted his share of Jeffcoat's twenty pounds.

"Well," I said, "outside of facing that captain in Jamaica, what more can I do?" I had to know his play before I could counter.

"I talked to Jeffcoat, too," Root said. "He-ah-described the thief. You fit."

That was easy. Many men were my size, weight and coloring. Some of the *Quarand's* company came close enough. I let my voice rise angrily.

"Now there's a grand argument. There must be scores of gentlemen on the account would pass as well. Aye, and more with the king's fleet, and more again on merchant vessels."

"Mayhap. But-ah-how many wear a gold chain and a Spanish doubloon around their necks?"

Logan Root asked the question softly, holding out his hand, palm up. The ship's company seemed to close ranks. Even Chips and Dago watched me suspiciously.

"A chain and doubloon?" I asked.

"Gold. It was-ah-this man's talisman. Jeffcoat remembered the day he won it. When the *Unicorn* took the *Santissima Caterina*."

He had the name wrong, perhaps because Dandy Jeffcoat trusted no one, but the substance was accurate enough. All the *Unicorn's* crew knew the store I set by my gold chain. Now, I could read the glitter in Root's beady eyes. Cupidity. The gold chain would be proof and prize.

Grinning, I loosened my shirt. "Sorry, Captain," I said, "I've sung the song on many a hoisting, but I've neither gold chain, nor wooden leg." Then I bared my neck and chest.

Root sucked his teeth, but his expression became blank. If he knew of the scar on my thigh—the thing that had tripped me in the fishing village—he gave no sign. He'd wanted the chain, all else could wait until I confronted Jeffcoat.

"Very well," he said, "I'll-ah-fetch the articles of agreement. You may have a vote in electing our new quartermaster."

[203]

"B'God and Davvy Jones," said Chips, slapping my shoulder. "There's one gold chain would have been unlucky."

Dago fingered an earring. Another pirate touched a hair bracelet. They were all superstitious enough to believe that a seaman would never part with a talisman. Jill, our wedding, had saved me for the moment.

There was only one course left to me, and nothing to gain by waiting longer. I had to take Turk's place now, and hope to escape later. In spite of my misgivings we would have to test Jill's disguise.

"Captain," I said, as Root turned away, "I've a shipmate with me."

He swung around instantly. "So did Irish Jack!"

"Turk said something of that." My laugh sounded genuine. "A Swede, wasn't it?"

"Aye. A giant of a man, who——"

"Wait'll you see my cousin Murdock!" Again, I laughed. "A poor half-wit of a lad with one eye. He's not much taller than Chips."

"I was taller oncet," said Chips.

"Why didn't this lad come with you?" Root asked.

"Captain," I said, knowing him better now, "I never care to put all my eggs in one basket. As it was Turk's reception left much to be desired. Besides, the lad's never been on the account, though he's willing enough."

"Hail him," said the captain. "Let's clap-ah-a sight on this lad."

"All right. I'll go fetch him."

The crew flared like poked embers. It was easy to see that their trust in me was small. Dago, frowning, shook his head till his earrings blurred. Old Chips munched his lips over his toothless gums worriedly.

"Now, look," I said, "stand by to come about, lads! You've my word and my lugger! I've stood up to every trial and question! I fought your quartermaster for his lie, and took your terms. I've no wish to be marooned, and I'll sign on. But either we're shipmates, members of the brotherhood, gentlemen on the account together, or we're not! I'll not be treated like a lousy impressed lubber and you can lay to that!"

They all listened intently; Logan Root cocked his head as he considered my speech. If I was what I claimed my indignation was understandable. Pirates, suspicious of each other, have a certain code. The most treacherous gave it lip service.

"But in the darkness," objected Dago, "if you run——"

"Run where, and to what? The lad will not come if I hail. Those were my orders. He was my anchor to windward. Aye, and still is. If I didn't mean to bring him back, why would I mention him?"

"You took-ah-long enough," said Captain Root.

"Granted. I came to parley about the lugger. Knowing nothing of this Jeffcoat business. You want me to ship because of it, so I'll ship. But I'll not leave my poor dolt of a cousin behind. If you don't trust me to go alone let Chips and Dago come with me."

"Done," said the captain. "They'll-ah-have muskets."

"You're a careful man, Captain," I said bitterly.

"It pays," he said.

We three left the fires and marched into the night. It was still too early for moon or starlight, and the darkness was thick. Dago marched at my left shoulder; Chips bobbed along on my right. Both held their muskets ready.

"You lads take many prizes?" I asked, as we walked along the beach.

Dago snorted. Chips was more expressive.

"Dammit, no! The sloop's a good ship for all her barnacles, but she was empty when we took her. We been having Jonah's own time since!"

"Thought so. Never saw such ado about twenty pounds." I was being pleasant, not sneering. "Especially twenty pounds that nobody's going to get."

"That Turk," said Dago, chuckling, "I never like him. But he never get so drunk he safe to fight. You do me favor there, *amigo*."

"Me, too," said Chips.

"All right." We had reached the foot of the ridge, and I stopped. "Do me one. Let me climb up here alone."

They were both veterans. The musket barrels swung toward me as they stepped away. Chips did the speaking.

"We can't do that. Cap'n would skin us."

"He'll never know. And I won't forget it. Dago, you can have your dagger back. Chips, you'll have to take my word that I'll pay you later."

"You won't," said Chips, "if you don't come back."

"Here's your knife, Dago," I said, and tossed it straight at him. He let go of the musket's trigger to catch the hilt. As he did, I reached and tapped the muzzle of Chips' gun.

"Hey!" he said.

"I could have grabbed and run. You'd never have hit me, or caught me. But I didn't. I'll be back, shipmates." Walking between them, I began to climb the slope. Without looking back, I heard their conversation.

"Dago?"

"Let him go. I trust him."

"But—— b'God——"

"Make once the gamble, Chips, why not?"

It was a good thing I'd read Dago aright, and that my move had worked. For when I reached the place where I'd left Jill, I found her crumpled in a dead faint.

Chapter 24

FRIGHT shocked me into violence, both word and deed. I cursed dead Turk and live captain, the *Quarand* and her crew, the lugger. I even cursed Jill for her weakness that deprived us of a last chance to flee. Only the grace of God saved me from using her name, or terms that would reveal her sex. For the two pirates were within earshot, and it was Dago's comment that stilled my tongue.

"*Madre de Dios!*" he called out in admiration. "You are one damn fine swearer, *Señor!*"

That brought me to my senses. My reply was deliberately annoyed, with a round oath to drive the point home.

"This fool lad went to sleep instead of standing guard!"

Then, I dropped to my knees beside Jill, took her in my arms. I was pretty sure she'd only fainted; my whisper was urgent, but very low.

"Jill. Darling, darling, wake up, please! We've no time."

She stirred; her eyelashes flickered, rose. "Oh, Cormac," she said, "that fight——" Her clutch was sudden, digging through my sleeve. "Don't ever leave me like that again!"

"Small likelihood," I said, bitterly. "We both have to join these cut-throats, Jill. They'll not loose the lugger. To leave here we must sail with them. Aye, and with the smell of danger in every breath we take."

"With you, I'm not afraid."

"Don't talk prattle, for I've fear enough for two! You must act the lad always, never forgetting, mumble through the bullet, keep the patch on your eye."

Jill nodded, reached up to replace the patch.

"You can't faint aboard that sloop, Jill. Nor show the chain and doubloon. You can't even be shocked at what you see, or hear. A blush can wreck us."

"I'll not blush."

A hail, shaken by nervousness, came from Chips.

"Say there! Hoist anchor, will ye?"

"We're coming," I called. "We're gathering our belongings."

And we took all the lugger's gear, except for one skin to protect Jill's chest. That we hid. No shipmate was supposed to rummage in another's box, but I couldn't risk discovery of petticoats and dresses. If we escaped early in the voyage, we might return for Jill's things.

Dago and Chips were waiting as we descended the slope. They were relieved to see me. Neither could understand Jill, mumbling around the bullet, when she spoke. Chips cupped his hand behind his ear, annoyed. The darkness made this meeting an easy test. In the firelight Jill's disguise would be subjected to a closer scrutiny. But she slouched along now as if she hadn't a care.

"Can't he even speak plain?" Chips asked. "Is his brain addled, too?"

"His father died raving," I said. "It's in his blood. But you can pass the word. Anybody making my cousin the butt of a jest, answers to me."

Jill trudged behind us, bowed beneath her bundle. When we reached the outer edge of the glow from the flames, she followed me without hesitation. The pirates had pulled Turk's body from sight; I avoided the smears of its trail. My glance at Jill seemed casual, but wasn't. In spite of all we'd done—dirt, eye patch, clothes—the disguise looked transparent, futile. Under it I could still see the limbs and features of the girl I loved.

I had reloaded my pistol on the ridge, and as the pirates surged forward my hand crept toward it. Surely someone would notice that the youthful suppleness of that body was feminine.

Captain Root gave her only a cursory glance. He shrugged, losing interest. "He sure ain't no giant Swede. What's your name, lad?"

Jill gazed at him vacantly through one eye. She had to turn her head completely to find me. Her play acting was well done.

"Your name," I prompted.

The bulge along her jaw worked; she smacked her lips several times before she spoke.

"Murdock." Both syllables were slurred.

"What?"

"Murdock," I said, translating.

"He can't talk so good," explained Chips.

Logan Root grunted. He said: "That ain't important. Can he work ship?"

"Good as any," I said. "I vouch for it. He'll pull his oar, Captain."

One of the pirates, scar marked from ear to nostril pushed forward. "How'd you lose your eye, Murdock?"

Jill hung her head, mumbled.

"Tavern brawl," I said. "Innkeeper caught him tumbling his daughter."

That brought a roar of laughter and several lewd remarks. Jill must have heard, but she paid no attention, turning her back to set down her bundle. They might have gone on with the jests and questions, but the captain silenced them impatiently.

They had set the document—the articles of agreement—atop a hogshead and quill and ink pot. It was little different from others I'd read. Article 5 was the one forbidding any member from smuggling aboard in disguise one of the other sex. Punishable by death. The crew had signed in round-robin fashion, with the names inscribed in a circle so that no man would appear more culpable than another. I signed, beckoned to Jill.

She dragged her feet as she approached. She lifted the paper from the barrel upside down, held it close to her nose as she pretended to read. Even the dour captain allowed himself a smile as I turned the paper around. The crew howled, laughed the harder when Jill cringed, threw up an arm to ward off a blow. They enjoyed such horseplay; they thought their new shipmate highly diverting.

"Don't overdo it," I whispered.

Her tongue flicked out at me for a split second. Then, taking her time, hunched over and straining, she drew an X with the quill.

I wrote beside it—M. Doyle his mark. It was just above my own C. Doyle, both on the fringe of the circle. According to custom drams of rum were thrust into our hands. I noticed the rum, too, was on short rations. This crew really had belts pulled tight. Jill raised her drink as I raised mine.

"Gold chains for all, shipmates," I toasted.

"Aye, aye!" The response came in chorus.

We both drank, took a place on the ground near the fire. Captain Root then called the pirates to council. These occasions always were held with strangely formal ceremony, with speeches and tedious arguments. Pirates never tired of demonstrating that they were as lawful as aldermen about their own affairs. Their discussions were long, loud, and full of cursing, but they were loath to end them. Even men with nothing to say said it. In the end everyone spoke but Jill and myself.

They elected Isaac Parrot, mate, to replace Turk as quartermaster. He was the scar-faced seaman who had questioned Jill. That made it necessary to elect a new mate. Dago, who was popular, refused the office, probably from laziness. They settled at last on a broad-shouldered man about my own age. His single name seemed to be Austin.

"Agreed then," said the captain, in conclusion. "We load ship at once, and sail on the first tide we're ready for. We need stores—victuals and rum—and we'll take them where we find them. Until we do Isaac parcels out the rations."

They broke up the council on that, after appointing sentries to keep the fires and guard against surprise. One, I noticed, was posted within gunshot of where Jill and I pitched our bedding. Another paced between the fires and the boats. Captain, mate and quartermaster went on board the sloop to sleep.

They trusted us, then, only a cable's length. There would be no chance to escape by sea.

Later, when snores of all kinds showed the camp asleep, and the guards murmured at a safe distance, Jill turned into my arms. No one had been surprised at our shared bed. The night was cold, more bitter as the hours grew smaller. Many messmates were bunking together for warmth. Some were packed four to a hut so tight they could only turn as one.

Jill spat out the bullet; we drew the blanket over our heads to muffle our whispering. Her shiver, and her kiss were indications of her relief.

"They don't suspect, Cormac."

"Not so far. But stay close to me ever."

"You know, they're not so bad. Except for the—the rough talk, they are no different than Alec, Hamish, or the other fishermen."

"They're like all sea-faring men, yes. But with a difference. They steal, and kill if opposed. If caught they will hang. They'd kill their mothers to avoid that. We are safe, Jill, only so long as we do not cross them."

"Cormac, if they take us all the way to the Indies——"

"I do not think they can. There's little shipping at this season, and they're nearly out of food. They will have to put in somewhere. And soon."

"New York?"

"Well, maybe not that soon."

"They won't just sail into a port, will they?"

"No, Jill. They'll land a foraging party. To buy, or beg, or steal. There are always merchants tempted by large profits. Now, go to sleep. Tomorrow's loading is hard work."

"My!" she said, flouncing around so her back was to me, "tired of me so soon, eh?" But she reached behind her to hold my hand.

We went to sleep like that. In the middle of that pirate camp!

Three days passed before the *Quarand* raised her anchor. Three miserable cold days spattered with wet snow flurries that made the crew sullen and mutinous. The captain, Isaac, Mate Austin tried in vain to get the sloop equipped faster. They were cursed for their pains, blamed for the plight and the weather. Indeed they were all to blame; they were Indies seamen who had never voyaged so far north before. They had started too late, stayed too long. Now, fingers stiff from cold, in clothes that never dried, they hated to leave the fires for work. Though Jill and I did more than our share, the delay delighted me. It made further inroads on the stores. On the last night the lugger was sacrificed to the need for firewood.

Captain Root watched me as he gave the order, but I swung an axe with the rest. If Jill had tears in her one visible eye when she dragged planks to the blaze, the biting wind had all eyes watering. The little vessel, which had served us so well, and on which we'd counted, deserved a better end.

I didn't encourage the crew's shirking. There was no need. Chips, for example, had his old bones crippled to uselessness by the cold. Dago did nothing but curse the climate through chattering teeth. Others were as bad, or worse. I have known crews, reeling from fever or racked with scurvy, that worked faster.

Jill, amazingly, was more hardy than most. For one thing she was no stranger to the weather; for another she picked her tasks, loads that wouldn't tax her strength, bailing the longboat, pulling on a halyard where she wasn't really needed. With discipline so lax, with Isaac unsure of his new duties as quartermaster, her methods went unnoticed.

Sure, she twitched in her sleep from fatigue, her face grew thinner and her hands chapped, but she managed. Her role as my addled cousin never slipped, she'd have made a great actress, that girl, barring her strict morals.

If Root was worried, so was I. I wanted no deposing of officers, no splitting of the crew into warring factions. The crew, however and thanks be to God, wanted to get away more than they wanted revolt. Slowly, but surely, the sloop was loaded and rigged. The cannon, three brass four-pounders, a brace and single, were finally hoisted on deck, and lashed in place amidships. There was a plentiful supply of powder and shot for these guns; pirates used cannon little, preferring to board their victims.

The fourth morning dawned bright and clear, a cloudless blue sky overhead. Though the weather was even colder—the bedding was starched with frost—the men's spirits rose. Wind and tide were favorable; the quartermaster doled out a tot of rum all around; cheers greeted the *Quarand's* anchor flukes.

As we passed through the narrow entrance of the bay, Jill, at my side, gazed back at the island dropping astern. She held the attitude so long that I nudged her. She gave me a misty one-eyed glance, pulled her hat brim lower, bent her head and pretended to fuss with the hitch on a belaying pin.

I knew how she felt. Gardiner's Island had been, for us, a safe haven and a place of beauty. Now we left its security, its memories, to voyage with a pirate crew. Privacy was impossible on board the *Quarand*, but I gave her elbow a quick squeeze.

"Lively there, Murdock," I said, in case any shipmate was watching.

"Aye, aye," she mumbled.

In the open sea, our course was southerly, though we fought a brisk head wind. I suspected that Root was afraid to order another steering. The hands that knew least of navigating would have raised a howl if he had. South was what they wanted, away from the cold, back to the tropics and the Indies isles. I know now that the course would have taken us straight into the southern prong of that Long Island where Jill lived, but I did not know it then. In any case I didn't care. The sooner an empty larder made a landing necessary, the sooner Jill and I would bolt.

"Sail ho!" cried the lookout.

That is the most stirring of all cries at sea! Officer, hand, voyager, honest seaman or pirate, heard it with excitement, a sudden lift of heart, a quick raise of head. It was a link with fellow humans, a break in the daily monotony, fresh fuel for conversation. This was the one time when, hearing it, my own heart sunk like the lead on the sounding line.

"Where away?" A dozen voices echoed Root's.

"Far astern to starboard!"

The deck shook as men raced aft to see. Jill, stirred by the commotion, stepped up on a cannon carriage for better sight. Sure, I shaded my eyes for a look myself. But my hope was that the strange sail was far away, and going fast.

It was not. Oh, it was distant enough, under full sail and scudding along on a north-easterly course, but it was not so far that chase was hopeless.

"What is she?" Root trumpeted through cupped hands.

"A schooner by her shape. Heavy laden and headed for the open sea!"

Logan Root collapsed his spyglass with a swift movement of his hands. His tone was as shopkeeper as ever, but raised to reach the farthest scupper. "Stand by," he shouted, "stand by to come about!"

The crew, faces turned aft, leaped into position. Root paced the afterdeck, raised an arm to point. His voice, unhesitant now, might have been checking pieces of cargo.

"There she goes, mates! Supplies, rum, and plunder. Making out from land, deep in the water with cargo! We'll not go home with hold and hands empty if we catch her! And catch her we will!"

A cheer, savage glee, rose from the crew. The mate bellowed his commands. They were obeyed with hearty haste. Dago, as helmsman, put the rudder hard over; Isaac, as quartermaster, told off men to bring the small arms from the hold. The *Quarand* was filled with loud boasts, hurrying sailors. *No prey, no pay* was the adage of all coast brethren. Here was the chance to make a bad voyage profitable.

The captain called me aft as we changed course. Jill pattered behind me.

"Doyle," said Root, "Turk was gunner, too. Can you lay a cannon?"

"Well enough," I said.

"Take the bow gun then."

With Jill and Chips as helpers, I stripped the canvas jacket from the gun. We wrestled it into position, but of course did not yet raise the hinged gun port in the bulwark. All pirate success was based upon surprise; colors or numbers were never displayed till the last moment.

The *Quarand*, no man-o'-war, was cleared for action by the time I rammed the round shot down the cannon muzzle. Fully armed the crew sprawled along the starboard scupper, hiding behind the raised bulwark. Commands weren't necessary; these were old hands.

Chips brought a cutlass for Jill from the ship's store, another for me. The rest had their own weapons. Jill, kneeling beside me as I readied the match in its sand bucket, began to tremble. That could be taken for a chill; I knew it wasn't. Our heads were close.

"Steady," I whispered. "Keep low."

"Cormac." She could talk around the bullet when she wished. "There'll be a battle?"

"Not if yon craft yields."

"Yield to—to pirates?"

"It's safest. These men want loot, not bloodshed. They'll not scratch a skin unless they must." Her expression was of total disbelief. " 'Tis true. They'll only empty that ship without harm. Unless it resists."

"What then?"

"Once fighting starts, anything can happen. We'll not board with the others, but stay on the sloop."

Crawling along the deck I found the other cannon loaded and ready, went aft to report. Isaac, sitting tailor-fashion with his back against the mast, had the red flag in his lap. It was already fastened to its halyard. The quartermaster grinned as I went by, a grimace that thinned the scar on his cheek.

Logan Root was pacing, singing softly in a deep, tuneless, chant. There was no hesitation in his voice now. He reminded me of a preacher enthralled by a hymn. His face was rapt, his eyes glazed. A nod greeted my message. The words of his song made me swallow hard.

> The broadside carried seven rounds
> And each was worth a hundred pounds.
> Dead men lay in every hold
> Stark among the glittering gold,
> As ransom for an Inca chief
> Was paid out by the Spanish thief!
> There was wealth for every man
> When our ship sank the *Yucatan!*

This one, I thought, is a fanatic. His greed gave him a battle lust that would be merciless if opposed. No wonder the *Quarand's* crew had chosen him captain. He was a practical, hard-headed mercenary who changed to a demon when he fought. God help the prisoner who tried to hide a guinea from Logan Root!

Feeling sick, I crawled back to my position. In the bow I peered over the rail for a sight of our prey.

The schooner, her sails stained to the color of weak tea, still held a considerable lead; we'd not speak her for at least another hour. But we were sure to close. Our wind was dead astern; she was quartering. With all sails set the sloop was faster, and the other had shifted her course to due north, probably making for Boston.

We were both far out to sea now. Block's Island had dropped from sight, as had Gardiner's. There'd be no witnesses to pirate perfidy except the waves, wind and the victims.

The distant crew made no effort to escape the following craft. Why should they? These waters were generally safe. From the schooner's deck the *Quarand* would look innocent enough. A small trader, empty, bound for home and coming up to exchange news. Only Dago, Austin and the captain would be visible to a spyglass.

Jill joined me, raising her head cautiously, aware we shouldn't betray our hidden mates. She gave the distant ship a long, frowning appraisal that must have strained her exposed eye. I finally pulled her down.

"Careful now, Murdock lad."

My voice was raised for listeners' ears, but Jill's was a worried whisper.

"Cormac! That schooner——"

"Will have to take her chances. We can't warn her. These pirates would cut us down like kindling!"

"But I think I knew her! I'm almost sure."

"You can't be."

"I am. It's *The Careful Mary*."

"*The Careful Mary*?" The name twanged a harpstring in my memory.

"Tobias Pemberly's ship. I've seen it often."

I had seen it once! And though that had been moonlight, and my stay aboard brief, I was sure Jill was right. I remembered the sturdy smuggler captain and his hardy crew of sons. My wrists had worn their iron shackles; young Pym had been my guard.

The Pemberlys! First and last they'd been a reef, and a torment. Grief they'd brought me only. Sure, it was deserving of heavy payment in return. Yet, as the *Quarand* ploughed toward them, the thought of vengeance never entered my mind.

"Jesus and His fishermen saints save us," I said, meaning it, "for they'll fight!"

Chapter 25

THAT hour or more of the chase, while the *Quarand* overhauled her quarry, seemed endless, as if the seconds dripped slowly from a leaking puncheon.

The crew made ribald jokes, bragged with round oaths about past prizes, speculated as to the value of the schooner's cargo. Jill was horrified by the change in our shipmates. These simple seamen, coarse and boorish but given to childish moods, turned into pirates under her gaze.

Chips was typical of the transformation. The old buccaneer, bent by cramped bones, wizened by age, thawed, minute by minute, into a younger villain, with useful muscles and an ageless, wicked leer. He crooned over his weapons, sharpening the barb of a pike with a whetstone. The rheumy, faded eyes were a brighter blue, hard as flint; his toothless grin was a buzzard's beak. With a brace of slung pistols, cutlass and pike, Chips looked like the Devil's oldest assistant. Aye, and impatient with his master's gentlemanly airs.

"Ye'll get blooded now, Murdock," he told Jill.

Jill, shuddering, turned away.

The *Quarand* was heeled slightly to starboard now, racing like a loosed colt. We could hear the water boiling past, as the prow cut its furrow. Above us the canvas, bellying full and taut, showed that wonderful white curve that only sails have. It was, as always, a thing of strength and beauty mixed, this captured power of the wind. Sure, it was as close to flying, to the graceful winged speed of birds, as man will come on this earth!

Others felt this power, too. The men spoke of the difference in the sloop since they'd scraped her clear of barnacles. They were proud of her now, sure she'd catch the schooner.

"Old *Quarand's* frisky," said one.

"Spanking clean," agreed another. "Take us down to the keys in no time now, eh, Chips?"

"Aye," Chips called back. "Once we have duff and goods there'll be no cause to go ashore. We'll be sighting the Bahamas in a month or so."

That jerked me from my pleasant contemplation of the glowing sky, a blue stressed by the pale winter sun. It was only too true. Once they took the schooner, Jill and I were in for a long voyage, with no escape and disaster at its end. Somewhere in the Indies there'd be an encounter with Dandy Jeffcoat or other old shipmates, and I'd be lucky to die as quick as hanging.

Jill had heard. She was gnawing her lip; the skin that showed through her grime was very white. But when my gaze met her single eye, she winked.

Now, did ever a man have a better wife, to put the heart back in him as needed? Whatever happened to the Pemberlys, nothing must happen to Jill!

"Cap'n's making signs," said Chips.

Root was pointing at me, gesturing over the side. With a wave, I rose for a sight on the schooner, blinked to find her so close. Her rigging was visible now, and figures standing on her afterdeck. They all looked to me like Tobias Pemberly, which was foolishness.

"Less than ten minutes," I said. "Pass the word, Chips."

As the mutter rolled along the scupper, we ran the gun forward to the closed port. Chips stood ready to raise the panel; Jill knelt by the sand bucket, watching me. I stood, my gaze on *The Careful Mary*, trying to judge range and elevation by hasty calculations.

Jill, wide eyed, mumbled something about sinking.

"No," I said. "Just a shot across her bow to tell her to drop canvas and quit."

Chips cackled. "A salute kind of, Murdock."

We were on her quarter now, almost blanketing her wind. There was only a strong swim between us, and that lessening. Her captain *was* built like Tobias Pemberly, but of course his face was a blob, featureless.

Tenseness could be felt on the *Quarand's* deck. The crew was up now, crouched behind the bulwark. A cutlass clashed against something; a hoarse voice cursed the offender. The sound couldn't have carried to the schooner but battle pitch turns a screw inside a man.

"The match," I said, holding out my hand.

Jill passed it to me. I held it behind a cupped palm, blew on it. Less than two lengths separated us from the schooner's stern.

Root was allowing them the first hail, waiting as long as he could. The nearer he took the sloop, the better the chance of surprise. At last it came, a carrying bellow that knifed through the clear cold air.

"*The Careful Mary* of Saybrook. Tobias Pemberly, Master. What ship?"

Root cupped his hands to return the answer. As he did I applied the match and Chips flipped open the gun port. The sputter of the powder was lost beneath Root's roar.

"From the sea!"

The cannon coughed, spewed smoke, kicked back in its harness. The crew cheered, brandished weapons. Isaac raised the fancy, blood-red pirate flag. When the breeze flapped it open the pirates yelled again.

Beyond the schooner's bow a white geyser spouted as my cannonball hit. The figures on her deck scurried as if it had landed among them.

Dago knew his job. A skillful shift of the helm brought the *Quarand* alongside her prey. The schooner was taller, but no more than five feet of freeboard above us. Wood screamed as we scraped. It was a fair catch!

Grapnels, gleaming in the sunshine like slimy starfish, were hurled upward, hooked onto the schooner's rail. The pirates kept up an ear-splitting din, intended to terrify.

"Boarders away!"

Root's command was echoed by a dozen throats, instantly obeyed. Chips, gibbering with excitement, leaped away to join the surge of boarders. Loose coin and finery went to the first man who seized it.

Jill and I busied ourselves reloading the cannon. I didn't think it would be used. The *Quarand* had managed as fine a surprise as I'd ever seen. Both ships were laced together, and the pirates were already clambering up the schooner's side.

"Cormac," Jill said, woebegone and tearful.

"This is better. If they fought they'd be——"

At that moment *The Careful Mary's* side exploded! Black smoke, slashed with jets of flame, erupted in the boarders' faces, hid them in an instant. That volley had the tearing blast of fowling pieces, with one deeper note, a cannon's thunder.

The shot, for the Pemberlys had loaded with scrap, rattled on the *Quarand's* deck like hail. But the cannonball struck higher. That four-pound pellet brought the pirate jib down on the run.

Screams rose from the wounded. Three bodies tumbled back onto our deck, bouncing off their comrades, limp as tossed wine sacks, torn ones spilling the reddest of wines. Others hung in the grapnel lashings. That first withering fire cost the pirates half their number, drove the rest back into their ship.

"Mother of God!" I said, grabbing Jill and diving for the shelter of the bulwark. The pirates' fine trap had burst in their clutches. And I doubted that canny old Pemberly had spent everything on one volley.

The *Quarand's* deck was a shambles. Logan Root was in among his crew, shouting, laying about with the flat of his cutlass. Men quailed before him, pushing like an unruly mob, seemingly too stunned to use their muskets.

Isaac Parrot, the quartermaster, lay under the wreckage of a fallen spar, head crushed. The *Quarand* was a bad ship for quartermasters.

Another volley, more ragged and without the cannon, blazed from the schooner, raking the sloop's deck. It gouged splinters from the wood, slashed through canvas. Austin, the mate, shook his head as if bothered by a fly, then slowly toppled. As he fell he twisted, his upturned face showed where a ricochet had driven in an eye. He was otherwise untouched.

The pirates were fighting back now. They had to; there was no surrender for pirates. Muskets and pistols slammed back at the schooner. But the pall of gunsmoke that hung over the sloop was too thick for accurate shooting.

[217]

Jill, half under me, had her face buried in her arms. She was plainly trying not to retch.

"Fight!" roared Logan Root. "Fight, God damn you! Do you want to hang like dogs?"

Chips burst through the smoke fog. He was bleeding down one cheek, but raging.

"The cannon, Doyle! Dammit, why ain't you at the cannon?"

"Stow it, Chips," I said. "See to the others. I'll handle this one!"

"Well, jump! We need all we got!"

He watched me slap match to touchhole, darted away as the cannon fired. He didn't know that Jill and I hadn't bothered to ram any ball atop the powder wad.

Jill crawled toward me, and I swore at her. "Get back there, and keep your head down."

The *Quarand's* other two cannon slammed. Those four pounders were meant for defense, but Root, learning a quick lesson from Pemberly, was hoping to hull the schooner. The range was point-blank; both shots rocked *The Careful Mary*. One merely scarred her, the other drilled a ragged hole.

There was no volleying from the schooner now. The pirates fired at will; the Pemberlys shot back the same way. If anything the pirate fire was heavier.

A gust of wind shredded the smoke. As I worked my ramrod I could see Tobias Pemberly slash at a grapnel line.

So could Root. His command shook with triumph.

"Boarders—*again!*"

They weren't lacking in courage, those pirates. Only the badly wounded didn't join the charge. Jill and I, of course, stayed behind. But Chips and Root himself led the rush.

Dago quit the helm, darted across the afterdeck on a run. A leap took him to the *Quarand's* rail, and from it, without pause, he hurled himself across the yard of water that separated the vessels' sterns. Cutlass dangling from his wrist by a thong, he caught the schooner's taffrail with both hands.

One leg was over the side when a defender rushed him. Dago, laughing, drove the man off with two flashing sweeps of his cutlass. The Spaniard's gleaming teeth still marked his laughter when Pym Pemberly shot him through the body.

Gaping, Dago went over backwards, fell between the ships. Sunshine, strangely, caught in bright pinpoint on one gold earring. That traced his course like a plummeting comet.

The main pirate charge, Root's crowd, had better success. They tumbled across the schooner's side, reached her deck. Steel clashing on steel replaced the rattle of gunfire. There was no time to reload in hand-to-hand fighting.

Again, that tearing volley of the Pemberly fowling pieces crashed out. Their cannon thundered, too, but I never saw that ball. I was busy.

A grenade looped onto the *Quarand's* deck, bounced high, disappeared down an open hatch, trailing a wisp of smoke from its fuse.

"Many thanks, my boyo," I said to the unseen thrower. For the path of that grenade, I thought, traced a way for us to help the Pemberlys, hurt the pirates, and attempt escape.

A gunpowder keg stood near the cannon; one kick stoved in its top. Then, raising the keg over my head, I pitched it into the hold after the grenade. Now, mind, I expected an explosion, a diversion, but I knew the magazine store had been stowed farther aft.

I was halfway to Jill when the grenade burst. It made a hollow boom like the beat on a big drum, but the sound was a finger snap compared to what followed a heartbeat later.

With a thunderous blast the powder exploded! A sheet of flame, flecked with debris, flashed up through the hatchway. The sloop rocked; the mast seemed to jump, shivering, from its bed. As I stared, openmouthed, the topmast came tumbling down. It was still falling when the magazine went off!

That explosion, more deafening than a joined score of thunderclaps, would have put the fear of God into Guy Fawkes himself! The *Quarand* was lifted by it, lifted toward a sky suddenly ripped asunder. The very force of its wind plucked me from my feet, slammed me into the angle of the bow.

Dazed, stunned by fall and noise, I lay in stupid inertia, dimly surprised at the havoc I had wrought. That was my only feeling, that and the ringing in my ears.

Jill shook me back to sense. She knelt beside me, hatless, speaking fiercely. There was a lurid glare somewhere behind her.

"Cormac, Cormac! Get up! The ship's afire!"

That roused me, brought me upright to stand, swaying, aghast and horrified. The *Quarand* was burning. Bathed in a weird, orange light the whole deck looked alive with flames. Screams from terrified wounded, the roaring of the blaze, drowned any din of battle from the schooner. Even while I gaped a sail caught; the canvas seemed instantly changed to a great crimson flake.

"God," I said. "Oh, God!"

"The wounded," Jill said. She started to turn away, and panic shocked me into motion. I grabbed her arm.

"No! We can't reach them!"

This was true. A barrier of fire fenced the whole starboard side behind its licking, leaping inferno. That red hedge reached from mast to rail. The only path possible, and that narrow, stretched along the port bulwark. We would have to go aft to find a boat; we were cut off from the schooner, whoever held her now.

Twice, in the furious seconds that followed, the heat drove us back. At last, arms linked, crouching, we raced through a shower of falling sparks to where the dinghy was berthed. The *Quarand* was doomed. No crew could quench such a conflagration. And her crew was battling aboard the schooner!

The dinghy's paint was already blistering, but the oars, fortunately, were under her. Panting from the intense heat, we loosed her, swung her over the side. Jill dropped into her first, I followed. The cool air nearer the waves was like a soothing draught to my lungs.

We shoved off, each with a pair of oars, Jill, on the thwart ahead of me, rasped in a ragged breath with every stroke, but her oars bit the water smoothly. I matched my beat to hers.

The sea was calm, with only a gentle swell, but a much duller blue than the sky. We rowed until we could see the burning sloop wholly reflected in the water. After the fire's furnace heat, the cold of the day seemed twice as biting.

When we rested, gazing back at the *Quarand,* a fireship from stern to bow, neither of us spoke. Jill, I think, was content to recover from the ordeal. For myself, I was cursing ashamed of Cormac O'Shaugnessy Doyle.

Mostly, I tried not to think of the wounded whose helplessness had prevented escape from a horrible death. Pirates they were, a hard lot and cruel, but not deserving of that. A long time would pass before I'd forget it was my doing that lit the torch.

We were not even free of the pirates, not if they had captured *The Careful Mary.* The schooner could easily overtake the dinghy. Nor was my own case much better if Tobias Pemberly was still master of his own vessel.

As if to settle the question, the schooner slowly moved out from behind the fire screen. *The Careful Mary's* sails filled; her prow sliced out an ever-broadening crest of white water. From her rail the cut grappling lines trailed like festive ribbons.

"Cormac, the schooner's loose!"

"Aye. Sure, it's lucky they are the fire didn't spread to them."

"But—who sails her?"

"Well, suppose we signal her and find out." I was half rising when Jill shoved me back on the thwart. Her eyes snapped; there was a streak of ash across her nose.

"Are you daft?" she asked. "Did you burn the sloop for naught?"

"For naught. And by mistake."

The weariness in my tone make her blink. She said: "What's done is done. I've seen enough piracy today to last me. We'll not return to that life!"

"As to that," I said, staring as the ship gathered speed, "all signs indicate the Pemberlys won. Her ensign's still flying, and she's back on the course she held before Root hailed her. The pirates wouldn't head north."

Sparks had scorched holes in Jill's head kerchief; she removed it, tossed her hair. She ripped off the eye patch, wadded it, dropped it over the side. It was a gesture of defiance.

"We're away free, Cormac! We'll stay that way."

"Tobias Pemberly knows you. You'd be safe with them. If we wave they'll pick us up."

"He knows you, too."

"Well, yes, but—I don't want you facing more dangers, Jill."

"I didn't don your gold chain to see you in iron shackles. That's what you'd get from Tobias Pemberly." She turned to gaze after the schooner. "They're wasting no time in leaving."

"Why should they? They've been through battle, probably have wounded. They're too busy to notice us."

"Or anyone else!" Jill stood up to stare at the *Quarand*. The sloop floated dead in the water, burnt to the hull, even the flames low now. "Cormac, suppose there are survivors?"

"From that fire?"

"We escaped. Maybe others did. Maybe those on the schooner fled when beaten. We can't leave them helpless." She pointed, voice rising in excitement. "Look, Cormac, there are things floating around the sloop!"

"Wreckage," I said, "flotsam."

"We'd better make sure." She sat down, worked an oar to turn the dinghy. "I thought I saw a man."

We rowed back, constantly scanning the water. There wasn't much heat now. The *Quarand* was a flame-filled hulk, not unlike a skillet in which fat has caught fire. Bits and pieces of wreckage strewed the waves, a broken spar, three barrel staves still circled by a hoop, rags of clothing.

"Junk thrown by the blast," I told Jill.

"Wait. What's that?"

Her gaze was fixed on a spot well astern of the sloop, where a flat slab of wood flashed on the crest of a swell. Something fluttered above the wood. Staring, I tried to believe it was an arm waving.

We pulled for it, driving the dinghy as fast as we could. There was a man clinging to a section of hatch cover. He evidently lacked the strength to wave again, just clung face down, awash more than afloat. His yellow cap, though sodden, was recognizable. It was Chips!

When we pulled the old man into the dinghy he seemed close to death. Chips was limp, and shivering, blue with cold. He could hardly speak and his eyes were wild. Strangely, he still had his pike, fixed by a lanyard to his belt.

"Are there any others?" Jill asked.

"Gone," he croaked. "B'God. All gone."

"Dead?"

He nodded, speaking in whimpers. "Every soul. Those—those damned buggers! They let us board apurpose. Rot 'em! They bunched at their mainmast. Hosed us with gunfire!" Chips seemed to gather strength as he continued. "A cannon, too. Loaded with chain links. B'God. Cap'n Root got it full in the face. Just as the sloop exploded. They riddled us fair. Only man standin' was me."

"You're safe now, Chips."

"Safe," he said. He was huddled in the dinghy's bow, staring at Jill's bright hair. "Aye. Safe!" He fumbled, untying the knots that held his pike. "Went over the side, I did! Where else? Killing before me, and burning behind. Jumped to my death, I did! Can't swim!"

"We'd better make for shore," I told Jill. "It's a long pull, and will take hours."

"Chips will freeze," she said, taking her place behind me.

"I'll lend him my coat," I said, and turned to him as I loosened my belt. To my surprise he reared up, hunching back in the bow like a cornered cat. Both fists gripped the pike.

"Avast!" he said, snarling. "I want nothing from you, nor your leman either!"

The epithet, sudden and startling, revealed his new knowledge of Jill's real sex. I have heard coarser terms, but this one angered me.

"Watch your tongue, old man," I said.

"Old, mebbe, but true!" Chips roared, with an oath. "Not like some. I saw you throw that keg, you sneaking whore's bastard! Traitor!"

He shrieked the last word, and swung. I saw the pike butt coming, but not in time. The old pirate had lashed out with all his strength. His clout caught me across the face, knocked me sprawling atop Jill.

"Cormac!"

Through a blur of pain, I heard Jill's cry, saw Chips reverse the pike, raise it. His wizened face was rigid with evil triumph, stony as carven gargoyle.

Sunshine gleamed on the pike's barb, became jagged lightning as he thrust!

The lightning struck me with a white, blinding flash! That was all I knew.

Chapter 26

SOMEWHERE beneath me the world seemed to be rocking, rocking to and fro with a motion at once frightening and painful. Helpless, without balance in this moving black void, I was afraid, with a vague, nameless terror. The pain, throbbing and intense, prevented thought. As the spasms racked my body I knew only fright and suffering. Torturers' hot irons stabbed my head, and shoulder; the heat spread from these to course along my veins until no part of me was spared. It was unendurable. I had to stop the torment.

With nightmare cunning, I shrieked and shrieked, and that was nightmare, too, for my screams took great straining effort, but the fear remained and the pain increased. Slowly, very slowly, I groped my way back to a form of consciousness.

I opened my eyes on more blackness, this one speckled with pinpoints of light. Now the world above me was rocking, too! That was too much. I began to weep.

"Cormac."

The voice was close; a hand stroked my brow. I tried to recall voice and touch.

"Lie still, darling," said the voice.

"Drink," I said, weakly demanding for I felt afire.

"Oh, please," said the voice with a catch like a sob. *"Don't* ask again. And lie still. I can't row while you toss about."

The sob did the trick. It puzzled me, and then reason forced through the pain. My head was pillowed on a soft cushion. Rowing meant a boat, which was natural in my trade. There was someone with me, and she—*she?*

"Jill," I said.

"Yes. Right here."

Her face was close, but blurred. Even the bright hair tumbled in dark strands. But I knew her, realized my head was on her lap.

"Jill, I—I can't—see——"

"It's night. It's all right."

"Night?"

"Yes. Don't try to talk."

I had to talk. For, all at once, I knew the reason for my fear, the cause of the pain. Suddenly, remembering, I tried to sit up, reeled back gasping. Movement seemed to make the pain boil over.

"Lie still, Cormac."

"Chips." The name was all I could manage.

"Don't worry about him. He's gone."

"Gone?"

"Dead," Jill said flatly. "I shot him. He tumbled over the side. He only came up once."

Impulse, in spite of my fever, made me want to reach out, to comfort her. "You had to," I said.

Jill didn't speak for a few moments. Then, the iron ring of the Covenant preacher, an echo of her brother Alec, was in her voice.

"Thou shalt not kill. That is the commandment of the Lord God of hosts. *Vengeance is mine, sayeth the Lord.* Yet I slew, raging, and rejoiced in the slaughter."

"Saul," I said, dredging the names from the dim recesses of my memory. "David. The Maccabees. The Covenant army."

"You don't understand. I—I thought he'd killed you. He stood gloating, waving that bloody pike. The pistol was in my hand, aimed and fired, before I knew I'd moved."

"He'd have killed you."

"Aye, he was evil. But—when his body rose in the water, I hurled the pike at it. To sink it. That was hate. And, God help me, I was unrepentant!"

[224]

She put her hands over her face, shuddered, though any tears were soundless. I thought her close to the breaking point. Her deed was brave and guiltless; her emotion an aftermath of violence. Raging at my weakness, I sought words that would distract her.

"Jill—my wound—how bad——?"

"Oh, Cormac!" The change of voice was immediate. Worry replaced self-condemnation. "It's—it's a terrible, deep gash. Just below your armpit. It bled so!"

"Bleeding's a cure."

"Not so much. I thought I'd never staunch it."

Now, I could feel the tightness of bandage around chest and shoulder, but my attempt to finger it ended in dizzy failure. The pain forced a groan through clenched teeth.

"Cormac, you mustn't move!"

"But——"

Her palm rested on my forehead. "You've fever. And if the bleeding starts again, we've naught left for bandages. I used both our shirts."

Dimly, in the daze of my misery, I was aware of the season and the weather. It was no time to be ill clad in an open boat miles at sea. For all her strength and courage, her seamanship, Jill was still a girl. It would be a long, cold row before we made a landfall.

"You need help," I said.

"I'm all right."

All right! I thought. A gallant lie! Due to my hasty foolish action with the gunpowder we were in dire straits. We had neither food, nor drink, sail nor covering. I was a sick weakling—again through my own carelessness in dealing with Chips—useful only as ballast. Fixing my eyes with effort, I peered up at Jill through the dim starlight.

Weariness showed in her slumped shoulders, her bowed head. Dark rings shadowed her eyes; the hand with which she brushed back her hair moved with slow, tired limpness.

"Jill," I said, "I've scuttled us."

She smiled, bent to kiss me. Then she said, very cheerfully: "We're still afloat, man. Far from beaten."

"Far from shore, too."

"That's no great problem. I have pulled a fair oar in my time, and with less need. My concern is your wound, Cormac."

"A fleabite."

"Aye, if you'll be still and not go bothering it."

We were both lying, of course, each trying to raise the other's spirits. Jill had seen the wound; I knew the fiery pain of it. The blow on my

[225]

head, too, had not helped my wits. From temple to chin one whole side of my face felt achingly swollen. The very effort of conversation took all my strength.

"I'll be good," I said. "I'll sleep now."

It was not sleep, but faintness that made the stars fade. My vision would not behave. I could feel my brain begin to reel; Jill seemed to dissolve in mist. Angrily, I shook my head to clear it. That was a mistake. I fainted.

The hours that followed were mostly delirium, broken by occasional minutes of clarity. Once I heard the oars creaking against the tholepins. The beat was very slow, dragging, so that I listened impatiently for the next creak. Another time I was aware of Jill holding me fast in her arms while we drifted, but I could not stop my thrashing.

In the end her talk proved the only means of quieting me. Somehow Jill's voice penetrated through the fog of fever, quelled my pain, soothed me. I did not understand much that she said. Endearments, prayers, encouragements all blended into senseless speech. But Jill kept talking.

Just before dawn my brain cleared for a longer period. I knew that the sky was paling to murky slate, and that it was beginning to snow. Such was my lassitude that I noted these things without worry. Both affected our plight, but that was not my concern. I merely lay and listened, receptive as a blank page under the press before the printer clamps tight.

❖

But once Jill stopped talking, I was aware of numbness creeping along my limbs. The feeling was welcome, a release from bitter chill, laudanum for my pain. Delirium still befuddled my thinking so that I did not recognize the deadly cold that drugs as it kills. Jill too must have been freezing; she sat up stiffly, beat her arms across herself. Daylight, sifting through the fine screen of snowflakes, showed her my true condition. With a cry she bent to pummel my thighs, rub life into my legs.

"No." My protest was a murmur.

"Cormac, I must!"

Moaning, I tried to win pity, find surcease. Jill didn't listen. No matter how I writhed there was no escape from her busy chafing.

Neither of us noticed the tall black shape that edged slowly through the storm. It was looming above us before, gazing past Jill, I saw it, first as a shadow, then a bulk, then a moving wall. Another figment of fever, I thought, and waited to be crushed into senseless comfort.

Something made Jill turn her head. Her scream was sharp with horror. "A ship! Sheer off! *Sheer off!*"

The dinghy was lifted by an invisible hand; a wave slapped across my face. That's wake, I decided with startled recognition. Wake from that black hull sliding past an oar length from our gunwale.

Jill plucked the pistol from her belt, fired it. Flash and report stabbed my eyes, rocked my reeling head. I struggled to sit up, only to topple into bottomless darkness away from a shouting voice that grew dimmer and dimmer.

Then, in what seemed an instant, the voice rose again, from silence through murmur to a roar. There was a light shining on my eyelids, and I raised them with effort.

"Pirates, no doubt," a man was bellowing. "Like the schooner said. To the brig with them both!"

"I'm no pirate," Jill said.

I was lying on a ship's deck, in the space between two cannon. Jill stood beside me, and sailors surrounded us in a tight circle. The roaring man, holding a lit lanthorn against the snow dark day, wore his majesty's coat. He was a short, keg-chested individual with a face as red as raw beef.

"Deny it, do ya?" he shouted at Jill.

"Aye," she said calmly, "what ship is this?"

"His Majesty's frigate *Rose,* ya scullion! John George is my name. Captain of this vessel. Cross me, ya scum, and I'll have ya flogged!"

"I am Judith Murdoch."

That caused a stir. George thrust the lanthorn almost in Jill's face. His voice was no lower, but it was surprised.

"Ya *are* a wench!"

"Lady," corrected Jill. "This wretch abducted me, and held me prisoner, but Providence has delivered him into my hands."

I couldn't believe I heard her right. Jill? My own Jill? She went on, as crisp and unfeeling as a turnkey.

"He is indeed a known pirate. His name is Cormac O'Shaugnessy Doyle."

"Damn all!" Another voice, high pitched and tight, burst from the group. "By your leave, sir, give me a glimpse of that lousy beggar!"

A red coat shouldered seamen aside. The tall officer plucked the lanthorn from Captain George as he passed. I barely had time to narrow my eyes before he bent over me. But I saw him as plain as he saw me.

Ensign Whitlaw himself! Sure, if ever a man sailed full circle to no purpose, I was that man. The ensign's nostrils quivered; the small mouth in that thin, narrow face widened with cruel pleasure.

"It is Doyle! I'd know the scoundrel anywhere!"

"Of course it is," Jill said. For all her ragamuffin clothes, she stood as proudly as a princess. "Wounded, and my captive. And since there's a price on his head in Boston, gentlemen, I mean to collect it."

George scowled from her to me. Whitlaw, smiling, swept off his hat and bowed.

Jill stamped her foot and said: "Enough dawdling. He needs a surgeon, Captain. Aye! I'll not be deprived of the pleasure of seeing him hanged!"

False, I screamed soundlessly. There was no speck of voice left in me! False, false, *false!* Lying, deceitful harlot! Give me back my doubloon, my gold chain!

The sailors, lifting me, sent me blessedly back to oblivion.

So, I came at last to Boston in great style, aboard a king's frigate, attended by a surgeon. It was too bad I knew nothing about it.

BOOK THREE

The Stone Gaol

Chapter 27

SURE, so much has happened since last I dipped quill in ink to chronicle this log, that there is scarce time left to relate it all. These Puritans of Boston town, clergy, gentry, and even females of different degrees, insist that my task must be finished before I leave the chill comfort of their new stone gaol forever.

One minister in particular, the grandest preacher of the lot, writes endless reams himself and considers an incomplete book an abomination. Since the gentleman in question is always after me to repent of my sins, to renounce what he calls "the bloody devotees of Papist Rome," and to accept his own crop-haired, psalm-singing kind of religion—before it is too late!—my scribbling serves me as shield and buckler. The scratching of my quill is respected; if my fingers grow cramped at least my ears are spared. That is reason enough to write on through these few remaining days.

They have propped the silver oar in one corner of my dungeon to remind me that those days are numbered. It is shining with new paint, and neat made, worthy of an honest seaman's stroke instead of making a holy show in a parade to the scaffold.

There is no need for such a reminder. Each changing tide draws me closer to my fate. But neither the running sands nor my situation will be allowed to fluster my narrative. Haste in high wind never yet made me tie granny knot for square, and the rule is as good for writing as for reefing.

My trial, the verdict and the sentence, are all recorded elsewhere. One Cormac O'Shaugnessy Doyle, a seafaring man, innocent as this spring's lamb, for all his nimble tongue, was found guilty of the crime of piracy, the same being a Papist.

Aye, there is nothing unexpected in that, but other events held some surprises. This year of our Lord 1689 will be remembered in New England's history. Few accounts will ever reveal the true details, the secret meetings, the dangerous plan. Mine tells how and why the happenings occurred.

And is not this the last book I'll set down on paper? Why, then, would I spoil it with lies?

One thing I wish stated, and understood. What I did was from necessity. I am no turncoat, and will face death when it comes with a loyal shout.

Long live King James!

❖

Of my transfer from the frigate *Rose* to a cell in the stone gaol of Boston, I knew as little as of the voyage aboard the vessel. Betwixt fever and spleen, wound and cracked skull, drugs and purges, my abode in the valley of pain and daze was the only fixed thing in my life. In fact, I almost became a permanent settler. The frigate's doctor, probably because of an overabundance in his apothecary chest, poured copious draughts of laudanum into me; the gaol surgeon continued the treatment, with variations.

Thus, while one year ended and the next drew near I lay for some weeks in stupor. Those who attended me have told of my ravings with awe, but, knowing myself closemouthed by nature, I have considered the reports exaggerated.

This period was peopled by faceless beings that had the guise of humans, and the tender touch of infernal fiends. They included the doctor, whose voice meant pokings, possets, and pain, the turnkey, known by the clatter of his keys, and two females. These last puzzled me; both seemed young and vaguely familiar.

Those were the regular visitants. Others came in groups, wearing the red of soldiery, or the black gowns of ministers. They crowded about my cot like different species of carrion-eating birds. The ones in the brighter plumage chattered less.

Once I thought dignitaries came, led by a resplendently dressed nobleman, but that stay was brief.

Physic's adage of kill or cure was never followed more diligently. In the end either nature proved stronger than my dosages, or the blessed angels refused to accept the cargo. At any rate I awoke one morning myself again. A weak self and weary, but clearheaded. The fever had fled; the wound itched amending.

As I gazed at the square of winter sunlight framed by the barred, paneless window high on one wall, I realized instantly where I was. Thick stone walls and iron bars made it a prison, but the clean smell refuted them. Though never incarcerated I knew Newgate to be foul as a sewer; the Indies dungeons reeked like pestholes. Here the air on my face, nipping cold, was untainted; the mortar joining the rough stones looked fresh.

Blankets were piled atop me for warmth, and even these, though worn and stained, were passably free from dirt.

By the well of Saint Kell, I thought, hearing the straw tick rustle under me as I moved, but I have bedded worse in inns where the score was figured in numbers that equaled the vermin. Someone had shaved me, dressed me in a coarse linen shirt.

Then, I remembered Jill, the betraying words spoken on the frigate's deck. A hollowness came into me that I could not inflate with anger. She had handed me defenseless to mine enemies, claimed the reward. Boston gaol held me at last, and the gallows waited.

Tears stung my eyes. Her deed made a whore of her, a fool of me. It sullied our love, tore the vows we'd exchanged to tatters. Jill! Jill, of all girls!

For a long time I stared, unseeing, at the window. So low were my spirits that I sorrowed over not dying, and didn't care how quickly they hanged me. Life in a world where Jill had used me for her lustful pleasure, and sold me for a few pounds, held little savor.

Hunger finally stirred me to action. Turning my head, I surveyed my dungeon. It was a stone chamber, raftered, with an uneven, flagged floor. Rings and shackle racks, unrusted iron, decorated the wall opposite my pallet. The only other furniture was a charcoal brazier that gave off more vapor than heat. The bareness upset my judgment of the room's size. My estimate was twelve paces in every direction, forming a perfect square, but later it proved two paces shorter.

The door was behind me. Twisting my neck I was startled to find it open. A man and a woman, she seated on a stool, he standing, crowded the portal. He held a skein of wool that she was winding into a ball.

Her back was to me, but there was no mistaking that blond hair, arranged in a coronet of braids, nor the plump busy little figure. Katrina Krön was guarding the gateway of my cell!

My amazement must have forced utterance. The man, a sallow-skinned individual, looked up nervously. His glance met mine over Katrina's head.

"He wakes," he said.

"*Ja?*" Katrina turned; her pleasant Dutch face dimpled at me. She tossed her yarn ball to the astonished man, flounced toward me. Her voice had the same gleeful breathlessness.

"Cormac! So you are better! Is good!"

"Katrina!" I said, "Katrina Krön. What are you doing here?"

"I live by Boston now," Katrina said, bubbling with merriment. Her palm felt my brow for fever, stroked for fun. "But is Krön no more. Mistress Neville now." She dipped in a curtsy. "Baby and me marry young Devon."

"The post boy?"

"*Ja.* Is nice."

The man shuffled beside her, hands still tangled in the yarn. By his leather jerkin, and the ring of keys dangling from his belt he was the gaoler. With his narrow, stooped shoulders, yellow complexion, and mournful countenance he seemed better suited to grave digging. He wore his hat indoors, brim straight, as if screwed on his crown like nut on bolt.

"Well, now," he said, twanging through his nose. "Well, now, you'd better take this here yarn. The felon's turn for the better calls for a turn of the key."

"Are you the gaoler?" I asked.

"*Ja.*" Katrina introduced him. "Master Mercy."

"Paulsgrave Mercy," said the gaoler. He raised a hand toward his hat, stared at strands of yarn as if they'd grown on him. "Well, now! This sort of thing ain't rightly a gaoler's duty. Besides His Excellency, the Governor, Sir Edmund will want to hear of this directly."

"About my yarn?" Katrina was bewildered.

"Well, now—no. About this here pirate, prisoner, miscreant. They'll hold the questioning now." Mercy dropped the wool on my cot, stripping his fingers as a farmer would a cow's teats.

"First fetch broth," Katrina said, "from kitchen."

Mention of food made my mouth water. My nod was eager.

"Well, now," Mercy sounded dubious, "that ain't rightly gaoler's work either. I know my duty. I've taken Sir Edmund's coin—Carolus, Unites, Pine Tree—and he's taken my service."

"Fetch!" Katrina stamped a foot.

"I'll have to shut you in, lock, bolt and bar." The gaoler fiddled with his key ring. "And this one's no ordinary prisoner gaoled for breaking Sabbath."

"Cormac?" Katrina laughed. "He not harm me."

"Nor could," I said. "I'm weak as a new-spawned kitten."

Paulsgrave Mercy sniffed, but shambled away. He shut the door; metal clinked, clanked, as he worked lock and bolt. It was a solid oak door, thick with studs; a barred wicket was set in the top panel. Sure, a dozen like me with crowbars couldn't force out through it.

"Katrina?"

"Ja?"

"I—I'm mixed up. What date is it?"

"Is December. Near over."

"It is?" I couldn't believe my ears. "Was it so great a wound, then?"

She shrugged. She was wearing a shawl against the cell's chill, but even under that the movement plainly stirred her bosom. She said: "Doctor think no. You get lung fever from snow in open boat. Cough, burn, and shake."

"Oh?" My distrust of all leeches showed in my voice. Doctors were ever great for drugging and bleeding. I fancied I'd have recovered faster if left alone. "Did he bleed me?"

Katrina shook her head. "Once only. Mistress Murdoch forbid. Say you lost much blood already."

"Mistress—Jill?"

"Ja."

"But—what had she to say about it?"

"Much. She oversee all." Katrina's mouth pursed with disapproval. "That one hard—hard as flint. Say she no have you die this side hangman."

"Aye." I had heard Jill say something like that. Anger began to warm me. I was hurt, and bitter. No matter how she felt now, our days together should not have prompted such vindictiveness. Was it revulsion from love because her Covenant deemed it sinful? Damned if I liked being used as a scapegoat, whipping boy for Jill's conscience!

"All Boston speak of Mistress Murdoch," Katrina said. "She capture pirate. She—how you say?—great warrior, only girl?"

"Heroine?"

"Ja. So. Preachers praise in sermons. Devon say she given five pounds for you."

"May it burn through her fingers!"

Mercy returned, made noises opening the door, brought in a steaming bowl of broth. He left without speaking, locking up carefully. Truly, Master Paulsgrave Mercy was going to be a severe gaoler.

Katrina sat on the edge of my pallet, propped me up against her, fed me with a wooden spoon. The broth was hot and nourishing. It revived my spirits. My head, pillowed on the soft cushions of Katrina's breast, shook off sluggishness, teemed with new plans.

"Katrina," I said, when the soup was finished, "I am not dancing on air yet. I'll get out of this stone box if only to spite Jill Murdoch."

"How?"

"You've got to help me."

"Cormac." She had her arms around me, her face above mine. The blue eyes were grave. "How help? They let me nurse, ja. I hear you very sick. I ask Devon, come. Mistress Murdoch let me help. But Paulsgrave Mercy watch me. Every minute."

"Jill nursed me too?"

"Ja. She demand. She make governor let."

That seemed a fresh betrayal. Jill had helped coddle me into a weakling unable to escape. My resolve hardened.

"This gaol can't hold me, Katrina."

"It is strong, new gaol."

"It is that. But I'll walk out singing when the time comes. Once I've my health back, I'll need but two things to escape. Clothes, and you."

"Me?"

"Aye. We duped them once before, we two. Remember?"

"Ja." She was gazing down on me, eyes twinkling as she smiled. Her soft whisper was merry. "Ja, I remember."

"They had gyves on me. And redcoat soldiers with guns. Paulsgrave Mercy will watch no whit closer than Ensign Borden Whitlaw. But I escaped. Over the hills I went, my heels to them, free as free."

"Lady Esterling——"

"Gave the chance. Aye. There must always be that—the right moment. We must think of another, Katrina."

"Different now."

"It needn't be."

Mind you, I knew the wench for an outcast like myself. Deviltry amused and excited her. Katrina's great heart put her always on the side of the hunted. She hid the hare and mocked the hounds. I'd not forgotten that.

"Needn't?"

"No."

God forgive me for a blackguard, but I slid my hand up along her side, slipped it under the shawl. Katrina's whims, I recalled, followed her senses. She gave the flesh free rein, and paid small heed to morals. As my palm rested on the bodice of her gown, ruching crisp against it, color tinted her cheeks.

"Cormac, now——"

"You will help, won't you?"

This was not all as deliberate as it reads. I needed Katrina, true, as an ally outside the thick stone walls. But some of my feeling was uncalculated. She was warm, friendly, softly feminine, and no stranger. All attractions for a man as recently sick as myself. My very weakness goaded me to test my manhood. And, though I'd have denied it on the Book, resentment toward Jill Murdoch was in the mixture, too.

"What can I do?"

"Many things."

I cupped my hand about one breast, felt the other's rise beneath my cheek. Katrina ran her fingers through my hair, smoothed it. She yielded to my caresses, visibly relaxed.

Then, she sighed, a long, hearty gust. That breath admitted present pleasure, mourned past memories, reluctantly dismissed both. Gently, but firmly Katrina removed my hand from under her shawl, plucked the other from her lap, held both.

"*Nein*. No," she said. "No, Cormac. Is nice, but no."

"But——"

"I am wife now. Mistress Devon Neville."

"A callow lad!"

"*Ja*, young." She grinned at me, unperturbed. "But not so young in everything. A good husband. Devon gave me his name. Brings home pay from post riding. He loves me. We marry for real. In church. Katrina good wife, Cormac."

"You love him?"

"*Ja*, I think so."

"I beg your forgiveness," I said, polite with shame. "I should not have——" My hands turned in her grip. She knew what I meant.

"No harm." Katrina chuckled. "But not *that* even except Devon away. He rides to New York four days ago." She flushed, giggling. "I miss. Besides you supposed sick."

My laughter joined hers, surprising me. Her candor was refreshing, her glee infectious. We shared the moment as old friends. Much of Katrina Krön remained in Mistress Neville, but I made no further attempt to touch her.

We were interrupted. Steps sounded outside the door, voices rumbled, Mercy's keys chimed. Katrina lowered me quickly, stepped demurely away from the cot. We had time for only a hurried exchange of whispers.

"Katrina, you will help?"

"*Ja*. What I can."

The door opened to admit a choleric bantam of a man in rumpled-black broadcloth clothes. He looked as if he slept in them; his mustard waistcoat was stained and spotted. His frame was spare, his face flabby, with pouches like proud skin under eyes and jowls.

"Mistress!" He spat the word in anger. "Do you think I have naught to do but trim this gaolbird's feathers?"

Katrina jumped, shied from him. "I—I don't know," she said.

"Ha! I'm not talking to *you!*" The man's head twisted as he glared back at the doorway.

Jill Murdoch's voice was calm, yet it sent prickles along my spine. "You failed to come yesterday, Doctor Oakes."

I dug my fingernails into my palms before I turned. She stood on the threshold, elegant in a new gown of dark-blue silk, with matching bonnet. Her gaze was on the surgeon so I could look my fill. The shorn hair was drawn back into a fish-net rigging, but its lustre was undimmed.

Dress and manner widened the distance between us. She was no longer my ragged shipmate, but a genteel lady who had decked herself in finery purchased by the price on my head. In that moment I hated her. She sensed my stare, for her eyes veered in my direction and widened.

"Ha!" Doctor Oakes cried. "Why should I come? To make potions for you to throw in the slop jar?"

Jill's face showed the briefest flicker of brightness, chased by a frown. She said: "Peace, Doctor. The gaoler told us true. Look, the rascal is better."

Alec Murdoch's tallness loomed behind his sister. His broad Scots burr rasped with eagerness. "Well enough to thrash, do you think, mon?"

"Aye," I said, "for a Murdoch. Now, there's a grand family for bravery. Cudgel a corpse any day, the Murdochs!"

"Why, you Papist——" Alec tried to push past Jill, but Paulsgrave Mercy grabbed his arm. Jill placed a hand against his chest, shook her head.

"Alec, you promised. His punishment will be according to law that the wicked may see, and seeing quail. For the Lord God is stern and righteous, and He said that the thief and the liar are vomit out of His mouth."

"He said something else, too." My jeer was deliberately barbed.

"About a woman taken in adultery. I don't think He expected her to cast that first stone."

"Ha!" Doctor Oakes showed his teeth. "The Devil quoting scripture, eh?"

"Is the fellow raving again, Doctor?" asked Jill.

"Oh, no." Katrina gave the question full value. "Cormac is weak but well."

"Cormac." Jill's glance flicked from Katrina to me. "Mmmm? I thought I heard laughter."

"*Ja.* We laugh."

"Indeed?"

The doctor prevented me joining that conversation. With fingers as blunt as pestles he was poking and probing. His method of raising an eyelid would have peeled a grape; he clamped on to a pulse as if determined to stop it. Simple modesty required all my attention. Doctor Oakes tossed coverings aside, unfastened my shirt. When he drew a villainous pair of scissors from his pocket, I was really alarmed, but he merely snipped away my bandages.

"Ha!" He sniffed my chest like a trailing hound. "No putrefaction. You can thank me for that. Spider's web never fails."

"Spider's web?"

"Best clotter there is." Oakes peered at the ceiling. "Too bad this gaol's so new. Had to fetch in a web. Generally handy."

The wound, visible when I craned my neck, was a raw, red furrow from high on my chest to my left armpit. There, I thought, is another scar to match the one on my thigh. It looked to be healing for it was closed and dry, but Oakes pinched it anyway. I yelped.

"Tender, ha! Good."

"Good be damned!" I said. "Keep your meat hooks to yourself!"

"The doctor is helping," said Katrina.

"More than you deserve," Alec Murdoch said.

"Well, now," Paulsgrave Mercy poked his long nose in, too, "gratitude ain't to be expected from miscreants."

"Nor wanted." Doctor Oakes dusted his hands, and turned away. "Though he should be grateful the pike barely grazed the bone. A neat thrust, Mistress."

"Thank you, Doctor."

Jill bowed as she spoke. Sheer surprise had me blinking. I said: "Neat thrust. Thank you. What talk is this?"

"Why, 'tis plain enough," Jill said, cool gaze meeting mine. "Though I take small credit for the Lord must have guided my hand."

[239]

"*Your* hand?"

"Aye. The blow was struck in righteous anger, but I'd not care to have your death on my conscience." She sounded prim, almost unctious. "Glad I was to capture you alive."

"You——"

The boldness of her lie robbed me of speech. I stared, gaping stupidly. From the other faces it was plain that they'd heard the same tale. Jill basked in their admiration. She gave me no chance to protest.

"What is it you say, Alec?" she asked, turning to her brother. "Hew to the line, and let the chips fall where they may?"

"Spoken like a true Murdoch," said Alec, putting a proud hand on her shoulder.

"Aye," I said. "Exactly! But——"

"I've said enough," Jill interrupted, with disdain. "Anything more would be unseemly."

Something in her attitude forced me to hold my tongue despite temptation. If Jill wished to claim my capture, ignoring Chips, she could not harm him dead and might help me living. A man struck down, and taken, by a mere girl might be less carefully guarded.

Paulsgrave Mercy took charge. "Well now," the gaoler said, "he's mending, healing, stronger."

"Ha! He'll live to be hanged!" Doctor Oakes seemed to relish the thought.

"Then," Master Mercy said, "there'll be no more need for nursing."

"No more nursing?"

Both girls spoke as one. Katrina was plainly dismayed; Jill looked startled.

Doctor Oakes laughed. "Fodder and exercise are all he needs. Like any brute. Ha! He's had enough petticoat coddling."

"More than he deserves," said Alec Murdoch.

Jill frowned at Katrina's protest. "But I will come," the Dutch girl said, "bring food. Calves-foot jelly, and——"

The gaoler shook his keys at her. "He can eat, chew, digest the regular prison fare. Eat it myself. You can come visiting if you like, but only on His Excellency, the Governor, Sir Edmund's say-so."

"Quite right," said Jill, sweeping forward and taking Katrina's arm. "Come, Mistress Neville."

"Cormac——"

"Good bye, Katrina," I said, noting Jill's wince. She was canny enough to realize that Katrina could aid me, so I said no more. Resentment at the way Jill herded the blond girl out would only promote suspicion.

Mercy slammed the door after them all, battened it down noisily. They clumped away, voices fading.

So, I was left to my thoughts. They were mostly of Jill. She was, blast her, still owner of my heart, the *cuilin* who could make me catch breath at sight. Of course, I ached to paddle Boston's new heroine until my hand blistered.

There was something just a bit puzzling about that role. Maybe it was her lying, mayhap her uneasiness in front of me. New England might call her heroine, but I knew her for a false jade.

I'd have time aplenty to figure it. The main thing was to get my strength back. The gaol wasn't built that could hold me long. Not if trick, or turn could prevent it.

I turned off my sore side, and went to sleep.

Chapter 28

FOR over a week I was left to the charge of the gaoler, Paulsgrave Mercy. That was both suitable and welcome. I needed a week to clear the last fog wisps of the drugs from my brain, to gain strength, tone muscles. The first morning that I rose from the pallet I tottered on legs as weak as the small beer that wet down the prison fare. When I demanded my clothes, Master Mercy fetched them, clean and brushed, with neat darns where Chips had rent them with his pike. Dressed, I felt more myself, though of course knife and pistol were missing.

The gaoler lent me a razor for shaving purposes, and stood armed guard while I used it. In fact, the mournful Paulsgrave's precautions so little matched his treatment that my curiosity was honed sharper than the razor.

"Thank you for refurbishing my garments, Mercy."

"Well, now," he said, "it weren't my doing, duty, service."

"Whose then?"

"Nobody's."

"Somebody sewed on this shirt," I said, fingering it, "with a neat needle."

"Likely. But the answer you got was paid for, purchased, bought." Mercy cupped a hand in the trade sign common to gaolers the world over. "Any other would come higher."

"I've no coin."

"Then you'd best be content." He knew my pockets were empty for he took his razor and left, playing his now familiar tune on the door locks.

That puzzled me, and my meals added to the puzzlement. My food was plentiful and good. There were savory, thick stews, sometimes with dumplings, fowls, mutton and beef, great lashings of turnips or squash. A fresh-baked wheaten loaf arrived regularly.

My sorest lack was decent drink. Small beer three times the day proved insipid on the tongue, bilge in the belly. Sure, it never yet inspired fight, frolic or song; the stuff would serve to scrub floors with, and that poorly.

Thinking I recognized my benefactor by her cookery, I passed such word to the gaoler.

" 'Tis bitter in here, Mercy. You might tell Mistress Neville a sup of warming drink wouldn't go amiss. A stoup of ale, mayhap, or some claret. Rum and molasses would heat best."

Mercy sniffed, frowned. "Well, now, beer is provided."

"Who can mull small beer? It chills the poker."

He shrugged, not looking at me. The shifty movement gave me an inkling of the truth. Katrina, I thought, knew too much of male wants to be niggardly with spirits. Master Mercy was decking his own table with bottles meant for me! I stored the suspicion away for future use.

It was blessed all I had to hoard. Except for two fellow prisoners who tended my cell under Mercy's glare, I had no other company. The skinny one who carried out the night bucket was serving sentence for drunken brawling. The other was an oafish orphan lad, born out of wedlock, confined as a charity; he brought fuel for my brazier. Neither was what you would call entertaining.

And few of the town's sounds reached me through the barred window, none through the thick stone walls. Besides, it was winter, and the winters of Boston in New England would put the fear of God into hardier sinners than me.

The weather was always freezing, had a full locker of blustery gales, sowed snow for days running. But tempest and cold were the least of my worries. I'd have walked into the teeth of the year's worse blizzard with pleasure. Gaol taught me a hard lesson. A man used to outdoors, to walking a deck or coursing a hill, who had glimpsed many a distant sail and far peak, shrivels when penned in a cell.

Ten paces from window to bolted door. Ten paces from solid wall to solid wall. Crisscross, then, corner to corner, for variety, like a lonely child amusing himself at a solitary game of puss-in-the-corner. Faith, it was poor amusement.

My pacing kept me warmer than huddling over the brazier, and the exercise made me stronger. But my hopes dwindled with each passing day.

Like all new prisoners bent on escape my first concern was to search for means, some flaw that would yield passageway. There was none. The window, reached by standing on my cot, had bars as thick as my wrist, planted firm. Closer inspection showed the door to be even more formidable than suspected.

Aye, the gaol had me stopped. Always, in times of stress, I have managed to whistle up a wind that changed my fortunes, but what kind of wind can blow a man through stone walls, through iron bars, past locks and bolts, to freedom? Especially a friendless man, without weapons or gold, marooned among strangers without humor.

I had not forgotten my sea chest. But I was not tempted to mention it. If Jill Murdoch could prove false for a paltry five pounds, there was no trusting anyone.

Oh, this time there'd be a great spate of whistling before I hit on the right tune!

❖

The first fair day beckoned me to the high window of my cell. By standing atop my pallet I could rest my chin on the lower edge of that deep-graved aperture. It was a cold perch; the bars, set halfway in the opening's four-foot depth, were tingling to the touch. From such a crow's nest it was impossible to see the ground that held the gaol. I was forced to gaze into the distance. My vista was to the south, narrowed by necessity, but sparkling clear under the cloudless blue of a sunlit winter sky.

Close below, past a tracery of bare branch tips that were my sole glimpse of a tree, was a corner of open square out of which rose a church. It was only a few rods distant, and on meeting days I could hear the singing plain, hymns and suchlike as is the custom with Puritans. When the wind was right I could sometimes distinguish voices. They all bellowed away heartily, with more lung power than skill, but the result was not unmusical.

[243]

That morn there was neither wind, nor song. Beyond the church square, and its fronting street, were several solid blocks of houses. These seemed narrow, two-storied buildings; the roofs, white painted by the snow, were as alike as new-minted shillings. Smoke plumed from every chimney.

Farther off, only visible because it topped a hill, was the fort. Even across a quarter mile its shape named it, and the king's jack on a tall flagstaff made it certain. The red cross was plain on its white field. I knew it faced the harbor, but could catch no sight of the water myself.

Whenever a Bostoner crossed my ken, I watched till my eyes watered. There were few enough passers. A skipping boy, a hurrying woman, a sedate preacher turning into the church.

They were human, and free, and I envied them. I tried to slow their steps with wishes, imagined their lives.

So, I was passing my time when the visitors arrived. Their coming was signalled by a murmur of voices, the clump of heels along the passage. Mercy's tinkling key ring summoned me down from the cot.

When the door opened redcoat soldiers marched in as if storming. They were a tight wedge of three. Sergeant Hanks led, carrying a stool. The other two held muskets. One was Sime; the third redcoat I didn't know. Sime gave me a baleful glare that recalled our last meeting, but the sergeant was impassive.

The trio was not alone. Ensign Whitlaw entered next, sneer twisting his mouth, with the stocky naval officer who commanded the frigate. Captain George was followed by the gaoler, and a man in the worn, dark suiting of a clerk.

Last to appear was a broad-shouldered, dark-visaged nobleman with a broad face and square chin. Stride and boots proclaimed the soldier; dress and bearing called him gentry. He wore a beautifully tailored chocolate coat over a gold brocade waistcoat. His hat was plumed, his laces spotless.

"You honor me, Sir Edmund," I said, with a bow.

He was about to seat himself on the stool Hanks had set out, but my remark checked him. Andros never took his sharp-eyed gaze from mine; he neither smiled nor frowned. "I do indeed, Master Doyle. Have we met?"

"No, sir."

"I was here once before, but supposed you in the grip of fever. You recall the time?"

"Very poorly, sir." This would be a hard man to fool. He tested each answer as a coiner bites a gold piece. "A dim memory."

"Yet you knew me?"

"A guess. Who else would come so escorted?" My gesture indicated the soldiery. "And, begging your Excellency's pardon, Puritan gentlemen dress a deal plainer." I made it a statement without impudence.

He considered, nodded, sat down and crossed his legs. Then he said: "Accepted. I'd not have liked to find your illness feigned. Your guess was shrewd. I am Sir Edmund Andros, his majesty's governor of this dominion."

Whitlaw's tight lips disapproved the governor's polite manner. Red-faced Captain George turned even redder. The clerk had a paper ready for Sir Edmund's hand.

I stood waiting while he glanced at it. Soldiers waited thus before officers. Andros had been an officer. I wanted approval without fawning for it.

"Your name?"

"Doyle, sir. Cormac O'Shaugnessy Doyle."

"Methinks you've worn other names at times."

"Aboard ship," I said, taking care with the reply. "Seamen have a habit of calling things and shipmates out of proper terms. A cannon will be known as Blowsy Betty, a tall man as Long Harry. Sure, and weren't there some that spoke of King Charles as Old Rowley?"

"Not in my hearing," Sir Edmund said. The twinkle that came into his eyes encouraged me, but not enough for carelessness. This was no carpet knight, nor official by favor; his next remark tried my guard. "Nor does the custom alter facts. A gentleman gone on the account, as seamen say, is still a pirate."

"And a forced sailor is not."

"Ensign Whitlaw."

"Sir?" Whitlaw's heels clicked. Hand on sword hilt he was the picture of the perfect subaltern.

"You held this man prisoner, I believe. Did he, before he escaped, argue then that he had been forced?"

"Not that I recall," Whitlaw said, his tight voice very sure. "His talk was the usual whining common to such wharf scum. Sergeant Hanks, and this private here will testify to his bawdy singing."

Hanks merely nodded, but Sime sniffed vengeance for the clout I gave him. He said, "Pirate songs, your Excellency, as the ensign remarked at the time."

"So I did," Whitlaw said, and nodded.

"Aye," my smile was deliberately amused, "I stood in Puritan stocks that eve, and wanted to singe their ears. Those tunes are sung in every fo'c's'le."

Captain George swore. "Not on my ship! I'd flog ya——"

"Raw," Andros interrupted. "We know, Captain." He turned back to me. "You knew the charge, Master Doyle. If you didn't fear it, why did you run?"

"Well," I said, "there were several reasons, and all of them good ones. I did not care for the shackles on my wrists. Nor did I fancy the long march to Boston with Ensign Whitlaw driving me with boot and spur."

Whitlaw clenched a fist, gave a short laugh. "A fussy pirate, this. Did you expect to be coddled?"

"No," I said, seeing Andros awaited my answer, "I expected to jump ship at the first chance. Which I did."

"*Touché*," Sir Edmund said. "My soldiers failed where Mistress Murdoch succeeded. Like better men, Master Doyle, your mistake was trying to hide behind petticoats."

"As you said, sir. 'Tis always a mistake. But that was fortunes of war, not choice. Surely, Mistress Murdoch has related how it happened."

"In detail." The governor nodded. "But I take it you'd have kept on running if she hadn't wounded you?"

"I would indeed. I'd no desire to hang by mistake."

"Mistake?"

"Aye, sir."

"Do you question the king's justice?"

"Not the king's, your Excellency. I'm a loyal subject of his majesty. Sure, if what I've heard is truth, King James, considering his leanings, would not be unfair to a man because he happened to be a Papist."

Sir Edmund Andros glowered. He said: "He is our king. He would not protect a priest who'd turned pirate!"

"I believe it, your Excellency. But he's an ocean away. I've been told that Papists get short shrift in New England."

"I rule here in the king's name!"

"And delighted I am to hear it. From the way the preachers thunder against the King's Chapel, I was beginning to wonder."

They all stirred. George and Whitlaw glanced at each other. The gaoler and the clerk stared. Sir Edmund leaned forward, aimed a finger like a pistol. The easy voice was shades brisker.

"What preachers? In which towns?"

"I know the names of neither. Wasn't I wandering, and not anxious to attract notice?"

"It doesn't matter. The like is said from the pulpits of Boston. These colonials find diversion in sermons. Their idea of obeying a royal command is to talk about it for ages."

"Aye, sir. They do go on about the new dominion of the provinces. Some even swear that they'll not give up their charters." I was using everything mentioned on my travels, catching at straws, but it seemed to be making a brick. "Of course it was just tavern gossip."

Whitlaw grunted; Captain George snorted. The governor merely said: "So? Among friends, I suppose?"

"Friends?" My blandness matched his own. "I'd not exactly call these people friendly. A mite stiff-necked to strangers. But it does help if your father supported the Protector, or if you'd a cousin who rode with Monmouth."

"Rebels, you think?"

"I'd not put it so strong, your Excellency. But hills that can hide regicides are many in this land." Andros was a loyal governor; to speak of the regicides was inviting trouble. To my surprise he laughed, a deep, pleasant laugh.

"Well done, Master Doyle," he said. "You have led us among the hills to hunt rebels, far from the sea and any talk of piracy. But you are bird in hand, my friend."

"Limed and taken," I said, recovering. "For all your net was cast for a falcon and caught a sparrow."

"Parrot," said Andros. "A talking bird."

"Parrot, then, but harmless."

"That's for the Court of Admiralty to decide. You will have a fair trial, a chance to plead. But let's have a few questions settled. First, you're an Irishman, and a Papist?"

"Aye, sir, to both."

"A sailor by trade?"

"These many years."

"What ships have you served on?"

"I sailed from London," I said. "On the *Happy Discovery*. For the Indies. Carrying hardware, wines, and cloth. After dyewood."

"Captain?"

George was ready for the governor's question. "The *Happy Discovery*," he said. "I think so. About three hundred tons. A bark."

"Brigantine," I said. "Thomas Stowe, Master. I learned my trade under him. We traded with all the islands, sir. English, Spanish, French. Port Royal. Hispaniola. Martinico. I made three voyages with Captain Stowe."

"Stowe's dead," said Captain George.

"Aye, sir. Of yellow fever in the Cayman Islands. The brigantine was sold to the slave trade. Not liking the life I took another berth."

"Honest work?"

"Yes, your Excellency. Aboard the trading pink *Rachel*. She was Dutch built but fine for island coasting. Trimble Coates, Master-owner. Charlestown born, Trim was."

"Captain?"

"Nay, Sir Edmund. Never heard of the craft."

"Other service, Master Doyle?"

"Well, sir, I'd barely signed aboard the *Bristol Merchant* when——"

George shouted, slapping fist in palm. "That's the one, Sir Edmund!" His red face was abeam with satisfaction. "I've papers on that one. The *Bristol Merchant*, three hundred fifty tons. Walter Heatheridge, Master. Taken by pirates in the Leeward Passage. Heatheridge was cast adrift in his longboat."

"He reached port safely then," I said. "I'm glad to hear it."

"I wouldn't be," Andros said, "for he reported one Doyle as gone over to the pirates."

"Forced, your Excellency."

"Willing!" Captain George bellowed. "It's written down!"

Whitlaw's grin was wolfish. Sime's was a thinned image of the ensign's. The gaoler licked his lips; the clerk scribbled a note. Only Sergeant Hanks and Governor Andros seemed a trifle sorry.

"Forced," I repeated.

"You'll have your chance to prove it," said Sir Edmund wearily. "That's all for now, gentlemen. I wished to be certain this was the same Doyle mentioned in Captain George's orders."

Whitlaw and George saluted, and left. The gaoler ushered them out. The clerk followed, but Sir Edmund made no move. Of course the three redcoats remained at their posts.

"Master Doyle," said the governor, removing his hat, "I confess that you've surprised me."

"I might say the same, Sir Edmund." More than ever I wanted this man's support. He had played his hand like a veteran officer and obtained his information. Now, his tone was friendly. There'd been no cause to deny the *Bristol Merchant*. My service aboard her had been so brief that Heatheridge was a vague memory.

"That," Andros said, "was no fair test. I had your name. But the surprise lies in your manner. I expected a cringing felon, a bravo, or a plain, blunt seaman."

"Plain, blunt and honest, Sir Edmund."

[248]

"You?" He laughed heartily. "That claim will never prove you honest. You're about as plain and blunt as a Cellini stiletto."

I didn't place the reference, but returned the compliment. Smiling, I said: "We've both been misled. Tyrant was the name these folk put to you."

"Tyrant. Yes, it would be." Andros rose and began to pace, swinging his hat. He had the old officer's trick of ignoring sentries; the three soldiers might have been statuary. Sergeant Hanks followed the governor with his eyes. Sime and his partner stared straight ahead.

"Popish tyrant," I said.

"You need not elaborate. I've heard worse. They speak so of the king himself, though couched in biblical language. Tyranny. That's when a royal governor gives an order."

To spread the fire, I blew on it, but gently, gently. My purpose was to win a confidence, not lose the confidant by brazenness.

"Not one who's met you, Sir Edmund, would believe——"

"Poppycock!" He flapped the hat plumes at me. "These settlers believe what their divines tell them! Those that aren't divines themselves. Why, at that Harvard College across the Charles they hammer out new ministers like an armorer makes swords."

"But——"

He never heard me. "Oh, they believe it, all right. The wives and children take it for Gospel. And all I've done is serve my king, and follow his commands. Not always the right commands, but the king's."

"As was your duty, Sir Edmund."

"As was my duty." Andros stopped ranting, stared at me, threw his head back to laugh. "O' rare, indeed! Master Doyle, you've a great gift for catching flies with honey! But you seem a reasonable man, pirate or no!"

"Thank you," I said.

Sir Edmund Andros laughed again. "You're a likeable rogue," he said, "but I'll uphold the king's law, as sworn. Which, of course, is another reason these Bostoners hate me. I'll be at your trial, but only as spectator."

"Sorry I am to hear that."

"Don't be. The magistrates are mostly native born. You'd be condemned out of hand if linked with Edmund Andros!"

I didn't believe that. For all his outburst he was royal governor, and would defend his prerogatives. As he made me a courtly bow, I spoke out.

"May I beg a favor, Sir Edmund?"

"Well?" He was instantly wary.

"Could I exercise in the prison yard? Fair days like these. Under guard, but, if you please, without irons."

"It would stir a rumpus. Master Mercy is my gaoler. The Puritan theocracy would much prefer their own man in charge here."

Hanks cleared his throat. "We soldiers could guard him in turns, sir."

"He got away from you once, Sergeant."

"Aye, Sir Edmund. It would not happen twice."

"Very well. Arrange it."

Sir Edmund clapped his hat on as he stalked out. The redcoats filed after him. Hanks winked over his shoulder as he closed the door.

So, I had met the governor of all New England. He'd had the best of the encounter. The favor of exercise would be a boon, but not toward escape. Hanks meant what he said. I thought Sir Edmund liked me, but thought too that he'd make sure I received my desserts.

There'd be no royal reprieve if my sentence was hanging.

Chapter 29

THE governor kept his word, but the foul weather returned to prevent my exercise for several days. Gales that blew in from the harbor seemed strong enough to rock the stone gaol itself.

Paulsgrave, still the mournful, careful watchdog, had evidently been impressed by Sir Edmund's friendly manner. A bottle of claret appeared with my supper a night later. The gaoler watched me uncork it with such woebegone greed that I poured him a bumper. He drained it at a gulp, but I rationed the rest.

There was only a swallow left when the sun came back again. Sergeant Hanks arrived in mid-morning. He had two redcoats with him, one a pudgy apple-cheeked Dutchman. Under their muskets, Mercy released me from my cell.

"No tricks now," Hanks said.

"Why, Sergeant," I said, "put the very thought from your mind. Would I give the back of my hand to those doing me this favor?"

The sergeant squinted at me, not smiling. "Not if they were looking."

He spoke without rancor, more like a fellow veteran than a captor. But he placed the two guards carefully at the corners of the prison yard, and kept his own musket on the half cock.

A foot or more of snow covered the ground and made walking difficult. The sun, for all its spun-gold handsomeness, lacked the warmth to melt the frosted crust. Outside, moving, the cold air had a cleaner, more intoxicating tang than when penned inside stone walls. And the feeling of release brought a gay lilt to my step.

Behind the prison the yard stretched to that of the schoolhouse on the next street. It must have been a pleasant walk in summer, for the area was studded with the trees of a small orchard. These were bare now, except for the white snow fur that coated the branches. They had been planted around the field's edges, and Hanks, thinking them cover, steered me into the open center.

He paced along beside me, his heavier weight breaking the deeper path. Some men added zest to a walk by their quiet presence; Hanks was one of them. He trudged in silence until we'd finished a complete circuit.

"Doyle," he said. "That day you escaped us. Remember?"

"Aye. With happy memory."

"Was the woman in on it?"

"Lady Esterling?"

"Herself. It puzzles me that you were so ready for flight when the occasion arose."

"Sure, you'd do better to blame the snake that frighted her."

"I saw no snake." Hanks tilted his head for a glance at my face. "And a soldier doesn't like to be fooled by a display of limbs. Not when the pretty sight costs him a prisoner."

"Mark you," I said, "I was set to run on the slightest pretext. At the first opportunity."

"You chose a good one."

"Did I not? Only my strong will kept me from gawking like the rest of you. But it's all old history now."

"No," Hanks said, shaking his head. "She's here at Sir Edmund's court, so to speak. Her husband has official post, and the ensign's still dancing to her tune."

"Fie, Sergeant! Scandal?"

The big shoulders moved in a shrug. "Don't put words in my mouth, sailor. For aught I know she keeps her laces knotted. She could make a fool of Ensign Whitlaw without putting horns on her spouse."

"Is it the slur on your army you resent?"

"It's not being sure she's to be trusted." Hanks frowned, kicked at a dislodged chunk of snow. "Boston is not a friendly town to the likes of you and me. A pirate to these Puritans is only a cut below a redcoat. Since that's the way the forces are drawn up, I'd like to be sure that everybody in my camp is truly on my side."

"Lady Esterling seemed no Puritan."

"Nor friend to felons! A woman who'll dupe you once, will try it again."

We were marching, slower now, across the far end of the yard. From the schoolhouse came the thin, shrill singsong of tots at their lessons. The sound carried plainly to our ears. I stopped to listen, and Hanks stayed with me.

> In Adam's fall
> We sinned all.

"There's your answer," I said. "Snake and lady put the old Adam in us all. You're fearful where you've no cause. Blame my heels and wits for my escape, not Lady Esterling's underpinnings."

"I'm not afeared," Hanks said. "I just like to know how the pickets are posted, and which are reliable. If the lady is skittish that's one thing, but if she's likely to cause trouble it's another."

"You expect trouble then?"

"Nothing open. More sneers at a soldier doing his duty. More complaints from the preachers when a man off duty takes a pint too much. These are a strange folk, Doyle. Their own New Model Puritan army was the first to wear the red coat, but all they recall is that the cipher on our flags and buckles is J.R. for a Stuart king with Popish bent."

"He's still their king."

Hanks held up a hand. The children had gone on with their lessons, and another scrap of it reached us.

> Young Obadias,
> David, Josias—
> All were pious.

"Using your own tactic," said Hanks, "the schoolboys over there prove my point. They recite all day out of a Puritan book, chapter and verse, about the evils of sin, and the joys of the pious. And those same little hellions when let out will snowball my patrols on sight."

"With rocks inside the balls," I said, laughing.

"Of course."

"Children are children, Sergeant. But few of them have routed troops."

"These are a different breed, Doyle. They fear the Lord, mayhap, for they tell us so often enough. But for the rest they're chosen people, and everyone else can give way or get sput on."

Hanks, from a barracks window, saw things invisible to Sir Edmund Andros, but his view of Boston was not dissimilar to the governor's. I began to realize how high the barrier was between the town folk and the town government. This thought I tucked away in my head, much as a housewife stores the live yeast borrowed from her neighbor against the day when she kneads dough for a loaf. Then I resumed my walk, feet crunching to the time of the small scholars' litany.

> Zaccheus he
> Did climb the tree
> Our Lord to see.

I was winded and damp, but not even the close guarding could dash my spirits. True, the yard had proved another disappointment. There was no easy way of escaping from it. Until a thaw the deep snow would slow running feet, and a daylight bolt was overlooked by the back windows of surrounding houses. Hanks at my elbow made such an attempt foolhardy. Unless my attack was overpoweringly sudden he was more than my match. And the other two guards would not be standing idle while we wrestled.

A pair of muskets I might have dared, not *three*. Not while the sergeant had the aiming of one, at close range. He was too complete a soldier to be a poor marksman.

"Say, there!" Paulsgrave Mercy called from the gaol's back door.

"Hour's up," Hanks said.

I nodded, wheeled about obediently. The more docile I was now, the better my future prospects. So I said: "Thanks, Sergeant. 'Twas pleasant. Will you come tomorrow?"

"If it prove fair." Hanks waved his detail closer, put a friendly hand on my shoulder. "And as for thanks, I'd do as much for any man smart enough to get away as you did. Not that it will happen again."

There were moments, and this was one, when I'd have preferred Sergeant Hanks less kind, and more forgetful of the stain on his record.

❖

The cell door was open awaiting my return. My meal, a kettle of stew with a mouth-watering aroma, stood steaming on the coals in the brazier. A fresh bottle, cork drawn, was warming beside it. Once I saw that I saw nothing else, but plunged straight in to seize it. Tilting the bottle, I ignored the slam of the door behind me, Mercy's drumbeat tattoo on the locks, the soldiers marching away. The wine was another, better claret, and I took a long pull to welcome it.

Then, I sampled the stew, found its taste outdid its odor, and was suddenly ravening. The meat was squirrel, the broth well laced with rum, the whole done to a turn. Without more ado, I fell to.

I had sunk the kettle's contents by a good inch when a chuckle chirped behind me. Spoon halfway to mouth, I froze, doubting my hearing. Another chuckle rippled into a giggle. I turned my head.

Jill Murdoch was standing flat against the wall inside the closed door!

"Is it as good as the rabbit on the island, Cormac?" Her voice was gay, her eyes tender.

My gaping was a grand foolish expression that brought her laughter bubbling. I shook the spoon at her, spilled stew in all directions, slammed the utensil back in the kettle. Anger flamed my face, slurred my speech. And all the time her hair had my vision fuddled as if I stared too long at the sun. Sure, I couldn't have named the color of her clothes.

"You!" I said, with fine wit. "What are *you* doing here?"

"Visiting my husband."

"Well, you can do your gloating elsewhere! You've earned my hate, and more, but I'd not soil my hands by giving you——" What she had said finally penetrated the blur of fury that possessed me. I choked on an epithet, coughed out a weak question. "Did—did you say 'husband'?"

"Aye. That I did." She was regarding me with demure gravity, and she dipped me a curtsy.

"The word should sear your tongue."

"Nary a sear," Jill said. "See?" She stuck it out at me.

"You sold me for five pounds!"

"'Twas all I could get. You were not in good condition at the time." Her calm look was jolted as I started for her; her speech changed to panicked haste. "Cormac, wait! Please! I was teasing!"

"Teasing! Put a noose around a man's windpipe and tease——"

Jill was faster than I was. Though I had her pinned in a corner, she ducked under my grasp, backed across the cell. Even as she danced away, she talked hurriedly.

"Cormac, I only pretended! For your sake! I had to pretend, to lie——"

I wasn't listening too closely. I was bent on revenge. She dodged again, but this time I jumped quicker. I caught her by the side of my pallet, held her fast with one arm. My bellow drowned her pleading.

"So you wounded me, captured me, and had me gaoled! Well, heroine, here are some wounds you'll remember!"

[254]

With that I tilted her, face down, over the cot, and walloped her bottom, swinging with all my strength.

She yelped, kicking. Jill was ever harder to hold than quicksilver, and she twisted from my grip in an inkling. She was on her feet, and her slap rocked my head, before I could deliver a second spank.

Her eyes blazed, then softened. Even as I reached for her, she stepped inside my arms. She clutched me by both ears, put her mouth on mine.

"Fool," she murmured, "doltish gowk of a fool! To doubt my love for a minute!"

"Love?" I said. But my hands had notions of their own, and they were not bruising her.

"Love," Jill repeated, whispering against my lips. "Did I not give you proof of it?" Her hands left my ears to clasp behind my neck. "Do I not now?"

The whole length of her was molded against me. When I spoke again, my voice still shook, but there was no anger in it, nor was there room for any.

"But, Jill, on the frigate——"

"Cormac." She placed her cheek against mine for easier speaking. "We were in sore straits. Aye, with you bad hurt and myself distracted with the fear of it. I'd have hailed a Sallee Rover, or the ghost ship of legend to get you out of the cold."

"I heard you tell Captain George——"

"A tale." A feather-light laugh tickled my ear lobe. "Sure, sick or well, I'd have thought you'd recognize a tale when you heard one. The moment I met that brute of a captain, I knew I'd be clapped in irons as a pirate lad or lass."

"Or flogged raw."

"His favored threat. You needed care, a surgeon. As my lady captor, I could command both. So, with my fingers crossed where none could see, I told of wounding you."

"Had I threatened your honor?"

"My dear man, of course not! My virtue and pious praying curbed any such inclinations." Jill pulled her head back to show her blush. "Oh, Cormac, darling, what a terrible liar you've married!"

"There are others," I said.

"Well, the bait was swallowed whole, hook, line and weight. I am celebrated, the wonder of Boston, and you are a scoundrel. And that will serve us, too. For they are counting much on my testimony to hang you, but surprised they'll be when they hear it."

"You could do naught else, Jill."

She'd bartered death in an open boat for death on the gallows, but I'd not reproach her ever. She'd had little choice, and done what she could. I loved her for it. But she overvalued her change of testimony. Neither Sir Edmund Andros nor any able magistrate would rely on one girl witness for a hanging charge.

"You don't believe me," Jill said, reading my thoughts.

"I believe you. But I wish we were both away out of this. Trials are strange, tricky affairs. I've no liking for any, and less for one of my own."

"Anyway, you're well again, and that was my first concern. You came near dying, Cormac."

By that time we had shifted to the pallet, and Jill was seated on my lap. When she mentioned my illness her hug was intense.

"Sure," I said, "a foot under the keel is as good as a fathom. With your help, and God's, we'll laugh at their silver oar yet. And aren't you rich as well as lovely?"

"Rich? Oh, you mean the five pounds."

"Blood money."

"Aye. But 'twas offered, and 'twas only canny to take it. Besides it was welcome. It paid for comforts and doctoring. Master Mercy had the last of it for letting me in today."

"Mercy will die rich. But I thank him."

"Cormac, you do understand that I must keep up my pretense. There's Alec——" She giggled at my groan. "And others. Daniel Bradish is here in Boston."

"Oh."

"Now, don't look like that. The wedding is postponed indefinitely. Poor Daniel is ill pleased by my sudden prominence. He thinks it unseemly for a minister's wife to be mixed up with a pirate."

"Why so it is," I said. "But you're not a minister's wife. You're Mistress Cormac Doyle, and don't you forget it!"

"Is it likely, the way you beat me? That was a lusty buffet you doled out."

"A love pat. Like this."

"Not like that!"

What with talking such nonsense, and the warm content of being in each other's arms again, the stone gaol could have changed to a marble palace unnoticed. We were so wrapped in each other that we were deaf to all else. Neither of us heard the keys at the lock, nor the sliding of bolts. For a poor excuse it was not the gaoler's familiar racket.

"W-well!" said a male voice, "no w-wonder Master Mercy did not w-wish to yield his keys!"

Jill shot off my lap as if flung by a catapult. She left her bonnet behind, her hair was disarrayed, and her cheeks flamed redder than the coals in the brazier.

"Reverend Master Mather!"

"Mistress Murdoch."

With a curt bow the man in the doorway seemed to lose his stammer. Since he wore the black and bands of a Puritan divine, I was not surprised by his flustered recoil at sight of us. Reverend Mather was young, only a few years older than myself, but held himself with a taut control that reminded me at once of a stretched cable spring. This made his moderate height appear tall. He had a thin face, well made, and his hair was already beginning to gray. His eyes were the most intense, gem-like, beacons.

"I come as is my duty to preach the solace of true repentance," Mather said, no trace of stammer in his preaching voice, "only to find that the misguided sinner has found his solace in another, wicked way."

"Now, don't jump to conclusions," I said rising.

"Cormac, this is the Reverend Cotton Mather." Jill meant to hush me with the name.

"How do you do, sir?" I made a formal bow.

That surprised him. Frowning, he glanced from me to Jill and back. "I know you're Master Doyle," Mather said, "for I was here during your illness. But something is amiss." The probing eyes narrowed. "Mistress Murdoch is supposed to be your Nemesis. Yet, I find her here with you in amorous dalliance."

By the way Jill paled, I knew the accusation was serious. This Cotton Mather, I decided, must be a dominie of some note. The preachers ran the town, and Jill exposed would be subject to punishment.

"Do not blame Mistress Murdoch," I said, trying to hit on an excuse. "She came for the same reason you did."

"Aye," said Jill. "To try by precept to wean the wrongdoer from his evil ways."

"But——" Cotton Mather shook his head. "I cannot disbelieve the testimony of my own eyes."

I would, if such eyes were mine, but that was not a politic remark. Jill looked so downcast, and the minister so righteous that I became belligerent.

"She is blameless!"

"I saw——"

"Something stronger than both of us."

Cotton Mather drew a breath; his glance sharpened. A finger was pointed at Jill. "Is this true?" he asked. "Were you in the grip of some unworldly power?"

"Why," said Jill, "I do not know." I was beginning to recognize her wiles, and saw her feeling her way, testing the path with each sentence. Was there escape here?

"Something came over you? Drew you to this—this pirate?"

"Oh, aye," Jill said.

"And you." He turned toward me quickly. "You exerted this power over the girl, deliberately?"

"No, sir. It overwhelmed me, too."

Cotton Mather clapped his hands together to form the attitude of prayer. His voice intoned his conclusion as if it were a text.

"Witchcraft."

"Witch——" Jill's jaw dropped, pulling her mouth to an O. She showed an instant fear, then her bright eyes flicked toward me, alive with merriment. " 'Tis true. I think I was bewitched."

That was dangerous jesting. A rope's end was bad enough, but burning at the stake was worse. I wanted no charge of witchery replacing one of piracy. Choosing my words, I tried to make that plain.

"I am no witch. This female is my enemy. Because of her I am in this gaol. I bear the marks of her thrust on my body. If she is bewitched, then I am in no better case, for I hate the sight of her."

"Interesting," said Cotton Mather. "Most interesting. Witchcraft is something deserving greater study. I have a young girl now, Martha Goodwin, staying my house. She too is subject to the strangest influences. And, in her case, the witch responsible was tried and executed."

"Yet she is still afflicted?" I asked.

"Yes." The word was slow spoken, considered. He seemed honestly and tolerantly puzzled. "The fire, I'm afraid, is not the solution to the problem. Witches should be restored to Godliness, not consigned to the flames."

That was his first sign of liberality, and it impressed me. Jill, however, was quicker at manipulating it for her own purposes.

"Reverend Master Mather," she said, with breathless respect, "could we not keep this secret until we discover the truth? I am, I admit, jealous of my reputation."

Cotton Mather nodded slowly. "There is no need for haste."

Whatever more he might have said was interrupted by loud voices in the passage. We could hear Paulsgrave Mercy expostulating, Alec Murdoch thundering. As one we turned toward the doorway.

Alec sounded furious. "What do you mean, my sister is in the cell with that son of Satan? Would you deliver the daughters of Israel into the claws of the Medes and the Persians?"

"Master Doyle," said Cotton Mather, "I think Mistress Murdoch would be thankful for her bonnet."

It was quiet done, and graceful. As I handed Jill her headgear, I stared at the clergyman. He met my gaze blandly. By the time Alec appeared in the doorway, Jill was properly covered.

"Jill!" roared Alec. "Are you daft to put yourself within reach of this villain's filthy fingers?"

Cotton Mather's tone was pitched low, yet sizzled like drops of water on a hot griddle. "Master Murdoch, I do not think your sister would come to harm in my presence."

"The Reverend Master Mather," Jill said, "has been my bulwark through this interview."

Neat, I said silently. Neat and tied with ribbon. Jill, with a sentence, had managed to link us with Cotton Mather as fellow conspirators. There was a girl to cherish! Alec's eyes got as round as olives.

" 'Tis Cotton Mather," said the young man with Alec.

"Aye, Daniel." Alec touched his hat.

Naturally, I took a good look at Daniel Bradish. There was a tall drink of water for you. In his clerical garb he resembled a black needle. Sure, if he closed one eye you could thread him!

"I think we should leave now," Jill said.

The Reverend Master Mather was the last to quit the cell. At the threshold he turned. He smiled, and it was a thing that flattered his face.

"You know, Master Doyle," he said, "that power we spoke of may not be unworldly at all. But the way of a man with a maid."

The slightest suggestion of wink flickered his eyelid. The sudden flash of good nature startled me. He was gone before I managed to think of a reply.

So I met Cotton Mather, who, with his father Increase, held a position of power and influence in the Boston hierarchy that was unequaled in his time.

I thought little of the meeting on that day. My thoughts were of Jill, of joy that her betrayal was a sham. That turned the squirrel stew, long cold, to ambrosia, and the claret into nectar.

Chapter 30

I⅂ was Cotton Mather, of course, a great scribbler himself, who provided the materials and insisted that I inscribe the record of my adventures that is this book. He persuaded the other Puritan dominies—and hardly a day passed without a preacher heavy with sermon who came to rehearse the next Sabbath's discourse in my lap—that my log was important.

I will say this for the theocracy of Boston: they would read almost any work if only for the joy of refuting the writer. Mayhap they expected a confession, or a memoir of a repentant pirate, but, though they all said much of salvation and repentance, none of them ever tried to change the style or matter of my writing. Quills were supplied by the pitcher full, ink by the bucket, paper enough to cover the stone gaol, inside and out, with a double-thick layer, but the suggestions were so few they could have been listed on a nail head.

Of Cotton Mather, a clergyman not without faults, my praise was, and is, without stint. I learned to know this young man in a way that I think few have known him. He came to the stone gaol several times a week, goaded by the desire to snatch a brand from the burning. His sermons bored me, his scriptural quotations plagued me, but discarding this chaff, his wheat was of purest gold.

He was as strange a mixture as Bumboo Punch, a concoction that always contained whatever was handy. Item: Cotton Mather was an ordained divine. Item: he had been destined for the church since childhood. Item: he had humor, learning, and too much adulation; the women of Boston thought the sun rose and set by the way he flipped his robe. But, through it all, as flavor laces a punch, the man had a quality that could not be missed.

For one thing he was surprisingly tolerant for his cloth and calling. Not about dogma! The good Lord's wrath was temperate compared to Cotton Mather on points of religion. Sure, he'd argue Saint Peter out of his keys, and post him for a heretic in the bargain. I had to steer him off that subject with gentle care. But on all other matters he talked freely and well, for he loved to talk; his questing, keen mind darted from topic to topic like a hummingbird among flowers.

There was a wealth of knowledge in his every discourse, and at times even wit. Only that they caught him fledgling, and trained him to the jesses early, he'd have soared wide and free. Children knew his kindness for he was easiest with them, but he had a ready smile for a pretty female too. He never shut his eyes at a wind-displayed ankle in his life.

I found him bluntly honest in his hatred. He hated Sir Edmund Andros just this side the Pope of Rome, and he hated King James well on the far side. He told me so.

"That fanged court tiger," Cotton Mather called the governor, "unleashed on this poor colony by that horned lecher on the throne!"

"Such talk is treason, Reverend."

"It is, Cormac, to James Stuart. But to be silent under tyranny is treason to God!"

"Tyranny? You walk about as freely as the watch. Sir Edmund hasn't banned you from your pulpit."

"He wouldn't dare!" Though we talked on friendly terms, Cotton Mather was vehement. "He chivvied my father out of the colony, forced him to fly in the night to take a just complaint to the king."

"To that same horned lecher?"

His grin flashed. "The very one. Philip drunk or Philip sober the appeal must go to the throne. Not that my father is making much progress with James."

"I'm the one should complain of tyranny. Penned behind bars and threatened with the gallows."

"Piracy is a heinous crime, Cormac. The path that leads to the silver oar is not one of righteousness."

"Nor primroses, Reverend."

"I pray for your acquittal almost as much as for your true repentance," said Cotton Mather soberly. Then, twinkling, he smiled at me. "Besides, I'd not like Mistress Murdoch left in a bewitched state after your demise. That is easier corrected while you live."

"I prefer it myself."

In such fashion, from kindliness, he gave lip service to Jill's fiction, though I was sure he knew it for falsehood. I was careful never to remind him of it, and he never mentioned finding us alone. Still, I was sure Mather was responsible that Mercy stayed in the cell when Jill came visiting. The gaoler was Sir Edmund's man, but he was deathly afraid of Cotton Mather.

"You may leave us," Jill said the first time this happened.

[261]

"Well, now," said Paulsgrave, "that ain't right, proper, permitted."

"But I gave you a shilling!"

"He gets his meals, don't he?"

"Master Mercy," I said, "suppose the governor should learn you take bribes?"

"From you or her?" The gaoler looked even sadder. "That don't make sense. I'd clap you in irons for lying about me. And folks'd wonder why the lady wanted to see you so bad she forked out hard money for it."

He had us, and he knew it. Jill was furious at being cheated, but we had to be content with whispers. Mercy made no attempt to listen, and sometimes we held hands behind Jill's skirt, but naturally there were no kisses.

My exercise in the yard on fair mornings was even better attended. In fact, except for prayer meetings it became the principal amusement of Boston. The neighboring schoolboys discovered that a live pirate could be seen during recess, and told others. After that there was always a crowd gaping at me from the schoolyard.

Sergeant Hanks didn't like the audience. He doubled his guard to be sure that it didn't give me ideas. Hanks knew that a curious crowd can be used by an artful fugitive, both as a screen, and as an obstacle to the pursuit.

None of the gawkers tried to speak to me. I was a freak attraction, like a two-headed calf at a fair, worth a peek even if fake. Then, one morning a couple waved and stepped forward. The crowd buzzed at such behavior, buzzed louder when the sergeant swore and leveled his musket.

"Stand still," Hanks said.

"I'm not moving," I said, "but it's only Katrina Neville and her husband."

"*Ja,*" called Katrina. "Just me and Devon."

"That's right." The young post rider was as delighted as his wife at the stir they were making. His baby face had the beam of a tickled cherub.

"What do you want?"

"To talk to Cormac is all, Sergeant."

I said, "I've missed seeing you, Katrina."

She dimpled at me, ready as ever to giggle. "First it was forbidden. Then Devon return." She fluttered her lashes at her husband.

They simpered like bemused rustics in a pastoral scene. Even Hanks couldn't keep his frown.

"You remember Katrina," I said.

"Sure," Hanks said. "The inn. I'd heard you'd married. I hope you keep her on a tight bit, young fellow."

Devon Neville laughed. For all his boyish looks he had none of the stripling's timidity. "A horse or a wife," he said, with authority, "is best gentled by hand."

"*Ja!*" said Katrina.

"They asked news of you," said the post rider, turning to me, "in every town from here to York. There'll be a passel of folk at your hanging."

"Devon!"

"It's all right, Katrina," I said. "After all Devon's the crier wherever he rides."

"And I must tell true, Kat-kit," said Devon, "though Master Doyle knows I wish him well."

"And thanks you."

"You're well remembered along the road." Devon burst into a guffaw. "If not too accurately. Some of the constables swear you were armed to the teeth. And Old Jotham Twigg has added a few stone to your weight and two feet to your stature."

"Twigg is pig," said Katrina, wrinkling her nose as if she smelled her former employer.

The rising murmur of the onlookers warned me, but Ensign Whitlaw's whiplash of a voice caught Sergeant Hanks by surprise.

"Damn all! What are you holding here, Sergeant? A convict coffee house?"

Hanks snapped to attention. "The prisoner is under guard, sir. And permitted visitors."

Whitlaw knew it, but Lady Esterling was on his arm and he was posturing for her. He gazed down his nose at the sergeant.

"By whose orders?"

"Sir Edmund's, sir."

"My Lady." Katrina made her curtsy. Devon raised his hat and bowed.

"Good morning, Katrina," said Lady Esterling. She had the bland, drawn-on-procelain loveliness I recalled. This time her riding habit was rich wine velvet. Even the feather in her broad-brimmed hat was carefully brushed. It was hard to believe she'd ever had a wanton thought, much less deed.

"Katrina?" The ensign pretended ignorance, snapped his fingers. "Ah, yes. The serving wench."

"My wife," said Devon Neville.

I could have hugged the lad. He stood, thumbs in belt, braving Whitlaw as calmly as he had left off the officer's title. The ensign's cheekbones reddened with anger.

Lady Esterling prevented his outburst. "Protégés of mine, Borden," she said. Her eyes flicked toward me. "So they have caught you again, fellow. And your downfall was a woman."

"Fate, my Lady," I said. Her faint contempt nettled me, but I was mindful of my debt. Her ingenuity had made my escape possible; she had the right to disdain my recapture.

"Fate is a coward's excuse for failure."

Her baiting pleased Whitlaw, but I kept rein on my temper. Hanks was listening so hard his ears quivered. However low Lady Esterling's opinion of me, I was not going to betray her trick in public. So I merely bowed.

Then, gazing past them all, I saw Jill Murdoch coming across the snow. The spectators practically cheered. Those poor theater-hating Puritans hadn't enjoyed such a spectacle since the burning of Boston!

Jill's appearance puzzled me. Her hostility to the pirate who'd abducted her was public knowledge; it served to excuse her visits to the gaol. Before this gathering we would both have to pretend, and so many watching eyes multiplied the risk.

"Ah, yes," said Lady Esterling, turned by the crowd's excitement, "the darling of the mob."

It was a cool insult delivered by a master, and it was capped by Whitlaw's titter. Katrina, who believed Jill my enemy, was female enough to welcome her ladyship as an ally.

"*Ja*, my Lady. Mistress Judas Murdoch."

The challenge was as plain as cats yowling at an intruder. Jill's step checked for an instant, her chin went up, and I saw her lips tighten. As I braced myself I was both proud and fearful. In temper she would say anything, might forget to dissemble.

She sailed up like a man-o'-war and opened with a broadside. Though she addressed Whitlaw her voice was pitched for the crowd to hear.

"What is the meaning of this, Ensign? My reading led me to understand that only Barbary pirates entertained harems?"

Whitlaw had no chance to reply. While Katrina merely looked puzzled, her ladyship purred a return.

"Mistress Murdoch forgets herself, Borden. Sir Edmund Andros governs here, not she."

"I need not the reminder, your Ladyship." Jill managed to make the title a slur. "'Tis obvious. Only those bred at a profligate court would allow consorting with criminals."

"Now, just a minute——" Whitlaw sputtered.

"Those who have never seen a court," said Lady Esterling, "are hardly capable of criticising it."

Katrina was out of her depth, but she tried.

"*Ja.* Is so."

Jill had no interest in small game. She kept her sights on the lady. "You misunderstand me, your Ladyship. What happens on the tiles of London does not concern me. The fate of this felon does."

"He's permitted exercise," Whitlaw said.

"Then, let him exercise."

"Right," Hanks muttered, under his breath.

By this time I was enjoying myself too much not to take a part. My glare was directed at Jill; my surly tone would have done credit to an abused apprentice.

"Some ain't satisfied with sticking a man, and gaoling him, but they even begrudge him a few kind words."

"You hold your tongue," said Whitlaw.

"But, Borden, the man speaks no more than truth."

"*Ja.*"

"Hush, Kat-kit."

The sergeant sighed.

Jill's glance barely touched me before it shifted. Then in spite of the general hubbub she managed to say what she'd come to say. Her message made my spine tingle.

"'Tis curiosity not kindness brings these folks to ogle you," she said. "The same was shown an hour ago when the whole North Side turned out to stare at twin Negroes. You'd have thought they were Castor and Pollux."

"Who?" asked Katrina.

"Stars," Lady Esterling said. "The Heavenly Twins."

"Nothing heavenly about these two," Jill said. "Slaves of a large man on a brown mare. A Rhode-Island horse breeder, I believe."

Jockey Grandison was in Boston! Jill had hurried to warn me. She, too, recalled his threat. I figured he'd let Jack Ketch have the killing of me, but I didn't relish a meeting that might include a beating. Jockey never forgave an injury; he was a great believer in the adage that a thick lip kept a mouth quiet.

"I think the hour's gone," I said to Hanks.

He stared. Never before had I failed to wait for a gaoler's summons.

Lady Esterling was not going to have Jill drive me from the field. She said: "I have not finished talking to you, fellow. Borden, tell him to stay."

"As you wish," Whitlaw said. "That's an order, Sergeant."

"Yes, sir," Hanks said.

"I would call it a whim," Jill said.

"Would you indeed?"

"Aye, your Ladyship."

"And is it your affair, pray?"

"Aye. More than any here."

"Methinks your recent importance has turned your head, Mistress Murdoch."

Knowing Jill, I could see her fingers itching to mark that placid cheek with a slap. Instead she glanced about desperately, smiled.

"Here comes the gaoler now, and——" Her voice trailed off slowly like the color ebbing from her lips.

"Gaoler or no gaoler," Lady Esterling said with quiet assurance, "I will not be rudely interrupted until I am quite ready." She didn't even bother to turn her head.

The plea in Jill's gaze made me glance over my shoulder. Paulsgrave Mercy was coming all right, but not alone. Swaggering beside him, larger than ever, was Jockey Grandison!

Sweet Blessed Bridget, I said silently. From the way the gaoler was scraping and bowing I knew Jockey, an artist at bribery, had been lavish. Castor and Pollux followed their master.

"It's a ruddy coronation!" Hanks, patience gone, sounded bitter.

And I'm to be crowned, I thought. Jockey's broad grin was toothy mean; it boded ill. Whatever he planned as payment for his cracked skull, I would not like the outcome.

"So here's a pirate bold," Jockey shouted as soon as he knew I saw him. "And keeping gallant company, too!"

Lady Esterling turned so fast that her coat tail swirled. The movement caught my eye, and it caught Jockey's.

He went gray, a sickly hue against the snow. The grin froze, trembled, slacked like a loosed line. Jockey's eyes seemed to bulge past his brow.

"Christ!" he said, a hoarse whisper, half prayer, half horror.

The lady swayed once, as if yielding to a sudden breeze. She wet her lips with the tip of her tongue. Otherwise her face never changed.

"Aggie," Jockey said. "*Aggie!*"

Ensign Whitlaw scowled. He said: "That's unduly familiar. Do you know the fellow, Lady Agnes?"

"No." Lady Esterling spoke coldly.

"God's teeth!" Jockey roared. "The voice even! And I thought you were dead! Dead!"

"The man is mad," said Lady Esterling.

"Dead by your own hand!"

"Quite mad."

[266]

Jill remembered first. Her look of unholy triumph passed the signal to me. A minute before Lady Esterling had been an overbearing noblewoman. Now, an ex-highwayman recalled her as his familiar!

"Not mad," said Jockey, "not me, Aggie. Diddled maybe, but not mad." Rage had restored the blood to his face.

"Look here," said the ensign, "you're addressing Lady Esterling, and——"

"Esterling," said Jockey. "So he married you. Well, you rolled high dice that night, Aggie. I'll give you that. You staked a lot on that throw."

"Borden, this grows tiresome."

Whitlaw agreed. He said: "That's enough. The lady has said she doesn't know you."

"Not know me!" Jockey's laugh was nasty. He'd lost all his discretion. "The lady lies! She rode with me, and bedded me, and diddled me with a scurvy trick. God's toes! You've misnamed her. It's not *lady*, but *whore!*"

The ensign rapped out an oath, went for his sword. The steel hissed from the scabbard, flashed in the sunlight. Jockey was as fast. He had a pistol out from under his coat, and cocked before you could blink.

Katrina gasped. Jill stiffened. Hanks and Lady Esterling moved.

The sergeant wheeled, musket at hip. The gun muzzle swung, steadied. Inches separated it from Jockey's waistcoat.

"No," said Hanks.

Whitlaw, white and cursing, tried to slip around Lady Esterling. She blocked him with the grace of a dance step.

"No, Borden," she said. "Please. Not here. The scandal. My husband."

The words were more urgent than her voice. Even now she was unflustered, quietly insistent.

"I'll kill him," Whitlaw said.

"Yes. But not a duel. A sword contest. Champion against champion." Again, she might have been arranging a table seating.

The watching crowd was silent, almost as motionless as Jockey. There was no telling how much they'd heard, but they'd seen the weapons. Mercy and the two slaves had heard everything, but were bewildered.

"You'll fight?" asked Whitlaw.

"A pleasure." Jockey's smile was grim. He glanced down at Hanks' musket, eased the hammer on his pistol, put it away. "Aggie won't save *you*."

"Make your arrangements elsewhere," Lady Esterling said. "Come, Borden."

I gave her credit. She left as if nothing had happened. The crowd parted before them; the rest of us stared after her.

[267]

Paulsgrave Mercy broke the silence by clearing his throat.

"Well, now," he said. "I guess your hour's run its course, prisoner. That's enough for now, today, this morn."

Enough, and running over.

Chapter 31

It took several weeks to arrange the details for the contest between champions, soldier and civilian, that was in reality a duel.

Boston's March, which had roared in like a lion, went out like a raging family of lions; April here was a misnamed month. The fight rivalled my trial in public interest, and, by happenstance, was scheduled for earlier on the same day.

My visitors expressed different views about the so-called exhibition. To a man the ministers disapproved. Cotton Mather spoke of it as a gladiator circus to distract the populace. The gaoler was frankly distracted, anxious to be present. Hanks, apologizing for discontinuing my exercise, reported the redcoats wagering heavily. Jill, atwitter with excitement, blamed it all on Lady Esterling who remained at home. Sir Edmund was said to be neutral. But the strangest reaction came from Jockey Grandison.

Jockey, known to the town as Master Anderson, was drained of every emotion, but a cold lust to kill. He forgot our quarrel, partly I think because he wanted to talk and I was from his past. He came often to my cell and stayed long.

"You're a good lad, Paddy," he said once. "You haven't peached, and neither has the girl."

"Nor will," I said, surprised by his older-man-to-younger attitude. Jockey, like Captain Quickly, had always played ageless.

"Nor will. As soon as I've settled some scores we'll get you out of here." He was sitting on a stool, balanced back against the wall, and he jerked a thumb toward the door. "That gaoler is half bought now."

"He won't stay bought."

"He won't have to. With Castor and Pollux we can crack this place like a walnut. All I need is Master Mercy's keys, and if he won't sell them, I'll *take* them."

My heart gave a bound. The colonies had never seen Captain Quickly in action. He could do it if he wished; he had the daring and he had the purse.

"And when we're out?"

"Horses. My own. And a fast ship out of Newport. I'll pay the toll. You can take the wench if you like."

"Aye. She goes."

"You're a fool, then." He clenched a big fist, chewed on a knuckle. "Still, you brought me face to face with Aggie, and I'm beholden."

God knows it was the best news I'd had in that gaol, but he was ignoring some problems.

"Jockey," I said, "if you kill Whitlaw——"

"No *if*."

"The man's an officer. Sir Edmund will rage. You'll probably end up in the next cell."

"They can prove nothing. We fight, get carried away, he gets killed. And the beauty of it is, it's her own sweet plan. She was ever sharp on plans, me boyo. This one will cost her dear." He tallied on his fingers. "First, this Whitlaw. Then, Esterling. Then—*her!*"

"You'd kill her?" I thought him crazy, but he sounded calmly practical.

"Better than that. When we go there'll be a letter left on Governor Andros's desk. He's conscientious, your Sir Edmund. He's no shielder of High Tobys on the king's roads! And I can name times and places, laddie. Times and places. God's fingers! I almost hope she escapes the gallows, for she'll have nothing left but her shift."

"What of your farm, the horses?"

He dismissed the years of safety with a flick of his wrist. "Worth it, and more."

"But——"

"I thought her dead, you see."

"How did she manage that?"

"Any of a dozen ways. It's easy to find once your eyes are awake. The dodge was old when the first brothel opened. No ball in the pistol. A bladder full of pig's blood. Or a vial of thin glass, easily shattered. The rest was acting."

Sure, it all sounded harebrained, but I was in no position to quibble. Jockey, once willing to murder to safeguard his new respectable station, was now eager to destroy it for revenge. I was not the one to be judging him. He must have loved the woman once, with a grand wild tide, for so much hate to be left when it ebbed.

Unhappily, Jill didn't share my enthusiasm for Jockey's assistance. When I told her she forgot the gaoler's presence; her head shake was violent, her voice sharp with worry.

"No, Cormac! No! Not that way!"

"Shhh! For God's sake, girl!"

She lowered her tone to a whisper, but it was crisply bitter. "I don't trust the man. He was no friend to us before. Why should he change?"

"He's forgotten everything but her ladyship."

"Well, I've not forgotten." Jill's hair tossed at the memory. "He's a dirty lecherous old goat. If we ran off with him, as you say, how long would it be before he came pawing at me again?"

"And would I be letting you out of my sight?"

"On his ship? With Castor and Pollux ready to break your bones at his word? No, I thank you! We'll not return to that Jockey's clutches!"

There was truth aplenty in what she said, truth I'd been avoiding. It brought me to my feet, to stride a pace and glare at Master Mercy. That worthy, pistol in lap, continued to pick his teeth. I swung back to my place beside Jill.

"Then it's holiday for Boston as I hang!"

"You'll not hang, Cormac dear. When the magistrates hear my testimony——"

"Jill, Jill. If talk could free me, I'd be reigning at Tara this day, and you a queen."

Tears welled, to make her eyes misty. Her fingers twisted among mine, gripped hard. She spoke around a lump in her throat.

"My own. I've not your gift with tales, but they'll listen. I'll open my heart, and they'll know it for truth."

"Aye. Who could doubt you?" I said. If ever God winked at a lie it was that one. For it wasn't in me to look on her tears, and bring more. Her dream of saving me—a proud, love of a thing, but still a dream—was her treasure. For a few more days she was welcome to enjoy it.

"Cormac, my way is best. Once acquitted we need flee no longer, but go where we will."

"Free as birds. We'll do it your way, Jill."

Then, Mercy or no Mercy, she kissed me.

Secretly, with the date of the trial drawing close, I devised a compromise. Since Jockey was willing, I'd let him waft me through the stone walls. Once mounted, Jill and I would ride our own way. Jockey, busy with his revenge on Lady Esterling, wouldn't care. Nor, once his letter went to the governor, could he waste time thwarting us.

After that, I was more cheerful. Breaking gaol was better handled by an expert like Captain Quickly. No matter how my trial was decided, and I was sure of the verdict, I'd be away out of Boston, Jill beside me, before they had the silver oar out of storage.

So, I wrote in my book, argued with Cotton Mather, had Jill avisiting, Katrina Neville, and a brace of strange preachers from some place called Salem. Jockey, staying away, sent word by Pollux that he was fit and ready.

And the days passed as days do.

❖

The morn of my trial dawned bright and cold. Hardly had the sun risen when Sergeant Hanks came with a redcoat squad to lead me forth. The Court of Admiralty was sitting in the Town House, no great distance, and magistrates were early risers. The soldiers were annoyed that the duty would prevent them from seeing the sword fight. Sime was swearing; Joe growled. Even the sergeant was frowning.

"Just like these blasted Puritans," said Sime. "Since they don't like no fun, they don't like anybody liking it."

Joe nodded. "They could have picked another day."

"It ain't often you can see an ensign get spitted."

"Stow that, Sime," said Hanks.

"You think he'll get spitted?" I asked.

Sime leered and winked. "Wagered my pay on it."

"Don't you mean pinked?"

That brought a laugh. "Contest between champions," Joe said, "is just sugar kisses for the governor, and the dominies. There's been talk."

"There's bad blood between the two," Sime said, "and it's gonna be spilt proper."

I looked at Hanks. He shook his head, whispered. "Not me. I trust the lady even less, but said nary a word."

Master Mercy rattled a pair of wrist shackles. "Well, now," he said, "you're summoned to appear in irons. That's the law, custom, procedure."

My face brought a chuckle from Sime, sympathy from the sergeant. Hanks took the shackles from the gaoler.

"I'll fix them loose," he said.

He was just hammering the last pin in place when we heard the drum. The drummer was rattling a march step—flim-flam, flam-flam-

flam! It was distant, but closing. You could tell where streets crossed by the extra riffle pattered by the drumsticks.

"What's that?" I asked.

"Rinty," said the Dutch redcoat.

"Company drummer boy," said Hanks.

"They're doing it high style," said Sime. "Drummer for each man. Ensign parades the North Side, the other fellow the South."

"Let's get out and see," Paulsgrave Mercy said.

We hustled from the gaol like a festive group instead of prisoner and escort. The drum was nearer now. People were crowding to windows, opening shutters to lean out. I'd never been in front of the gaol before, in my right, well mind that is, but soldiers and gaoler carried me along.

Facing down Brattles Street we could see the procession coming. The drummer boy, a scarlet elf scarce taller than his drum, was flourishing his sticks as he strutted in front.

"Flim-flam! Flam-flam-*flam!*"

Behind the drummer, pacing through the mud in the middle of the street, marched Borden Whitlaw. I never liked the ensign, but he was all soldier now, a credit to the king's coat. He wore full-dress uniform, with borrowed scarlet hat and gloves. The sword, sheathed, was tucked under his arm, swinging in the rhythm of his stride.

"Other fellow's wearing white," Sime said.

Joe nodded. "Master Anderson paid for the drummer's dress. Some town lad."

Master Anderson was Jockey's New-World name. As if an echo to the drum we watched, though the beat was wrong for an echo, we heard the faint tap-tip-tap of another, distant drum.

"There's the other one," Joe said. "Meeting's on the Common."

The scarlet pair had almost reached us. There was a crowd following the ensign. Running boys, truant apprentices, idle men, jostled each other as they hurried.

Young Rinty, fully aware of the watching rank of redcoats, paused before our group, made his riffle with a blur of sticks, snapped through a military right turn.

"Right to Treamont," Sime said. "Left to the Common."

Whitlaw made the turn as precisely. The ensign's face was as white and drawn as the drumhead.

He marches to his death, I thought, and the taste of it was sour. Whitlaw was an arrogant bully, a stupid brute, but he was young. The parade, with its show of drum and scarlet, made a false mockery of dying. Jockey, Lady Esterling, Whitlaw were all masking bitter motives with pulse-quickening sounds, and gaudy colors.

Of the three the ensign's motive was the least shabby. He fought, or thought he did, as he had been trained and bred, for a lady's honor. Poor fool, he was the serf thrust into a battle between powerful lords; he no more belonged in the clash of those two than a rabbit interfering with snapping mongrels. And it was going to be the death of him.

Sure, the sun was too bright, the sky too blue, to be smiling down on the likes of that.

The scurrying crowd poured after the principals, a human flash flood that filled the street.

Sime spat into the mud. "I hate to miss it," he said.

There was a compulsion on me, too. The speech came of itself.

"Need we?"

"Town House is t'other way," said Paulsgrave Mercy, plucking at his lower lip.

"You march me in procession. Past the Common."

Mercy's eyes glittered. Hanks bowed in a slow nod. "Orders," he said, "were to escort him. There was no mention of a route."

The squad was delighted. Sime chortled, and shouted.

"Fall in!"

We formed in the now empty street. A few women stayed in their windows to stare. Hanks placed me in the middle, a brace of redcoats before, another behind. He led, with the gaoler. At the command we marched briskly in the direction taken by the crowd.

Brisk as we were, the champions proved brisker, evidently brusque with ceremony. By the time the squad halted, the fight had begun.

This Boston Common was a stretch of open grazing with a slight and gentle slope. In summer, mayhap, it was good pasture, but that morning it looked sere and drab. The turf was heavy with thaw; a few snowdrifts remained like forgotten laundry. One of these formed a bowstring for the arced rank of spectators, and the level space between was the arena.

Jockey's white costume made his bulk seem even larger. His wig was as new as his garments. For the look of it, they both fought fully clothed, not even discarding hats. Amazingly, neither appeared to be bothered by the mud underfoot.

I am no great judge of swordplay. Hit or miss, trip and duck, was always my method of fighting, and I preferred a loaded pistol to the finest blade that ever left Damascus. But that fight had me staring, with dry throat.

[273]

There was a kind of deadly beauty in it, and a speed of movement that made my hair rise. The swords themselves darted in and out, back and forth, like thin segments of lightning, flashing bolts without pause. And the two swordsmen, the red clad and the white, were a single, graceful unit held together, blended and controlled, by those quivering blades.

Before I drew two breaths Jockey attacked. He moved forward, thrust, thrust, and thrust, from this position or that, lithe as a panther, quick as an accident.

I know not how many came there to watch an exhibition. Those who did knew better after that first assault. The bright steel clashed, slithered, rang and tinkled; it was not unmusical but the tune played was a death dance.

Jockey was master, dominant, eager to kill as soon as possible. Whitlaw gave ground, falling back before the fury of it. The ensign was no novice; his step was as light as Jockey's.

Still, the scarlet looked smothered by the white. Suddenly, I did not wish to see it, and shut my eyes. A gasp from those around me impelled me to gaze again.

Whitlaw was wounded. The rip in his left sleeve, a white scar that turned dark, showed where. But the ensign was on his feet, circling and parrying. Jockey shook himself like a doused mastiff, and attacked again.

He seemed to stretch himself with each succeeding lunge, extending reach and height as he glided forward. Whitlaw was hard pressed, but untouched. The ensign, fighting for his life, was a superb swordsman.

Again and again Jockey attacked, coldly, furiously, with obvious skill. Whitlaw met every foray, parried it, held it.

The crowd's growl, that instinctive salute that greets the moment when the fortunes of battle change, warned me. Whitlaw was no longer retreating; he was sliding forward now.

Captain Quickly had been out of the saddle too long. For all his skill Jockey had forgotten the passing years, the unused muscles, the added inches of girth. Whitlaw was just as skillful, and he lacked some twenty years weighing down his hilt.

The rest was not short, nor, to my gaze, handsome. Jockey fought with fading desperation. I shall not forget the look on his face.

He did not yield. When Whitlaw lunged for his middle, Jockey's parry was speedy. But he flicked the ensign's blade high, and the point took him in the throat.

There was a frozen instant of stillness. Nothing seemed to move, not the red figure slanting toward the white one, not the dark, fixed sword, nor the clean.

Then a gush of crimson stained Jockey's lace. The big body turned slowly, and collapsed into the snowdrift. A streak spread across the snow.

"Jesus!" said Sime.

"Bless us, save us, deliver us!" Mercy said.

"March!" Sergeant Hanks ordered.

We went along streets I would never recognize. I marched in a black daze, past faceless buildings, under a cloud sky. All I saw was the heels of the soldier ahead of me.

So died Jockey Grandison, also known as Captain Quickly and Thomas Anderson, highwayman and horse breeder. With him died my best hope of escape.

As we turned the corner to reach the Town House, the sergeant edged to my side, nudged me.

"Don't go in there hangdog," he said. "You look like you'd lost your last friend."

In a way, I had. But I raised my head, and squared my shoulders as I climbed the steps.

Chapter 32

THE room in the Town House of Boston where a Court of Admiralty sat in session to try me for the crime of piracy was a large chamber, but unmistakably a courtroom. If a ball had been held in it, a banquet or a prayer meeting, the place would have imposed its gloomy character on the occasion.

It was panelled in some New-World wood, already darkly weathered; the furniture was sturdily uncomfortable. Dust clotted shadows in corners, peppered the musty smell from legal tomes, the cadaver stench of long-dead laws. Somehow, in a short span, the colony jurists, copying the pattern common to their craft, had managed to make the room ancient, tired, and depressing.

Two features only marked the justice dispensed there as English, and

Puritan. The first, the one colored patch against the dingy walls, was the king's jack: red and white—blood on snow!—with the gold cipher JR surmounted by the golden crown. For the second, these Bostoners, by carpentry or prayer, had turned the judges' bench into a pulpit.

During the wait that precedes all trials, I lounged in the dock, stared about me, and thought of Jockey Grandison. The irons on my wrists weighed less than the lump in my stomach. Jockey lay dead in the April sunshine with my hopes as cold as his lips. I had not realized how much I'd relied on the highwayman's promise.

The courtroom was not crowded. Jill was there, of course, cheering me with looks, a lone bright egg in a nest of witnesses. Captain George and Jotham Twigg were among them; the rest I did not know. Alec Murdoch sat on the front spectator bench, with his little partner, Hamish MacInnis, pecking bird-like glances around, beside him. My redcoat escort was lined behind me. Mercy and Hanks chatted while they waited.

From a rear corner Cotton Mather's face showed, clear as a fresh painting in a smoky gallery. It was as welcome as a ship to a maroon. The Reverend Master Mather might think me destined for eternal damnation, but he wanted me to escape execution.

Lawyers appeared, gowned and wigged. One of them, a young Scot named Fraser, introduced himself. He'd been summoned to represent me.

Sir Edmund Andros entered with retinue. The governor took an armchair on a dais near the side wall. He was careful not to glance at me.

"Oyez, oyez!" cried the clerk, thumping his staff. He then prattled a description of the court, but so fast that, except for the words 'Dominion' and 'New England', it was doggerel to me. The scuff and scrape as the assemblage rose sent dust motes flying; before they settled the magistrates were ranked behind their long, high bench.

There were five of them. While they took their chairs, with a rustle of robes and papers, my advocate whispered their names. Only two, Waitstill Winthrop and Samuel Shrimpton, were of Puritan stock; their own hair and rugged features made them conspicuous, flint pebbles on an amber necklace. The others were bewigged Andros imports, professional colonizers, servants of the crown. Justice Francis Foxcroft, Justice John Palmer, and, presiding, Sir William Esterling.

The last suprised me. I took a long look at Lady Esterling's husband. He had a thin, pallid face, buffed by years of government service until nothing showed in it but fine-boned intelligence. Sir William's well-set eyes had drooping lids, from true fatigue or posed indolence.

That type of government official could be met in any British colony. Conscientious, clever, and high strung, they did prodigious work, and were seldom popular.

Somewhere I'd heard that Sir William's post dealt with shipping, or harbor fees, or the Navigation Acts, which might account for the governor's appointing him president of this court. I wondered if Cotton Mather, who resented all Sir Edmund's appointments, approved this one.

If he'd heard of Whitlaw's victory, Sir William gave no sign. He tapped a knuckle on the bench, spoke in a quiet, cultured tone.

"Order. Arraign the prisoner at the bar."

I left the dock to stand before them. Gazing up, I felt that the bench dwarfed me like a small boat under the stern of a merchantman.

"The clerk will read the articles of arraignment."

Master Clerk launched his reading with such zest down ways greased slick by practice that I missed the opening rigmarole entire. I began to understand him when, after slowing for breath, he reached my name.

"—and that said Cormac Doyle, also known as Mac Foyle, also known as Irish Jack, did commit said crimes of felony, piracy, robbery, murder, and abduction against his majesty's welfare, and this royal dominion."

"How pleads the prisoner?"

"Not guilty," I said.

"Strike off his irons. He stands arraigned."

As Paulsgrave Mercy came forward with the tools, Justice Winthrop stirred. His protest was not against the custom that a man face trial unshackled, but against an omission in the articles. He made it in a precise, dry voice, the sound when one sands a parchment.

"There was no mention that the accused is a Papist."

"Is it germane?" asked Sir William.

"To the welfare of this realm—yes."

The other Puritan Justice, Shrimpton, nodded. Palmer and Foxcroft exchanged a glance and a shrug. It was more than a difference in attitude; it was a faint trumpet signalling another skirmish in the long dispute between Boston and the governor.

"The evidence may show it," said Sir William.

Winthrop was leaning forward, watching Sir Edmund Andros. The governor, arms folded, glowered, but stayed motionless. His public manner was formidable, without charm.

"And may not," said Shrimpton.

"Is he, or isn't he?" Again, the dry sifting of sand on paper.

"Aye," I said, loud and clear. "That I am."

[277]

Sir William frowned; the Puritan pair sat back. Winthrop favored me with a cold smile.

The attorney for the crown, one Randolph, an Andros man to his expressive fingertips, briskly efficient, opened the trial by calling Captain John George. The naval officer clumped to the stand, was sworn, gave his testimony in a quarterdeck bellow that would have filled his frigate's mainsail. In the orders that sent the *Rose* to Boston, one Doyle was mentioned as joining the pirates who took the *Bristol Merchant*.

Fraser rose to cross-examine.

"Are you sure the accused is the same Doyle, Captain?"

"Aye. The bast—" George checked himself. "He admitted it."

"The *Bristol Merchant's* master, Heatheridge, was cast adrift, wasn't he?"

"Aye."

"Then how could he know if the men left aboard were or were not forcibly detained by the pirates?"

"Wrote it down, didn't he?"

"But how could he know?"

"God damn it!" George exploded. "My job's catching pirates, not explaining them!"

Fraser saw the Puritan justices wince at the profanity, and dismissed the captain. The young Scot was a canny advocate.

The next witness was a limping, small man with one eye. His patch made me glance at Jill, who smiled. He gave his name, hoarsely, as Silence Scates. From his weathered, salty look I recognized him for an old seaman, but he claimed to know me better.

"Aye," he said, "I seen him afore." He pointed me out with a finger stiff as tarred hemp. "Him, there, the accused. Jamaica, it was. In the Wench's Butt. A tavern like."

"Was he with anyone, Master Scates?"

"With Jeffcoat's crew off the *Unicorn.*"

"And this Jeffcoat was known as a pirate?"

"*Dandy Jeffcoat?* Was known! 'Twas his brag!"

"Would you say the accused was constrained by these pirates?"

"Huh?"

"Was he forced to keep their company?"

"Him? Naw! Him and his messmate, a big Swede giant, took naught from nobody. You couldn't force those two with a regiment."

"He moved freely with the others?"

"Aye, spending and drinking." The venom of envy flashed. "Gold coins. Lace cuffs!"

[278]

"This man Doyle?"

"Doyle, Foyle, some-such. I weren't social with them."

My whisper gave Fraser a course to follow. I didn't know the man, but I knew the time and place.

"Master Scates, you were familiar with this tavern you mentioned?"

"I was on the beach. Worked there."

"And you saw the accused there often?"

"A dozen times."

"Ever see him—brawling?"

"Him and the Swede near wrecked the place!"

"Just once?"

"They were always fighting."

"I see. Against whom?"

"Why, Jeffcoat's whole crowd——"

"*Jeffcoat's?* You mean they *fought* these pirates?"

"Well, sure, they was all pirates and——"

"And Master Doyle brawled with them, fought them, shed their blood?"

"Hell, yes!" said Scates. "Only the Swede did triple duty to this lubber."

"You wouldn't call that friendly, would you, Master Scates?"

"Well," Scates didn't want me off the hook; he used truth for a gaff, "they was all uncommon drunk at the time."

"Witness dismissed," Fraser said.

Samuel Quimby was sworn next, identified himself as the master of the *Brothers' Venture,* a Banks fisherman. With other similar vessels, while resting on the Sabbath in a Newfoundland harbor, Quimby's ship had been surprised by a pirate fleet. This skipper was a good deal sharper than Silence Scates; he'd not forgotten details.

"A sloop, Jeffcoat's flagship, the *Unicorn.* A smaller sloop, the *Bumboo Queen.* A Bermudas boat, the *Melissa.* And a ketch, *Fancy.*"

The pirates had boarded the fishermen, Quimby related, but because his cargo was codfish, they hadn't bothered to loot the *Brothers' Venture.* They had all lain together in the harbor for two days and nights, during which time Quimby had talked to Jeffcoat, and others.

"And is one of those others in this court?"

"Not as I talked to. But one I saw."

"Will you kindly point him out?"

"The prisoner in the dock."

Sir William took over the questioning. "You are sure of that?"

"Aye, aye, sir."

"What was his position among these pirates?" asked Sir William. "I mean was he mate, bosun, common deckhand or what?"

"I don't know how he was listed," Quimby said, "but he appeared, at the times I saw him, to be in charge of revels, sir. At least he was dispensing spirits freely."

"Ah. You may continue, Master Quimby."

Quimby continued. The pirate captain, Jeffcoat, had told him that the renamed *Bumboo Queen* was a recent prize, and in the taking seven men, crew and officers, had been slain.

"He seemed to relish bloodshed," Quimby said, understating Dandy Jeffcoat's boasts while in his cups. "He spoke of other vessels burned, and scuttled with great loss."

During the second night the ketch had disappeared. Jeffcoat was angered by the desertion of two men.

"The accused and another, a Swede."

Fishing fleet and pirate left the harbor together. Quimby wished to escape, but the *Unicorn* was too fast to elude and stayed alongside for three days cruising. Quimby's heart sank when Jeffcoat hailed, and came aboard. But the result was release for the *Brothers' Venture*.

"He wished me to lay information against the two who had stolen the ketch. Jeffcoat claimed they had robbed him, and the company. He was very wroth. His language is not repeatable, but it indicated a painful loss."

I wagered it had. I realized that Quimby had hurt my case, when Fraser dismissed him without questioning.

The rest of the prosecution witnesses came in quick succession. Hamish MacInnis testified to my taking at Southold; Jotham Twigg testified to my escape on the road. The latter was leaving the stand without mention of Lady Esterling when Justice Winthrop stopped him.

"One moment, Master Twigg."

Twigg sat down again.

"The accused escaped from you, five armed soldiers, and an ensign?"

"Yes, your Honor."

"Would you say the soldiers were careless?"

There it was again, the quiet filing on the pilings that upheld the governor. Small raspings intended to annoy, not yet capable of undermining.

"Well, we was all—well—diverted like." Twigg was squirming. He knew Sir William for her ladyship's husband; he didn't want trouble.

"Diverted? From duty?"

"There was a snake, you see—a poisonous reptile—we ran to scotch it. The prisoner struck down a guard, and fled."

"One snake," Winthrop said, musingly, "against a whole squad of the king's regulars. An Indian would require a company."

"Have you finished, Master Justice?" asked Sir William, politely.

"Quite."

The prosecutor had nearly finished, too. He had built the crown's case into a nice, solid structure, tight as my stone gaol. His witnesses had placed me among known pirates from the first, traced me to the present. Fraser had reason to look defeated. There had been evidence presented to support the charges of felony, piracy, robbery and murder. All that remained was abduction, and I knew who they'd call for that.

"Mistress Judith Murdoch."

Jill rose, flashed me a tremulous smile, dipped a curtsy to the judges. She was sworn on the Book, sat down. The progress of the trial, as weight after weight of testimony tilted the scales against me, had shaken her confidence. She was brave—God love the lass!—but she knew now what I'd always known. She, alone, could not win my acquittal.

"Mistress, you know the accused?"

"I do."

Jill was calm, speaking clearly.

"This man, Cormac Doyle, is the one who abducted you?"

"No, sir."

There went the mainmast, man the pumps! All five justices acted as if the platform had shaken under them. Alec Murdoch sat bolt upright. The crown prosecutor stood stunned, openmouthed. Everyone else in that chamber, barring myself and Jill, gasped.

"No?" asked Sir William Esterling.

"There was no abduction," Jill said. "A horse ran away with a chaise we were both in. Master Doyle could no more have prevented that, than I could."

Sir Edmund Andros smiled. He had heard that much before. Even the prosecutor seemed relieved.

"Your fairness does you credit," said Sir William, "to a man who held you hostage until you wounded and captured him."

"My lords," said Jill, twisting to face the bench, "I am under oath here, and I had Godly upbringing that taught an oath as a serious undertaking before the face of the Almighty. I was also taught *Thou shalt not bear false witness!*"

She had both Puritan justices nodding, and the others bemused by her loveliness. Sure, there was eloquence in her, and fire, but she was hacking granite with a feather duster.

"So we all," said Sir William, friendly but puzzled, "understand such teachings."

"May I then speak in my own words?"

"Of course."

"Cormac Doyle did not hold me hostage at any time. I went with him and stayed with him of my own free will."

"What?"

"Jill!"

The question was Winthrop's; the groaned name came from Alec Murdoch. But the Heroine of Boston had thrown her cap over the windmill, and could not be stopped.

"The wound he took was in fighting a pirate named Chips, after he, Cormac, had sunk the pirate sloop that attacked *The Careful Mary——*"

The rest of it was lost in hubbub and chatter as the courtroom lost all decorum. Sir Edmund Andros had a hand cupped behind an ear as he bent forward to hear. Sir William was pounding for quiet. The soldiers behind me were buzzing like hornets. Alec Murdoch had his face buried in his hands.

"Order!" cried Sir William, hammering with his fist. "Order in the court!"

As the mutterings died to silence the quintet of justices turned to Jill. But my girl was battling with what craft she had, and she beat them all to the punch. Her voice rang out, a triumphant announcement.

"So you see Cormac is neither an abductor nor a pirate!"

"Mistress!"

Both Puritan judges thundered the title. Shrimpton, grimacing, yielded to Winthrop. The sand in the latter's voice had become gravel.

"This is not the tale you told at first!"

"No, my lords. I spoke in falsehoods. There were reasons that made it necessary."

"Reason," said the crown attorney bitterly. He took his wig off, threw it on the floor.

"Order!" Sir William hit the bench. "I will have order!"

Justice Winthrop pointed an accusing finger at Jill. It shook as badly as his voice.

"You, a decent, Puritan maid——"

"Covenant, my lord."

"Covenant be—don't interrupt! You, from a God-fearing family, raised in the way of righteousness, *admit* you accompanied this pirate, this Papist—willingly?"

"I accompanied Cormac Doyle, no pirate, and a gentleman whatever his beliefs or his religion." It was a grand, proud thing to hear. "And I would do so again, my lord."

"For whole weeks," Winthrop said. "Days and nights, *nights*, on end! Be you shameless?"

Jill flushed, but gave no inch. "I have naught to be shamed with. Cormac fought for me, saved my life at risk of his own, had no thought to harm me. I would be ungrateful indeed, my lord, did I not speak for him."

Her very boldness left Winthrop speechless, but Sir William was more worldly. Smiling, he said: "A pretty speech, Mistress Murdoch. One question, pray."

"Aye, my lord?"

"Do you love the accused?"

All those Cormacs had betrayed her. Jill turned from the judges to gaze at me. For one long moment, while the silence grew, there was no one in that place but we two. Then, still looking at me, she spoke.

"Aye, my lord, I'll not deny it."

"Love?" Shrimpton cried. "Lust of the flesh!"

That brought her head around, with her eyes blazing, and all her glorious red-haired temper flashing through her answer.

"If you do not know the difference, Master Shrimpton, *I do!*"

Sir William bowed to her. "I am satisfied. There was no abduction. That charge will be removed from the articles."

From the look on Winthrop and Shrimpton, poor Jill had hanged me higher than Haman, and done herself no good either. Alec, her brother, had the pale stiffness of a condemned man. Sinful dalliance was ignored sometimes in Boston, but never when publicly flaunted. Jill left the witness chair without further questions, in an ominous silence.

"His Majesty's government rests," said the crown attorney.

"The defense," Fraser said, "calls a single witness. The accused."

So they swore me, and let me tell my story.

❖

The only, true real name in the articles is that of Cormac O'Shaugnessy Doyle. Aye, and the case against me contains about the same amount of truth, a cinnamon stick's worth to sweeten the toddy. Sure, even how a rainbow looks depends on where a body stands, so maybe you won't mind hearing about things from my side.

First things first. If I'd not gone to sea, I'd not be standing here this day, fearful of hanging for a slip of the tongue. But I went, afore the mast, and was tricked aboard by a press gang, like others before me and since.

It was not a regular naval press gang and therein lay the trick. For I knew these bully boys, cutpurses and footpads, with no love for the navy. What I didn't know was that a nimble, strong lad was worth six shillings delivered on a deck.

I woke on the *Happy Discovery,* out past Land's End, with a lump on my head, and sick at heart as well as stomach. Instead of a printer's apprentice, overnight I became a cabin boy.

Captain Stowe was master, a hard taskmaster but fair. "Lad," he said, "you can sulk and feel a rope's end, or you can learn and feel it."

"Do you call that a choice then?" I asked.

"Aye," said the captain, "for if you learn, the sea can give you much. Hard work, poor food, scant pay, and some moments never matched ashore."

Right he was. All those things I found aboard his vessel. And by the time we sighted Dover Cliffs again, the love of the trade was in me, and I was a seafaring man.

For two more voyages I sailed with Captain Stowe. My work was honest, as honest as any seaman who ever put out from Boston. Aye, and I had written lines to prove it once, but fathoms deep long since. I was acting coxswain when the captain died.

My other service, among the Indies islands, need not be mentioned here. But it was honest, too, and there are sailors and masters would say so in this hall, living men but far distant and ignorant of my trouble.

Then, I signed on the *Bristol Merchant,* may the man who laid her keel never know a day's peace! An unlucky ship with a dolt for a master.

Heatheridge! Sure, the man was stupid enough to spit into the wind. Myself it was who sighted the Bermudas boat in the Leeward Passage.

"Captain," I said, "I don't like the look of her."

"Doyle," said he, "you're a fool. She's scarce bigger than a smack, and only five aboard her."

His five were thirty-five when Dandy Jeffcoat clapped alongside, and sent them over our rail. And Heatheridge on his knees begging mercy with the keys to the arms chest in his pocket!

That it took four to down me, and me unarmed, made me conspicuous. Jeffcoat noticed me.

"Fetch that man aft," he said.

Aft I was dragged, and we looked each other over. The pirate was the taller, wide shouldered but lean in the flanks. He had a great lump of head, tanned to saddle leather, a bashed-in nose, squinty, mismatched eyes, one brown, one gray. There was a scar on his chin, another on his forehead, and the top of his left ear was missing.

Ugly as sin was Dandy. And wasn't that why he decked himself in such finery and fancy raiment? The blaze of his waistcoats was meant to blind the beholder from having to gaze on his phiz. He was a great one for changing clothes, too; he'd be dressing, undressing and redressing the livelong day!

That afternoon he was wearing a pea-green coat, frogged in yellow, a lavender waistcoat, sky-blue breeches and candy-striped stockings. Over all this was a crimson sword sash, and gold cords to hold his pistols. He had a big, native-made straw hat, that he'd decorated with ribbon, lace and feathers.

Dandy they'd named him! Peacock would have suited better!

"We can use you," Jeffcoat told me, "for you fight like a man, instead of whining like a dog."

"I'm an honest seaman," I said. "I must refuse."

With that he swore horribly, and clapped a pistol to my head. "Refuse, then, and sign on with the Devil! Since you prefer a voyage in Hell to our company!"

"It's not so much your company," I said, for I was thinking my end at hand, "but I don't like your flag."

"Don't you?" asked Jeffcoat. "What's the matter with it? I picked the colors myself."

Their jack was black with crossed cutlasses in yellow stuck through a great red bleeding heart.

"It's not the colors," I said. "It's bad drawn."

"You're right, it is! Could you do better?"

"Aye," I said, not thinking.

"You'll have the chance," Jeffcoat said. By that time Heatheridge and a few others were in the longboat, and Jeffcoat ordered it away. "Cast off! The rest stays."

For there were six crewmen who knew Heatheridge so well they preferred the pirate. I struggled, but was held fast.

"You'll bear witness," I cried, "that I'm forced."

"Forced you are," said Jeffcoat, "till I get that new flag."

So I sailed with Dandy Jeffcoat. After the flag was made, a black skull with a red knife in its teeth on a mustard field, he would not let me go. The *Bristol Merchant* was the first rich craft they'd taken, and they took two more as soon as they ran up my flag.

"You're a lucky piece," Jeffcoat said. He had as many superstitions as waistcoats. "I'll not lose you, Mac."

He even ordered my name changed in case there was search for me. Aboard the Bermudas boat I was Mac Foyle. When he took the *Unicorn,* and made her his flagship I became Irish Jack.

"To change a ship's name," Jeffcoat explained, "is bad luck. But to change a man's is good."

"How do you figure that?" I asked.

"Stands to reason," Jeffcoat said. "There's many walking around would be rotting in chains under their right names. Besides, if you don't fetch prizes as Irish Jack we can always change you back."

Now, it's hard to believe but from that day on the prizes came to him like sharks to blood. Within the week they took a Spaniard so loaded with plate that half Madrid felt the pinch. Aye, it made Jeffcoat's reputation, that haul!

He needed a reputation, as he needed luck, for if ever a pirate chief was all filagree outside, and nothing inside, like an empty Venetian flask, it was Dandy Jeffcoat. Faith, he could swear to curdle your blood, and his face would gray a saint's hair, but he couldn't tie a decent bowline.

The crew, and it grew with success, were dazzled by his dress, and believed his every word. They held me lucky, too.

My own desperate attempt to escape fixed that. We put in for water at an island, and I hid in the jungle. For forty days I was marooned on that spit of land. Forty days living on berries. I was crawling and helpless when they put back for me. By the strangeness of Providence they hadn't made a capture in all that time!

We took the Swede off a Rotterdammer in the gulf a fortnight later. He was forced, too, wanted for his great size. We became comrades because of that bond. For I needed those giant muscles to assure a successful escape.

Neither of us ever signed articles, nor accepted prize money. When there was fighting we watched, or cared for the wounded.

There was little fighting. Pirates do not attack even numbers or near. In my time with Jeffcoat, out of seventeen-odd prizes, three were burned, two scuttled, the loot ran into thousands of pounds, but less than a dozen humans were killed or wounded.

The *Bumboo Queen* was a good example. Jeffcoat, to scare Captain Quimby, made a grand yarn out of her taking. She was the sloop *Miriam S.* out of Newport and her master was killed. He tripped on his cutlass, fell down the companionway, and broke his neck. Nobody else was scratched.

Jeffcoat was so upset that, one superstition outweighing the other, he changed the sloop's name. That she carried a hold full of rum made the choice easy.

It also gave the Swede and me our chance. In that Newfoundland harbor, we made sure that the rum flowed free, and the merrymaking lasted long. Then, we sneaked the ketch away.

Sure, true it is that we took a few things with us. Provisions like, and clothing. Necessities. No more than would fill a single sea chest.

Dandy Jeffcoat, as I said, always was a great liar.

The ketch, *Fancy*, was wrecked; the Swede went down with her. And all the rest you know.

Chapter 33

IT took far less time to decide my fate, than it did to tell my tale. The justices didn't bother to leave the bench. Five heads, three wigged, two cropped, were joined for about the interval that a man might bunch his fingertips to pluck down from a goose. Chins waggled as they whispered. To me, it was obvious that they didn't believe a word I'd said. Not that I'd truly expected they would, mind, but a man must strike with what he has though it be only a split reed.

Sir William Esterling dipped quill, wrote, sprinkled with the sand box. Then he linked his fingers, cleared his throat.

"Bring the prisoner to the bar."

Out of the corner of my eye, I saw Jill rise. Not a single judge as much as glanced at her. I know, for the whole ten eyes gazed down at me like a line of open, hostile gunports.

This was no place to beg or crawl. I spread my feet, clasped my hands behind me, and waited.

"This Court of Admiralty," said Sir William, "in discharge of its duty doth find as follows. The articles charging felony, piracy, and robbery are judged to be proven. The article charging murder is judged unproven, that of abduction having been removed."

Now, there, I thought, is a fine, scrupulous distinction. Instead of five reasons for hanging me, they were satisfied with three!

"We, therefore, of the aforesaid proven articles declare the accused, Cormac Doyle, also known as——"

"May it please the court," I said, "but I would prefer to take this in my true name, and that only."

Sir William's bow was his only notice of the interruption.

"—the accused, Cormac O'Shaugnessy Doyle, to be—Guilty."

There it was. For all my twisting and turning, fine speech and great plans, I had come to the end of the road. Nothing remained now but the silver oar, and the gibbet. No matter how long awaited, nor how often dreaded, the terrible, terrible words of sentence must be heard to shake the soul. A man condemned did double dying. This was the first.

The faces above me blurred; the calm voice was unheard. When I returned to life, a matter of seconds, Sir William was still speaking.

"—in solemn procession from the prison to Scarletts Wharf whence, the silver oar being carried before him, the procession shall proceed by boat to the place of execution, the same being between highwater mark and low, on the point of land this side the Charles, below Copp's Hill, about midway between Hudson's Point and Broughton's warehouse."

Sir William paused. There was no sound.

"There, on a gallows erected for the purpose, he shall be hanged by the neck until he is dead."

While Boston watched. And children held up for better view would still have nightmares when the corpse in chains was rotted beyond human semblance.

"And," said Sir William, "may God have mercy on his soul."

"Amen." The four other justices rumbled in unison.

And wasn't that a grand, charitable wish, from them to me? Sure, it was about the only prayer those five were in agreement on.

The court rose, the justices filed out. While Mercy was putting my shackles back on, I stole a quick glance at Jill. She was standing, Alec and Hamish behind her, with a desperate white clutch on a bench back. The blood had drained from her face making her hair a borrowed wig.

Sir Edmund Andros paused beside me. Once he put aside his official manner, he looked no more forbidding than any courtly gentleman. His smile was kindly, and he spoke me fair.

"I am sorry, Cormac Doyle."

"And I, Sir Edmund, with greater cause."

"The trial was fair," the governor said. "The king himself could find naught to fault it."

"Well," I said, "we could wait till he had the chance to say so."

He shook his head, stepped back, doffed his hat. He bowed low, till the plumes swept floor dust, an elegant leg! Straightening, he turned and strode away.

I appreciated the gesture. With it the governor meant to acknowledge my jest, salute my courage, express his sadness. It was a fine, generous act, from one gentleman to another.

Of course, as I well knew, it was also his farewell.

Any wishful thinking I'd nourished concerning a reprieve departed with Governor Andros. When a statute was royal he was the most law-abiding tyrant's satrap that ever walked. I'd not ask the good Lord on His throne of judgment to be less stern than Edmund Andros, but He might think of it Himself.

Jill was gone by the time they led me out, and glad I was. There was a group of small boys gawking at the Town House entrance, but Paulsgrave Mercy shooed them away.

The sky had darkened while we were inside. A black fleet of clouds was scudding inland from the harbor. There was a quick spatter of raindrops across the mud of the streets.

"Come on, come on," Sime said, pushing me, "we'll get caught in a downpour."

"Leave him alone!" Sergeant Hanks rapped out the command.

The apple-cheeked Dutchman nodded. Except for Sime, my escort seemed disturbed by the verdict. Mercy, of course, looked the very same. The gaoler was probably mournful in his cradle.

"So a wetting makes no difference to him now," Sime said. "The rest of us got more living to do."

"Shut up, Sime," Joe said.

Somehow, I didn't want their pity. The thought was kindly, but Sime's jeers suited my mood better. He, at least, treated me the same as ever. The others were figuratively tiptoeing around my death bed.

Yet, the next procession, from prison to wharf, would be my last walk in Boston. Neither rain, nor Sime, nor sympathy, was going to hurry me.

"Wait a minute," I said. "What's the news on Whitlaw and Joc— the other fellow?"

"Cost me," Sime whined, "he did. Lost a month's pay on the blighter."

"He lost more," said Hanks.

"Rinty stopped in at the trial," Joe said. "They ain't holding the ensign. He's facing a tongue lashing from Sir Edmund, but that's all. It goes as an accident."

Sime snickered.

"And the other?"

"Give his body to his slaves, Rinty said." Joe was marching sideways to reach his audience. "Appears the man, Anderson, didn't leave no instructions or nothing. At least none ain't been found."

"Cocky," Sime said, "sure he'd win."

"That he was," I said. I doubted that Jockey had ever drawn a will. His plans were all for life, as highwayman or horse breeder. His success at both had led him to consider Whitlaw merely the first step in his grand scheme to destroy Lady Esterling.

By the direct route it was little more than a saunter from the Town House to the stone gaol. The rain was beginning to fall harder, and it linked Jockey's end with my own.

The sunken sea chest was all I had to leave. Mayhap it was beyond reach, but Jill should have it, written down and legal.

"Sergeant," I said, "did they set a date for my execution?"

Hanks was so surprised he stopped. They were all staring at me. "Didn't you hear?" Hanks asked. "Sir William said."

"I wasn't listening."

"Wasn't——?"

"They just give time for praying at you," Sime said.

Hanks nodded. He turned away as he spoke.

"Five days hence."

Five days.

❖

Jill was waiting when I reached my cell. Alec and Hamish were with her, and Katrina. In fact it seemed wetter inside the stone room than out, for the two girls were weeping on each other, and the fishing partners were blowing their noses in alternate blasts, as if hawking their wares in the street. The place had the smell of a wake before a cork gets drawn.

"Cormac!" cried Jill. She was in my arms with a leap. It was fortunate Mercy had removed the shackles.

"It's all right," I said, patting her.

"All right?" She split the words with a sob.

"Expected, then."

That sent her off into a wild burst of tears. There was naught to do, but hold her tight, and let her have it out. I was not exactly feeling merry myself, but Jill's keening put the starch back into me.

Katrina was hovering around us, sniffing helpless.

[290]

"Poor girl," she said. "Poor, poor girl."

That being the first kind word she'd ever had for Jill, I realized Katrina had been in the courtroom. Nothing less than Jill's testimony would have changed the Dutch girl's attitude.

"Thanks for coming, Katrina," I said.

"Oh, Cormac!"

Hearing Katrina go off behind her, pulled Jill together. She ceased wailing and sobbing, wiped her eyes on my neckcloth. A hand rose to smooth her hair; she drew back, fitting herself into the curve of my arm.

"Enough, Katrina," Jill said. "We've no time for caterwauling."

"I—I can't help!"

"Then, cry quietly."

Seeing my grin, Jill tried one of her own, a bit damp, but pleasant. Just touching each other put heart into us both.

"Cormac," Jill said, "you were right, and I was wrong. They believed all that was said about you, except by you and me."

"The more fools, they."

"There's only Jockey now."

Of course she didn't know. She hadn't seen, and nobody'd thought to tell her. I kissed her to ease the shock.

"Not any more. Jockey was killed this morn."

She gulped, clutched me the tighter.

"Whitlaw?"

"Aye. Fair fight called accident."

"Then—there's nothing we can do!"

"You can wed."

Alec Murdoch's vibrating voice shook through us. He stood, still the prophet, under the barred window, heedless of the rain drifting in on him.

"*Ja,*" said Katrina, interested, "is so."

"Mind," said Alec, raising one long arm, "I like ye no better. You've brought naught to my house but desolation and misery. But the lass has chosen, and she's my sister, and the Murdochs stand by their blood."

Hamish MacInnis, deaf to the skirl of the pipes, was more practical. "Aye," he said, "it's the least you can do to save her from scorn and contumely."

"Whose?" said Jill. "Yours?"

She was out of my arms like a fishwife, crouched, fingers curved into talons. They had done that, at least, and I blessed them both. But I reached out to grab her before she flew at them.

"Not mine," said Hamish, quailing before Jill's wrath, "but the elders of Boston."

"Susannah's elders! Hypocrites!"

"Jill!" Alec was shocked.

"Hypocrites!" she repeated, louder. "Would you have me cringe before them, and thank them for hanging my man?"

"I'd have you show decent respect," said Alec, "for those who preach God's word, and His commandments. There'll be a dreadful reckoning for what you did this day."

"Is that it?" said Jill. "Their five pounds? Well, they can whistle for it."

"Aye," agreed Hamish. "She did deliver the man, Alec."

"You misread me apurpose," thundered Alec. "Whatever is between this man and you, Jill, is for the Lord God to judge. It was sin enough for you to avow your love for the Papist publicly."

"Sin?" I said. "It will warm me on the gallows. But enough. The argument is fruitless. I will wed Jill, with all my heart, if she will have me."

"To be your wife, gladly," Jill said, "to be your widow, no."

"Is five days," said Katrina.

"You refuse me, Jill?"

"You know better. But I want you for life—life, Cormac!—and to wed you now is to admit we're beaten."

That brought silence. For we were beaten, and all the fine talk ever spoke wouldn't change the fact. Katrina knew it. Alec and Hamish knew it. Only Jill refused to accept it.

Mercy, arguing in the passage, shattered the quiet. The gaoler was shrill with protest.

"There's too many in there now."

"Aw, cease your whinnying, you old thief. If it's toll you wish, here. Now, step aside."

Katrina brightened to the voice. "Is Devon."

Devon Neville it was, in a rain-soaked leather cloak, and a shapeless, dripping hat. His spurs tinkled as he squelched across the flagged floor.

He kissed Katrina, briefly though wetly, and turned to me. Devon's scowl was that of a boy who had lost a most important game.

"I've heard," he said, "as I rode in. 'Tis the talk of Boston. You've the Devil's own luck, Cormac."

"And I wish he had it back."

He glanced at Jill, grinned like a street imp. "You had us all fooled, Mistress. It was as good a dupe as this town's seen."

Alec groaned; Hamish shook his head at him. Jill's temper flared again. She swung round, but the post rider wasn't one to let his news grow cold.

"If only there was more time," Devon said, removing his hat and wringing it out. "Five days is not enough."

"Enough?" asked Jill. "Enough for what?"

"For a ship to get here from London. If we only knew for sure Cormac might have a postponement."

"A post——" Jill's eyes widened.

"But so far," Devon said, "it's just another rumor. They can't act on a rumor."

"Devon," I said, annoyed, "slow down, rein in, and breathe your horse. *What's* a rumor?"

"Why, that William of Orange is landed in England with an army, that James has fled, and William and his wife Mary are to share the throne."

"William——"

"Aye," said Alec, "you called it rumor true enough. Would it was so, but it isn't."

Hamish shook his head. "James is too strong."

"Wait," I said, "just wait now. Devon. Where'd you hear this—this rumor?"

"Well, there was a man new arrived in Providence Plantation. Just in from Nevis. That's an island in the——"

"I know Nevis. Are you telling *me* about Indies islands?"

"Hush, Cormac. Listen to Devon."

"*Ja.*"

"Well, this man, name of Winslow, believed it. He had a copy of some proclamation replacing magistrates. Of course it was in Winslow's own hand, and mightn't be true."

"By the stones of Iona!" I cried, for the great thought had burst on me like sunrise. "By the fort of Aenghus, and the well of Kell! We'll diddle the Sassenach yet!"

I grabbed Jill and whirled her around.

"Cormac, Cormac, what is it?"

"Sure," said Hamish MacInnis, "his brain has snapped."

"I don't doubt it," Alec said.

"Cormac, what is?"

"Didn't you hear Devon?" Sure, the plan was sprouting so fast within me, I had trouble getting the words past it. "Nevis! Nevis near Saint

Kitts! 'Twas in the islands my troubles started, and from the islands comes my deliverance!"

"Deliverance?"

"Yes, Jill!"

"But, Cormac," said Devon, "didn't you listen? New magistrates might mean a new trial. I worked it that far myself. But they'll not postpone execution on a rumor."

"Postpone, be damned," I said, "and triple damned be rumor! Devon, have you mentioned this to anyone else?"

"Nay. I came straight here."

"Do you remember the words of the proclamation?"

"Aye. The gist anyways."

"Well, then!" Jill dancing beside me, flushed with new hope, I moved to the table piled with manuscript. Her belief in me showed in her eyes; that and the wild gamble of it drove me beyond logic. "There's paper here, quills and ink! Aye, and I've become practiced at writing of late!"

"Darling what do you mean to do?"

"Jill, betwixt Devon and me—he to swear it true, and me to set it down—I'll write such a proclamation that will turn rumor to fact! Aye, and forge the key will free me!"

Alec and Hamish were staring. Katrina, watching Devon, smiled when he did. Jill, of course, was beaming, clinging to my arm.

"And then, my own?"

"And then—if you have to tell him I need salvation—just fetch me Cotton Mather!"

❖

"But is it true?"

The Reverend Cotton Mather held the sheet of paper so tightly that it fluttered. His eyes, glowing, shifted as he read the written lines for the fifth time. It was not a forgery; Jill had copied what I'd devised and Devon remembered only because Mather knew my script. The part about restoring all magistrates unjustly turned out was directly derived from the Nevis man's document. That was a lever tooled for Cotton Mather's grip; he was violent about Sir Edmund's appointments replacing good Puritans. If William was in, and James out, Boston would have to declare itself for one or the other.

"Devon swears to it, Reverend."

"Winslow thought it true," said Devon Neville. "They believe it in Nevis."

Cotton Mather raised his head. I very nearly blew my relief in his face. He wanted it to be true so badly, that he was already convinced. His arguments and questions were those of a man wanting reassurance that he was reasonable, not rash.

"Why bring it to Cormac?" he asked the post rider.

"So he could bargain," Devon said, with a shrug. "Changed kings means changed courts. William will not hang his friends."

"Friends?" Mather's eyebrows rose. "You prefer the Protestant to the Papist?"

"Aye," I said. "Sir Edmund is James's man, and under Sir Edmund, I die, and soon. Besides, if you truly wish to unseat Andros——"

" 'Tis my daily prayer!"

"Then you'll need somebody running things that knows how and can be trusted. A man with some knowledge of striking fast, without warning, and seizing what needs to be seized before force can be brought to thwart him."

"In short, a pirate!"

"I don't deny I've learned their tricks." I knew my own worth. "And I've other value too. This, if James comes uppermost again, is treason." Devon stirred, but I didn't glance his way. We were far from sure that James was down. "Who better to blame for any—disturbance—than a condemned pirate who broke gaol?"

"For the first time," said Cotton Mather, "I begin to think you should hang. You're dangerous."

"Most men fighting for their lives are."

"Esterling," said Devon, at my pinch on his leg. He'd been well coached, and was enjoying himself. "Palmer. Foxcroft. All James Stuart's justices. But if James is dethroned——"

"You needn't belabor the point," said Cotton Mather. "If I thought Cormac could do it, his life would be a cheap price, granted gladly."

"Do it I can," I said, "on that promise."

"It's a promise. But—haven't you forgotten the frigate?"

"Neither fort nor frigate. But, first, Paulsgrave Mercy must be put in a cell, and another in his place. He's Sir Edmund's gaoler. I'd not be talking so free this minute only Jill and Katrina are keeping him from the door."

"That's easily done. Then, naturally, you must be released."

"Lord, no! Begging your pardon, Reverend. But you really do need a man like me in this. My face is a giveaway, known to half Boston. And what safer place to meet than here?"

"This cell?"

"This cell! With a pirate in it who's to hang in five days. There's a reason for men to come for a look at the knave. Aye, and preachers to come to exhort him."

"Would you make a mockery of the Lord's work?"

"Are we not doing the Lord's work?"

It was the right answer to give Cotton Mather, but I was far from as certain as I sounded. Still, there was no time for me to indulge myself in religious scruples. If James Stuart couldn't win his throne back in spite of one man's work in Boston town, he didn't deserve a kingdom.

"There's still the frigate," said Cotton Mather. "It can blow down the walls of the whole waterfront. With Sir Edmund in the fort and the *Rose* in the harbor——"

"What about that, Cormac?" asked Devon.

"Simple. Captain John George commands the frigate. Ensign Borden Whitlaw commands the redcoat guard. We take them both beforehand to keep them from mischief."

"Take them?"

"Yes, Reverend. At some quiet rendezvous ashore. Say, the Red Lion Inn. And I've just the lady to get them both there when wanted. One for love of her ladyship, and the other for love of her rank."

"Lady Esterling? She'll not do it."

"She might," said Devon.

"She will after Jill Murdoch talks to her. Very sympathetic to young love is her ladyship. She was young once herself."

"What else?" Cotton Mather was a picture of mixed emotions. His cloth was outraged by my proposals, his humor was tickled, his brain saw that the plan might work. Aye, and every so often a shrewd glint from the bright eyes made me suspect he was using me as much as vice-versa.

"Give Devon a note to ride with that will summon the militia from the farms. Send Alec Murdoch and his friend Hamish to the waterfront with enough coins to treat the frigate's crew. Print that proclamation, and see that it reaches the proper hands in Boston, and only the proper hands."

"No man reads it I cannot trust."

"Then, Reverend, fetch me a few leaders. Soldiers and captains. Those of your persuasion. Have them here tomorrow night, armed, ready to replace Mercy."

"Tomorrow night? You don't give us much time."
"And how much have I left to be throwing it away?"
So, it was decided.

Chapter 34

THE day after my trial passed so slowly that the morning seemed to last a century. Others, outside the stone gaol, were busily working, but the plan was mine and I was forced to sit in idleness.

My imagination traveled the streets of Boston with Cotton Mather as he carried the broadsides of the proclamation from the printer's, waited with Jill in Lady Esterling's anteroom, helped Devon curry his horse, bought sailors rum beside wee Hamish MacInnis.

I stopped that nonsense when my mind saw Mather pass a handbill to Borden Whitlaw who brought the redcoats arunning. To write more in my log proved impossible, thrice the quill dried before I began. There was naught to do but pace, watching the shaft of sunshine on the wall, cursing its laggard changes of position.

For a man with only four days to live I was surely spendthrift with my hours. How they stuck to my hands till I gnawed my nails to the quick!

Jill brought my dinner at noon, and I near blurted my questions in front of the gaoler. As Mercy sat in the doorway, and I pretended to eat, we whispered. Paulsgrave was used to that, but this time an overheard word would be our ruin.

"You saw Lady Esterling?"
"Aye, Cormac."
"And?"
"A strange woman."
"She is, but——"
"You'd have thought me her laundress."
"Jill, for the love of——"
"Shhh, Cormac, Mercy."
"All right."

"Don't you know how to whisper?"

"I said, all right!"

"Shhh."

"Will she do it?"

"Aye. She called it blackmail, but she agreed."

"Both Whitlaw and George?"

"Both. The Red Lion. A midnight supper, after her husband's abed."

"Then, that's done."

"Aye." Jill frowned. "You know, she hardly changed countenance through it all. And yet——"

I could see her ladyship, the handsome clock-like face, with no sign of the works whirring behind it. "And yet, Jill?"

"I've the feeling she was *pleased* to do it."

Time didn't drag so with Jill beside me; her excitement was infectious. She had dressed in her best for the interview, the blue silk, though I recalled brown linsey, very plain, at my trial. I hadn't been thinking of her clothes, then, so I queried her.

"Aye," said Jill, smiling, "it was brown."

"Why not this? It's my favorite."

"But, darling," her laughter rippled, "the brown was more suitable. And today, it was Lady Esterling."

That was supposed to make sense, I knew, so I changed the subject. We whispered of ourselves, and of the future. We were still at it, holding hands, when Katrina arrived an hour later.

Katrina, of course, never had to guess about lovers. She took one look at us, whirled on Mercy like a small, blonde hurricane.

"You," she said, "shoo!"

"Well, now——"

"I am here. Is proper. Shut door."

While Jill and I gaped, Mercy meekly went out, locked the door. Katrina beamed at us.

"First, of Devon. *Ja.*"

"He's away?"

"*Ja*, Cormac. Hours."

"Wonderful," said Jill. "If the militia comes in——"

"They come," Katrina said, "tomorrow. Now is now." As she spoke she pounced on a stool, carried it in front of the door, plumped herself down on it. There she sat, back to us, glaring up at the wicket, the gaoler's peephole.

"Katrina," Jill said, "what in the world——"

"Now," said Katrina, a giggle jiggling her spine, "is private. Is nice. Use!"

We looked at each other, blushed, and used. So there were kisses to add spice to our danger, zest to our plans, pleasure. Neither of us, myself especially, trusted Katrina not to peek, but we were ardent enough for Jill to end flustered and rosy. I must have been the same to judge by Katrina's laughter when told to turn around.

Both girls left in the late afternoon. The days were growing longer, but even so dusk seemed to dawdle coming only to stay like a newsfull gossip. When the gaoler made his last rounds, I was scratching away busily by candlelight. The quill was tracing nothing but loops, circles, and curlicues, but Mercy could not tell that through the wicket.

Then, I settled myself to wait. It wasn't long before the scrape of metal on metal as key sought lock brought me upright. Bolts were eased back, hinges squeaked.

There in the doorway, candle raised in one hand, the gaoler's key ring dangling from the other, stood the lean figure of Justice Waitstill Winthrop, the judge with the sand-dry voice!

God, I thought, bounding to my feet, we're caught!

Winthrop peered at me from under his hatbrim, nodded. He spoke as I remembered from the trial.

"Master Doyle, good evening. We meet again."

The justice stepped forward, and Cotton Mather was behind him. From the tilt of Mather's head he wasn't in custody.

"You've a new gaoler," Cotton Mather said. "Paulsgrave's tied to his bed."

"Gagged," said a young man, cheerfully, as he entered, "with his own nightcap. Give those keys to Scates, Judge."

"Scates?" I said, dazed. "Silence Scates?"

"The same, cock," said the one-eyed witness who'd helped convict me. He took the key ring, touched his cap in salute. "I'm gaoler now. Today, ain't yesterday."

"Tomorrow is our day," said the gay young man.

Others came until my cell was thronged with the cream of Boston's Puritan gentry. Mather might have picked them as trustees for that Harvard College he was so fond of; it was that exclusive a roster. Yet, I must say, they were all grimly amused at the turn events had taken, and willing to risk their heads. Treason was no petty crime, nor was it petty punished.

Samuel Shrimpton was present, colonel of militia as well as justice.

Doctor Elisha Cooke. An old gentleman with a skin of fragile parchment, Simon Bradstreet, a former governor of the colony.

Three militia commanders, fully armed were the most capable looking of the group. These were Major John Richards, Captain James Hill, and Captain John Nelson. The last, the youngest, was the cheerful young man. I took to him at once. Nelson was merry for a Puritan, a quality very refreshing in a risky enterprise.

This trio came to business at once, listing available troops, dividing the town into sections, arranging for the arrest of Andros supporters. The older men contributed names to this last.

"Dudley's in Southold," Winthrop said, "on circuit. He should be taken."

"We can send word," someone suggested. "But to whom?"

"There's a family named Pemberly," I said, "this side the sound——"

"Of course!" Nelson clapped me on the shoulder. "Old Tobias! He'd be delighted to cross over and take Joe Dudley right out of his courtroom."

Nelson and Hill were to lead the party to capture the pair at the Red Lion Inn. I was going with them. They wanted me, and I didn't want to miss it, though I'd be careful to keep my face hidden.

Scates limped in with a steaming bowl of punch, and Hamish MacInnis. The wee man was a good six sheets to windward, but his report was carefully clear.

"Alec has half the *Rose's* crew ripe for mutiny," Hamish said, with a hiccup. "And t'other half dead-drunk. For a God-fearing Covenanter, Alec's a mighty swiller. He's downing rum like water. It don't make him happy, it don't make him sad, it don't even make him sing!"

I took a swig of Silence Scates's punch, and nearly dropped the mug. He'd mixed Dandy Jeffcoat's favorite tipple as served at the Wench's Butt! He was waiting for my amazed look, grinned, and winked his good eye.

"Hello, brother," I said when he sidled close.

"Shh," he whispered. "Sorry about that testament yesterday. They *said* you'd robbed your shipmates." He gazed at the company he was keeping, chuckled.

"You old pirate."

"I'm proud to be with you," Scates said. "Hell, I ain't never been in on the taking of even a *Spanish* governor!"

Cotton Mather tapped for quiet, rose. He had a paper in his hand. "This, my friends, is the statement of our aims to be read to the people of Boston tomorrow. It's called 'Declaration of the Gentlemen, Merchants, and Inhabitants of Boston and County Adjacent!' "

"Hear, hear."

He started to read, and he read well.

"We have seen more than a decade of Years rolled away since the English World had the Discovery of a horrid Popish Plot, wherein the bloody Devotoes of Rome had in their Design and Prospect no less than the extinction of the Protestant Religion:"

Popish Plot! 'Twas that devilish nonsense of Titus Oakes he meant; a spate of lies spewed from a diseased brain!

As Mather droned on, my thought, head cupped in hands, was of a tired priest riding the Irish hills.

Now, the winds in their whims blow a man down strange ways. But it was a hell of a queer Protestant wind that blew me into Boston, to sit listening to the likes of that!

❖

The Revolution of Boston in New England took place on the eighteenth of April, 1689, a date that will be celebrated in that town as long as it stands. Even when Bostoners have forgotten who marched that morning there'll be songs about the eighteenth of April. Not that there'll be need to forget me, for my name was known only to a few fellow revolutionists.

We left the stone gaol in the pale mists before dawn, separating on our different missions. It was a raw April morn fit for treason. I was with Nelson and Hill, feeling our way through silent, deserted streets packed tight with the dirty fleece of fog.

The town still slumbered. There were no sounds but our own; the triple slap of our heels through mud, the rattle of our weapons. A borrowed cutlass was in my belt, a horse pistol almost as long in my fist.

I'd no intention of using either, but a rebel does not beard a king with empty hands.

John Nelson halted us at a corner. He peered at nothing in four directions, then whistled. It was a sharp, quick three notes of signal.

"Soft," I said. "What of the watch?"

"It's the watch I'm calling," said Nelson, laughing. "He's one of mine."

A rum town Boston, when it had the mind.

The fog was brightening, through gray to yellow. It was thinning too, for a tavern sign became gradually visible opposite. Under it an eddy of mist jelled suddenly into a man. We crossed to join him.

"Still there?"

"Snug, Captain Nelson."

"And the boys?"

"Ready and waiting, Captain," said a hidden voice.

Another said: "Flog ya raw. That I will."

Unseen chuckles stirred the fog. Captain George's catchword, it seemed, had made an impression not intended.

"Let's go," said Hill.

Around us, then, were the muted small stirrings by which men prepare for action: a drawn breath, a whisper as blade left scabbard, the cricket clicking of hammers cocked on firearms.

We pushed through a door into a hallway. Mine host, in apron, waited to greet us with lighted candle.

"The captain's snoring below," he said, nodding us on. "The others upstairs."

Hill, sword bared, stepped to a latch, lifted it. Light, widening as the door swung, streamed into the dark hall. The room was a private dining chamber, hazy with stale smoke; in the fireplace a mound of pink embers was cooling to ash.

Head on arms, Captain John George slept at table amid the debris of a meal and guttering candles. The naval officer's lusty snores paid tribute to the several empty bottles among the litter.

"Thus did David gaze on Saul sleeping," said a voice.

Nelson snorted. "Don't insult Saul."

Scripture or no, the Bostoners moved into the room with a stealth worthy of pirates. There were a dozen solid-built militiamen, homespun clad in yarns as varied as their weapons. They had muskets, new and old, fowling pieces, pistols, pikes, clubs. One brawny fellow even swung a calking maul.

George was an easy prize. He started up when they touched him, and, though sodden with wine, was veteran enough to realize on the instant he was boarded and at bay. When he opened his mouth to roar the calker stuffed a gag in it. The chair, overturned, crashed, but they had him trussed like a fowl with no more ado.

"One," said Nelson.

"The ensign's another kettle of cod," said a man. "He's mighty handy with a sword."

Several nodded agreement.

"Well," Nelson said, "I expect he isn't wearing one at the moment."

Single file, we climbed the inn's narrow stairway. All was quiet above;

the creak of a floorboard seemed loud. Hill listened at a door, placed us with fluttering fingers.

"Rush," he whispered, easing up the latch hook. "We don't want bloodshed."

Our rush nearly tore loose the hinges! We exploded into the room, turned to a bumping mass as we stopped. For one, I felt a fool.

Borden Whitlaw, in shirt and small clothes, sprawled across the canopied bed. His head was burrowed deep in a pillow, and he lay in the sleep of the stunned.

From the candlelit mirror where she was pinning her hat, Lady Esterling turned. I had not expected to find her touseled in her shift, forwarned as she was, but I'd not expected such completeness of attire. The woman was cloaked, and half gloved!

"Mary of Scotland," she said, in cool, unruffled rebuke, drawing on the second glove, "was at least embarrassed by intruders with noble blood."

Embarrassed, my foot! We were the embarrassed ones. Under that placid gaze we turned to boors. Hill flushed. Nelson's bow was awkward.

"Now, if you please," said Lady Esterling, "I will take my departure." She might have been ordering her coach, and we her footmen.

"Escorted," Hill blurted. "We want no premature alarm."

"As you wish. But your fears are groundless. If you succeed today, Sir William will go home. The dullness of Boston has made me your ally."

She swept toward us, passing the bed without a glance. The men jostled each other to give her passage. At Hill's nod, two preceded her down the stairs. I followed; Whitlaw, who hadn't twitched, would be no problem.

At the Red Lion's entrance Lady Esterling paused. "Master Doyle," she said, "you are a blackguard."

"Aye, my Lady."

"You need expect no more favors from me."

"No, my Lady. Sorry I am that my plight made it necessary. To escape hanging a man grasps any means."

"There'll be more hangings than one, if James regains his throne."

"Aye, if he has *lost* it."

Her expression didn't change, but, after a pause, she laughed, soft as cooing. "A knave *and* a blackguard. Are your promises as false?"

"No, my Lady. Your secrets are safe. Even tonight's. These men are pledged to that."

"The pledges of men!" Lady Esterling shrugged, glanced up into the shadowed recess of the stairway. "Poor Borden. So much for so little."

With that she stepped out into the morning. Breeze had thinned the mist to wisps, and I watched her to the corner. Somewhere in the brightening town a rooster crowed. Sure, the bird's single cry held more emotion than all her ladyship's speeches.

Revolutions by farmers wait upon chores. It was nine o'clock before the drums of Boston rattled their signal. North Side, South Side, the streets filled with scurrying men. Across the Charles an army of militia grew larger by the minute. One company on the waterfront, young shipwrights, summoned recruits with a rallying cry.

"Town born, turn out!"

I have seen London mobs growling with a grievance. In Boston revolution was classless, less disorderly, something of a lark. Wealthy Puritan merchants marched beside their clerks; apprentices joined shopkeepers; clergymen, without gowns, brandished guns instead of hymnals. There was no looting. The patrols that arrested the Andros men moved swiftly from home to gaol. There was much good-natured banter, in spite of grim purpose.

Keeping from sight, I took a station in a chandler's shop at the foot of Oliver's Wharf, overlooking both the fort, and the South Battery. Major Richards used it as a headquarters; the other leaders came and went. The only order I gave concerned the ultimatum sent to the frigate.

"Tell George's lieutenant if he touches match to a single cannon, we will shoot Captain George at once."

The boatman looked at the major.

"You wouldn't?"

"Tell him anyway," said Richards.

"And command him to surrender his sails," I said. "Without sails, the frigate's helpless."

In spite of the order, the frigate lieutenant, with Alec's mutineers protesting, tried to reinforce the fort. Sir Edmund himself led a detachment out to meet this succor. They numbered only half a score. Nelson, with hundreds, intercepted the boat, and the governor retired.

That was as close as things came to a clash, and happened around two o'clock, well after the "declaration" was read from the gallery of the Council House. Jill, who heard the speech, said it was received with cheers.

By four, when Jill joined me at the chandler's, John Nelson had several thousand militiamen surrounding the fort, outside the palisades. Two men went in with a demand that Sir Edmund surrender.

Nelson gave me a diverting account of the conference.

"Old Andros wanted to fight, but his gentlemen had no stomach for it."

"What about the soldiers?"

"One sergeant tried to rally them."

"Hanks," I said, and Jill nodded.

"He got his answer from a Dutchman with pink cheeks." Nelson chuckled, tried to mimic an accent. "'What the devil,' says Dutch, 'should I fight a thousand men?'"

"And the frigate?"

"Now, there's a strange thing. Captain George managed to get his gag out. Asked for quill and paper. Sent a message to the *Rose*, begging his second to quit."

"What?"

"Gospel truth. George was afraid if we damaged his ship, he couldn't collect his pay."

Together, Jill and I watched the royal standard flutter down the fort's flagstaff. A moment later another ensign was jerking its way upward.

"Oh, Cormac, Cormac!" Jill threw her arms around me. "You did it! You did it!"

"Hush," I said, "that's not to be known. The Puritans did it. Cotton Mather, Governor Bradstreet, the militia. In fact, the town of Boston."

"But you're free!"

"Aye!"

Despite the happy captains shaking hands around us, we kissed on that. John Nelson only waited for Jill to step back, then grabbed me.

"Cormac," he cried, thrusting a noggin of rum in my fist, "some of us know who laid the plans, lit the match. Your health, Cormac O'Shaugnessy Doyle! And a health to King William! Long may he reign!"

"Long live William and Mary!"

They shouted the toast in chorus.

Jill and I exchanged a look that shared the unuttered hope that the honored couple were really reigning in England. I drank to them, against my principles and feeling a traitor. And I'll wager I was the lone man in the group with that feeling.

It was good rum, though.

So ended the Revolution of Boston without a drop of bloodshed, without a shot fired, without anything even bruised save a few feelings.

Once in a long, blessed while, a man finds a task peculiarly suited to his talents, and his training.

Chapter 35

AND now, a month and more since the government of Boston was turned topsy-turvy, with little left to write and less time to do it, I sit in the stone gaol for the last few hours.

Outside, it is spring, a fair May day. It may be because of the winters, but there seems to be a special lilt to New England's springtime. The air is softer, the birds sing louder and better, the green buds are greener even to eyes that remember Ireland. At least it is true when you're young, in love, and a silver oar is a curious piece of painted handicraft designed for some other poor devil's procession.

The one in the corner of my cell was brought by John Nelson. He carried it in on his shoulder, presented it with a bow.

"Here, Cormac," he said, "I found this in the fort storehouse, all freshly painted just for you."

Jill, who was with me, shuddered.

"Take it away, John."

Nelson looked hurt. "He ought to keep it as a reminder, Jill."

"Of what?" I asked.

"Why," he said, grinning at Jill, "that your days of single blessedness are numbered. Mayhap it is better to be married than burn, but there's some would choose the gallows to either."

"Not Cormac."

"Not Cormac," I agreed, "nor any man who has stood as close to the scaffold steps. But prop it in the corner, John. It's a trophy now."

I was far from sure it wasn't meant as a different reminder. On the day of revolt I was escorted back to gaol with cheers, but back I went. Silence Scates was an easier gaoler; the cell door was never locked; visitors came without hindrance. I even strolled in the yard with only Scates to keep his one eye on me. But gaol is gaol.

Legally, I was still a sentenced pirate though no longer condemned. One of old Master Bradstreet's first acts, as new governor, was to revoke my death sentence. This, of course, was the agreed payment for my part in the revolution, and was done, following proper procedure, on the petition of certain outstanding citizens of Boston. The signers, my fellow conspirators, made great mention of mercy, and none of rebellion.

Still, the Puritans did not let me off scot free, and I suspected Cotton Mather's well-kept hand in the result. I was reprimanded, admonished, dismissed from the township of Boston, and fined. The fine, suspended but on the record, made my return to the town highly unlikely.

That was the way it was written down, in fine legal script and lawyers' terms, for any king to read if the changed administration were questioned. Meanwhile I remained a prisoner in my stone cell.

"We must avoid scandal," said Cotton Mather.

"How long?" Jill's question was a wail.

"Oh, just till the first ship arrives from England. Justices Winthrop and Shrimpton thought it advisable."

Winthrop and Shrimpton, of the five judges who tried me, still held office. Fooling Puritans was no great task, keeping them fooled was another matter. Cotton Mather had jumped at the assumption that William of Orange was King of England. He wanted me handy until that assumption was confirmed as fact. He had, for reasons of his own, accepted my word on the matter; all Boston had accepted his. Until an official report crossed the ocean I was the Reverend Mather's hostage.

A canny man, my preacher friend. Mayhap I'd sold him a pig in a sack, or thought I had, but he was waiting for its delivery. I didn't relish my prospects if the pig turned out to be the wrong color.

"How long in time?" Jill asked, aware of my situation.

"Only a month or so."

"A month!"

Cotton Mather smiled at our unison exclamation. But on matters of religion he was adamant. "My dear children, the banns alone take three weeks. I couldn't marry you in less."

He used his preacher tone that always tripled the few years' difference in our ages. It made me want to rip the clerical bands from his gown. But Jill, mainly for Alec's sake, wanted a proper wedding, which settled that.

Some things of moment helped pass the time. For one thing I had a new suit made, by the best tailor in Boston, dove gray with a buff waistcoat. For another, Jill burst in one morning, squired by Castor and Pollux.

"Cormac, see who I've brought!"

Her expression was about as apt as the oarsman rowing herd on twin whales. I had never been completely unawed by Jockey's slaves, and I greeted them gingerly.

"Thought you went back to Rhode Island."

"Did, sah," said either Castor or his brother. "Took Master back. Buried him where he wished."

The other one nodded.

"They've no place to go, so they came to us!" Jill explained.

I doubted that, for the twins were valuable, but it was true. Jockey had died intestate; everything he'd owned had gone under the hammer. A Narragansett Quaker who didn't hold with slavery had purchased the Negroes and set them free.

"And," concluded Jill, "he gave them a wagon, and a horse!"

"A mare," said one.

"Best in stable," the other said.

They both grinned. I gathered they'd managed to select a nice bit of horseflesh.

"We're going West," I said, "once I'm out of here. A new settlement. We'll have to clear ground, plant, build. It won't be anything near what Jockey—your master—had."

"We can work."

"There'll be Indians, too. Real savages, not like around here."

"We can fight."

The quieter twin glanced at the open door. He said, seriously: "Want to go now? Pollux and me fix."

It was tempting, but Jill refused.

"Thank you, Castor. We won't be leaving for a few weeks."

Still, it was settled that they go with us when we leave, for keep at first and wages later. Jill, who tells them apart by some magic of her own, insisted that the mare and wagon remain their property. Neither of the brothers has much idea of wages, or ownership. They want guidance; in return we get those magnificent muscles and, in Jill's case anyway, loyal devotion.

Piracy was never match for such fortune. In a few weeks the gallows bird has become a man of means, well dressed, with an equipage and body servants.

Aye, I said *means*.

Jill brought part as her dowry. Whatever my opinion of her brother, and it's below the bilge, Alec was more than generous.

We were married a week yesterday. The wedding was in the South Church, Cotton Mather's, and he officiated. They let me out of gaol for the occasion. Enough rumors have followed that first one for my preacher friend to increase his belief in my veracity. Increase, not convince.

Though the service was private to avoid scandal, the church was filled. Alec gave the bride away. Devon Neville and Katrina were our attendants. Jill wore brocade, not the blue, but sort of a Lincoln green shot with something else. I must ask her the name. I saw only her hair, and the gold chain, and the doubloon gleaming on her bodice.

I received as a wedding gift a purse stuffed with gold coin, from the men who met in my cell on the eve of Revolution.

So, I did not come to Jill empty handed, after all. In fact, I didn't come to her at all. I'd gone back to my cell, at Cotton Mather's mild, iron insistence, and was staring at darkness when the door opened and closed.

"What is——"

"Hush, darling."

"Jill! Are you daft?"

"Aye. 'Tis a happy state."

"But, if anyone should discover——"

"There was only old Silence," cloth rustled in the room, "and he shut his one good eye."

Then, she was in my arms.

"Besides, Cormac, I want to tell our children I spent my bridal night in a stone gaol."

"We had our bridal night long ago."

"Aye, but I shan't tell them *that!*"

❖

Yesterday, a ship anchored in the harbor. William and Mary reign in England all right. The Bostoners are heroes. Cotton Mather nearly squashed my fingers with his handshake. The new sentence is now official, and my exile begins.

Jill is outside now. I can hear her directing Castor and Pollux with her boxes. We can't take the silver oar. These Puritans may find need for it in the future. But we are packed, and leaving immediately, inland, until we reach the Connecticut River.

We will build there, Jill and I, on the banks of the most splendid river I have ever seen.

Besides, I mean to have a boat. Nothing big, a small sailboat of decent build that Jill can handle, too. That grand stream of a Connecticut will provide many happy hours of sailing for a retired seafaring man. Why, it would be no trouble at all to cruise down to where it empties into the sea!

From there 'tis but a bit of a sail to the rocks that wrecked the *Fancy*.

Now, I'm not saying I will, mind, for I've put all that life behind me. That sea chest, after all, contains pirate loot, ill-gotten gains. Such wealth has yet to bring good luck to anyone.

Still, it is nice to have an anchor to windward.

So the voyage is ended, and the log is closed.

The End